SIGNS
in the
WILLOWS

J.A. FAGAN

Paperback: 979-8-9985391-2-1

eBook: 979-8-9985391-1-4

Book Cover Concept by Jan Fagan

Book Cover art created Yulya at Miblart

Illustrations by Jan Fagan

To my daughter Heidi.

Elswyth
From the Anglo-Saxon name *Ealhswiþ*, which is made up of two words: *ealh* meaning "temple", and *swiþ* meaning "strong".
Also, sometimes translated as Elf from the Willows.

"A woman with a voice is, by definition, a strong woman. But the search to find that voice can be remarkably difficult."
Melinda Gates

CONTENTS

PROLOGUE

Maybe living with the witch will be better than living with Mother, the child thought as she looked up at the ancient face staring down at her.

The crone glared at the girl's mother. "When was the last time you fed her? There's hardly an ounce of meat on her bones."

The small girl shivered and averted her gaze from the witch. To mask her fear, she squared her bony shoulders, raised her chin, and shifted her attention to the dark room around her—this place that was to be her new home.

Clutter and dust covered every corner of the dark cottage. Herbs and other plants hung from the log rafters. Shelves lined the walls upon which sat containers and bundles of every kind, each labeled with symbols she couldn't read. The windows were closed to any fresh air from the outside and tattered lace curtains hung over their dirty panes.

Across the room stood a heavy wooden table and a single chair. However, there was no room on the table for a meal. A few bowls and plates sat scattered among mortars, pestles, baskets, and utensils of every description. On the back wall, a small cauldron hung on a wrought iron crane over crackling flames in the stone fireplace.

Something bubbled away in the pot, and its aroma made the child's mouth water. She gulped a swallow. *Is that meat stew I smell? When was the last time I got to eat meat?* She heard the all-too familiar loud grumbling from her stomach, then noticed the crone's gaze shifting to her noisy belly.

"Go sit at the table, girl," the old woman said quietly.

The mother shoved her daughter forward. "Do as you're told!" She rubbed her hands on her apron as if she'd touched something unclean. The child shuffled across the room, sat and crossed her arms over her chest.

"The brat eats just fine," the mother growled. "So, if ya want her, she's yours and good riddance, I say. Maybe you'll be able to teach her your healin' ways, maybe not. Either way, ya can put her to work. She ain't no good to me with her being cursed without a voice and all. Ya remember she won't speak, right? She ain't never spoke a word. The girl is an ornery brat, so ya can't say I didn't warn ya! I don't want ya backing out on our deal." She licked her lips and eyed the cauldron in the fireplace. "And, by the way, some of that stew might be good to throw into the bargain, too!"

"She won't, or can't speak?" The witch let out a heavy sigh.

The mother grimaced. "It don't matter. Either way, she ain't got no voice and never did. That just ain't natural, so like I told ya, she's cursed. Ya said you can use her to help around here, so, Agnes, do we still got us a deal?"

Agnes looked at the girl and said nothing for a few moments. The child glared back at her with defiance, focusing on the wild, gray hair that framed the old face deeply lined with wrinkles—wrinkles that didn't look like those made from years of smiling.

"Yes, we have a deal! Here's the bag of potions we agreed on," Agnes said, as she shoved the sack into the mother's chest. "And as far as what's in that pot—it's a dark potion I'm working on, and I'm not sure I've got it right yet. Of course, if you really want to, you're more than welcome to try a big bowl of it," she said, jutting her chin toward the bubbling brew.

"Oh! Then, no—no," the mother stammered. "That's OK. Come to think of it, I guess I ain't as hungry as I thought! This'll do fine, thank ya!" she said as she shrunk backwards, clutching the sack to her chest.

Across the room, the little girl smirked with satisfaction at seeing her mother afraid of something for a change.

"Fine. Then our transaction is done. You can leave now," Agnes said, waving the mother off.

Looking at her daughter one last time, her mother threw her a triumphant glare. "Behave yourself, Elswyth." She spat her daughter's name out as if it tasted of bitter apple. "Do what Agnes tells ya or else!" She shook her fist, cackled, then scurried out the door, slamming it behind her.

The only sound was the crackling of the flames in the fireplace as Agnes and Elswyth stared at each other.

"I suppose you're hungry, judging from the sounds your stomach keeps making?" Agnes eyed her new charge while she walked to the table, picked out two bowls from the pile, and rearranged the mess to clear some space. Elswyth looked like a frightened rabbit as she shrunk back into the chair and stared wide-eyed at Agnes.

"Ah, that's right. You can't speak. No matter." Agnes shrugged and walked over to the fireplace, her steps slow and measured. She pulled a ladle from the mantel, served generous servings from the pot into the bowls and shuffled back to the table. "Here you go. Now eat and fill up that belly. We'll worry about what comes next in the morning," she said, and handed Elswyth a spoon. "You can sit on that crate, though. The chair is mine."

Elswyth slid the crate over and sat in front of her bowl. The stew smelled so good it made her lightheaded, and her stomach growled again as she picked up her spoon.

Wait! Isn't this poison? she wondered, her spoon still raised to her lips. As hungry as she was, she was more afraid of what the concoction in her bowl might be. She gawked at the old woman, who slurped big spoonfuls into her mouth and waited for her to drop dead or burst into flames. Nothing happened. The old woman just kept eating. *Maybe it doesn't kill witches? Just children? Maybe it doesn't kill at all! Maybe it turns children into cockroaches or spiders—or something worse!*

Her imagination ran rampant, so Elswyth set her spoon down and stared at her bowl. As she fidgeted with her long, red braid, Agnes looked up at her.

"Oh, sorry, child," Agnes chuckled, and the wrinkles around her eyes deepened even more. "Don't worry. It isn't lethal. It's only venison stew. I just didn't want to give any of it to that mother of yours. Eat up. Tomorrow you will start earning your keep."

Elswyth returned her attention to her meal, then scooped up the biggest spoonful she could and quickly put it in her mouth. It tasted so good she almost cried.

She would worry about tomorrow in the morning. That night, she was going to eat the best meal she'd had in a long time.

PART ONE

J. A. FAGAN

ONE

H er mother's shrill voice ricocheted off the bleak walls of their house. "Can't ya do nothing right, ya little brat? Why can't ya ever speak? Ya just ain't natural, I tell ya! If it weren't for that curse of yours, I'd be happy now! By the Fates, I wish I never birthed ya!"

Ten-year-old Elswyth curled up in a tight ball in a corner of the room and covered her head with her frail arms. She didn't dare cry. It just made her mother even more angry, and it was never good when that happened. That was especially true when she came home stinking of rum, like now. All she could do was silently plead with the Fates to save her, but they never did.

She looked up. Her mother's hand was raised and ready to strike. Just as it came close to making cruel contact, Elswyth awoke with a jolt and sat up in bed, gasping.

It had been two years since she'd had the nightmares but this one brought the past back as fresh as if it were yesterday instead of eight years ago, when she first came to Willow Grove. But with every awful dream, Agnes was there, lighting a candle to banish the dark shadows, gently urging her awake. She'd rock Elswyth in her arms, brushing the sweaty strands of hair from her face, and reminded her that her mother was not coming back, and all the lies

2

she heard in her dreams were not true. Agnes always stayed with her until Elswyth's tears had dried and she'd fallen back to sleep.

Desperate to clear her mind of last night's terrors, Elswyth stood at the well and breathed in the fresh spring air while she pulled the bucket up. She closed her eyes to ground herself in the familiar sounds of home: their goat shuffling in the pen with the chickens, birds singing in the branches, and the nearby stream bubbling over the rocks. The nightmare from last night faded as she opened her eyes to watch the willow tree branches sway in the gentle breeze.

She was happy here. Safe. But she was also afraid it could all go away. This place was where she found a new life and an escape from her mother's cruelty. Here, she also found acceptance and purpose. Most importantly, she found family with the first person she had ever trusted and loved—Agnes.

Agnes did more than soothe her nightly terrors. She taught Elswyth to read, write, and communicate through hand signals and gestures. She taught her the healing arts using nature's abundance. And, although King Markan outlawed the use of Majik (except by himself), Agnes instructed her how to practice the sacred art in secret. To Elswyth's surprise, it came easily to her. Of course, she could only do simple things like help herbs grow more potent or light a fire, but she looked forward to her eighteenth birthday when, (according to Agnes) she would have full access to her own Majik. And her birthday was only days away!

Together, they had transformed the cottage into a home that was warm and orderly, the dust and clutter from the early days gone. The windows were open to the fresh air when the weather permitted. The table was a place to come together to share their meals. They had even bartered with the village carpenter to build some extra furniture, like her bed, more chairs, and a new worktable installed on the back wall near the storage shelves.

And, over time, Agnes's wrinkles had somehow softened into those made by smiles.

Elswyth's reverie broke as she heard and felt the loud flapping of wings to her right. She turned and saw the raven perched on the edge of the well, his head cocked to the side, looking straight at her. He spread his wings out and bowed.

"Morning to you, Cicero!" She sent the thought to him and raised her hand in greeting.

"And a good morning back to you, Elly!" he answered and bobbed his head towards her, signaling for a head scratch.

"Well, okay. We only have a little time, though. There's a lot to do today!"

She reached out, gave him a gentle ruffle of the feathers on his neck, and he reciprocated with a soft caw. She smiled down at him, then put her hands on her hips.

"Sorry, my friend, but that's all for now," she said as she took the bucket off the rope. *"I have to help Agnes with rounds today in the village. Mr. Baines's arthritis is acting up, and he needs some willow bark tea. Widow Craig needs feverfew tincture for her headaches again, and..."*

"Elly! Come inside and eat your breakfast. We still have a lot to do before we leave, for the village," Agnes called from the front door. The morning light turned her now white hair into a gossamer halo around her face.

"Be right there," Elswyth signed back to Agnes. Cicero flew ahead into the cottage and settled on the back of a chair at the table.

Agnes shook her head at the bird and smiled. "Morning, Cicero. I should have known you would be the first to show up for breakfast," Agnes said and gave him a gentle pat on the head as she walked by.

"Well now, Agnes, is it my fault you are such a wonderful cook?" he asked.

"Flattery will get you nowhere, my dark friend! Well, at least it won't work with me!" Agnes said. Truth be told, she was a little flattered that he liked her cooking, though.

Elswyth came in and set the water bucket on a small table near the fireplace, and then the two women sat down to eat. It was a perfect breakfast with eggs from their chickens, milk from their goat, cheese, butter, and Agnes's freshly baked barley bread. What more could she want? When she thought Agnes wasn't looking, she snuck an extra piece of bread to Cicero.

"I saw that! Elly, you do spoil him!" Agnes chided.

"It's only a small bite," Elswyth signed back with an impish smile.

Cicero puffed out his feathers. "What are you saying? I'm not spoiled! I just happen to like your bread very much, Agnes!"

"All right, all right. Don't get your feathers in such a fluff!" Agnes said. As she spread butter on her bread, there was a loud knock at the door. "Huh! We rarely get visitors this early unless it is urgent. Elly, would you see who that is?"

Elswyth went to the door and opened it just enough to see who was there. She gasped and threw the door open all the way and spun back towards Agnes. Her eyes were wide and her hands shook while she signed, "No! No! No!"

Agnes narrowed her eyes at their visitor, slowly got to her feet and gripped the edge of the table, her knuckles turning white. "What are you doing here?" she snapped.

Elswyth turned to face the visitor, her worst nightmare standing before her in the light of day. There, in the doorway, was her mother.

Two

Agnes walked around the table, stood next to Elswyth, and put a protective arm around her. She could feel her trembling. "I said, what are you doing here? What do you want?"

"Now is that any way for ya to greet me? After all, I am the mother of this here young lady," she crooned. Elswyth's mother had aged over the past eight years, and not gracefully. Any physical beauty she once owned had gone stale and haggard; the stench of sweat and cheap rum rose like steam from her threadbare clothes. She tried to step over the threshold, but Agnes stepped in front of her and barred the way.

"You aren't welcome here and you know that! Our deal was for you to leave and never come back. So, I will ask one more time before slamming this door in your face. What. Do. You. Want?!"

"I ain't wanting anything. Can't a mother come see her long-lost daughter? Just checking to see that ya done right by her, that's all." She sniffled and put her hand to her chest as if her feelings had truly been hurt.

"I know you," Agnes said. "Everyone knows you. Unless there is something in it for you, there is nothing you do from any good place in your heart, if there is such a place in that body of yours!"

"Well now, that's just being mean. I got half a mind to not tell ya what I done on her behalf. I just come to let her know that she's got some fine things in store for her—all thanks to me, of course."

Agnes felt a chill. "What have you done?" She reached for Elswyth's hand.

"Well, okay. I'll tell ya, if you insist." She paused for dramatic effect and adjusted her natty collar. "I was doing my usual entertaining at the village inn—ya know how I love to entertain—and these gentlemen came in who were, let's just say, obviously very well off and not from the village." Not once did Elswyth's mother look at her while she spoke.

Agnes snorted. "Yes, everyone is well aware of how you like to—entertain at the inn."

"As I was saying," her mother said and huffed indignantly, "these gentlemen came in and was very finely appointed. So, I being the curious one when it comes to out-of-towners, listened in to see what they was up to. Turned out they was from the king's court and the king was looking for some new healers! Of course, I broke into their conversation right away to let them know I knew the whereabouts of a young lady that was a very good healer. Taught by the best, I told them!"

Agnes leaned forward and spoke through gritted teeth. "Why would you do that? Markan's known for his cruelty. He publicly hangs people he isn't happy with, especially court healers, and goes through them like water through a sieve." She pinched hard between her eyes in order to control her temper. "They can't help a king who is a drunk and an addict. You've signed a death warrant for Elswyth! What, in the name of all the Fates, is wrong with you?"

She knew that the last question was rhetorical. No matter what she said, it wouldn't make a difference and gave up. Besides, none of that mattered now. The deed was done. Agnes was so angry she wanted to smack the smug look off the woman in front of her. She looked over and saw that Elswyth's face was red and her jaw clenched as she glared at her mother. "Tell me," Agnes turned back to the woman, "what did they pay you? I know you'd only do this for a price!"

"Of course, a lady's gotta take care of herself." She chortled and patted her ratty hair. "So, yes, I did ask for a small payment for the information. They was more than glad to oblige me with a few gold coins but, out of the goodness of my heart, I came to give you a day's warning so ya could say some proper goodbyes. Ya should be grateful to me for that, right?" She held out her hand out as if looking for compensation, and Agnes fought the urge to slap that greedy hand down right then and there.

Elswyth stepped towards her mother, her eyes narrowed, and pointed a shaking finger behind her mother, showing the way off the property.

"What's she going on about?" her mother asked Agnes, still not looking at her daughter.

"I think it's pretty obvious. She is telling you to leave, and I would do as she says." Agnes folded her arms and looked at Elswyth with pride for standing up to this excuse of a mother. She rarely saw her girl asserting herself in any situation, much less this one.

"Why, ya ungrateful little wretch! Looks like you never did learn to respect your elders! I should—" Her mother raised her hand to Elswyth.

That's all it took. Elswyth exploded and signed wildly in her mother's face, *"GET OUT! I HATE YOU! JUST GET OUT AND NEVER COME BACK HERE!"* Angry tears streamed down her face as she lunged toward her mother.

The woman stumbled backwards, shocked at her daughter's response. "Oi! Is she putting a hex on me?! Tell her to take it back! I done her a favor by sending her to the king's court and she'll be living in luxury! She should be grateful!" She screamed and held her arms up in front of her, trying to ward off the imagined curse.

Agnes knew what Elswyth was really saying but lied, "Yes, she is, and I don't blame her! And you should know that her Majik has become powerful, so I'd just be watchful from now on, if I was you, because your days are about to go horribly wrong. You may even notice your teeth—what's left of them—falling out."

Elswyth's mother clamped her hands over her mouth and stared at her daughter, bug-eyed. "She wouldn't dare do that to her own dear mother!" Elswyth just sneered at her in answer and crossed her arms.

Agnes couldn't help herself and continued. "You'll also soon notice horrible rashes and boils appearing all over your body. Oh, and don't bother coming to me for any relief because you won't find help or compassion here!" It was all Agnes could do not to use her Majik to make any of that really happen.

Her face a mask of dread, Elswyth's mother recoiled backwards off the small front porch, jabbing her finger at Agnes and Elswyth. "How dare ya!" she hissed as she tried to step in the door again.

With a wide grin, Agnes leaned out, flicked her fingers in the air, then whispered, "Boo!" The woman turned and fled, screaming obscenities at the top of her lungs as she ran down the path from the cottage, her arms flailing over her head. Cicero took off from the chair and flew after her, croaking and pecking at her from every angle. Agnes shut the door, turned to Elswyth and pulled her into her arms as tightly as she could, working to calm her own pounding heart. "I'm so proud of you, my girl. You stood up for yourself! Now, we have some planning to do and I don't believe we have a lot of time."

THREE

Cicero flew back in through the window, perched on a chair at the table, and hopped from leg to leg in agitation. "She won't be coming back this way anytime soon, I'll wager," he said. "I left a few marks on the old biddy and I think she's still running down the road screaming her head off!" He puffed up his chest with satisfaction.

Agnes held Elswyth tight for a few moments more, then sat her down at the table. "Elly, your mother did not come here to give us a day's warning," she said, and sat in a chair facing her. She took Elswyth's hands in hers. "I think she just came to make sure you were at the cottage so the king's men could come collect you. We need to get you out of here, and we need to do it quickly."

What? No! I don't want to leave, Agnes! You're my family! This is my home. Where will I go? Please!" Elswyth signed frantically.

"I wish with all my heart, my girl, that there was another way, but there isn't," Agnes said as she choked back tears. "If we're going to save your life, we have to prepare, and you need to leave as soon as possible. Cicero will go with you."

"Of course I'll go with you, Elly! Where else would I be?" Cicero ruffled his feathers, then paused. "Um, Agnes, where exactly is it we're going?"

Instead of answering him, Agnes stood and pulled Elswyth up with her, issuing orders while running around the cottage. "Cicero, go watch the road. Let us know right away if you see anyone coming."

"Of course!" he said and flew back out the window.

"Elly, we need to make it look like you don't live here anymore," she said. "Make your bed and pile some of my things on top of it. I'll clear your breakfast dishes off the table and leave mine. Then I'll pack some food and a blanket for you. I'll gather some herbs and potions for you to take, too, in case you need them. And your Little Book of Healing! Be sure to take that since you may need that as well. Now, get your clothes together in a backpack. Hurry! Oh, and I need to hang the teakettle on the crane, so it's hot and ready. When they get here, I have a plan I hope will work."

"But where am I going? Please tell me!" Elswyth signed frantically but, Agnes wouldn't look at her while she continued to dash around the room. Then Elswyth tried knocking on the table, but even then, Agnes kept her back to her. Finally, Elswyth jumped up, grabbed her by the arm, and turned her around. *"Where are you sending me?"*

Agnes paused, took a deep breath, then said, "You have to escape up into the mountains."

Elswyth froze and stared at Agnes in disbelief. *"What? But—but no one goes up there! The mountain elves—they hate humans, don't they? They're our enemies! Their Majik is not our Majik and—"*

Agnes put her hands over Elswyth's to interrupt her. "I promise I'll tell you more in a moment, but first we've got to finish making it look like it's only me here. It will give you more time to get away." Agnes wouldn't look her in the eyes and, instead, kept gathering supplies from around the room. Within fifteen minutes, they had taken care of all the preparations—all Elswyth's earthly belongings were next to the door in two packs.

Agnes returned to the table and motioned for Elswyth to sit next to her. "I wish we had more time, Elly," she spoke quickly, looking down at her shaking hands. "There are some things I haven't told you, my girl—things you need to know before you go. I'd promised not to tell you any of this until your

11

eighteenth birthday and, well, you would have learned the truth in a week, anyway." She looked directly into Elswyth's eyes before she continued, "I need to tell you all I can now before you go."

Elswyth hesitated, not sure she wanted to hear what Agnes was going to say. *"Who did you make this promise to?"* she signed.

Agnes took in a quivering, deep breath. "Your father. I promised your father."

FOUR

E lswyth felt like the very air had been sucked from the room. *"My fa-ther?? You—you said no one knew who he was."* She couldn't help but feel the familiar stab of betrayal. First, her mother's cruelty and for abandoning her without so much as a second thought, and now Agnes had kept this from her all these years?

Agnes got up and walked over to her bed. "I know, Elly. But I had to tell you that because I promised him I'd wait until you turned eighteen. I'm sorry. It was for your own protection and I'll tell you all I can, but first I have something he left for you." She knelt before her bed and pulled out a small wooden box from underneath. "Come here, my girl. This is for you."

Elswyth got up and went over to kneel next to the bed, and Agnes handed her the box. She opened it and inside was a green crystal pendant set in silver filigree on a chain. She felt drawn to it and reached in to pick it up. At first, it felt cold to the touch, but within seconds, it warmed up in her hand. She dropped it and looked at Agnes.

"What is this?"

"Elly, your father left this for you, and you need to wear it up the moun-tain." She picked up the pendant and put the chain around Elswyth's neck. "Your father came down from the Elven kingdom in the mountains nineteen years ago and—met your mother. As the story was told to me, he was young, reckless and idealistic. Even though he'd been warned not to come here, he was curious to see what we humans were like and decided he wanted to see for himself. He even wondered if there could be a way to unite our two kingdoms, so he snuck down here to our village."

She took a deep breath. "Unfortunately, the first person he came in contact with was your mother at the inn. She plied him with rum and afterwards, took any gold he had in his pockets and left him there, passed out in an alley. Well, unbeknownst to your young father, the mountain elves can't drink human rum. He remembered very little about his time with your mother, but recalled enough to be ashamed to have ignored his elders. He left disillusioned about our people ever becoming allies and returned to the mountains." Agnes looked to see how Elswyth was taking this all in and squeezed her hands. "Time passed and your father finally learned he had a daughter. You."

"How could he know that if he'd gone back to the mountains?"

"Majik. Your Majik," Agnes replied. "It called to him. Because you are half Elven and half human, your Majik was, at first, not very strong. Eventually, though, it reached him and he wanted to do right by you so he sent his most trusted regent to come and look for you. It was impossible for your father to come himself, but know that he was desperate to find out where you were."

"Regent? What do you mean, regent?" Elswyth interrupted.

"Your father is—a prince in the Elven mountain court." Elswyth quickly began signing again, but Agnes stopped her."I know this is a shock but, please let me finish, my dear girl, so I can get you safely on your way. You'll get more answers when you see him." Agnes continued, "When his regent found you, he was furious about how your mother treated you, so he searched for a haven, someplace where you could grow up in safety until you could return to your father. Even though I've always been able to shield my Majik from humans, apparently elves can sense it. He explained that even though our Majiks are different, he sensed I would protect you with mine and after learning what you'd been through, of course, I didn't hesitate and told him I would. Your father's agent then persuaded your mother to bring you to me. Predictably, all it took was a pouch full of coins from him and she was ready to be rid of you." Agnes paused and smiled." For me, my girl, you coming here was the best day of my life!" She cleared her throat and went on. "Your mother thought he was simply another rich traveler she could take advantage of while, at the same, give her the freedom from motherhood. She never let on he paid her to bring you here, and made it sound like it was all a trade for some of my potions."

Elswyth's mind was swimming with question after question, but time had run out. Cicero flew back in through the window, squawking loudly, and settled back on the chair. "Agnes, you were right! The king's men are coming! They're still at the bottom of the hill but on their way up with a prisoner's carriage. It won't be long until they're here. We have to leave now, Elly!"

Agnes and Elswyth looked at each other and clasped hands. *"Oh, Agnes. I'm scared. I don't know how to live without you!"* Her hands shook as she signed.

"My dearest girl! There is so much more to tell you but, we don't have time. Be sure to wear the pendant under your blouse and keep it on you at all times while you're traveling up the mountain," she said, holding her hand over Eslwyth's heart. Agnes choked with emotion as she struggled to go on."Please know that I love you so very much and that hopefully, someday soon, it will be safe for you to come home. Until then, remember everything I've taught you." They wept as they clung to each other.

Elswyth pushed back from her and signed, *"I love you, too."*

"Now, Elly. Please!" Cicero said, flapping his wings. "We have to go now!"

Elswyth slung one pack over her shoulder, tied the pouch full of herbs and potions onto her belt, and picked up her second pack before they walked out the door. She turned one last time over the threshold to look around the cottage, her heart aching, and her mind racing, wondering if she would ever see it again—if she would ever see Agnes again.

They rushed out back to the edge of the grove, hugged each other fiercely, not wanting to let go. Agnes then gripped Elswyth's shoulders. "Follow the stream north up through the forest and keep going until you reach the two standing stones, about two days' journey. Take the path between them. Be sure you go between them and not around!" Agnes hurriedly advised. "You'll know when you are close. Now go. Hurry!" she said through her tears.

The sounds of horse's hooves and wagon wheels echoed from the bottom of the hill from the cottage.

"Run, Elly! Run!" Agnes choked out the words and gave her a gentle push. As Cicero flew overhead, Elswyth ran through the willows into the forest, barely able to see the way ahead through her tears.

FIVE

A gnes ran back into the cottage a mere moment before she heard the
sounds of a carriage and horses come to a stop out front. She looked
around to make sure she hadn't forgotten to arrange anything in the room,
ran to her workbench, and chose a box of powder from the top rack. Working
quickly, she chose a teacup from the shelf, sprinkled a generous pinch of the
powder into it and returned it to its place. Then she brought the box of mix
to the water bucket and stirred a hefty measure into that as well. Just as she
finished, someone banged on the front door.

"Open up by order of King Markan!" bellowed a loud voice.

She pulled from her heart center to summon all of her Majik, and called
out as sweetly as she could. "Coming!" Without rushing, she went to the door
and opened it. Standing on the front porch was a hulk of a man, taller and
wider than her door, wearing the black and gold uniform of Markan's army.
Glad she'd put an extra measure of her mix in the teacup, she realized this
might take more effort than she first thought because the soldier reeked of
stale mead and sweat, and didn't seem like the type for a simple cup of tea. He
glowered down at her, then focused his squinty, bloodshot eyes past her into
the cottage. *Not to worry*, she told herself with confidence. *This will work! It
has to.* She trusted in her Majik, and he *would* drink the tea.

"By the Fates! To what honor do I owe a visit of such a handsome young man and an officer from the king's army, no less?" She bowed her head to him, trying to appear as feeble as she could. "Your mother must be so proud of you, young man. If my dear son had lived beyond his boyhood," she sniffed a little for added effect, "I would've been so happy for him to be in the king's service like a man such as yourself!" she said and sighed, wistfully. Agnes never had a son, but she hoped the ruse was believable enough. Instead, he grabbed her arm, roughly shoved her aside, and stomped into the cottage.

She glanced outside and saw two more soldiers on horseback, equally intimidating as the one now in her home. A black prison carriage, emblazoned with the king's gold double-dragon crest, stood parked out front as well. From his seat up top, the driver craned his neck in every direction as he looked around the yard. Not one of the men looked happy to be there.

At the back of the carriage, there was a padlocked door with a barred window. A frightened young woman looked out, her hands gripping the bars. *Maybe I can help her*, Agnes thought. *Maybe*.

Her attention snapped back to the officer in the cottage when he barked at her, "I am here on orders from his majesty, King Markan, to collect the young healer living in this cottage. She's to come with me immediately to be transported to the king's dormitories." He glared at her for a moment and then continued to look around the room. "Where is she, old woman? Where is she hiding?" He stormed around the space, tossing things left and right.

Agnes shut the front door, then rubbed her arm where he'd grabbed her. The brute obviously had no reservations about hurting women. "Oh my. No need for all this extra fuss, young man, I assure you. Please come and sit, even if just for a moment. It must be such tiring work to be out on your horse all day riding around the countryside," she crooned, while she sent her Majik in his direction. "It's rare I get visitors, and when I do, it's no one as important as you! I would consider it an honor to offer refreshment to one of the king's bravest and finest, of which you are obviously one. I've just made myself some tea and I'll be happy to make you a cup."

"I ain't in need of no tea. I just need to collect the healer and be on my way. So, where is she? I was told she lives here!" he said. The veins in his neck bulged from his reddening skin and he flexed his fists. Agnes needed to work fast for her plan to succeed, so she went to the shelf and took down the cup she'd already prepared. Once she got him to at least get a whiff of the tea, she knew she'd have him and her Majik could finish him.

"Such a dutiful young man," she said while pouring tea in the cup. The fragrance from the brew swirled into the air between them. She watched with satisfaction as he breathed in the aromatic wisps that encircled his head, and then he stood stock-still while the angry brute's face softened and his arms relaxed by his sides. *Ah yes. Works every time*, she thought, pleased with herself.

"Please make a lonely old woman's day. Here, come sit for a quick cup," she purred. "You remind me so much of my son, and it would mean the world to me." She sniffled, dabbed her eyes with her apron, and gave him a shy smile. "Oh, and I also have some sweet butter and freshly made barley bread. How does that sound, young man?" She held up the loaf, waved her hand over it, and the warm, baked aroma intensified and surrounded his head in a wispy cloud.

He hesitated, then stepped closer to her, looked at the bread and swallowed. "Well, maybe a wee bite wouldn't hurt," he said. The brute was fighting it, but she knew her Majik had already won.

"Now there's a good lad! Have a seat right here and I will take care of you as if you were my beloved son!" He grabbed a chair at the table, sat, and looked around the room again with a befuddled look. Now, with the tea in front of him, he breathed in the steam and a sappy smile spread across his face. Agnes could see that his eyes had become unfocused as she sat down across from him. His breathing had slowed, and he sat back in the chair.

"Now, dear, drink up and tell me again why you've come such a long way. I will be most happy to assist you however I can," Agnes said as she patted his hand for extra motherly effect while resisting the urge to recoil when she touched him. She watched him as he took a loud, slurpy sip from his cup.

"This is some of the best tea I have ever tasted!" His voice softened even more. He paused, then looked perplexed. "Um, why was I here?" He scratched his head. "Oh yeah! I was, um, told you have a young healer living here and I've come to take her into the king's service." He took another big, sloppy gulp from his cup, picked up a piece of the bread and slathered a generous dollop of butter on it. The bread disappeared in one bite.

Agnes nodded. "Ah, I see. Well, sadly, it appears you've come too late and I'm so sorry about that. There was an apprentice healer staying with me but, she left to travel somewhere down south about a month ago. Or was it west that she traveled? Oh, my. I'm so sorry, but this old mind of mine is not what it used to be, I have to say! In any case, she wanted to find a larger village to practice in." It hurt her arm to pick up the teapot, and she was sure there'd be a bruise where he had grabbed her. "Oh, I do chatter on, don't I? Would you like more tea? I make the blend myself."

He held his cup up for more. "Yes, please. I'd love some." He let out a loud giggle, then slapped his hand over his mouth, his face red with embarrassment. "Excuse me! I don't know where that came from! Your tea is delicious—wait! She's gone, did you say? The healer?" He looked around the cottage again, but saw no evidence of anyone but Agnes living there. Not only that, but he then decided he no longer felt the urge to get up and look for his prisoner.

Agnes nodded again. "Yes. And she was quite the talented young lady, too. I was sorry to see her go. I'm not sure where you heard she was still here, but whoever told you that was very mistaken." *He is ready!* she thought. Agnes pushed some stray white hair from her face, smiled sweetly at him, and peered into his eyes. With her voice lowered and her Majik focused, she spoke in a kind manner. "Such a hard job you have! I suppose you will just have to say you couldn't find her here. Isn't that right?"

"Yes," he said absently. "I couldn't find her. It has been a wasted trip."

"Not so wasted. After all, I got to meet you and reminisce about my son. Thank you so much for that, my dear. You made this old woman very happy," she said softly while maintaining eye contact.

"Yes, you're right. There is no healer here, but I have had a lovely time with you." His mouth twisted into an idiotic grin. The vacant look on his rugged face would have been comical at any other time. Today, however, she just needed to plant the idea of there not being anyone here for him to take, then get him and his cohorts to leave.

She got up and went to the small table by the fireplace, pointing to the bucket of water. "Oh my. Where are my manners? We should give your men some of this water. Don't you think so? After all, they've been out there sitting in the sun in those hot uniforms."

"Yes, yes we should do that," he said as his grin grew even wider.

"All right, young man. Just take that bucket of fresh water outside for me and I'll bring the ladle."

The soldiers were sweating in the warm morning sun, so when they saw there was water to drink, they didn't hesitate to step forward. Agnes waited while they had their fill and gave the drugged water enough time to do its job. Then, gathering her Majik again, she suggested they open the door for the young woman in the carriage. The soldiers were only too happy (giddy, in fact) to oblige her. One of them unlocked the padlock, opened the door, and another pushed him out of the way. That soldier held his hand out to help the young prisoner down, who descended into the yard and looked to Agnes for clues about what to do next.

"Oh, the king's men are so chivalrous, indeed!" Agnes said, wiping alligator tears from her eyes. "Hmm. Well, look here," acting as if she were assessing their prisoner. "I can tell you that this one is no healer, so I have saved you the embarrassment of delivering an imposter to the king. Isn't that right?" They all nodded with toothy grins, thanking her for the favor. "Oh, your mothers must be so proud!" That last statement made them all blush, which looked out of place on their rough, grizzled faces.

"Now, I know you're all very busy and must be on your way. You won't have any need to come back here in the future, isn't that right, boys?" She made sure each of them looked her in the eyes as she spoke. Again, nods of agreement. "Well, then, may the Fates bring you a blessed future. I'll let you all be on your way now! And you, young lady, please come over here and stand with me."

Together, the two women watched the soldiers leave until they disappeared down the hill. Then the young woman collapsed to her knees in relief.

Six

After walking uphill for what felt like hours, Elswyth's legs burned and her lungs were greedy for air, so she looked for a place to rest. Cicero had flown back down the mountain earlier to make sure no one was following them, promising he wouldn't be long, so it felt safe to stop and rest. A large fallen tree lay on one side of the trail, and she took off her pack and set everything down next to it. A drink of the cool, clear water from the stream helped to slow down her breathing and pounding heart.

Her heartbeat may have calmed, but the many questions and worries that swirled around inside her head had not. *Why did Agnes have to keep all this from me until my eighteenth* birthday, *and why did I need protection? Couldn't I have lived with my father—my Elven father—all this time? Why didn't he come looking for me himself instead of sending someone else? How could Mother have done this to me?* When she imagined what may lie ahead, the elves that have always been the enemy of humans, she shivered. As a half elf, would she be just another outcast in the mountain kingdom, as she was in Carthia? Were the stories she heard as a child true? Did they enslave humans? Were they evil? The other choice was to remain in Carhtia where she risked being taken by the king and, most likely, never see Agnes or her home again. Terrified of going back, but just as afraid of what may be ahead of her, she tried to make sense of it all, but it only made her head hurt. Elswyth went back to the log, rested against it, and looked up through the trees.

The forest was much denser here than closer to Willow Grove. The tree canopy overhead painted everything in dappled lights and deep shadows that moved with the gentle wind. Breathing in the rich scents of damp soil, water, and vegetation calmed her, and the sounds of hundreds of birds in the branches made her smile. Was that the promise of rain she smelled? She closed her eyes and lost herself in her surroundings.

"Cis, I need to stop for just a little while," she called up to him, her eyes still closed. *"I'll be ready to go in a few minutes."*

"Okay!" Cicero landed on the tree near her. "But, also, I think you should eat."

"Do you mean WE should eat?" Elswyth smiled and opened one eye at him. Having him with her was an added balm to her frayed nerves, and she had to admit, now that they had stopped, she was a little hungry. They'd never got to eat their breakfast.

"Well, yes. I don't mind if I do! Did Agnes pack any of the barley bread and cheese? I am famished. All that flying has given me quite an appetite," he said, leaning toward her pack.

Elswyth shook her head, laughed and opened the bag. *"Let's see what Agnes packed for us,"* she said while she rummaged through it. Then she paused and looked up at him. *"Cis, I am so glad you're here with me."*

"Really now, Elly. Where else would I be?" He shrugged his shoulders.

Elswyth pulled out the bread and cheese, set it on top of the log, and shared it with him. She watched him for a moment, then, after taking a few bites, asked, *"Cis, I have to ask—did you know about my father? About the arrangement with Agnes?"*

"No, Elly. Agnes kept it all close to her heart, as she told you, and shared none of that with me. I think she knows me all too well. You know I could never keep secrets, especially from you," he said. "Remember the time I ruined your birthday surprise for Agnes? Ha ha! That ended up being a fun day, though."

"I remember that!" She smiled at the memory and suddenly missed home deeply—missed Agnes. To keep from thinking too much about it, she stood up and packed everything back in the bag. *"We need to keep going, Cis,"* her sense of urgency had returned. *"Agnes said the standing stones are a two-day journey, and it looks like it's only a little after midday. We've a way to go yet."* Determined not to crumble, she put her backpack over her shoulder, picked up the extra bag, and started north along the stream again. Cicero flew from tree to tree close to her, chatting the entire way.

What they didn't see was that their every move was being watched.

When they finally stopped again, she noticed the dense tree cover dimmed what little she could see of the light from the sky but, she could tell it was probably even later than she thought. Her legs felt like lead weights and her arms ached from lugging her bags up the steep incline of the trail, so she looked around for somewhere to stop for the night while they still had enough daylight to see. Large rocks, some as tall as her, jutted out of the thick cover of bushes, trees, and wildflowers. Mushrooms sprouted everywhere on and near logs that had long ago fallen and rotted. The stream bubbled off to their right, which gave her some comfort and connection to Willow Grove.

"Look here, Elly! This should work for tonight," Cicero said, as he landed on one of several small stone huts set back in the tall evergreens. As ancient as they looked, they still appeared to be sturdy, well-built, and just big enough for two people to lie down in, each with its own fire pit near the doorway. The shelters were crude, with no doors or windows, but at least they offered protection, shelter, and warmth for the night.

"That looks perfect. I wonder who built these and why? They look like they've been here a long time, don't they?"

"It could be a place for people to rest on the journey up or down the mountain? That's my guess, anyway."

"Huh. Maybe. You could be right but, who would want to come up the mountain? I'm just glad they're here for tonight, no matter who built them."

Elswyth was grateful their Majik allowed Cicero to hear her thoughts, because she didn't have the energy to raise her hands to sign, anyway. She dropped her bags inside the small structure and eased her tired body to the ground. Cicero hopped onto her lap and cuddled as closely as he could, while Elswyth hugged him close.

Cuddling under her chin, he tried to comfort her. "You know we're going to be okay, Elly. After a decent night's rest, you'll feel better and we can start out again early in the morning."

After all that had happened that day, she doubted anything and everything at the moment. *"But we still don't know where we're going! All we have to go on is to follow the stream up the mountain. We still have to reach the standing stones. After that, where it leads, how much longer we need to travel and where we'll end up, we don't know. It's getting cold the higher we go. I'm hungry, dirty, and tired, Cis. So tired. I miss home and Agnes. And, well, I don't know if I can do this without her."* She wept and Cicero snuggled under her chin again.

"Hey! I know what will help you feel better."

Elswyth looked down at him and smiled through her sniffles. *"Just a wild guess—food!"*

"How did you know what I was going to say?!"

"Because food is always your answer to life's problems! All right. Let's get something to eat, then." She pulled out the bread and cheese, set them on a scarf, and added a few edible mushrooms that helped round out their little feast. After they were done, she had to admit she felt better with something in her stomach.

"I think it's safe to light a fire, Elly, since I saw no soldiers following us. How about I get us some kindling and you can collect a few larger pieces of wood? We'll be warm and toasty in no time."

"I don't know what I would do without you, Cis."

"Of course you don't. You'd be lost without me," he said and puffed out his chest. "Don't worry. I'm not going anywhere—well, except to get the kindling!" He laughed and flew off into the forest. Once they had gathered all they needed, Elswyth cupped her hands over the pile of kindling and wood, focused on a single point, and a small flame jumped to life. After adding more wood, they soon had a crackling fire going.

"Well, what do you think, Cis? Not too bad, if I do say so myself." She sat back to admire her Majik handiwork.

"Perfect fire! Excellent job, Elly!"

Elswyth pulled out the blanket from the bag, covered them with it, and the two of them curled up inside the rock hut and watched the flames dancing in the darkness.

"Remember when you first came to me, Cis?" She smiled at the memory and he nodded in answer. *"I think it was only a few days after my mother—after I arrived at the cottage. Agnes was kind to me, but I was so scared, lonely, and angry at the world. I had no way of saying what was going on in my head and heart, and I'm ashamed to say I wasn't very nice to Agnes in the beginning. Then you showed up. I think I was gathering eggs, and you landed on the fence post in the pen. You wasted no time in introducing yourself and, of course, asked when dinner time was. Do you remember that?"* She beamed at the memory. *"I was so shocked a raven could talk and I thought as much to myself. Then you remarked on what I was thinking! It was the first time in my life someone actually heard me. It was amazing!"* She petted his head.

"Our Majik's were meant to connect, Elly."

She hugged him close in response and stared at the fire. *"Did you know Agnes's complement? Wasn't it an owl? She's never wanted to talk about it, so I never pushed her about it."*

"Yes, I knew her owl for a short time. She was magnificent, by any account. When she died, it broke Agnes," he said sadly. "It was during the Great Royal Cleansing. At least, that's what Markan called it—a cleansing!" He spat out the last words and shivered. "The king ordered all complements to be destroyed and then decreed we were illegal from that day on. The rest of us are now matched in secret. It was a terrible time, Elly. She was so sad and lost until you came along. I really think you saved her."

"I can still remember the state of the cottage when I first got there, and I hope she's going to be okay by herself."

"Not to worry. Agnes is a strong woman and her Majik is even stronger. She raised you, didn't she?" he said and laughed.

Elswyth yawned. *"I'm getting really sleepy, Cis,"* she said, struggling to keep her eyes open.

"Okay. Enough talk, then. Sleep well, Elly. I'll be right here next to you until the morning."

Over the sound of the hissing and popping of their campfire, they heard rustling in the nearby bushes and snapped to attention. *"Cis, did you hear that?"*

"I don't think it was anything to worry about, Elly." Cicero whispered, his tone not entirely convincing. They peered past the flames into the dark. After a few minutes of silence, their fatigue got the better of them and they fell asleep together.

Beyond their campsite, a low shadow moved away through the underbrush.

SEVEN

Agnes helped the young woman to her feet, and they went into the cottage. Closing the door behind them, she asked, "What's your name, child? How old are you?"

"I'm Sarah. I'm fifteen and I'm from Engstrom Village. My mother is—I mean was—a healer," she said as a tear rolled down her cheek. "The king's men arrested her for secretly teaching Majik to others, and she died in prison last month. They didn't know she also trained me, because we kept that a secret. Ever since I could walk, though, she taught me all she could about the healing arts and Majik so I could carry on for her some day. Our village loved her, but now that I'm gone too, they have no one to help them," she said with a tremor in her voice.

"Ah, I'm so very sorry about your mother," Agnes said, and hugged her. "Sarah, you must realize you can't return to your village or you'll only be taken again. You need to go into hiding for now." Sarah nodded and looked down at the floor.

Agnes walked her to the table, and they sat down together. "How about this? My Majik will have convinced that last group of soldiers that they didn't find anyone worth collecting here and that you actually aren't a healer. Of course, that doesn't mean they won't send other soldiers, but I think we can

29

make things work if you want to stay here with me. What do you say? Would you like to do that?"

"I don't want to put you in any danger!" Sarah said.

"I think we're both safe for the foreseeable future. Let me think about this. Most of the time, we'd go into the village to see our clients rather than them coming to us so I'll just keep doing that alone. And if anyone comes up here, we'll tell them you're my niece. Not a healer. We'll keep your healing skills and Majik a secret and in the meantime, you could be a help to me around here, if you're willing?"

"Oh, yes! Thank you! I'll be more than happy to help however you need me to." She let out a breath and sat back in the chair, then looked at Agnes with concern. "May I ask who was it the soldiers came here to collect?"

Agnes considered just how much she should say. "It was my—daughter," she answered, because truthfully, that was how she thought of Elswyth. Her chest twisted a little at the thought of having to send her away. "She escaped south to the coast, and that is the last I saw of her," she said. It didn't feel safe for anyone else to know the actual story yet, if ever.

"I'm so sorry. I hope you'll get to see each other again soon." Sarah fidgeted for a few moments, uncomfortable, and seemed unsure of what to do next.

Agnes folded her hands in hers. "You must be hungry. Why don't we get something to eat before we decide anything else? We can worry about what comes next tomorrow." Agnes got up from the table to start the meal.

"Yes, please. I've eaten nothing since yesterday morning."

"Perfect," Agnes said and got a second plate and cup from the cupboard. "How about you clean out that bucket and fill it with some fresh water from the well for me?"

"Yes, ma'am. Right away!"

"Just Agnes will do."

After Sarah went outside, Agnes took a moment to collect herself. She could feel tears fighting their way to the surface, but she held them in. "Oh, please keep my Elly safe," she whispered to the Fates.

Sarah interrupted her prayers. "Agnes? I think you need to see this," she said, coming back inside. "I saw something out by the willows and went to look closer and—well, you just need to come see for yourself," she beckoned Agnes to follow and stepped back out the door.

They walked out past the well, and there, under the nearest willow, was an enormous white owl perched on a log. Agnes could sense the Majik surrounding it and knew that was no ordinary wild bird. "Stay here, child. I'll see about this." Sarah stayed back by the well as Agnes approached the owl. It seemed to watch her as she neared it, but otherwise, it just stood there, unmoving until she got closer.

"Hello, Agnes. It is an honor to finally speak with you," the owl said, his voice deep, and very proper.

"Oh! Hello? To finally speak with me? What—what can I do for you?" The owl was stunning, and it reminded her of her old complement, whom she still missed dearly. *Why would this handsome creature of Majik be visiting me now, of all times?* Her eyes grew wide and her hands grasped at her chest. "Oh no! Is it Elswyth? Are you here about her? Is my girl safe??" Her heart was pounding.

"Not to worry. The princess is safe so far. She's not quite halfway with her trek but, I will be told how she is doing and inform you of her progress."

"Oh, thank the Fates!" She squeezed her eyes shut to compose herself. *She's all right. Just breathe!* "But, wait! How do you know this? Who are you?"

The owl slowly blinked a few times before answering. "I am an envoy in the Royal Order of the Mountain, a network of animals and Elven that live along the path to the summit and for over two millennia. It has been our sworn duty to deliver news, intelligence, and messages between Glenorim and Carthia. While she was living with you here in Willow Grove, we kept the prince apprised of Princess Elswyth's continued progress and safety, which was all due to you, of course."

"I don't understand. How did you do that?"

"I have been watching over you both. Each week, I delivered a willow twig from the grove as a sign of her well-being to the prince via a relay of fellow envoys in our network. The twigs were always delivered to him within a few hours. We are very swift, you see," he said, spreading his wings out in a show of pride. "By the same token, if we felt the princess was in any kind of jeopardy, I was to send a thorny twig from your blackberry brambles as a sign that help was needed. To your credit as her caretaker, I never had to send one thorny twig! That being said, please know that members of our order would also have stepped in to defend her—or you—if it became necessary. I must say, today's events happened quickly, but you handled it all spectacularly. We were watching and ready to intervene, but saw you had things quite in hand. Well done on your part, Agnes. I know it was difficult for you! We've sent an account of your brave actions to the prince." He blinked again and bowed.

She ignored the compliment and instead felt irritated. Couldn't the regent have let her know about this at the very beginning? "Why was I not told about this—network?"

"Please trust me when I say that it was safer for you, as well as us, that you had no knowledge of our existence," he said firmly. "That being said, I will now continue to send him the signs from the willows, letting him know of your well-being, since you're an important part of the royal family. He will also provide us with news regarding Princess Elswyth's welfare for us to deliver to you. In addition, we can occasionally act as letter couriers between you and the princess. That must, however, be something that doesn't happen often. It would be unsafe to have a lot of written correspondence to connect you both until it is wise to do so."

She took in a deep breath and let it out, relieved she would at least be able to know her girl was okay. "Please thank His Highness for me."

"Of course. It would be my honor to relay your gratitude. However, I have one more reason for talking with you today—one more reason to reveal myself to you."

"And what reason is that?"

He paused and then added kindly, "Agnes, it has been a long time since you've had a complement. The prince desires to reward you for loving and caring for his daughter all this time." Agnes was going to say she'd cared for Elswyth out of love, but he held up a wing to stop her from speaking. "At the behest of His Highness, I will proudly act as your complement until it is safe for you and the princess to see each other again. After that, it shall be up to you if you wish me to remain in your company."

Agnes sat down heavily on the log next to him and felt some of the weight lifted off her heart. The owl's gigantic eyes followed her and despite his intense stare, she could feel the kindness in his Majik reaching in to calm her heart. Even though she was still worried about Elly, he'd given her a measure of peace, and it meant the world to her.

Agnes bowed her head to him. "Thank you! Thank you so much and it would be my honor to have you as my complement."

"There is no need to thank me. The honor is mine."

Agnes tapped her finger on her cheek. "Well now, where are my manners? You know my name. What is yours?"

"I am called Tallon," he replied, his chest puffed out.

Agnes smiled. "It's my pleasure to meet you, Tallon. I think we'll get on just fine." She glanced at Sarah, still standing by the well. "We were just about to sit down to a meal, if you'd like to join us."

"Thank you, but no. I prefer to provide my own meals, if that is agreeable with you."

"Yes. Absolutely," she smiled, thinking about how Cicero loved to eat human food. At least he certainly seemed to like her cooking, silly raven! "Please come in when you're ready and I'll leave the window open for you. You should know that I've told no one about Elswyth—only that she has escaped."

"Of course, that is the wise thing to do for the time being." With that, Tallon bowed, turned and flew back through the willows. She got up, walked Sarah back inside the cottage, and they set the table for an early lunch.

"Agnes? Is everything all right? Were you talking to that owl?" Sarah asked.

"Yes. He's my complement and you will most likely see him around here quite often." They sat at the table and ate a long-overdue meal together. It reminded Agnes of that first night she and Elswyth shared a meal, and she sent silent prayers up for her girl's safety.

EIGHT

C icero awoke with a start to the deep rumble of thunder. "Wake up, Elly! We've got to get moving. There's a storm coming," he shouted, hopping around their small campsite. Elswyth stirred from a deep sleep and, for a moment, couldn't remember where she was. The early hour and gathering clouds shrouded the forest in darkness and their campfire had gone out long ago, making the morning air extra chilly and damp. As she opened her eyes, the events of the last twenty-four hours came crashing back in on her. Determined to not let panic overwhelm her, she pivoted to what needed to be done at the moment and threw her blanket off.

In short order, they were once again following the stream up the mountain. Then the rain started—in torrents. Sudden wind whipped her wet skirt around her legs, making it difficult to walk. Her clothes quickly soaked through to her skin, her wet bags weighed heavier, and her hair plastered against her head. It became impossible for Cicero to fly in the storm, so Elswyth held him to her chest as she trudged up the now muddy, steep path.

As if the drenching rain and violent gusts weren't enough, lightning ripped through the sky, and the earth trembled with the thunder that followed each bolt. Soon, she couldn't even see a few feet ahead through the wall of water, and walking became treacherous. CRACK! BOOM! Lightning and thunder exploded around them, the full fury of the storm right on top of them.

"We need to find shelter away from the trees, Cis! Maybe one of these large boulders—" She froze, knowing it was too late.

Ozone. Tingling. She saw the blinding blast a millisecond before the ear-splitting boom exploded in her ears and they were both slammed onto the ground, unconscious.

Deep in her foggy mind, Elswyth dreamed Agnes was there, in the middle of the storm, stroking her cheek and encouraging her to wake up.

"Elly, use your Majik to pull yourself up, my girl. You need to wake up!" The stroking on her cheek continued.

"Agnes? What happened? I need you!" Her thoughts felt disconnected and fragile, and there was a strange vibration centered in her chest. She couldn't hear anything but a loud ringing in her ears. When she tried to move, her limbs refused to cooperate.

"Wake up. You can do it. Draw on your Majik. You have more than enough to help yourself," Agnes encouraged her.

But was that really Agnes? Something wasn't right about all this, but Elswyth did as asked and worked to gather her Majik. It took all she had at first, but she concentrated and pulled from her heart center. Finally, a glimmer of power gave her enough energy to move—but only a little. Slowly, Elswyth reached up to meet the hand on her cheek, but it wasn't a hand, and it most certainly was not Agnes.

"What? Who's there? What is going on?" she asked, fighting to regain full consciousness. The harder her mind struggled to climb out of her fog, the more she remembered what had happened and where she was. Agnes wasn't there, so who was that? In a clumsy effort, she tried to reach up again to whoever was there and touched something slippery and warm.

Then she felt fur! Something was licking her, some kind of wild animal! Elswyth trembled with the effort to make her limbs move, spitting mud from her mouth and coughing as she fought to push herself up from the wet ground. Finally able to sit up, certain she would face the gaping jaws of some horrific beast, she gathered the courage to open her eyes.

Now completely aware, she snapped her head around, looking for the ferocious creature, but whatever it was, she had scared it off. Not a ferocious, or otherwise, animal lurked nearby. No tongue. No fur. No teeth. Was that a dream?

Not twenty feet away, however, she saw an oak tree split down the center, still burning and smoking from the lightning strike. She shivered at how close she and Cicero had been to it. *Where is Cis?* Then she saw him—lying still and unconscious, half buried in the muck near her.

"Cis!" Her energy instantly returned, and she scooped him into her arms, terrified she'd lost him. Leaning over him to offer at least a little shelter from the beating rain, Elswyth stroked his head and chest to encourage him to wake up. Panic threatened to overtake her, but with a little more coaxing, he shook his head and looked up at her, dazed, but very much alive.

"Elly?"

"Cis!" She breathed a sigh of relief.

They sat recovering on the cold wet ground, relieved and grateful. Then, they had no choice other than to get up and slog through the rain and keep going. At least the wind had died down some, and the lightning was much further away. They stepped around the still smoldering downed oak and shuddered at what could have been had they been even a few feet closer to it.

As they moved on, the pouring rain muffled the sound of something, or someone, moving away from them in the underbrush.

Hours had passed by the time Elswyth noticed the vegetation had changed. Towering pines outnumbered other trees, but even those were becoming farther and farther apart as they moved up the mountain. Now she could see more of the gray sky through the treetops. The forest floor had less undergrowth and the many more large boulders looked like miniature mountains emerging from the ground. And there was more mud. So much mud! With every uphill step, she had to work to pull her foot out of the greedy muck as it tried to suck her shoes from her feet.

Elswyth figured it was probably close to mid-afternoon by the time the rain let up. Every muscle in her body was sore and tired from the extra effort it took to walk through the deep, earthly sludge. Even poor Cicero was ready for a break.

"Elly, we need to stop, at least for a little while. My wings are tired and my poor stomach is beyond empty! Can we spare some of our food now?" he said, as he landed on a rock near her.

Yes, you're right. I'm exhausted, too. We'll rest for a bit and then we have to keep going and find those standing stones. Hopefully, we aren't far now. Agnes said we would know them when we get there. She walked over to one of the taller pines and chose the driest spot she could find underneath it. Looking in her pack, she saw they only had enough for one last meal, so she brought it out and split it up between the two of them.

Cicero stepped away from her as she handed him his share. "Why don't you eat it all, Elly? After all, I can find something to eat in the woods and you need your strength!"

No, Cis! I know how much you love cheese and Agnes's bread! I'll be fine. Really! I want you to have some. She knew how much he preferred to eat the food that she and Agnes ate. He abhorred scavenging for his meals.

"No, really. You eat. I'll go look around for berries and bring them back if I find any," he said. She knew his cheerful act was for her benefit.

All right, all right. Cicero was stubborn, and she knew she wouldn't change his mind, so she gave in. He waited to make sure she ate every last piece before he took off to find something else edible in the woods. After he left, she got up to get some water from the stream when, off to her right, she heard some rustling in one of the nearby straggly bushes. Thinking Cicero was already back from foraging; she turned with a smile and then froze. It wasn't Cicero.

A fox, still as a statue, stared back at her with one blue and one gold eye! It was a stunning animal. She dared not move a muscle so as not to frighten it away when she heard Cicero croak and land next to her. The fox was gone in a flash.

"Look what I found!" he said proudly as he dropped a branch full of berries. "There are lots just beyond the trees back there." He noticed the smile on her face as she peered into the woods. "What?" he asked, looking in the direction of her gaze.

"There was a fox over there near that tree, Cis! It was beautiful. It only stayed for a moment, and then it was gone."

"Well, then. Sorry I missed it. I can't say that I've ever met one face to face," he said, and looked around the area.

"I have to admit, it did lighten my mood. Let's get some more of those berries. They look delicious! " They gathered more berries, then set off on the trail again. Not much farther up the path, the rain lessened to a misty drizzle but, Elswyth was still drenched to the skin and cold. All they could do was keep working their way up towards the end of the pathway where the standing stones were supposed to be.

NINE

The drizzle never let up, but Elswyth was grateful that at least the torrential downpour had stopped. The walk through the mud and steep incline over the last couple of hours had been arduous. Exhaustion was, once again, taking its toll as her thoughts tumbled around in her head like pebbles in a rushing river.

As instructed, they kept the stream in sight, but she wondered if they had perhaps missed the standing stones—or maybe they were no longer there? Now, near the end of the second day of their trek up the mountain, she felt utterly drained and was not sure just how much longer she could push herself.

Almost imperceptibly at first, she felt a growing energy building in her heart center and the hair on her arms stood up, alerting Elswyth to her Majik being awakened. Then she felt a slight warmth against her chest and remembered she was wearing the pendant her father had left for her. She pulled the chain out from inside her collar and put the stone in her hand. It felt warm, and the faint glow was unmistakable. She stopped walking and held it up on the chain to look closer at it.

"Cis! Where are you? You have to see this!" She turned around on the path, thinking he was in the trees behind her, but when she did that, the stone

became cold again, its light dimmed. *That's curious!* she thought and turned back around in the direction they had been heading. The stone warmed again and the faint glow returned.

Cicero landed next to her. "What is it? What did I miss? Is there another fox? Are you OK?"

"It's the pendant. Look! It's glowing and getting warmer." She showed it to Cicero, who hopped around her, unsure what to make of it.

"Why is it doing that?" he asked, clearly worried.

"I'm not sure why. But watch this," she said, turning back in the direction they had come from. Once again, it was as if the crystal went to sleep. It cooled, and the glow died down.

"Elly, I'm not so sure about this. Should you be wearing that?"

"Agnes said I shouldn't take it off. My Majik doesn't sense anything harmful, at least so far, and it only started reacting the farther up the mountain we got. Besides, why would my father leave something for me that was harmful if he went to all that trouble to find me in the first place? Maybe this is a good sign."

"Hm," Cicero said. "I suppose if you say so."

"You're such a worrier, Cis." She tucked it back inside her blouse as they continued up the mountain, the stone in the pendant still warm against her chest.

"I'm going to fly up ahead on the path a ways and see what I can find," Cicero said.

"Thanks, Cis. It's getting late, and we've got to be close." He took off, and she continued to trudge uphill while working hard at keeping her shoes from getting sucked off her feet in the mud.

He was gone less than fifteen minutes when she heard him call to her in the distance. At first, she couldn't make out what he was saying and panicked. *"What is it? Are you OK? Did you find something?"* No answer. *"Cis?!"* Just then, he landed at her feet, hopping around excitedly in the mud.

41

"Up ahead, Elly! They're up ahead!" he said. He was so excited he had trouble catching his breath. "I saw the standing stones. At least I think that's what they are. Come on! We only have a little farther to go, Elly!"

"Oh, thank goodness! I was starting to worry that we had somehow missed them or that maybe they were no longer there."

"We'll be there well before dark but," he said and shifted nervously from foot to foot. "Elly, there is nothing else up there. And I mean nothing! Just rocks, sand, the standing stones, and the mountains beyond that. No people, food, or shelter. Nothing!"

Elswyth considered the news for a moment. *"Well, we can't go back and we can't stay here. So, forward it is."* She was muddy, tired, hungry, and soaked through to the skin in the chill mountain air. She shifted the weight of her bags, looked up the hill, and took a deep breath. *"Lead the way, my friend. Let's see what's next."* She nodded forward, trying to sound braver than she felt.

Thirty minutes later, they reached a large circular plateau on the side of the mountain, completely bare of trees or vegetation. Rocks and boulders jutted up from barren, sandy ground everywhere and the stream they'd been following since they left the grove sliced through the plateau diagonally. Up ahead, positioned center stage, were two towering, ancient monoliths, stationed parallel to each other like silent colossal sentries. They stood far enough apart from each other for a small cart or wagon to pass between them. On the other side of the plateau, they saw a narrow waterfall that plummeted down the sheer rock wall of the towering mountain. That waterfall was the source of the stream they'd been following up from Willow Grove. Worst of all, there was no path or road beyond this point. It was a dead end!

Navigating around all the rocks and boulders in the sand, they made their way until they stood in front of the standing stones, which were even more monumental up close. Not wanting to alarm Cicero, she didn't tell him that the crystal had now become quite warm against her chest, not enough to burn, but enough to feel the heat. She was sure now the stone was letting her know they were in the right place—at least, that's what she hoped. But what

42

is this place? Cicero was right. There was absolutely nothing here but sand, rock, and gray. Everything was dirty and gray!

Cicero landed on a small boulder next to her and spoke in a hushed tone. "Elly, I can sense Majik here."

"I can, too, but it feels safe somehow," she said. *"We have to walk between the stones, Cis. Agnes said once we reach them, we have to go through."*

"I know. Let me go first, though, since we don't know what's going to happen and—"

"We go together, Cis," she interrupted. *"Just like always, we will go together."* She offered her arm, and he flew up and landed there. The surrounding air began to buzz and vibrate as she stepped closer to the stones. Then, even if she had wanted to, she could no longer turn back as the Majik in the monoliths pulled them into the path between—and they disappeared from sight.

TEN

Everything around them went fuzzy and white, like they had fallen into a dense, soupy fog, and breathing was difficult. Impossible to tell which way was up or down, Elswyth became disoriented and nauseous, her stomach doing flip-flops. Majik buzzed around them, like thousands of bees whirring through the air. She couldn't see Cicero, but she felt him hug up against her chest, his talons clinging to her sleeve. Worried he'd fall, she dropped her second bag and reached up to hug him closer.

Then, as quickly as it appeared, the fog lifted, and she stood staring at her surroundings, blinking in bright sunlight. When the dizziness subsided, she looked around, wide-eyed in disbelief. They were on the opposite side of the standing stones, but everything had changed.

Gone were the rocks and sand. The plateau was now full of green grasses and colorful wildflowers. Birds were singing in clumps of trees that dotted the area, and the sky was a brilliant cerulean blue, with not a rain cloud in sight. The waterfall still cascaded down the mountainside at the far end of the plateau, but now lush vegetation framed the falls all the way to the bottom. And, of course, the stream was still there, but now it flowed under a quaint stone bridge that stood in front of her, giving her access to the opposite side of the stream. Beyond the bridge was a road that led off the plateau via the side of the mountain.

Across the bridge, stood a man. No, not a man. He had pointed ears! He was an elf! Tall and handsome, dressed like royalty, and smiling at her and Cicero. *Could that be my father?* Even though he looked no older than forty, his hair was as white as snow. Sitting next to him on the ground was a fox. Not just any fox—THE fox she saw earlier. She could see its unusual colored eyes, even from where she stood.

Next to them stood a pair of magnificent cream-colored horses hitched to an elegant mahogany carriage trimmed in gold. Up in the driver's seat sat the coachman, also an elf, smiling down at her and Cicero. He looked as though he enjoyed his food quite a bit because the buttons on the jacket of his uniform were struggling to stay closed. "Hello, Your Highness!" the coachman waved and tipped his purple velvet hat to her and Cicero. He chuckled and his gray, handlebar mustache wriggled. "My name is Sedge. It'll be my pleasure to deliver you safe and sound tonight."

"Cis, he called me Your Highness. Me? Well, at least the elves here seem friendly," Elswyth thought to Cicero, *"wherever here is!"* It all felt like a dream, and she wondered if the last two days had finally made her mind snap. This place couldn't be real, could it? She turned around to look back at where they had come through the standing stones. The other side was a wavy, hazy vision of the plateau as it was before they stepped through—all rock and sand.

"Please don't be afraid, Your Highness," the elf next to the carriage spoke up. She spun back around as he continued. "My name is Caden and I am your father's regent." He bowed his head to them. "Your father wasn't expecting you for a few days and is up north in Belnoir until tomorrow."

"Okay. So, I guess that's not my father, Cis."

"This is Ruby," Caden said, gesturing to the fox at his feet. "She's been trailing you in case you needed help and tells me you had quite a scare with some lightning. I'm glad you're both all right! Ruby also made sure that Agnes knows of your progress. She's fine, incidentally. Her ruse went well with the soldiers and she even rescued another young girl destined for the king's dormitories. Agnes is an amazing woman, Your Highness, but I'm sure you already knew that."

Ruby stood up and wagged her tail. "Hello and welcome to you both. I'm so glad you've made it here safely! We've been looking forward to this day for a long time! I hope I didn't frighten you on the trail." Both Elswyth and Cicero were too dumbstruck to respond, and they just stared at Caden and Ruby. The last few days were already crazy, and this just topped it all off!

"Ruby also let me know how difficult your trek up here has," Caden continued. "I'm sorry I couldn't have brought you up here myself but, this has all happened so quickly I couldn't escort you here properly. Please know, we had originally planned that I would come to get you once you were ready and—" He stopped talking, finally acknowledging Elswyth's wide-opened eyes and Cicero's stare. "I'm sorry. I am rambling and I know you must be hungry and tired. Please, let me help you with your things." He crossed the bridge, picked up the bag she'd dropped, and helped her remove the backpack. "Please come this way," he said, as he gently led Elswyth towards the carriage, Cicero still firmly cradled in her arms.

Caden opened the door and helped the weary travelers into the carriage. "Ruby and I are going to ride up top with Sedge so you can have plenty of room to spread out and rest." Caden bowed before he closed the door.

Elswyth settled onto the soft bench seat, covered in beautiful purple brocade with gold trim. The windows on either side had ivory silk shades with fringe on the bottom that were pulled down all the way. It made it comfortably dark after being thrust so abruptly into bright sunlight. She then felt self-conscious of the mud covering her from head to toe, especially next to all the rich fabric and ornate trim.

"Hi! I'm Pic."

Both Elswyth and Cicero jumped at the sound of the voice. There, in the shadows of the corner opposite them, sat a smiling Elven girl who looked about twelve years old.

ELEVEN

Elswyth hadn't noticed the young elf sitting in the darkened corner when she got in the coach, but she noticed her now and pulled the shades up so she could see her better. The elf had a warm smile and freckles that covered her plump cheeks. The tips of her pointed ears blushed a deep pink and her long, braided hair was as white as Caden's.

"My father said it was okay for me to come along to meet you today. I hope that's okay with you, Your Highness?" Elswyth cringed at the title. "That's my dad who you were talking to out there. Oh, what a handsome raven you are, Cicero! I thought you two might be hungry after your journey, so I packed a dinner," Pic spoke quickly, barely taking time to breathe, and held up a food hamper for them to see. "I hope you like what I put in here. I love to cook. Do you? I wasn't sure what people in Carthia eat but, my father said I did a great job with my choices. He has to say that as my dad, though. Right?"

Cicero interrupted before she could go on. "Um, thank you for your kindness, Pic. I am Elswyth's complement and best friend. So you know, Elswyth does not speak, at least not with a voice. She never has. But I am connected to her thoughts and happy to help you talk with her."

"Thanks, Cicero. But, you should both know there are many elves here who don't have a speaking voice just like you, Elswyth. Lots! Father told me that's unusual where you live, but it's not here. We can still talk with each other. All you need to do is direct your thought to the person you want to talk with and we'll hear you in here," she smiled, tapping her head. Just then, the carriage lurched forward, and they were on their way, but to where, Elswyth couldn't imagine.

"I don't know if I like that, Cis. They can read my thoughts!?" she asked, looking down at him.

"Elswyth wants to know if her thoughts are still private? Can anyone hear them?" Cicero asked Pic.

"Oh, no. They can't hear your thoughts unless you want someone to hear them. You just use your intention to speak to someone, though, and they'll be able to talk with you. If you want, you can also ask others to only speak in thought and not out loud," she said, smiling. "It's up to you!"

Elswyth gave it a try and asked, *"So, Pic can you hear my thought to you now?"*

"Yes! I can!" her smile widening. "Perfect."

Elswyth couldn't believe she could talk that easily with someone other than Cicero. She looked down at him as he let out a loud huff. Their conversations had always been their private activity. *"Don't worry, Cis. What we have is always going to be precious!"* He huffed again, then eyed the basket of food.

"I sure would like to see what you have in your basket, Pic," he said. Elswyth smiled to herself. Cicero was never shy about asking for something to eat, but in all fairness, the aromas were tantalizing.

"Of course, Cicero! You both must be starving. We have a bit of a ride left, so why wait until we get home to eat, right?" Pic reached into the basket and pulled out plates, napkins, and forks, laying them out on the seat next to Elswyth. Next came herb crusted lamb chops, venison medallions, crusty bread, butter, and fruits (some of which Elswyth had never seen. There were baked desserts that almost looked too beautiful to eat! Almost. Pic even produced a capped bottle of cold water and crystal glasses. Last to come out was a package wrapped in brightly colored paper.

"I made this especially for you, Cicero. I had to go to the royal library to see what ravens ate, but found a recipe for a seed mix I hope you'll like." She opened the paper folds and held it out to him.

"Um, thank you but, no," he said, backing away. "I appreciate your efforts, but my Majik allows me to eat pretty much what I want. Except for lentils and beans. They give me gas!"

"Oh, my yes. Please never give him lentils or beans!" Elswyth shook her head and rolled her eyes.

"Duly noted!" Pic said and chuckled. "I'll remember to never include either of those on any menu!"

"Pic, how, in the name of the Fates, did you fit all that in there?" Elswyth asked, peering into the now empty hamper.

"Just a little simple Majik the chefs in the royal kitchens taught me. It's very handy for packing lots of stuff in small containers. And I can keep the food warm and fresh with it, too."

"I would love to learn how you do that!"

"I'll be happy to teach you." Pic beamed, blushing ear tip to ear tip.

Cicero bounced up and down with delight at the feast in front of them, unconcerned with the how the Majik worked and only wanted to eat. "Elly, I would like some of that! Oh, and a little of that, too!" Cicero said and pointed his beak excitedly at everything, ready to try it all.

"Cis, you're going to burst if you eat all that!" Elswyth said while filling a plate for him. *"Honestly, I don't know where you put it all in that body of yours!"* She started plating a few of the delicacies for him and then filled a plate for herself. *"Pic, did you say you cooked all this?! This is marvelous,"* she said, tasting the lamb chops.

"Thank you, and yes! I've been cooking for some time. My father says that I'm very accomplished in the kitchen for only being twenty years old!"

Elswyth almost choked on her food. *"You're twenty? I'm sorry but, I thought you were—much younger."*

"Ah, yes. You're going to find that we age differently than humans. And we live a lot longer, too. A lot. But you'll have all the time in the world to learn about us. Actually, now that I think of it, since you are half elf, you will probably live longer than many humans, too. Of course, I am not an expert. Your father can help you with all that, I guess."

"My father! Do you know if I will meet him soon?" Elswyth asked. Cicero was listening while he munched away, sampling everything on his plate.

"I only know you will meet with him tomorrow afternoon. When we get back to the castle, I'll help you get settled into your room. You're going to love it! At least I hope you'll love it. I helped to decorate it for you," she said proudly.

"You obviously have many talents, Pic!" Elswyth said, and served herself a second helping of a small cake topped with icing shaped into delicate flowers. She felt herself warming to Pic as they talked. Images of the village children that used to shun and torment her for being different flashed through her mind, the memories still painful. Pic was different. She was treating her with kindness, and it felt good.

When everyone had their fill, Pic could see her guests were tired and pulled a quilt from under the seat. "We still have a way to go, so why don't you both nap? It'll be dark by the time we get there, but I'll wake you just before we arrive."

Elswyth had so many questions she wanted to ask but, by the time she'd eaten her last bite she had run out of energy. She looked down at Cicero, already asleep on her lap, snoring away, noticed a piece of cake crumb on his beak, and brushed it off. Laying down on the soft bench, she adjusted him so he was curled up safely in her arms, while Pic tucked the blanket over them both. As she closed her eyes, dreams of Agnes and home came almost immediately for Elswyth as the motion of the carriage rocked her to sleep.

TWELVE

P ic shook Elswyth's shoulders. "Time to wake up, Your Highness! We're getting close to the castle and you have to see the view!"

"Okay, Pic! I'm awake." Well, more or less, anyway. She was still groggy and her legs were sore from slogging through all that mud up the mountain. It was dark inside the carriage except for two small, dimly lit crystal lanterns on the back wall. Judging from the rumbling and bumping of the carriage, they were moving quickly along the road. She sat up, looked around, and saw that Pic had pulled the shades up on the windows. Cicero was already awake, perched on the sill on the right, intent on gazing outside.

"Elly! You have got to see this!" he cried. "It's fantastic!"

She moved next to him, looked out, and took in the sight before her. The night sky was alight with a thick blanket of stars and a thin crescent moon that hung low in the sky. They were traveling on a narrow road next to a steep drop that plummeted thousands of feet down the side of the mountain to a bay below. Turning back around towards the opposite side, through the left window she saw a rock wall, only inches from the carriage, zooming past as they sped through the night.

Back to the right side, she looked out again and saw the expansive bay below, many miles wide and sheltered by tall mountains on all sides. Except for a protected marina where ships were docked or moored close to the shore, the edges of the bay were rocky and alive with crashing waves. The salt air was invigorating. She craned her head a little further out and down, gasped, and pulled her head back in. The sheer drop from the road to the rocky shores below made her stomach drop to the floor.

Pic smiled and patted Elswyth's hand. "Don't worry. Sedge has driven this road for over a hundred years and could navigate the way with his eyes closed." When Pic saw the startled look on Elswyth's face, she added, "Oh, but he'll keep his eyes open. I promise!"

"Wow, Elly, look up ahead! It's beautiful!" Cicero said. She gathered her courage and craned her head out the window, looking straight ahead in the direction they were traveling, determined not to look down again.

Cicero was right. She couldn't believe what was coming into view! The road along the side of the mountain made a wide curve to the right and, in the distance, she could see a city and a castle built into the sheer face of the pinnacle. Myriad twinkling lights shone from top to bottom, so many that, even in the dark of night, she could see the hundreds of streets, terraces, steps, and walkways carved into the side of the rock. Trees and gardens fit the vertical landscape everywhere. Beautiful marble facades marked the entrances to dwellings and other buildings. Colorful awnings lined streets here and there that looked to be bazaars or shops during the day. It was nothing like she had ever seen in her life.

Pic pointed out the window. "Elswyth, that's the city of Glenorim below and the castle up above. Isn't it amazing to see at night? And all the lights you see? They're powered by our collective Majiks! I always thought it looked like the stars fell down from the sky and landed onto the mountainside. Don't you think it looks like that?" Pic's pride shone on her face as she described this place—her home. "And that's just what you see from the outside. There's even more built into the mountain," she said.

"Oh, Pic. It's amazing! Never in my life did I imagine a place like this existed! I can't wait to see it all."

Pic gave Elswyth's arm a gentle tug. "You two should put your heads in now. The tunnel to the castle is coming up, and it is pretty narrow," No sooner had everyone sat back in their seats when the carriage entered a dark passage carved into the rock. Sedge apparently knew it well because he didn't slow down, guided only by the lanterns he had at the front of the coach. "We're almost there now. Just a few more minutes." Pic said, almost bouncing up and down in her seat with excitement.

They soon emerged from the tunnel into a massive cobblestone courtyard built into the side of the mountain. Hundreds of lanterns lit a perimeter lined with purple and gold standards, the image of a gold wyvern, its wings spread wide, adorning each flag. The coach pulled to a stop, and Elswyth craned her neck farther out the window. Along one wall, steps lead up to an entrance to the castle. Tall stone arches framed intricately carved wooden doors with filigreed Elven steel handles and hinges. Servants dressed in cream-colored silk with purple trim stood ready to open them. Another wall led to stables, the groomsmen already rushing out to unhitch the horses and lead them to water.

Caden opened the door to the carriage and offered his hand to Elswyth and then Pic.

Thirteen

C aden spread his arms wide and announced, "Welcome to Glenorim Castle, Your Highness! I hope you find your second home to your liking!" Ruby stood by his side, wagging her tail.

"Thank you. It's beyond what I could have imagined and I am at a loss for words!" She said as she directed her thought to him. Cicero hopped out and sat on her arm, gawking at everything, and everyone, around him. She looked down at the fox. *"And Ruby, I didn't thank you earlier for helping us in the storm. I'm not sure we would be here if you hadn't helped me wake up."*

"Think nothing of it, Your Highness. I sensed the strength of your Majik and knew you could help yourself. You just needed a little nudge, is all. I'm glad you and Cicero are safe." She winked her gold eye at her.

Caden spoke up. "And don't worry. You'll know your way around here in no time. Let's get you and Cicero to your rooms. A servant will bring your things up for you." Caden turned to Ruby and whispered something to her. She nodded, turned and ran ahead into the castle.

Pic cleared her throat. "Did I tell you that I helped to decorate your sitting room and bedroom, Your Highness? I hope you like everything!" Pic said.

"Yes, you did and I'm sure I will," she said and smiled. Elswyth couldn't put a finger on why yet, but she not only liked this young elf, she felt a connection

through her Majik that resonated with her own. *"And Pic, how about you call me Elly? It seems like we are going to become good friends. What do you say?"*

Pic's face lit up and the tips of her ears blushed even deeper than they already were. "Thank you, Your High—I mean Elly!" She walked a little taller as they entered the castle through the large doors at the top of the steps.

After winding their way through arched hallways filled with paintings and ornate portals leading to who knew where, Caden stopped in front of a wooden door with a carving of a raven flying above a willow tree. "Home sweet, home, Your Highness! The door will open for you and Cicero, using your Majik. You can grant anyone else access, too. It is completely up to you."

"Look!" Cicero cried. "Hey! That's me on the door, and quite a handsome likeness, if I do say so myself!" He puffed out his chest. Elswyth grinned at him, then focused on the handle, and the door opened.

She stepped over the threshold, flabbergasted, as she looked around. *"All this is for me and Cicero?!"* Her eyes grew wide as she surveyed the marvelous room before her, which was larger than the entire cottage back home, with ceilings twice as high. Soft greens, ivory, and gold complemented each other throughout the space.

A crackling fire had been lit in the carved stone fireplace and two over-stuffed chairs sat on either side of the hearth. On one wall was a towering floor-to-ceiling window, framed in dark green velvet drapes, with a view of the night sky and the city lights below. On the other side of the room was a dining table big enough to seat six people with room to spare. Behind that, against the wall, stood a beautiful burl wood desk. And especially for Cicero, set near the table, stood an elven steel perch trimmed in gold. He flew right over and settled on it.

"Well? What do you think? Do you like it?" Pic asked, wringing her hands. Elswyth could only nod in amazement. "Oh, I'm so glad! Now come through here to see your bedroom and bathroom," she said and beckoned Elswyth to follow. Caden smiled while his daughter continued with the tour.

Elswyth stepped in behind Pic and was, once again, at a loss for words. Another tall window looked out on the spectacular view below, and opposite that was an enormous four-poster bed covered with thick down comforters and fluffy pillows. In the nearby corner was yet another ornate perch for Cicero next to an enormous wardrobe with carvings of willow trees on the doors. A dressing table and dresser completed the furnishings.

"I helped pick out some clothes for you in the wardrobe, but if you don't like any of them, or want more, we can take care of that later. I just wanted you to have something nice to wear. Now let's go through here to the bathroom." Pic pulled Elswyth through a door on the back wall. It seemed there was no end to being surprised at this apartment, and the bathroom was no exception. A large brass tub filled with hot water and bubbles stood on cream-colored tiles. Lavender infused the steam rising in the air and a nearby table held thick towels and a basket of soaps. Across from the tub was an elegant brass sink set into a marble countertop, and next to that, yet another door that led to a water closet.

"Pic, this is too much! I don't know what to do with all this." Elswyth felt lost in all the luxury.

"Oh, no! You don't like what I've done? I'm so, so sorry!" Pic placed her hands on her heart. "I can change anything you want. Just let me know and—"

"No! It's not that! Please don't worry." She felt bad for hurting her new friend's feelings. *"I love it! I do! It will just take me a bit to get used to all of this, I think."* Elswyth smiled as she hugged Pic. *"Thank you so much for all you've done. I truly love it!"*

Pic sighed, visibly relieved. "You're welcome! I'm so, so happy you like it," They walked back into the bedroom and Pic showed Elswyth a gold rope that hung from a lever on the wall. "I almost forgot! If you need me for anything, anything at all, you can use this," she explained, and pulled its tasseled end down once. "It rings a bell in my room. I'll be here in one blink of a wyvern's eye, if you ring it."

They went back out into the sitting room and Elswyth noticed her bags had not only been delivered, but someone had even cleaned all the mud off them. Caden asked Elswyth to join him in the chairs by the fireplace.

"Ruby let your father know you've arrived safely and you'll see him tomorrow afternoon at 2 pm," he explained. "I want you to know he is very much looking forward to meeting with you. He's been waiting a long time for this day. And, so you know, Ruby is also making sure Agnes is notified of your safe arrival."

"Thank you for everything, Caden."

"Of course, Your Highness. Someone will bring up breakfast for you in the morning and leave it at your table. And—for your own safety—I urge you to stay here in your rooms at least until after you see your father. No one but us knows who you are yet and that you're going to meet with the prince. Your family has placed a protective Majik shield around you, so you'll be safe here. I know this is all probably overwhelming, but, again, your father will explain everything tomorrow," he said with a smile. Then Caden stood up and reached out for his daughter. "Pic, why don't we let the princess and Cicero settle in for the night? They've had a long few days!"

"Okay. You're right," she said with a heavy sigh. Clearly, she didn't want to go, and turned back to Elswyth one last time. "I'll come help you get ready in the morning. Remember, just pull the rope and I will be right over. My apartment is only a few doors away. Night, Elly! And to you, too, Cicero. I'm so glad you're finally here," she said.

After they left, Elswyth walked through the rooms with Cicero on her arm, missing Agnes and their cottage deeply. As stunning as everything here was, it still wasn't home, and she didn't know when she would see it again. She looked through the dresser and found a silky white nightgown with blue ribbon trim and considered wearing it. Instead, she opened her bag and pulled out the cotton one that Agnes made for her. It was a bit of home—of comfort—and she laid it across the bed. Then she went into the bathroom and took a long, relaxing bath. The hot water helped to soothe her sore muscles, aching joints, and busy thoughts. Majik was keeping the water comfortably hot until she was ready to get out, so she stayed in until her fingers and toes turned pink and wrinkly.

When she was done and dressed, she crawled onto the bed and snuggled under the thick comforters. After fluffing up the pillows, she patted the bed, and Cicero flew over from his perch.

"Elly?" he began and stopped.

"Cis? Is something wrong?"

"Well, no. Yes. It's just that—" He paused again, not looking her in the eye.

"Cis, please. Just tell me. It's okay!" she said, pulling him closer.

He cleared his throat, didn't respond right away, and fluffed his feathers out. "I've always been the only one who could hear your thoughts. We always had that together—no one else, and I felt that made us special, you know? Now you can talk with anyone here you want," he said, still not looking up at her.

"Oh, my dear friend. That you could hear my thoughts is not what makes us special, although that is pretty incredible. It's our friendship. You are so precious to me and we'll always be together." She placed a gentle finger under his beak. *"You have nothing to worry about. No one could ever take your place. Okay?"*

"Okay. I love you, Elly."

"Love you, too, Cis."

They both snuggled under the blankets. Then, *"I don't think I'm ever going to get to sleep tonight, Cis. My mind is still churning!"* Elswyth said.

"Same with me. It's been a long couple of days and I can't stop thinking about it all. And this place! Wow!"

"I know, my friend. I know."

Within minutes, they both fell fast asleep.

FOURTEEN

"E lly! It's time to wake up! I smell food! Elllllllyyy," Cicero sang in her ear. The sunlight was so bright she could see its light through her eyelids, so she put her pillow over her face and made a mental note to pull the drapes closed on the windows before they went to bed that night.

"Cis, it's early! Do we really have to get up now?"

"Elly, come on! It smells delicious, and I don't like to eat by myself. Besides, I can't open the bedroom door on my own, you know. Please, can't we get up?"

"All right, Cis. I'm getting up!" Elswyth thought to him. *That bird and his stomach were going to be the end of me!* She sat up and looked around the room, which was even more grand in the morning sunlight. Her own stomach then growled in agreement with Cicero, so she arose to investigate those aromas.

She swung her legs over the edge of the bed and padded over to open the door. Once in the sitting room, she noticed that someone had already lit the fireplace, which warmed the space to a perfect temperature. It may have been late spring, but the air was cooler higher in the mountains, so she was glad for the warmth.

Then the wonderful smells from the table wafted over her, beckoning her to hurry over to see the eggs, cooked ham, juices, fresh-made breads, and fruits arranged on the linen tablecloth. Steam from a brass teapot sent the warm, spicy fragrance of cinnamon into the air. She noticed two crystal cups attached to Cicero's perch in the corner, one with water and the other with seeds and berries. *"Cicero, I think there is something for you over there,"* she said and pointed, knowing full well what he would say.

"I saw that. Not interested. That's just snack food," he sniffed with his beak in. "I'm eating with you. I'll just use your saucer as my plate for now. Next time, though, we need to let them know I should have my own plate."

Elswyth smiled and served him a few small portions on a saucer, which he starting eating almost before she set it before him on the table. *"Slow down, Cis! You're going to get fat. What would Agnes say to feeding you all this?"* Mentioning Agnes made them both go silent, and their mood sunk. *"Hey, let's finish up and have Pic come in for a visit. I'd like her to help me with what to wear today, anyway."* She was getting nervous about meeting her father later, and needed the distraction. Besides, she enjoyed Pic's company.

"Brilliant idea," Cicero said, then helped himself to another bit of egg.

After they finished eating, Elswyth unpacked her belongings, her own homespun clothes appearing out of place and plain next to all the finery Pic had left for her. But Agnes had made so many of her things, so she still folded everything carefully and put them in the dresser drawers. The desk in the sitting room was a perfect place for the pouch of herbs and powders that Agnes packed for her and she set the book of potions next to them. She chose the simplest dress in the wardrobe (which was still very elegant, by her standards) and put it on. She assessed her new look in the wardrobe's full-length mirror and shook her head. *I don't look like me!* Her curly red hair was a bit of a mess as she worked to comb it out, but no matter what she tried, it still looked unruly.

"Oh Cis, I don't look like I fit in here. It is a beautiful dress, but it isn't me!"

Cicero flew in from the next room and landed on the dresser. "Wow, Elly! You look wonderful! Really, you do," he said with approval. "You'll get used to it. Don't worry. It's going to be all right."

"Thanks. You know, this is a wonderful place, and everyone has been really nice so far but, I miss Agnes. I miss our little cottage."

"I do, too. I miss Agnes fussing at me, but we'll see her again," he said.

"I have to keep believing that, Cis." She turned, walked over to the rope on the wall, and pulled it. *"Maybe Pic can help me choose something appropriate for today. I want to look perfect to meet my father!"*

Pic must have been waiting for her to ring the bell because less than five minutes later, there was a knock at the door.

"Oh, you look wonderful in that dress! And how was your breakfast?" Pic declared as she swept into the room. Elswyth just smiled as she whizzed by and closed the door.

"Don't tell me, you picked the menu, didn't you?" Elswyth said, already knowing the answer. Pic nodded enthusiastically in response. *"It was delicious, but I do have one request for our meals.—rather, the request is Cicero's. Can we please set a plate for him, too, when we have meals here? He would appreciate it, if that's okay."*

"Of course! That's easy. I'll be sure that's taken care of from now on. Anything else?"

"Well, yes, as a matter of fact. This is all so new to me and I don't know what to wear. Everyone I see here dresses so stylish and is so distinguished. I'm used to simply braiding my hair and wearing my comfortable, cotton clothes. I don't know where to start with those lovely dresses in the wardrobe. And my hair? I'm at a loss with that, too. Can you help me? I want to look perfect when I meet my father this afternoon."

Pic put her hands on her hips, cocked her head, and looked at Elswyth, appraising her from all sides. "We have a lot to work with here! You're so beautiful, even if you don't have pointed ears." She caught herself at the last comment. "Oh, I didn't mean to offend! That came out wrong and I just meant that people might notice." Pic grimaced and put her hands to her face. "Oh bother. I'm going to shut up now!"

Elswyth chuckled and pulled Pic's hands down. *"Pic, I am very aware I'm not like everyone else here—in more ways than just my ears. I'm used to being different and I will be fine. Now let's get busy,"* she thought to her as she gave her a hug.

The morning flew by with trying on clothes, deciding which ones they would keep, and putting the others in a pile to be taken away. The whole time, Pic offered tips and suggestions about the accessories that went with each dress, pulling jewelry pieces from the dresser one by one. Once Elswyth decided which dress she liked best, Pic sat her down at the dressing table.

"Now. What to do with your hair," Pic mused, eyeing Elswyth's curly red mane. She played with putting it up, braiding it and tying ribbons through it. Nothing seemed to make Pic happy, and she was clearly growing frustrated with her efforts as she mumbled the entire time. "That's too fancy. Oh, that won't do at all! Oh, what was I thinking?'

Amused, Elswyth watched the process in the mirror. Twenty minutes later, Pic exclaimed, "I know what to do!" She went to the dresser and pulled out multiple strings of tiny pearls and held them up for Elswyth to see. "These will go perfect with your dress and show up nicely against your red hair! I'm going to turn you around so you can't see until I'm done."

Elswyth sat still while Pic wove the beads in and around her hair. It took thirty minutes, and she began to wonder how long it would take to remove it all later. The whole time, Pic mumbled to herself again, standing back to look at her work and retrying something she had already done. Finally, she announced she had finished and turned Elswyth around so she could look in the mirror. "Well? What do you think?" she asked, holding her breath.

Elswyth reached up to touch her hair, careful not to muss up anything and couldn't believe how stunning it looked. Multiple strands of the tiny pearls crowned her head and then, woven through the rest of her hair, were more pearls. Her hair also had a sheen to it that gave it a subtle sparkle. She had never felt so pretty.

"Pic, I love it! Thank you. I never would have been able to do this on my own."

Looking over from his perch, Cicero exclaimed, "Elly, you look amazing! I must say, Pic, excellent work."

Letting out a loud sigh, Pic put her hands on Elswyth's shoulders. "I'm glad you like it. Oh, and I used a little Majik to add the sparkle. I may not be that great with my own Majik yet, but I can do that," she said.

Servants were bringing in the afternoon meal, so Pic went out to ask for the extra plate for Cicero (who was already at the table waiting, of course) and a plate for herself. Elswyth looked down at all the food and wasn't sure how much she'd be able to eat. Her stomach was in knots.

In one hour, she would meet her father.

FIFTEEN

As a servant removed the last of the lunch dishes from the table, there was a knock at the door. "That should be Caden," Cicero said, turning to Elswyth. "Are you ready, Elly?"

"No but, I guess I'll have to be. This is all so unreal! You're coming with me. Right, Cis? I really don't think I can do this alone," she said, while holding her arm out.

"Of course I will. I won't leave your side." He fluttered over and landed on her arm. "You're going to be fine. And don't worry. We do this together!"

Pic hugged Elswyth tight. "I'll be here for you when you get back," she promised. Elswyth smiled at her and opened the door.

A few minutes later, she was walking down the corridor with Caden, their footsteps echoing off the lofty, arched ceilings of the castle halls. Elves passed them coming and going as if nothing was out of the ordinary, which made everything feel even more surreal for Elswyth. She wondered what those elves would do if they saw her rounded ears under her hair, and then hugged Cicero close to her chest.

Caden cut into her thoughts. "Your Highness, we go up this stairway." Her mind was so far away she almost missed him turning left.

"Sorry! I'm coming." She turned back and followed him up the steps.

"We're almost there. His study is at the top of the landing." He looked over at her. "If it helps, your father is just as nervous as you are."

She nodded, grateful for his kindness, but bit her lower lip, her nerves threatening to get the better of her. Her father had the advantage of her knowing of her existence all these years and had the time to get used to the idea. She'd only just found out about him a few days ago. *Just concentrate on getting through this, Elly,* she told herself. *Wait a minute! What do I do when I first meet him? Do hug him? Shake his hand? Curtsy? After all, he is a prince. Maybe I should wait for him to make a first move.* She could feel a bead of sweat rolling down her spine as her thoughts buzzed around in her brain like a shaken hornet's nest. Cicero leaned into her again to remind her he was there for her, and it helped, at least a little.

When they got to the landing, they walked up to two heavy wooden doors at the end of the short hallway. On each side of the doors stood a soldier, their spears crossed over each other, blocking the way in. Upon seeing Caden and Elswyth approach, the guards snapped to attention and righted their weapons.

"You'll be fine," he said and smiled, while knocking on the door. She squared her shoulders and looked straight ahead as the doors opened. An older, plump elf wearing a jacket, vest, and knee breeches bowed, smiled and ushered them into the hallway. The tips of his ears flopped over and his bald head reflected the bright lights above.

"This way, please. His Highness is expecting you," the elf said with a tilt of his head. They followed him to the end of the corridor, where he opened another set of enormous doors. As they stepped into the room, the servant bowed and left through a door off to the right.

Caden faced Elswyth. "I'll be back to escort you to your rooms when you're done. It will be okay. I promise you." He walked out of the study and closed the doors behind him.

Elswyth turned back around to take in the space. Even with six two-story windows, the room was darker than the hallways, so it took her eyes a moment to adjust. As she stepped further into the vast wood-paneled room, she looked up at the high cathedral ceilings, and marveled at the ornate animal carvings that decorated every beam. Shelves full of books and scrolls lined the walls. Maps, both ancient and modern, hung in niches throughout the room, one of them being Carthia. An elven steel staircase led up to a second floor, where there were even more books, and she realized there had to be thousands of them here. In the center of the first floor stood a massive ornate desk, its top full of more maps, books, and parchments, with a beautiful chandelier hanging over it for light.

She didn't see anyone at first, but then, from the corner of her eye, noticed movement near a set of chairs in front of the monumental granite fireplace to the left. Then she saw him. He had dark auburn hair, broad shoulders, and he stood tall and strong. If she were to imagine what an elven prince should look like, he would be it. While she could sense he was nervous, he exuded strength and power. Underneath all that, however, she could sense a gentle spirit and his Majik felt—familiar and connected to hers.

"Hello, Elswyth. I'm your father. I'm so happy we finally get to meet!"

Sixteen

T hey stood in awkward silence. Prince Dayel then reached up to rub the back of his neck and gestured to one of the two chairs next to him. "Please, Elswyth, come sit down. I'll tell you what I can, and then you can ask all the questions you want. I imagine you must have many."

Elswyth sat ramrod straight on the edge of the chair while Cicero hopped onto the arm, as close to her as possible. She watched her father closely. When he looked up at her, his bright green eyes shone with a kindness that put her at ease and she wondered if she should say something first, but didn't.

Prince Dayel then acknowledged Cicero. "Hello, Cicero. I'm glad we also finally get to meet. I hope you know how indebted I am to you for how you have taken care of Elswyth all this time."

Cicero puffed up the feathers on his chest. "Of course. Elly and I are the best of friends and I will do anything to protect her." Elswyth looked down and patted his back.

Dayel nodded. "I can see that you're both very close." The awkward silence stood like a wall between father and daughter until someone cleared their throat to the left of the prince's chair. "Oh yes! I almost forgot! I'd like to introduce you to my complement, Ratheus," her father said.

A large brown bear shuffled forward on enormous paws, sat down next to her father's chair and raised a forepaw in greeting. "Dayel has told me all about you, Your Highness and you, Cicero. I am honored to meet you both and look forward to getting to know you." His voice was low and gravelly, but not unkind.

The floppy-eared servant came back into the room with a tray of tea and cakes and set it on the low table between the chairs. He bowed to the prince. "Would you like me to pour the tea, Your Highness? I can stay and make sure you have everything you need."

"No thank you, Samésh. We'll make do ourselves. Why don't you take the rest of the afternoon off and spend some time with your wife?" Dayel said.

"Thank you, Your Highness. You're always so thoughtful." Samésh bowed and smiled. He turned towards Elswyth, but his smile was gone and his eyes downcast. She wondered if he had noticed her ears earlier and reached up to make sure her hair covered them. The elf lingered for a moment in front of her, then turned to exit through the servant's door on the far side of the study.

Dayel rubbed the back of his neck again and said, "I guess I should first ask what Agnes told you?"

Elswyth took a deep breath. *Well, here we go,* she thought, then recounted all she'd been told before her escape. She watched him while she sent him her thoughts, and he listened patiently, nodding occasionally. When she finished, she relaxed and sat back in the chair.

Her father also slid back into his seat and sighed. "Yes, I had to keep you, all this, a secret for your protection. There are actually several things I've been shielding you from." He rubbed his hands together. "I don't know where to begin!"

Wanting to make him feel less nervous (because, in truth, it would help her, too) she joked, *"Well, I've heard it said that the beginning is among the most popular places to start."*

"Indeed. You are correct," he said, chuckling softly. "I don't know how much you know of the history between our two kingdoms."

Elswyth shook her head. *"I learned nothing about it growing up. We humans are taught to fear elves. I never knew why. It is just the way things are."* Saying that out loud suddenly sounded so ignorant to her, especially since she was now getting to know them. People just accepted the idea that elves were frightening and horrible beings. She wanted to hear what her father had to say.

"There was a time when our two kingdoms worked together in harmony. We shared resources and information. Our healers learned from each other and there were even some elves and humans that married. Both our lands flourished together. Then, a little over 200 years ago, King Markan's ancestor, King Richtor, became greedy and wanted both nations for himself. He sowed division and hate between elves and humans. He sought power and control. We came close to war and finally, my father, our king, and your grandfather, severed all contact with Carthia. Unfortunately for us, it was too late, and that hate had poisoned even some here."

"Willow Grove used to be the key passage between the two kingdoms. The way up the mountain was a well-travelled thoroughfare that went all the way to Glenorim and the standing stones were the portal through which everyone passed back and forth. Then, on the day we cut ties, my father put a spell on the stones. Unless you wore a royal crystal, like the one I left for you, all you would see from the human side of the plateau was barren rock and sand. By the same token, no one from this side could pass to the other side. Both kingdoms were cut off from each other from that day on." He paused, lost in thought for a moment. Elswyth tried to picture the muddy path she had come up on as a well-cared for road and couldn't imagine it.

"Closing the portal angered Richtor beyond measure," Dayel said. "He hated us for what he called our act of defiance and took out his frustration and malice on his own subjects. While your people suffered poverty and hunger at his hand, he blamed it all on the elves and openly vowed that if he discovered any elves in his kingdom, he'd hang them from the castle walls for everyone to see. He passed the lies and cruelty down through his descendants—to Markan, who still spews hatred for us."

Dayel picked up the teakettle and poured them each a cup. After taking a sip, he continued. "If Markan had discovered there was an elf living in his lands, even a halfling, your life would have been in danger. You were safe, however, until your eighteenth birthday. Until then, your Elven energy was indistinguishable from that of a human's. But, after your birthday, I knew that the stronger the Elven side of your Majik grew, the easier it would have been for him to find you. He would have done anything to make an example of you, and I couldn't let that happen. That is why you're here now." He shook his head for emphasis.

"You could have rescued me yourself when I was ten! Why couldn't I come to Glenorim? Wouldn't I have been safe here? I don't understand why you left me there. Why did you abandoned me?" she blurted out the thoughts to him in rapid succession, her hurt and anger bubbling up. Of course, she was eternally grateful to the Fates for Agnes, but Elswyth still struggled with being so easily left that night eight years ago, the abandonment, her mother's last way of telling her daughter she had no worth. Although she'd come a long way towards healing, all thanks to Agnes, Elswyth still carried that pain and its consequences. Now, to discover that she had a father who left her behind, it felt like being abandoned a second time and it tore the wounds her mother inflicted on her heart open again. Hot tears threatened to stream down her flushed cheeks, but she willed them to stay inside. She did not want to show weakness. Cicero glared at the prince in support.

Her father clasped his hands across his lap and looked down before he started talking again. Then, looking into her eyes, he continued. "As much as I wanted to, especially when I learned how badly your mother was treating you, I couldn't rescue you myself without endangering you further."

"When I came down the mountain nineteen years ago and met your mother, she was lovely and could be quite charming, but I didn't see her devious side until it was too late. I was naïve, and foolish, Elswyth. I thought I was being so smart," he sighed and shook his head at the memory. "Since I was only just twenty years old, my Majik was still indistinguishable from a human's. Markan would not have been able to sense I was in his territory. But I was strong enough to glamour my ears to look rounded so I wasn't obvious to the villagers. Elswyth, I should have listened to my father."

He cleared his throat and continued. "By the time I learned about you, you were ten years old and I was well past my Awakening, my Majik at its fullest. Not only that, the matured Majik of the royal house is far stronger than other elves in the kingdom, even if we use a shield, so Markan would've immediately sensed I was coming. He would have either intercepted me at the base of the mountain or found us when I got to the cottage. Either way, both you and Agnes would've been in danger of being imprisoned or executed. That is why I sent my regent, Caden. His Majik is less strong and he could shield it enough to arrange to have you brought to Agnes. He knew she was a healer and sensed her kind Majik, her strength. He sought her out and knew you would be safe with her. She did not hesitate to take you in."

"As for coming here, sadly, we couldn't do that either. You were safest with Agnes. As I mentioned, Richtor's hate had infected some of us here, as well. It took time, but most elves have learned to let go of their hostility for humans. We finally understood that what happened before closing the portal stemmed from one man, Richtor. Unfortunately, there are some here who still harbor that hostility and want to use it for their own desire for power. They want to declare war on Markan and take his lands for the elves. One of those elves is my younger brother, Prince Terrick, and he sees you as much of a threat as I am to him."

"How can that be? He doesn't even know me and I've done nothing to him," she said as Cicero cuddled up closer to her.

"Terrick has resented me as the firstborn, and next-in-line to the throne, for as long as I can remember. He aspires to be king someday, and he wants that above all else. You would just be an additional threat to him because you are also in line for the throne, even though you're only half Elven."

71

"Why would he care about me? I'm no threat to him. I don't even care about being royalty or about any claim to the throne. My home is in Willow Grove with Agnes! Can't I just tell him that? Maybe I can convince him."

Dayel shook his head. "Unfortunately, no. As my daughter, the reality is you're in line for the throne. Except for two other people here, I've kept your existence a secret so he wouldn't go looking for you and—" He looked down at his hands. "Elswyth, I'm afraid he could hurt you—or worse—in an effort to keep his path to the throne clear."

"I don't understand. Why wasn't he dealt with if he is that much of a threat?"

"For several years he's kept more to himself, but I don't trust him. He is cunning, intelligent, and knows how to control others. One of his many dark talents is to invade the minds of other elves and then know just what to say to get what he wants from them. And I can't prove it, but I fear he's embraced Dark Majik." Elswyth shivered at that last statement. "He has many fooled, including our mother, it seems. Or at least she doesn't want to believe he would go against the throne or his family. Sadly, he has deluded some in the kingdom into thinking he has Elven interests as his highest priority when all he cares about is power. Among other things, he has preached war and division and there are those that support him."

"You said there are two others here that know about me?"

"Yes. They've kept your secret all these years and are eager to meet you and welcome you to the family. They're your grandparents, Elswyth, the king and queen of Glenorim."

Seventeen

"Elswyth," Dayel said, "aside being the king and queen, they are good-hearted, loving elves who value family above all else. As soon as I knew about you, I went to them with the news that I had a daughter. Of course, it was a shock at first but, they wanted to do all they could to keep you safe. They also wanted to meet you today, but thought it might be overwhelming for you. Besides, I wanted us to have this chance to connect first—just us." He avoided her eyes and said. "I hope that was okay to do. You'll meet them soon and I know you'll come to love them as I do."

Elswyth sighed. *"I'm sure they're wonderful!"* she said, stumbling with her words. *"The last few days have* been—*I don't know what to do or say or even feel right now. Agnes is my family and always will be."* She stared off in the distance, wishing she were back at the cottage, gathering herbs and chicken eggs.

"I know this has been a tremendous shock for you and I can't even imagine what you're feeling. I know you miss Agnes because, after all, she is your family. Know that we consider her family, too, and that we are watching over her, but I want you to remember that she is a powerful woman with very strong Majik; stronger than most humans. She is going to be fine, and someday, you *will be* together again. I promise you that!"

Elswyth reached out and brought Cicero to her lap. *"So, I am still in danger, then?"*

He met her eyes again. "Yes. Unfortunately, you are. But in two days, you'll be eighteen and, on that day, your Majik will mature. You'll need to learn how to use it to protect yourself and grow stronger so, you'll get training here in the castle while I continue to help and protect you."

"I already learned about Majik from Agnes and she was—is an amazing teacher!" Elswyth said defensively. She sat up tall in her seat and Cicero ruffled his feathers, glaring that the prince.

Dayel put his hands up. "Of course she is, and she did an outstanding job of it, too, as I knew she would! But, our two Majiks, human, and Elven, are very different. Our Majik is far more powerful than that of humans, and if I am right, your power will be much more than you ever expected it would be. But, don't worry. We have an excellent teacher here for that. As a matter of fact, she was my teacher. Your grandparents were her students as well!"

"You're forgetting to tell her about Pic, Dayel," Ratheus said. Both Elswyth and Cicero jumped in their seat. He'd been so quiet that they forgot he was even in the room.

Her father nodded. "Oh yes. That's right. Thank you, Ratheus! Elswyth, I understand you and Pic have hit it off well."

"Yes, we have! She's delightful, and I think we're going to be good friends! Pic even helped me get ready to meet with you today. She did my hair and helped me pick out this dress." Elswyth said, grateful for the change of subject.

"And you look lovely. I had hoped that you two would get along. I've known Pic since she was born and she's the ultimate aspiring chef, ambassador, encourager, organizer, and master student of all things, as I'm sure you've already discovered!" Elswyth rolled her eyes and chuckled in agreement. Dayel laughed and nodded knowingly. "Yes, we all love her, too. Since your birthday was coming up and we had already planned for you to be here for that, Caden thought you and Pic might be good for each other, so he told her all about you a month ago. As you can imagine, she's been a whirlwind of preparation since then."

"But there's something I need to ask you about Pic. We haven't spoken to her about this because we wanted to check with you first. You see, in a few weeks she'll be coming into her own Majik, as well. Unlike humans, that happens when an elf reaches twenty-one years old. Caden and I were hoping, though, that she could start her studies early and you two can take your classes together. Would that work for you?"

"Oh yes! I would love to do that, and it is a wonderful idea. Thank you."

"Perfect! It's settled, then. I'll let you break the news to her since I think she'd like hearing it from you. One last thing and then I believe you've probably had enough for today, haven't you?"

Elswyth nodded gratefully. She had more questions, but they could wait since she had plenty to work through for the time being.

"Your grandparents want to have a royal fete in your honor. It will be a way for them to announce you to the court and once they've done that, no one can dispute that you are a member of the royal family. It's planned for three days from now, the day after your birthday. Don't worry," he said, seeing her hand go to her mouth and her eyes opened wide. "You'll be fine. Pic will help you with what to wear and what to do. That morning, I'll escort you to your grandparent's chambers and you'll be able to meet them before the evening's festivities. And I promise you'll love them. They already love you."

He stood up and offered his arm to her. She hesitated before rising, but then took his arm, and they walked together to the door. Ratheus followed close behind while Cicero flew to a nearby chair and waited. After another awkward moment of silence, her father reached up, once again, to rub his neck. Turning to her, Dayel said, "I want you to know how very proud I am of the young woman you've become, and I am beyond happy to have you here!"

"Thank you. I had a wonderful teacher and mentor all these years." She didn't yet feel comfortable calling him father and wasn't sure how to address him otherwise, so she just left it hanging. Cicero cleared his throat and cocked his head at her as Elswyth added, *"Oh yes, and of course, I've also had my best*

friend, Cicero with me, as well. He's always been there." The raven puffed up the feathers on his chest.

Ratheus sat next to the door and added his goodbyes. "We shall see you again soon, Your Highness. And you, too, Cicero."

"Thank you, Ratheus. We're glad to have met you. We both are, aren't we, Cis?" She looked down at Cicero and raised her eyebrows when he didn't answer right away.

"Oh yes. Sorry! Me, too. Glad to have met you, Ratheus," Cicero said. Now that the meeting was ending, he was more interested in the uneaten pastries on the table.

Elswyth turned to her father. *"This is going to take some time to get used to. It's all—so much. But I'm glad we finally got to talk."*

"Me, too. Oh and, Elswyth, for your own safety, please be sure to stay in your rooms at least until the fete. I know it's a lot to ask, but we're still keeping you a secret until then just to be extra safe. Okay?"

"I understand. I'm sure Pic and I can come up with some things to do!"

"I'm sure you two can! And speaking of Pic, I have one favor I need to ask of you: do tell our Pic that I think she did a lovely job helping you with your hair and dress today. I will never hear the end of it if you don't," he said, and winked.

They laughed together. *"I will. And thank you, again."*

They stood together, awkward gain, then Elswyth impulsively reached out and gave her father a tentative hug. Dayel paused, then hugged her back.

Unnoticed by the four standing there, the servant's door, left ajar earlier, slowly closed completely.

Eighteen

At least Pic waited for Elswyth to get one foot in the door before bombarding her with questions. "Welcome back, Elly! How did it go? Was it very difficult? Did you like your father? He's really nice, don't you think? Everyone thinks he's a kind elf. Isn't his study amazing? He's let me borrow books from there sometimes. Did you meet Ratheus? He looks ferocious, but he's actually very sweet. Tell me *everything*! By the way, I made a late afternoon treat for us. It will probably ruin our dinner appetite, but sometimes you just have to splurge, you know? I hope that's okay?"

"Oh, my goodness, Pic. Let me get in the room first," Elswyth said, laughing as she shut the door behind her. She was beginning to wonder if Pic ever breathed when she talked.

All Cicero heard was the part about the treat, so he flew to his perch next to the table, ready to eat. Set around a beautiful floral centerpiece were three white China plates covered with tall silver cloches, each plate accompanied by a linen napkin trimmed in gold thread. Tall crystal glasses full of sparkling water and long-handled teaspoons completed the festive setting. Cicero hopped onto the table, leaned forward, and tried to get a whiff of whatever was hidden under the nearest cloche, but there was no aroma, no scent at all escaped from under the metal covers. "Pic, what is it? What's under there?" His curiosity was getting the better of him.

Since the cloches seemed more important at the moment (at least where Cicero was concerned) it looked like the answers to Pic's questions were going to have to wait, so she went to the table and lifted the covers up off their dishes. "Tada!" she announced with fanfare, waving her arms wide. Three long-stemmed glasses held something that looked, disappointingly, like mashed up potatoes.

"Ummm. Pic, what is that?" Elswyth asked. She and Cicero went silent and stared at the strange food set before them. Neither looked impressed so far.

Cicero moved closer to the dish and shivered. "It's cold! Freezing, in fact!" he said. Pic stood nearby, a huge grin on her face while he stretched his neck closer and sniffed. His head snapped up. "Vanilla? I smell vanilla! You mixed vanilla with—cold potatoes? I don't know about this, Pic." He shook his head.

"Just give it a try, Cicero! Go on!"

Elswyth watched, curious, and Pic clasped her hands under her chin, suppressing a giggle as Cicero stuck out his tongue to taste it and—"Pic, is this Majik food? It is amazing!" he said, and began eating.

"No. It's not Majik. Well, Majik is what's keeping it cold but, otherwise, no. I call it frozen cream with vanilla for the time being. I need to think harder on that name, but it works for now. It's a cold treat, and it's one of my favorites. It's the only flavor I know how to make so far, but I'm trying some new recipes. If I have a stressful day, I eat a dish of this and it pretty much fixes everything for me. Well, most of the time it does!" she pulled out two chairs. "Come on, Elly. Let's sit down and eat. You can tell me how it went with your father after we're done."

Elswyth had to admit that Pic's treat was not only delicious, but it made for a nice ending to a very long day. When she finished hers, she dabbed at a small bit of cream on her chin and pushed back from the table. *"Thank you, Pic. You were right. That really was one of the best things I've ever tasted!"* Then she tapped her forehead and remembered what her father had asked her to do. *"Pic, I almost forgot to tell you! My father wanted me to be sure to let you know he thought you did an outstanding job helping me with my dress and hair today."*

Pic's usual smile grew even wider, and she blushed crimson from ear tip to ear tip. "I am so honored he thought so. You're beautiful anyway, Elly, so I can't take all the credit. I just added to what you already have." Modesty aside, it was obvious Pic was happy her efforts were acknowledged. "Um, did you want to talk now about your meeting with the prince today? I'll understand if you don't want to."

Elswyth felt Pic's sincerity like a warm hug. *"Actually, I do want to talk about it and I think it will help to get it out of my head! Let's go sit by the fire,"* she said. *"Cis, how about cuddling up on my lap?"*

Cicero flew over to the fireplace chairs. "Just waiting for you, Elly!"

She snuggled into the chair and turned towards the warmth of the fire, petting Cicero's back as he settled into her lap. Gathering her thoughts, she glanced at Pic, who waited patiently across from her. Once Elswyth started talking, it all came tumbling out, and the more she shared, the lighter she felt.

Pic listened to every word; her care and concern shining through her eyes. Then she got up from her chair, walked over to Elswyth, and hugged her. "I'm not going anywhere, Elly. I'll be here for you. Okay?"

Elswyth needed that more than she realized and hugged her back as tightly as she could.

"Hey! You're squishing me!" Cicero said from between them.

Pic jumped back. "Oops! I'm so sorry, Cicero."

"I suppose you're forgiven," he said with a grunt. "Just give me a little notice next time, ladies. Okay? I'll get out of the way."

Pic gave him an apologetic smile; her head tilted to the side. "Oh, Cicero. We don't want you out of the way! We'll just be sure to be more careful next time. All right?"

"I suppose that will work," he said, still miffed.

"Sorry, Cis!" Elswyth laughed and stroked his head, and felt better than she had in days. Lighter. *"So Pic, my father also said I need to start Majik classes soon, and it sounds like it would take up a lot of my time."*

Pic's smile faded. "Yeah, I knew you'd have to start your studies soon. I'll miss being able to spend time with you during the day, but I completely understand." She reached down and picked at the hem of her blouse.

Elswyth folded her hands on her lap and put on as serious a face as she could manage. *"Yes, well, about that. It appears we'll both be busy with studies because, well, only if you want to, mind you—"* she glanced up at Pic, who was holding her breath and staring wide-eyed at her. *"Oh, I can't keep you in suspense any longer. What would you say to the both of us taking our classes together? You'd be starting earlier than planned, but—"*

Pic jumped up to hug Elswyth again, squealing. At the last-minute, she held back and embraced her carefully so as not to squish Cicero again. "Yes, oh, a thousand times, yes! It's going to be fun, and we can practice our lessons with each other! This is even better than frozen cream with vanilla!"

Cicero bobbed his head. "I can help you with your homework if needed," he said and looked at Pic. "Both of you."

"Thank you, Cis. I will probably call on you for that help!" Elswyth held him close.

"Me, too, Cicero! I will definitely want your help." Pic added.

The frozen cream with vanilla had, indeed, ruined their appetites for dinner, but they didn't care. As they talked long into the night about Elswyth's father, the king, the queen, desserts, and imagined the Majik they would master in their classes; all three became closer while curled up next to the fire.

Nineteen

Terrick stood in front of the towering window of his darkened office, looking down at the glitter of the city lights below the castle, his mind anywhere but on the beauty of Glenorim. No, what he saw was simply his rightful future: his riches, possessions, subjects and, most importantly, his seat on the throne. He'd worked too hard for too many years, paving the way to his ascension, to waste his thoughts on something as trivial as a marvelous view of his home, castle, and city.

He brushed a strand of hair from his eyes and turned from the window to face the full-length mirror on the adjoining wall. Terrick smirked at his image as he reached up, smoothed his long black mane and noted with pride the red streak that blended in at the top of his head. He gazed with admiration at the dark eyes staring back at him, his chest swelling with hubris. "Yes. I will be an imposing king, won't I? I will show them all."

He tore himself away from the mirror and scowled at a large hourglass on his mantle. "Why hasn't he returned yet?" he said, shaking his head, anger building in his chest as he paced in front of his massive desk. "That imp should have been back here hours ago!" As if on cue, there was a tentative knock at the door. "It's about time!" he growled, grinding his teeth. "Enter!" With a wave of his hand, the door creaked opened.

Silhouetted against the light from the hall stood a short, plump elf who stepped into the room, his head bowed and his hands clasped at his chest. His floppy ears trembled. Terrick crossed his arms over his chest and peered down at him. "Where have you been, Samésh, you miserable imp? You took your time reporting to me!" he said through gritted teeth.

Samésh did not dare look up and wrung his hands together. "I'm so sorry, Your Highness, but I had to wait for everyone to go to bed so I could come here without being seen." A sheen of sweat covered his bald head. "But I do have news for you. Your brother had the meeting with the young guest he brought to the castle. She and Pic, his regent's daughter—"

"I know who Pic is!" Terrick snapped. "Get on with it and tell me what happened at the meeting."

"Yes—yes. Begging your pardon, Your Highness!" he whimpered and bowed his head further. "I think she may be more than just a friend of Pic's, but I'm not sure. The meeting seemed tense and important to both her and your brother. I tried to stay in the room while they talked, but Prince Dayel dismissed me before he would have any discussions."

"So, you're telling me you failed? You have no information for me?" Terrick's voice rose as he stepped menacingly closer to Samésh. "That doesn't help me. I need to know who she is and why she's here."

"Please, Your Highness." Samésh raised his hands protectively over his head. "I tried to discern something of her Majik, but it is unlike any I am familiar with. She is certainly Elven, but not from Glenorim, at least as far as I can tell. And she has the protection of royal shields so that made it more difficult for me to read her." He blurted. "The prince sent me from the room, but I stayed behind the servant's door and tried to listen to what they were saying. Unfortunately, I was too far away and could only hear a little of what they talked about."

"And? Spit it out, you miserable creature. I am growing tired of waiting for you to get through this!" As annoyed as Terrick was, he also enjoyed watching the old elf squirm.

"I—I can tell you she's invited to the fete the king and queen have planned in a few days." Samésh said, his words rushed. "They apparently know about her, too, but that's all I could really get from the conversation. I'm sorry, but I could hear no more." He finally dared to look up at Terrick.

"Is that so? My parents know of her, do they? Of course they do!" he said. Terrick felt the now familiar inky black tendrils curl up and around his ankles. He was losing control of his emotions—giving his anger the power, so he was grateful he was the only one who could see the tendrils, the outward proof of his descent into Dark Majik. Turning back to the window, he focused on a point in the blackness of the night sky, and slowed his breathing down. The darkness writhing around his legs retreated into the stone floor and he took in a deep, cleansing breath, and continued to gaze out at the window. "No need to worry. I plan to deal with them with in time, anyway. Especially father. Yes, especially him," he muttered.

Having calmed himself, he faced the elf again. "Samésh, you will continue to be my eyes and ears. And don't worry. I'll keep a protective shield on your Majik to hide your—complicity. No one will discover you're a *traitor*. At least not for now." He leaned in close to Samésh's face, grinning as the old elf pulled back ever so slightly. "But remember, if you dare cross me, it will not go well for you—or your wife. You know that, don't you? Work harder at getting information. Do you understand?" Without waiting for an answer, Terrick turned back to the mirror, patting back his hair as he admired his reflection, and the door to the hallway swung open on its own, signaling he was done with the conversation.

"Yes, Your Highness. Of course. You—you can rely on me," Samésh sniffled, bowing repeatedly. He stepped backwards towards the door and stopped, once again wringing his hands. Taking in a shuddering breath, he asked, "May I request one thing? A favor, please, Your Highness?"

Terrick slowly turned to face the elf, his eyes flared, dripping with avarice. "A favor? You DARE ask me for something when you haven't given me what I needed?" he asked and cocked his head at the elf.

"Please, Your Highness. May I please see my wife? You said you would let me see her soon." He placed his hands in prayer and took a tentative step forward. "I beg you. I only want to see that she's well."

Terrick turned back to the mirror and waved his hand dismissively. "She's fine—for now." His words filled with menace. "I told you, as long as you do as I ask, she'll be unharmed. You'll see her when I say you can see her. Not before."

"But—"

Terrick stiffened, his eyes turned completely black and his fists clenched as he eyed Samésh's reflection in the glass. The air in the room grew heavy with Dark Majik and the black tendrils returned, making their way up the prince's body. "Leave now, elf, before I change my mind about keeping her safe at all!"

"Yes, Your Highness. I'm so sorry, Your Highness!" Samésh wept.

Terrick grinned in amusement at the servant's tears as he watched him back out of the room. The door slammed, and he continued to admire his reflection once again.

TWENTY

E ven after staying up late the night before, Elswyth awoke just before sunrise. Cicero was still snoring away on the pillow next to her, so she slipped out of bed and tip-toed to the front room. She snuggled into a chair by the fireplace to enjoy what would be the only few minutes of peace in the busy day ahead and went over the to-do list in her head one more time.

There would be new dresses to try on because Pic informed her that nothing in her wardrobe was appropriate for either meeting her grandparents or the fete. The dresses were to be delivered here right after their breakfast. Of course, there would be lots of jewelry to try on, too. Hairstyles would be an important discussion as well. Elswyth planned to let Pic take the reins on that since she did so well last time.

Next, Pic was going to teach her how to conduct herself in court. Those lessons included everything from a proper curtsy to using the correct utensils at the dinner table. And then, there was the lowdown on who was who, how they were, or were not, related to each other and their titles or stations within the court. How in the world was she ever going to remember all that?

Later in the day, both Elswyth and Pic were also expecting a visit from the official court Governess of Majik, who would talk to them about their upcoming classes. Pic couldn't tell her much about the instructress other than her Majik was very powerful, and she was rumored to be over 2500 years old. Elswyth was already having trouble getting over the fact that her grandparents were well over three hundred. She had to admit she was curious about that meeting on many levels.

And last on the docket, Pic needed to know what Elswyth wanted for her birthday dinner tomorrow. Pic planned to do the cooking herself as a gift, instead of having the staff cater the food, and she was very excited about doing it. As much as Elswyth loved Pic for wanting the make the day special, the idea of spending her birthday without Agnes made her heart ache. But she also knew how much it meant to Pic to do this.

"I'm already exhausted. Oh well. I'll get through it all one step at a time. I'll just have lots of stories to tell Agnes when next I see her." She rolled her eyes and put her hands to her cheeks just as a servant was rolling in the breakfast service.

Mistaking Elswyth's actions, the servant stopped short with the cart and apologized. "Begging your pardon, Miss! If this is a bad time, I can come back later."

"Oh no. I'm so sorry! I didn't mean that look towards you. Please, do come in." She smiled at the elf and got up from her chair while the food was being arranged on the table. And then, right on time, Cicero flew into the room and sat on the back of a chair.

"I smell breakfast!" he said.

"I figured you would." Elswyth laughed. Then, before the servant had finished placing the service, Pic walked in through the open door.

"Morning! I'm so ready for today. How about you?" Pic announced with the usual bounce in her step.

Elswyth smiled and nodded at her friend. *And so it begins,* she thought.

Hours later, two new beautiful gowns hung in Elswyth's wardrobe, jewelry to complement them sat arranged on the dressing table, and loads of notes about court etiquette sat stacked on the desk. She gave up worrying about remembering all the rules and asked Pic to just show her the bare minimum of things she had to remember. If there was anything of grave importance she needed to know during the fete, Pic could send her thoughts and help that way. As for a birthday meal, Elswyth asked Pic to surprise her, and that checked off every item on the list but one, the one they both were most looking forward to.

Elswyth and Pic sat facing their governess at the table. Careful to keep her thoughts to herself (because she didn't want to offend), Elswyth stared in wonder at the ancient elf across from her. If their teacher was as old as Pic said she was, then she certainly didn't show it in her movements and personality. Despite the deep lines, wrinkles and the sagging skin over her frail-looking bones, the elf moved with the grace of a dancer. Her voice was soft, yet conveyed strength and confidence. And those eyes! Her silver eyes were beautiful but penetrating. With all that, Elswyth only felt kindness and patience emanating from her and was at ease in her new teacher's presence.

"You may call me Madame Teshka," she began. "And you're both quite mistaken. I am not 2500 years old, although that would most certainly not be considered old in my book. I'm only 2127." She sat back in her chair, folded her hands in her lap, her lips curled up at the corners. Even her eyes smiled!

What?! Elswyth felt horrified that the governess could read her thoughts, even though she was sure she had guarded them. She was embarrassed and glanced at Pic, whose ear tips blushed a bright scarlet.

"One thing you must learn right from the start, ladies, is that you cannot hide anything from me. I shall teach you all you need to know, and then some, about your Majik, but I will require you to work hard and always be honest with me. And, no. I will not always read your thoughts. That will only happen when we are together in classes. I need to know how your lessons are affecting you at all times in order to keep you safe. Are we understood?"

"Yep! I mean, yes, Madam Teshka," Pic said.

"Yes, Madam Teshka!" Elswyth echoed.

"Lovely! Today I shall go over a few things and then you'll be dismissed. First, here is the textbook you'll be working from during your studies," she said and handed them each a very heavy, leather-bound tome she took from a large brocade-covered bag. As frail as she appeared, she picked them up as if they weighed nothing. "These are yours to keep, and if you take excellent care of them, they will do likewise for you. Your books are imbued with Majik and will help you as you progress in your studies. Know that there is no use trying to skip ahead in the chapters. In fact, if your book determines something is too difficult or dangerous for you to try, it will not allow you to see those pages until such time it deems it is wise to do so. Is all that understood, ladies?"

They both nodded to their new teacher.

"Now, I would like to talk briefly to you about what you could expect on the first day your Majik completely opens to you. It is called your Awakening. Elswyth, this is more for you at the moment because you're on the cusp of your eighteenth birthday. Pic, you must pay also attention because you only have a short time to go before you'll also need to know this." Madam Teshka shifted to the edge of her seat and leaned in. "You may experience an episode or occurrence of Majik that is new to you. I want you to know that is perfectly normal, so don't let it frighten you. Quite the contrary, anything that comes up could very well signal a Majik strength or talent you will need to hone or work on. And, please know, ladies, if you ever have questions or fears, you have only to reach out to me in thought and I will be there for you." She sat back in her chair.

Elswyth had to admit this made her a little nervous. *"What kind of episode are you talking about?"*

"Please don't fret too much about it, Elswyth. You will be fine, and when you do experience something, remember it will be brief and we shall sort it all out together. Yes?"

Elswyth nodded, then Madame Teshka reached across the table to pat her hand. When the governess touched her; she felt calmed and assured. Then, their teacher gathered up her voluminous bag and rose from the table.

"Thank you for the tea, ladies. I shall take my leave now and look forward to us working together. Before we meet next, I want you to read the first two chapters in your text: The Five Tenets of Majik and Majik vs. Dark Majik. The readings will be short but important. Ta-ta, my dears! Until we meet again next week!" And with that, she practically floated out the door.

"Well, then. That was interesting!" Pic said as the door clicked shut.

"Yes, it was!" Elswyth agreed.

"I wonder what's in our textbooks? We don't have to study them now, but I am curious," Pic said.

"Yes! Let's take a peek," Elswyth agreed. Curious, they each tried to open their enormous tomes, only to discover their covers wouldn't budge.

TWENTY-ONE

Elswyth awoke in a cold sweat, trembling from the inside out in terror. Something was wrong. Terribly wrong! She opened her eyes as wide as she could in an effort to see something—anything—in her room, but it was no use. The darkness enveloped her in a deep, inky black, the air dank and heavy. If she hadn't been able to feel the bed beneath her, she wouldn't have known which way was up. The silence in the room was deafening, the only sound her labored breathing and her pounding heart. *"Cis? Cis, are you here? I can't see you! I can't see anything!"* No answer. Could he not hear her?

The temperature in the room had plummeted. Sitting up in her bed, she felt for her blanket and pulled it tight around her shivering body. She smelled death in the air and tasted metal on her tongue. Dread gripped every part of her mind and body, and she froze in position, afraid to move. *"Cis? Oh, please be here, Cis,"* she said, reaching a hand out in search of him.

Then, a few feet beyond her, a swirling, foggy ball emerged from the blackness. She couldn't look away as it spiraled larger and larger. Voices flowed from its center, vague whispers, like she was hearing them through water—garbled and distorted.

As if floating up from the depths of a deep murky pond, a disembodied face emerged from the fog, its image fuzzy in the swirling gray mists. All she could make out were two black holes where eyes should be—two black holes that appeared to bore into her soul through the darkness. As terrified as she was, she couldn't look away, needing to know who she was facing. She pulled her blanket tighter around herself and trembled as the face grew nearer to her. Suddenly, she knew she had to escape, and do it now! If she didn't, she'd be lost to whoever—or whatever—that was forever. She squeezed her eyes closed and willed herself to be back in her rooms. Then, with renewed panic, Elswyth realized she was powerless to do so.

Was this real? A nightmare? *"Wake up! Wake up, Elswyth!"* her mind screamed, as it became impossible to breathe. The bed started to spin and felt like it was dropping through the floor. It was getting hard to breathe, so she loosened her grip on the blanket, clutched at her chest, and attempted to will the air into her lungs, but nothing worked. *"Cis, help me! Cis!"*

A voice slithered from the void. "You can't escape me. Just give in and let go."

And then...

"LEAVE HER BE!" The command exploded through the dark and the vision recoiled. Its two black orbs grew wider. *"Go! Go NOW!!"* The voice rumbled like thunder and the darkness split into a blinding white light. Elswyth brought her hands up to cover her eyes against the brilliance as she recognized who that voice belonged to. Her governess!

"Elly, it's Pic! Can you hear me?"

"Elswyth, it's Madame Teshka. Focus on my voice and listen to me, my child," she said. "You are safe in your rooms with me, Cicero, and Pic. Elswyth? I have you, my dear. Come back to us and everything will be fine in a few minutes." The thunder in her voice was gone, replaced with a tone and timbre that pulled Elswyth gently back into the world she knew, to a place of safety.

As she brought her hands down from her face, Elswyth could finally breathe again. She took in a few deep, sobbing gulps of air and felt someone's arms wrapped around her. Dizzy and disoriented, Elswyth looked around and realized she wasn't in her bed. She was in the middle of her sitting room in her nightgown and bare feet. Cicero sat perched on Pic's arm, and they both stared at her. Pic's red-rimmed, puffy eyes shown with concern and worry.

"Elly? Are you okay?" Cicero asked as he choked on a sob.

"I—I don't understand what happened. How did I get out here? I don't remember leaving my bedroom. How—why are you all here?" Her head felt like someone had shaken it severely and she couldn't think straight. She looked up at her teacher, who still held her in her arms.

"It seems, my dear, that you've had a monumental Awakening of your Majik," her teacher said with concern. "In all my years as a Majik teacher, I've seldom come across a student with such a strong connection to—well, more about that later. You first need to rest and recover, and I'm here to help you." She stroked Elswyth's hair and guided her towards a chair next to the fireplace.

Elswyth could feel the vertigo and fear draining from her mind with Madame Teshka's gentle touch. "You've had quite the scare, young lady, and I must say, you had us all a bit worried, too. Cicero found you standing out here in the middle of the room and he wasn't able to get you to respond, so he rang the bell for Pic. Neither one of them could snap you out of your trance, so Pic contacted me and I came straight away. I want you to know that I could see what you were seeing just now." She helped Elswyth settle into the chair and sent Pic to get a blanket.

Cicero snuggled into Elswyth's lap, not ready to leave her side any time soon. Elswyth reached down and stroked his feathers, then picked him up and hugged him to her chest. Still shaken to the core, she needed to know what had happened. If that was what her Majik was going to be like, she wanted nothing to do with it and looked up at her teacher.

"What was that? I've never been so terrified in my life! There was a darkness I couldn't escape, and I felt lost! Like I would never get back here. If you hadn't come when you did—"

Their governess pulled the other chair closer and sat in front of Elswyth, her ever-watchful silver eyes still full of concern. "There are several layers to go through here. Not only has your Majik fully awakened tonight, but it is showing you an ability, a powerful gift, if you will, that will be important for you to learn about and work with."

"A gift!? That was no gift I want! How do I give it back?" Elswyth's heart started pounding in her chest again.

"I am so sorry, my dear, but this is something that is now part of you. I shall promise you this, though," she gently took Elswyth's face in her hands and looked deeply into her eyes. "you will be able to control it and use it for the good of yourself as well as others. It will not be the horrible experience you had tonight—not once you have the proper training. This I promise you." She touched Elswyth's hands, and relief flooded through her. "For the time being, I'm going to give you a potion to help you sleep and when you awake, you'll feel much better in the morning light. I assure you."

Something about her teacher made her believe what she was telling her. Feeling more drained than she ever had in her life, she wanted nothing more than to sleep but was afraid to close her eyes. *"What if it comes back?"*

"It won't come back, my dear. It won't. The potion will ensure you get a good night's rest, and I've already added my shield around you. It will stay there until you no longer need it. You are safe and you'll be able to rest peacefully."

Pic brought a blanket in, tucked it around Elswyth, then sat on the floor next to her chair. Madame Teshka took a small pouch and a teacup from her bag, then poured the contents of the little bag into the cup. A pleasant-smelling steam rose into the air as she waved her hand above the cup.

"Here you are, my dear. Drink this up. It will help," she said, handing it to Elswyth. "When you awake, you'll feel much better. Don't fret about anything else tonight. Trust in me and I'll take you through this. Can you do that?"

Elswyth nodded her head and drank the potion her governess offered her. Once Elswyth finished the drink, Madam Teshka hugged her and gave Pic and Cicero strict instructions. "Help her to her bed and stay with her until the morning, you two." Then she hugged her patient one last time and left.

Once in her bed, Elswyth lay her head on her pillow. *"Please stay with me, both of you!"* Elswyth said, groggy from the brew.

"We'll be right here, Elly," Cicero said.

"We aren't going anywhere, my friend," Pic whispered.

Elswyth drifted into a deep sleep.

Twenty-Two

T he morning sun peeked through the gap in the curtains, waking El-swyth. She yawned and heard Pic's gentle snores next to her. *"Hey, Pic, you're snoring!"* Elswyth gently nudged her. Pic just grunted and rolled over, smiling at someone or something in her dreams while Cicero, on the other side of her, had just opened his eyes.

At seeing her awake, he popped up. "Elly! Are you okay? How are you feeling?" He hopped onto her chest and tucked his head under her chin. "I was so worried!"

"Shush. Let's not wake her just yet," she said, smiling down at her friend and tucking the blanket around Pic. She scooped Cicero into her arms, went out to the front room, and saw breakfast already on the table with an especially lovely bouquet in its center. Elswyth noted Cicero wasn't at all interested in eating yet, so she knew he was worried. He tucked himself closer in her arms.

"I'm still a little shaky, but I'm fine, Cis. At least, I think I am. Whatever tincture Madam Teshka put in that tea gave me the best rest I've had in a long time. And, strangely, I also feel—" She searched for her words. *"It's hard to describe, but I also feel— more whole. Maybe that is because my Majik is fully open to me now? I can still remember every moment of what happened last night, though, Cis. I never want to go through that again, but I also want to*

95

understand what it was. It's all so confusing. If I didn't completely trust in the governess to help me, I'm not sure what I'd do."

"Elly? Oh my gosh, I panicked when you weren't there when I woke up." Pic stood at the bedroom door, her hair sticking out in every direction and her eyes still puffy. "How are you? Can I get you anything? How about some tea? Here, I'll butter some toast for you! You should eat something." Pic ran to the table to pick up the toast, dropped it, and instead rushed over to hug Elswyth.

"Careful!" Cicero yelped and hopped out of the way. "Once squished was enough!"

Pic smiled and held on to Elswyth a moment longer. When she pulled back, she looked her friend up and down, checking her over. "You look all right, at least. You had us really worried last night, Elly!"

"As I was just telling Cis, I'm okay," Elswyth said. *"Shaken up quite a lot, but I feel like I will be fine. Really, I do. It will take a while to rid myself of whatever that was. I can still see and feel it all if I close my eyes."* She shivered and shifted her attention to the table and changed the subject. *"Pic, did you order these flowers? They're so unusual and beautiful!"*

Her friend's face transformed into the Pic Elswyth knew and loved. "Yes, I did order them. Actually, I picked them myself yesterday, especially for your birthday! Those are all from the royal gardens and only grow here in Glenorim. They're very rare. Don't worry," she saw Elswyth give her a look and added, "I had permission to pick them!"

Then all three of them stopped for a moment, remembering this was a special day.

"Your birthday! It's your birthday. Happy birthday, Elly!" Cicero sang.

"Yes, happy birthday, Elly!" Pic chimed in, transforming into the organizer. "I have a wonderful evening planned for you. We're going to have an early dinner and I've invited just a few people since we still have to keep things quiet until you're officially announced at the court gala. Your father will be here and my father, too. I was going to ask Madam Teshka to come, if you'd like?"

"Of course. I'd love for her to be here."

"Perfect! You're going to have a wonderful time and there will be gifts for you, too, but I don't want to spoil any surprises, so that is all I'm going to say!" Then Pic became serious. "I know you miss Agnes, especially today, but Ruby brought back a birthday letter from her for you. I can let you know about that gift, at least. Just don't tell anyone I told you."

"And you thought I was the only one who couldn't keep a secret!" Cicero said, and chuckled.

Elswyth smiled at them both. *"Pic, if you are the one that planned everything, I know it's all going to be perfect and I can't wait!"*

The three finally ate their breakfast and chatted about the rest of the day, but unspoken in the back of their minds, was last night's terror.

TWENTY-THREE

Of course, any time Pic was involved in planning something, she put her all into it. Throughout the day, she went back and forth from her apartment to Elswyth's, with decorations, dishes, sweets, and treats. Pic arranged everything in the room precisely where she needed them to be. Servants brought in an extra table and candle sticks so there would be a place to set a buffet service.

Cicero wanted to sample every goodie Pic brought in, prompting her to issue strict instructions (especially for him) not to touch any of the food until the guests arrived. Of course, he couldn't help sneaking a few bites here and there, just to give "things a taste," as he put it, but Pic had planned on him doing that and made extra, anyway. When she had to check on the food cooking in her apartment, Pic made sure not to be gone long so she could keep a watchful eye on Elswyth. Last night was still fresh on her mind.

Just as Pic finished creating another work of art with Elswyth's hair, there was a knock at the front door. Instructing Elswyth to stay in her bedroom until she called for her, Pic went to let everyone in. "Come on in!" she sang out as she bounced with anticipation for the party to start. The first in the door were her father and Prince Dayel. Then, like a dandelion seed floating on air, Madame Teshka made her entrance, toting her ever-present large brocade bag.

"Welcome everyone," Pic announced with her usual dramatic flair, arms spread wide. "May I present the birthday girl?" She turned towards Elswyth's bedroom and added a dramatic wave of her hands.

Elswyth felt silly making a grand entrance, but Pic had insisted she must do it. She had to admit it did make her smile when they all applauded and wished her a happy birthday as she stepped into the room. Then everyone gasped over her dress and hair. Elswyth thanked them for coming, and Pic for all her hard work putting the party (and her hair) together.

Pic pulled Elswyth over to the bedecked buffet table, and with exaggerated ceremony, placed her hand on one of the many cloches. "I have two gifts for you on the table, Elly. First, Agnes sent me the recipe for her venison stew weeks ago and I hope I did it justice. I've practiced it a lot." Off came the lid, and the aroma rose from the pot, filling the air with mouth-watering promise. More applause erupted as Elswyth smiled and gave Pic a massive hug.

"Pic, of course you did it justice. It smells divine!" Everyone in the room agreed and leaned in to serve themselves a bowl, eager to try it, but Pic stopped them.

"Wait! I have one more surprise," she said and pointed to the adjacent cloche. "She also sent me the recipe for this!"

With a flourish, Pic pulled off the next lid. The warm yeasty scent of barley bread brought Elswyth right back to the cottage, and she felt her eyes water with precious memories. *"Oh Pic!"* Elswyth sighed happily and breathed in the scents of home.

"I practiced that, too, before you came here and it took me quite a lot of tries to get it right, but I finally did it. I hope you like it." It was a definite crowd pleaser as they all bent in to get a better look at the perfectly shaped golden loaf.

"Oh Pic. This means so much to me." She gave Pic the tightest hug she could and then everyone piled their plates high with a little of everything, both savory and sweet, from the table. It was a grand meal, and they all ate their

fill. Then the time came to move the party across the room, so Pic arranged all the chairs to form a circle around the fireplace.

Presents were next on the schedule, and Pic orchestrated that with her typical panache. Placing Elswyth front and center at the hearth, she called each of the three guests to come up and present their gifts, Prince Dayel being the first. He stepped up to his daughter and placed a beautiful gold circlet, made to look like braided willow branches, on her head.

"For you on your birthday, Elswyth. I am so happy you're here and blessed by the Fates to have you as my daughter. It was made by the artisans in Belnoir and I was picking it up the day you arrived." Of course, Pic just happened to have a hand mirror ready so Elswyth could see herself.

"Thank you so much! It's stunning!" she beamed. She looked into the mirror, turned her head from side to side, amazed at the workmanship of the delicate piece.

"Elly! You already look like a princess, and that just makes it even more so!" Cicero said.

Her father presented her with two more gifts in small boxes. She opened the first and found a pair of delicate gold filigree earrings, each held a red stone in the center. "These are from your grandmother, Elswyth. The earrings belonged to her mother, and have been passed down to the daughters and granddaughters for thousands of years." They were so beautiful it took her breath away.

Then he handed her the second gift. "And this is from the king," he said, handing her a small mahogany jewelry box decorated with gold inlaid willow trees on the outside. "This is so you have a special place to store your earrings."

"These are beautiful! I'll be sure to thank them!"

"They wished they could be here, but thought it would not be safe for you just yet. You will see them soon, though!"

Next up was Caden, and he presented her with a gold bracelet that had a heart-shaped locket on it. When she opened it, there was a cottage engraved on the inside that looked remarkably like her home in Willow Grove. "This was Cicero's brilliant idea, Elswyth, and I had it made for you," Caden said, while placing it on her wrist. "This is to be a reminder that wherever you are, home is in your heart. And it is also a promise that we will all work towards you, one day, being able to return there."

Elswyth choked back grateful tears, thanked Caden and Cicero, then let everyone see the bracelet close up.

And last to offer their gift was the teacher that both Elswyth and Pic had come to love. From out of her bag, she held up a simple, oval white amulet on a long silver chain. "This, my dear, is for you." She smiled and put the amulet in Elswyth's hands.

Elswyth felt a slight vibration coming from it. *"Thank you so much Madame Teshka! And thank you, everyone. This all means more than I can ever say."* Elswyth put the chain around her neck and let the stone go.

"Just a moment, my dear," the governess said. "Gaze into the center of the stone and tell me what you see."

Elswyth picked up the amulet again, looked into the milky white surface, and then gasped. There on the surface, an image of Agnes appeared, looking back at her with a warm smile on her face. *"Agnes! It's Agnes! Oh, thank you so much!"*

"You are most welcome, child. I must tell you I sent a similar amulet to Agnes, so she will have an image of you, too. I'm sorry you can't yet see each other in person, but I thought this Majik would be a comfort until that day comes."

Elswyth flew into her teacher's arms and there wasn't a dry eye in the house.

"I have one more gift for you, but it's not from any of us," Madame Teshka announced. She reached into her bag and pulled out a thick, pillowy quilt, and an envelope. "Why don't you sit in the armchair, Elswyth, so you can see this more easily?" she directed. Elswyth sat down and her teacher handed the quilt to her.

"Oh my gosh, it's incredible! Each square has embroidered willow trees on it! Who is this from? Who made this?" She pulled the blanket to her cheek and noticed the familiar scents of herbs and wood smoke.

Her father spoke up, "Agnes made it for you, Elswyth. She's been working on it for years, knowing that someday you would have to come up here for this birthday. She worked on it in the evenings after you fell asleep."

Elswyth held the quilt to her heart and couldn't meet anyone's eyes for a moment. *"Is the letter from her, too?"* Madame Teshka nodded and handed it to her. *"I'll read this later, if that is okay."*

"I think that is more than okay," her father said quietly. "She'll be so happy you loved her gift."

Pic jumped up and announced she had coffee and hot chocolate for everyone, which started talking and laughter that lasted another hour. Elswyth looked around the room at everyone and felt blessed. She would see Agnes again and would do whatever she needed to do in order to make that happen. But for tonight, she would find joy in her new friends—her new family.

To that one person who was missing, though, she sent a silent message. *"I miss you so much, Agnes. Every time I look at my blanket, I will think about when we see each other again."*

Elswyth looked around the now silent room, enjoying the peace after everyone had said their final "Happy Birthdays" and left for the night. It made her smile to relive the evening with them all, but the one person she wished was here—wasn't—and it hurt.

Cicero looked over at her from his perch. "I know she misses you, too, Elly, but we will see her again. You have to believe that."

"I do, Cis. But I've looked forward to sharing this day with her for so long. Please understand that I really do appreciative everyone here. I really do. And I had the best time with them tonight, but—" She held up the stone her governess gave her and looked at Agnes's smiling image as it materialized.

"I know, Elly. And I think they understand, too," he said.

Elswyth sat down in the chair near the fireplace and wrapped herself in Agnes's quilt. She brought a corner to her face and breathed in the familiar scents of home as she brushed the soft cotton on her cheek. Cicero flew over and nestled in her lap as she finally opened the letter that came with it. Seeing Agnes's neat handwriting made her heart dip, making it hard to read it through her tears.

My Dearest Elly,

I feel a piece of my heart is missing without you here! Everywhere I look, there are reminders of you. Today I will cook your favorites, venison stew, and barley bread. I know we can't be together for your birthday, but making your special meal will at least help me feel nearer to you. Afterwards, I'll sit under the night sky near the willows and ask the stars to send you my love.

I'm sure the quilt is nothing like the finery you are now getting used to in the castle but, it comes from my heart. Knowing the day would come when we'd have to say goodbye, I wanted you to have something from me for your birthday.

Elly, I've watched you grow up to be the kindest, bravest young woman I've ever known and I'm so proud of you. Your strength and determination brought you this far and will take you farther still. You're destined for great things, my girl. You need to believe that.

My dearest Elly, remember that I have every confidence we'll be together again. Don't ask me how I know it will happen. I just do. Until then, I love and miss you so, so much,

Your Agnes,

P.S. Remind Cicero not to eat too much! He will be happy to know I miss him, too.

Twenty-Four

Agnes sat next to Tallon on the log nearest the willows, looking up towards the bright ceiling of twinkling stars in the night sky. Unfortunately, the celestial show was lost on her tonight. Just cool enough for her to wear her shawl in this late hour, she pulled one corner of it up to wipe her tears.

"So, she truly liked the quilt?" Agnes asked, still focusing upward.

"She did, Agnes. As a matter of fact, from what I was told, she quite loved it very much. I expect it's now her most cherished possession," Tallon answered. Agnes gave him a slight nod, still staring at the sky, afraid she would cry if she spoke further. Tallon moved a little closer to her on the log. "And I know it will be difficult for you, but try not to worry too much about her first Majik episode. Her father thought it was important for you to know all that was going on with the princess. Yes, it was quite challenging for her, to say the least, but he also wants to assure you she's in excellent hands. The royal governess is more than capable of giving her the guidance, training, and protection she will need going forward." He paused, "Agnes, it appears her Majik will be very powerful. So again, rest assured, she is in the right place for now."

"Thank you, Tallon. And please make sure the prince knows how grateful I am for keeping me informed of all that's going on. I need to know, good or bad, how my girl is."

"It is his intention to always keep you informed as he considers you family, but I will most certainly pass your message on to him."

Agnes was still for a moment. "I miss her so much, Tallon. Especially tonight, on her birthday." She looked down at the pendant the governess sent her, and Elswyth's image beamed back at her on its surface. She touched the stone tenderly.

"I know you do, Agnes. I know you do." Tallon stepped next to her and leaned against her side.

TWENTY-FIVE

Elswyth stood in front of the two massive carved doors to the royal chambers, a guard stationed on each side. With one arm through her father's and the other holding Cicero, she steadied herself for whatever was to come. Prince Dayel looked down at his daughter and put his free hand over hers. "Ready?"

"Yes, I think so," she said. *"How about you, Cis?"*

"I'm ready, too. Let's do this, Elly!"

Her father smiled at them both. "Then here we go," he said and patted her hand.

He nodded to the guards, and the doors opened before them. As they stepped in, it wasn't the splendor of the room that made her stare in awe, but, in fact, the king, and queen before her. They were magnificent, and she had to stop from staring open-mouthed at them. *Poise!* she said to herself. She felt Cicero shift closer to her side.

Both the king and queen rose from matching embroidered armchairs trimmed in gold and smiled as the trio entered the room. Elswyth's eyes went to the queen's vibrant red hair that spilled over her shoulders to her waist and realized with a start that this was where her own red hair came from! The queen was stunning, but she was so much more than a physical beauty. She radiated an aura of grace, power, and confidence. And her Majik? Nothing but kindness and warmth. But the most important thing Elswyth felt from her was joy—directed at her being there. Despite trying to be the picture of composure, Elswyth's smile spread across her face, and the queen's smile, in return, grew even wider.

Elswyth turned her gaze to the king, whose salt and pepper hair framed a handsome face, and she could see where her father got his strength and presence from. Although the king's Majik was more reserved than the queen's, she felt his joy at her being there as well, and his amiable smile just confirmed that for her. They made her feel accepted and comfortable in their presence.

"Elswyth," her father said, interrupting her thoughts, "May I present His Majesty, King Garreth, and Her Majesty, Queen Araleia, your grandparents." Elswyth performed a flawless curtsy she was sure Pic would be proud of.

The king spoke up first. "Welcome, Elswyth. We've looked forward to you coming for a very long time! I hope you found your quarters comfortable. I understand our Pic worked diligently to impress you."

"Yes, she did, Your Majesty! My rooms are beautiful and Pic has been wonderful. We're becoming fast friends!"

"I'm glad to hear that." He smiled.

The queen broke into the conversation. "Oh, my dear girl, we are so happy you're finally here!" She stepped towards Elswyth and swept her up in a gentle embrace, being extra careful of Cicero. "I've looked forward to meeting my beautiful granddaughter for so long!" Then she reached down and gently stroked Cicero's head. "And this must be the famous Cicero we've heard so much about!"

His chest puffed out to twice its size. "I am honored to meet you both, Your Majesties!" he replied as he bowed on Elswyth's arm.

Elswyth reached up to touch her earrings. "And thank you so much for the earrings and jewelry box! I love them and am honored to wear your mother's earrings!"

"I'm so pleased you liked them, my dear, and they look lovely on you." She nodded her approval. "Please, let's all get to know each other over some refreshments," the queen offered as she directed everyone to the opposite side of the room. They each took a seat at a large round table, the queen sitting next to her granddaughter. On the other side of Elswyth, there was a beautiful gold and mahogany perch for Cicero that even had a little tray fitted with a small plate!

On cue, three servants entered the chambers. Two of them wheeled in carts full of teas, a samovar, and an assortment of luscious cakes and cookies. A third servant followed them and began directing where to set items on the buffet. Elswyth recognized the last elf as the floppy-eared one who ushered her into her father's study and brought the tea service to the meeting.

Araleia turned in her seat towards the buffet. "Oh Samésh, that all looks wonderful," she said. "Thank you for organizing everything and please tell chef I am most appreciative of the wonderful delicacies she's prepared today!" Turning back, she said, "Elswyth, I would like to introduce Samésh. He's been a loyal personal servant of the royal family for many, many years. I rely on him for, well, everything. Don't I, Samésh?" the queen gushed.

"You're too kind, Your Majesty. It is always my honor to serve!" he bowed respectfully.

"And how is your lovely wife, Justa, Samésh? I haven't seen her in the gardens as of late. I miss our chats and the lovely bouquets she always brings me," the queen said.

"Oh, um, she is w-well, Your Majesty. She's visiting family up north for a bit." Samésh stumbled with his words and looked down at the floor. "I will tell her you asked after her when I write to her."

"Please do. She is such a dear." Then the queen added, "And, Samésh, I would like to introduce you to our granddaughter, Princess Elswyth! She's been living abroad until now and has come to Glenorim to stay with us for a while," she said, squeezing Elswyth's hand on the table. "And while she is here, I hope you will serve her as honorably as you serve us all."

Samésh looked shocked, but recovered within seconds. "It will be my honor, of course, Your Majesty." He turned to Elswyth. "May I extend a warm welcome to you, Your Highness!" he said respectfully, and bowed to her.

"I believe we've already met, Samésh. It was in my father's study and you were kind enough to bring us tea." Elswyth smiled at him, but he merely bowed again and stepped backwards towards the wall. As he moved away, however, she felt something odd about his Majik, as if an invisible, thick blanket covered him, one she couldn't quite get through.

Samésh dismissed the two other attendants and then served everyone from the buffet. As the family enjoyed their time together, he stood at his station at the side of the room, ready to refill cups or plates when asked. Soon, though, everyone forgot he was there—invisibility being the mark of an excellent servant—and they resumed their little party. The entire time, however, Samésh kept stealing furtive glances at Elswyth, occasionally wiping beads of perspiration from his forehead with his handkerchief.

For the better part of an hour, Queen Araleia focused much of the conversation on Elswyth, interested in her life in Willow Grove, Agnes, and how she liked Glenorim so far. The king joined in occasionally but most of the time, just smiled at his wife with a sparkle in his eyes as she talked. Even if he had wanted to speak up more, Elswyth was sure he wouldn't have been able to get a stray word in between her sentences, anyway. He didn't seem to mind.

When her grandmother began a boyhood story about Elswyth's father and Terrick, the king cleared his throat and tenderly put his hand on her shoulder. The mood shifted as an awkward silence took over the table. Even though he looked at his wife with love, there was a stern plea in his eyes. For the briefest of moments, Elswyth felt a heaviness in the queen's heart. Then Araleia reached up, squeezed her husband's hand, and pivoted to stories of only Prince Dayel when he was five, leaving Prince Terrick out. Things went back to being lighthearted and fun, with Dayel occasionally begging his mother not to share a particular memory, which encouraged her all the more, to everyone's delight.

Agnes would love them, Elswyth thought. Except for the grand and rich setting of the castle, this gathering felt much the same as sharing stories over a meal back home at the cottage. She looked at Cicero, hoping he was enjoying himself, too, and he certainly seemed to be. He laughed at the stories and joined in the conversations. Although the party was going well, Elswyth wondered about the reasons for her grandparents' reactions regarding Terrick and resolved to learn more. But now, she wanted to ask for something that felt more important.

"I—I would like to make a request about the fete tonight, if that's allowed," Elswyth asked, her hands clasped tightly in her lap.

The queen set her hand over Elswyth's. "Name it, my dear. What is it you need?"

Elswyth took a deep breath, looking down at the table. *"I don't want to hide who I am and, well, I'd like to wear my hair up tonight so everyone can see my ears. I understand there will be some here in Glenorim that don't like me for being a halfling and I'm fine with that. It's just important that I am accepted, or not accepted, for who I am. If you think it's wise for me to keep that a secret for now, I will, of course, do as you ask, but—"*

Araleia reached under Elswyth's chin and lifted it. "Please look at me." Elswyth looked up to meet her grandmother's eyes. "If that's what you need to do, then I—we—support you! Actually, I'd hoped that would be your decision, but was waiting for it to come from you."

"And Elswyth, you're right," her grandfather said. "There will be some that won't welcome you. But the mark of a true princess, and a strong elf, is to know herself and take pride in who she is. Of course, we will honor your request—as a family. We are proud of you and I'm sure that Agnes is, too!"

Elswyth let out a breath she didn't realize she was holding. *"Thank you so much! It means a lot to hear you say that."* She could feel grateful tears threatening, so she changed the subject by asking for more stories about her father. Of course, the queen was happy to oblige, while her father just laughed and shook his head.

They continued talking for a little longer when Araleia exclaimed, "Oh my. I think it may be getting quite late! We should retire to our rooms so we have plenty of time to get ready for tonight!" She stood up from the table and everyone followed suit and made their way towards the doors, Cicero flying to his place on Elswyth's arm. "We look forward to introducing you to the court tonight, Elswyth," her grandmother said and reached out to embrace her in a tight hug. "And welcome to the family, my dear," she whispered into Elswyth's ear. Then she held her at arm's length and exclaimed, "We must get some time together soon, just for us girls. Of course, we would need to include our Pic, yes?"

"Oh, she would love that! Um, Your Majesty, I have one more question for you. Would it be okay if—I mean—would it be proper for you to call me Elly? Would that be allowed now that I'm a princess?" Elswyth asked. She surprised herself by asking, but she wanted it very much.

"It is absolutely okay for you to ask and of course I will! But only if you call me Grandmother. I've waited so long to hear you say that!" replied Araleia.

Elswyth's smile grew wider. *"Thank you—Grandmother!"* That earned Elswyth one extra grandmotherly embrace.

"And thank you, Elly!"

"Wait until I tell Pic about all this, Cicero!" Elswyth thought to him on the way back to her rooms.

TWENTY-SIX

Elswyth stood next to Cicero near the tall, double portcullis, waiting with the rest of the royal family to make their entry into the grand ballroom. Dayel and Ratheus stood close by, deep in conversation while her grandparents were on the other side of the room, talking to each other. There was one elf who had not joined them yet, and they were all waiting until he arrived before the festivities could begin. Elswyth reached up to touch her hair one more time, hoping she'd done the right thing by having it up tonight—by having her ears be so obvious. *Was this the right decision?* she asked herself for the hundredth time.

"Here we are again, Cis, waiting outside yet another set of doors in the castle," she said to Cicero, who sat on a wheeled golden perch next to her.

"Yes, indeed. We've made a habit of that here, haven't we?" he said, under his breath.

"I bet you're loving this! You'll be making a grand entrance right along-side me! How does it feel to be royalty?"

"It feels quite good, actually, but don't worry. I would never let it go to my head, I assure you!" he said, holding his head high.

If ravens had fingers to cross, she was certain Cicero would have been crossing his behind his back. She laughed as he bobbed his head and hopped back and forth, trying to hold his elation at bay!

Adjusting the golden willow circlet on her head yet again, she knew she was as ready as she'd ever be, thanks to Pic teaching her all there was to know about how to behave as a princess in public. Who knew there were so many rules to standing, sitting, walking and talking? She hoped she'd remember everything! At least both Pic and their governess would be in the audience if she needed any extra help. She looked back at her father, standing with Ratheus, and he sent her an encouraging wink.

"You look lovely, Elswyth. Try not to be too nervous," he said, as he noticed her touching her hair again. "Remember, once the rest of us are on the dais, Mother will introduce you to the court, and that's when they'll escort you in." She nodded her acknowledgment. "Just remember I am proud of you. We all are," her father said and smiled.

"Thank you. I'll try not to embarrass you!" She laughed, trying to make light of her worry.

"That's something you never have to worry about." he said and gave her shoulder a squeeze.

The side door to the anteroom then opened and in stepped the elf they'd been waiting for. Even though she hadn't met him yet, Elswyth recognized Terrick not only from the description her father had given her, but from his smoldering and angry Majik. He swept into the room, his black, and purple robe trailing behind him, and his face a dark mask that obscured any emotion.

"Hello, dear," the queen called softly to Terrick. "Are you ready?"

"Yes, mother." He stepped over to Araleia and kissed her on her cheek, avoiding any interaction with his father, who was standing close by. The king glanced away as his son came near. Elswyth noticed Terrick's countenance soften around the queen, but after turning away from her, a stoney veil covered his face once again.

Then Terrick's attention snapped to Elswyth, and an icy shiver raced down her spine as she saw his eyes go wide. A faint but insistent, angry voice invaded her thoughts as she locked eyes with him, unable to look away, her feet riveted to the ground.

"You! You're a human girl? What are you doing here? Why are you standing with the royal family?" Then a moment later, *"And why can't I read your Majik?"* Terrick's eyes narrowed to slits as he attempted to worm his way into her mind, without success. Then his eyes shifted to her ears. "And why are you wearing our grandmother's earrings?"

Elswyth tried to read his Majik, but it was a solid black wall she couldn't get past. She finally pried her eyes from him and then turned to Cicero, shaken and pale. *"Cis, Prince Terrick just tried to force his way into my mind!"*

"What? Tell your father, Elly! Now!" he whispered back. Cicero glanced back at Terrick and then sidled closer to Elswyth on his perch.

She heard Ratheus growl under his breath and pivoted back toward the enormous bear. The dark prince sneered at Ratheus, but he finally turned away. The entire interchange lasted only a few moments, and escaped the notice of her grandparents, who were still busy in a discussion of their own on the other side of the room. Dayel, unaware of the exchange that had just happened with his brother and Elswyth, thought Ratheus was angry at Terrick's presence.

"Easy, my friend," Dayel whispered while patting the bear's muscular furry back. "All is safe at the moment. He won't dare do anything, especially today. And our Majik is still protecting her."

"I don't like the way he was looking at the princess," the bear grumbled quietly.

Dayel then noticed his daughter looking at him with alarm, not realizing that his brother had just tried to connect with her. "I promise it will be OK," he tried to assure her. Just as she was going to tell her father what had happened, the doors swung open toward the festivities. The evening had begun.

Looking out, she could see several hundred elves as they stood on the floor beyond the stage. Ten servants flanked each side of the path from the anteroom to the dais, leading to the royal table. The decorated ballroom, its ceiling festooned with forty gigantic twinkling chandeliers, was breathtaking! Exquisitely decorated tables lined the edges of the space, framing an immense mosaic-tiled dance floor. A quartet that was playing music at the opposite end of the hall paused their performance and waited for the royal family to enter. The entire room went silent and looked up at the dais.

"Their Royal Highnesses, Prince Dayel, and Prince Terrick!" a servant announced loudly, his voice echoing to the back of the hall. Attendants conducted a ceremonial escort for Prince Dayel and Ratheus to their places at the table, but Prince Terrick refused to be ushered and made his way to a seat at the opposite end, his face hard and unreadable.

Once again, shouting at the top of his lungs, the servant called out to the crowd from the side of the stage, "Good elves of the Court of Glenorim! Pay honor to Their Royal Majesties: The All-Powerful and Just, King Garreth" The crier paused while the king walked out, followed by the queen. "And Queen Araleia, the Benevolent and Peace-Bringer!" The elves in the room bowed or curtsied deeply until the royal couple had taken their places at the center of the table. Queen Araleia sat in her chair with Terrick to her left and Garreth to her right. One empty chair sat between the king and Dayel, Ratheus sitting behind Dayel.

Terrick touched his mother's shoulder and whispered, "Who is the human, Mother? Why is she up here with us and why is she wearing the earrings?"

"In just a moment, dear. It is a—it's a surprise. It's one I've been excited to announce for some time," she said in his ear and patted his hand. She avoided his eyes and looked down at the table as she spoke, though.

The king and queen rose from their chairs as one and walked to the front of the stage. Then Garreth's deep voice rang out to the waiting crowd. "It is my honor, this evening, to welcome someone of utmost importance to the court of Glenorim, and to the royal family." He turned and motioned for a servant to fetch Elswyth to the stage.

An attendant escorted her up front, with Cicero pushed on his perch beside her. Once she reached the front of the dais, the room became so quiet one could have heard a feather as it fell through the air. All eyes were on Elswyth, shocked to see the human in front of them. A collective murmur spread through the crowd, and the room buzzed with questions and comments.

"By the Fates! She's human!"

"Look at her ears!"

"We haven't seen a human for so long. Why is she here?"

"She is beautiful!"

"Look at that hair. It's like Queen Araleia's!"

"What is happening?"

Elswyth held her head high, keeping her posture straight, and her gaze leveled just above the audience. Her naked ears felt like they were on fire, making her feel more vulnerable than she ever had in her life. Still, she was determined they did not see weakness.

Araleia put her arm around Elswyth's back. That brought even more wonderment from the crowd and Garreth raised his hand to hush the crowd. Terrick sat straight up in his chair, finally beginning to guess at what was coming. He looked at his mother's hair and then Elswyth's. Then at his brother. It was all he could do to keep the fury from taking possession of him, and he worked to keep the dark tendrils at bay.

"Good elves of Glenorim," Garreth began. "The queen and I have an announcement to make." He turned to his wife and nodded for the queen to begin.

"My fellow citizens of Glenorim," Araleia's voice rang out, strong and clear. "King Garreth and I are proud to introduce to the court, Princess Elswyth, who has been living abroad until now." The elves in the room shifted on their feet, utter shock on their faces. "She is the beloved daughter of Prince Dayel," she continued, and gestured to him as he joined them center stage, "and our cherished granddaughter. I know you will show her the respect and honor you have always shown us." Araleia and Garreth started the applause and a few heartbeats later, the guests joined in—at least most did.

Elswyth took in an enormous sigh of relief that at least this part was over. She looked out into the audience for Pic and their governess and there they were, right up in front of the crowd, looking up at her with bright smiles spread across their faces. Pic mouthed, "I'm so proud of you!" and added a thumbs up for extra measure.

Garreth then spread his arms out wide and announced, "In our grand-daughter's honor, let the fete begin!" With that, the musicians began playing their happiest dance tunes, and the crowd swarmed the floor all at once as the family went to their seats. Laughter and merry-making echoed throughout the space. Even so, many cast furtive glances at the new princess on the stage while they danced. Some sat at their tables, looking her way and talking amongst themselves. But Elswyth noticed others who looked at Terrick with veiled, angry looks on their faces.

After an hour of dancing, servants brought out a sumptuous twelve-course meal for all in attendance. Everyone proclaimed it the best meal ever served at a royal function. Of course, that was the same thing said after every party the crown threw.

Terrick, on the other hand, enjoyed neither the merriment nor the food and left the stage before the dancing and dinner had ever begun.

Twenty-Seven

Terrick glared into the flames roaring away in his fireplace, working to control the fury he felt roiling within his mind. Reaching towards the fire, he tried to warm his icy hands, but it was no good. He was always cold now and no amount of heat helped. With a disgusted snarl, he stepped away and fell heavily into the tufted chair at his desk. He gripped the arms so tight the leather tore under his nails. The familiar black tendrils curled up from between his fingers and he took in a deep breath, willing them back to where they came from. He needed to get his emotions under control.

"Once again, Dayel strikes again!" he said out loud to himself. As far back as he could remember, his brother could do no wrong, and it galled Terrick beyond his endurance. "He spawned a halfling and, if that wasn't bad enough, he's brought her here to live amongst her betters. She should've been destroyed long ago." He ground his teeth and rubbed his fist into his forehead.

And how far back did his parents know about her? How could his mother and father agree to even bring her here? A dirty halfling! And, of course, technically, she was another obstacle, another heir to the throne. This was disastrous.

"Not to worry. None of this will deter my plans. This is just a minor bump in the road and I need to think this through."

Keeping his breathing steady and measured, he replayed the evening's events at the fete over and over, his fury still simmering just below the surface. His mother's betrayal was almost too much to bear. His father keeping silent about his brother's halfling daughter is something he would have expected, but his mother? He always thought she was on his side. Terrick squeezed his eyes closed and rubbed his forehead again, trying to make sense of it all.

At the fete, he could sense his mother's nervousness, especially when she wouldn't look him in the eyes. Their connection, which had once been strong, easy, and full of laughter when he was a child, had profoundly changed over the years. There were moments here and there when he truly missed those days, but those moments were fleeting now.

He loved his mother (as much as he could still feel love now that he had given himself over to Dark Majik) and he knew she loved him, too. However, he now sensed a heavy sadness that covered her love for him. He mistook it as disappointment which wounded him deeply, but what Terrick failed to understand was that, for her, it was more a sense of deep loss. A grief. The little boy she had once cherished had morphed into someone she no longer recognized. Someone she was afraid for—and of. They were a complicated pair and because of that, they rarely talked anymore, but missed each other, or rather, who they once were, all the same.

Then a thought occurred to him that eased at least some of his ire. "It was probably you, Father. You probably forced her to do it—to keep things from me. That has to be it. Yes." That is the idea he decided on and clung to. Shaking his head, he sat up and put his elbows on the desk and his head in his hands. "Think!" he whispered to himself. "The goal hasn't changed. Things have just become a little more complicated, but nothing I can't handle. I will still be king and just need to adjust my plans!" Someone knocked at his study door.

"Enter!" he called out as he waved the door open. In walked a burly soldier, hauling Samésh by the back of his collar.

"I found him, Your Highness. What would you like me to do with him?"

"Leave him with me," Terrick ordered. And then looking down at Samésh, "You! I have several bones to pick with you," he said with a menacing hiss as he rose from his desk. "Thank you, Sergeant. Wait outside until I am ready for you to remove him."

The soldier pushed the quivering elf to the stone floor in front of Terrick and bowed. "Your Highness!" he grumbled and left. The door closed behind him, sealing with a muffled click. Terrick stayed silent and stared down at the hapless elf and swore he could hear the elf's heart pounding in his chest. That made him smile with delight.

"We have to talk, Samésh. I think you may have been keeping things from me."

TWENTY-EIGHT

Terrick scowled at Samésh as he sat shivering in the middle of his office floor. "So, Samésh, how much did you know about the halfling?" he asked, his hands clasped behind his back while slowly circling the kneeling elf. He could feel the dark tendrils beginning to writhe between his fingers. Terrick stopped in front of him and took a deep breath before speaking. "And exactly when did you know?"

The elf looked up and his words tumbled out. "Please, Your Highness. I only found out just before the fete! The king and queen met with Princess Els—"

Terrick stiffened, and his eyes widened at the mention of her name and title. Samésh changed course and continued. "That is—they met with the young halfling in their drawing room before the evening's events. I was only told to plan for an important guest and didn't know who it would be. I assumed it would be someone from the court. Please! I knew nothing about who she was until then."

"Then why did you not come to me after they were done? You had plenty of time before the fete!" Terrick loomed over him, deciding whether he believed what the elf was telling him.

"After everyone left the royal quarters, I couldn't leave because your father required my services as valet for the gala. There was no way for me to get to you before the fete, Your Highness."

Terrick eyed the elf for a moment and then turned towards his mirror. He glanced at the reflection of Samésh trembling on the floor behind him. "I see," Terrick said, as he admired his own mirror image. "This may all work out better for me after all! This halfling could be just the thing I needed." He started chuckling to himself, a low, menacing rumble in his throat. "Yes! She is the answer, isn't she?!" A thin crack of a smile crept across Terrick's face and he looked down at the old elf again.

"Well, Samésh. It's your lucky day because I believe you, which means you—and your wife—will live to see another day." Terrick waved his hand, and the door opened, signaling he'd finished with Samésh, at least for the moment. "I'll let you know if I have further need of your services."

Samésh slowly got up from the floor, his knees wobbly. "Yes, Your Highness. Whatever you need."

"Guard! Kindly escort our little friend back out!"

The guard stepped in and shoved Samésh into the hall, and the door closed. Terrick's icy laughter echoed against the walls of his study as he returned to his reflection, his mood improved. "Yes. It appears I was given a gift with that halfling! Yes, indeed I have," he mused aloud to himself.

PART TWO

J. A. FAGAN

Elswyth sat in a chair by the window, staring out at the afternoon sky, while Cicero snoozed in the sunlight on the arm of her chair. It had been a couple of days since the fete, and except for her father visiting one afternoon, the frenetic activity of the previous week had died down. Her textbook sat ready and waiting on the table, but she had no interest in opening it. She looked down at the pendant with Agnes's image and squeezed it to her chest.

Pic sat across the room at the table, watching her friend, trying to think of some way to cheer her up. Then she sat up straight, slammed her hand on the table, and leaped from her chair. Both Elswyth and Cicero flinched at the noise.

"That's it! We are getting out of here! We've got places to go and things to do!" Pic announced, her finger pointed up in a declaration.

"But shouldn't we be studying today?" Elswyth asked without conviction.

"Oh please, Elly. We don't meet with Madam Teshka until the end of the week so we've got plenty of time to study! Admit it. It would be good for all of us to get out, and now that your father said it was okay, there are some places in the castle I've been dying to show you!"

"I don't know—" Elswyth waffled and gazed back out the window.

"Cicero, help me out here! Convince her we all need this."

"I think exploring the castle is a perfect idea, Elly. Besides, I'll help you both study later this week. Let's do something fun today!" he pleaded.

Elswyth let out a heavy sigh. *"All right. I guess I'm outnumbered. You both win."* She shrugged her shoulders and got up. *"Where to first?"*

Before Elswyth could change her mind, Pic hurried her out the door, Cicero flying alongside.

Elswyth was not only shielded with Royal Majik now, but accompanied by two guards whenever she left her rooms. The soldiers kept a respectable distance, but it was another aspect of life as a princess Elswyth didn't enjoy. She missed the simple life of Willow Grove. She missed Agnes even more.

Cicero, however, enjoyed playing the role of royalty, delighting in every minute of notoriety, except for the negative moments, that is. And those happened enough to put them all on alert as they walked the halls.

Many elves they passed in the busy corridors bowed or curtsied to Elswyth and a few even sent her a "Good day, Your Highness!" using their thoughts. But others scowled and refused to meet her eyes when they bowed—if they bowed at all. A few hissed, "Dirty halfling!" as she passed them. Elswyth had to keep Cicero from flying after them, so he wouldn't peck them into apologizing. Pic also wanted to join him and say something to those elves, but Elswyth forbid it. Masking her hurt was a skill she'd learned as a small child living with a mother that ridiculed, mocked, and beat her. *Never let them see your pain. Be stronger than them and hold your head high,* she repeated to herself with gritted teeth as she walked through the halls.

Then, like the moment before the lightning strike on the mountain, Elswyth knew too late that something bad was about to occur. Then it did. Prince Terrick rounded the next corner in the opposite direction. He was in deep conversation with several high-ranking soldiers and court officials—until he saw her.

Everyone in the hallway froze in place as Terrick stopped, his narrowed gaze locked on Elswyth. Her royal guards stepped closer to her, their hands on their swords. Pic grabbed Elswyth's hand, and Cicero landed on her shoulder. The huge hallway instantly felt narrow and claustrophobic, with Terrick and his entourage blocking their path.

"Well, look who we have here," he announced to his retinue. He offered her a curt bow, never taking his eyes off her. "Princess Elswyth. What a—pleasure it is to run into you today and I trust you're enjoying getting out and about in our beautiful castle?" His words oozed with a feigned warmth that sent icy shards through her chest. It took all she had to meet his dark gaze and not look away.

"Good day, Prince Terrick," she said, bowing. *"The pleasure is mine, and yes, I am enjoying myself. I trust your day is going well, too, but we should be on our way. We've got lots to do."* She forced the words out in thought publicly so everyone would hear her reply. Holding her head high and forcing her fear as deep as possible, she reminded herself to keep breathing under his dark, suffocating energy.

No one dared move in the corridor as Terrick's slash of a grin spread across his face. *"Ah. I see you are trying to put on a brave front. That will change in due time, halfling!"* his thought hissed privately into her mind.

Elswyth's gaze moved to his collar, where shadowy, black tendrils emerged, slithering up Terrick's head and neck. She watched in horror as the writhing shadows inched up, covering all but his face.

Terrick lost his grin and his thought pierced her brain. *"What are you gawking at, you half-breed brat?"*

"Your head! There is something crawling around—"

His jaw clenched, Terrick took a faltering step back, reached up to his collar, and cleared his throat. A moment later, he regained his composure and blurted, "I have pressing business to attend to so I will wish you a pleasant rest of your day!" Signaling to his soldiers, he rushed past the trio and hurried down the hallway. As he passed them, though, Elswyth noticed one of her guards give a slight nod to the prince. The hall went silent, and everyone's eyes were on Elswyth.

Cicero broke the silence. "Okay, everyone, move on. Show's is over. I'm sure you have plenty enough of your own business to tend to today!" It took a few moments, but the small crowd broke up and everyone went their way.

"Pic, you can let go of me now. I don't think I have any feeling left in my hand." Elswyth said.

"Elly, how can you be so calm? Did he say anything to you? It looked like he did," she asked, visibly shaken.

"Trust me. I'm not as calm as I may look. And yes, he did. It was definitely a threat. And did you see those black snake-like things coiling around his neck?"

"No, I didn't. And I didn't take my eyes off him. What snakes? Did you see anything, Cis?"

"Not me. Are you sure you saw something, Elly?"

"Yes! I thought at first that maybe my eyes were playing tricks on me, but I know I saw something. I don't know what it was, but I saw something." She shuddered at the heavy, dark energy she felt from Terrick.

"We should tell your dad, or at least Madam Teshka. They could warn him to stay away from you. Maybe you should have told everyone he just threatened you! Elly, he scares me down to my bones." Pic grabbed onto Elswyth again.

"Me, too. He knew just what he was doing then. As far as everyone standing here heard out loud, he said nothing intimidating. If I try to make a fuss about this and involve my father, it would be the halfling's word against Terrick's—at least publicly—to other elves. My father would believe me but, I don't want to cause him any problems. Besides, I'm going to have to get used to Terrick being around since he lives in the castle, too. Right? I'll just try to be better at avoiding him." She looked over at her two guards, who nodded and stepped back, straight-faced but alert.

Cicero fluffed his feathers and shook his head. "I don't know, Elly. I think you should still let your father know what happened today."

"I agree!" Pic said emphatically.

"No. Please. Let's forget about Terrick for now and enjoy the day. I need to have some good things to focus on! I'll tell my father later but, for now can't we just go have some fun?"

Pic and Cicero reluctantly agreed to not say anything for the time being. Relieved, Elswyth pulled Pic along, but inside she was still shaking and her mind was churning. Whatever that was she saw, it scared her!

THIRTY

O ver the next few days, they toured the enormous royal library, a palatial art gallery, and the multiple kitchens, where enticing aromas hung in the air, begging them to enter. Pic knew every chef (since she had been their eager student over the years), and they served the trio their best culinary delights. Of course, the kitchens became one of Cicero's preferred places to visit in the castle.

For Elswyth and Pic, however, the royal gardens were their favorite choice. Acres of amazing plants and trees, many Elswyth had never seen before, as well as some she was familiar with, greeted them in abundance. She learned elves had brought plants from Carthia to Glenorim long before the portal closed on the plateau two hundred years ago. Since that time, they'd been cultivated and cared for on the castle grounds.

On their third visit to the royal gardens, as they sat on the gazebo steps, Pic was not as talkative as usual and Elswyth gave a playful tug on her long, white braid. *"Hey you. What's up? Is everything okay? You've hardly said a word all morning."*

Cicero tilted his head towards Pic and said, "Yeah. I was wondering the same thing, It's strange for you to be so quiet!"

Pic twirled a small blossom between her fingers. "I was just wondering. Be honest, Elly. Do you think I would be good at being a healer?"

"Absolutely not!"

"That's what I thought. I probably shouldn't have brought it up." Pic got up, but Elswyth held her arm, then gently pulled her back down.

"Pic, you would most definitely not make a good healer," she said and looked Pic directly in the eyes. *"You'd be an amazing healer and it's the perfect calling for you! You're intelligent, compassionate, creative and you love to make people happy."* She looked to Cicero for help. *"Don't you think she'd be amazing, Cis?"*

"Well, I don't know about amazing—" Cicero said.

"Don't tease her, Cis!"

"Okay. Yes, I agree with Elly, Pic. I'd probably even come to you if I was sick and needed a healer."

"Only probably?" Pic asked. "I'll take it!" She said and pet him on the head. "Seriously, Elly. It's something I've thought about since I was little. I was already excited about you coming here because I was finally going to have someone close to my age in the castle, but then Dad told me you were a healer and, well, I've wanted to learn from you and just been afraid to ask for your help."

"Pic, I'd be honored to teach you what I know. Of course, that will just be the start for you. I mean, look around us. There is so much here from both our worlds!" Elswyth had barely gotten to her feet before Pic rushed out into the garden.

"Oh, thank you! Could we start today? For instance, what about this one, Elly? I love the delicate purple flowers!" Pic gushed over the plant, gently cupping the small blossoms in her hand.

"That's called sage, and it's used both for medicine and cooking. For instance, some use it to help relieve a sore throat. Pick two of the leaves, rub them together, and smell them. You can even put the flowers in a salad."

Pic inhaled the scent and smiled. "Oh yes! That smells wonderful," she said as she reached in to cut a stem off the plant, then laid it in a basket Elswyth brought with them. Pic dashed over to another plant. "And what's the name of this flower? I've always liked them because they look like little sunbursts to me. So that's what I named them—Sunbursts!"

"Actually, that is called chamomile, and it's been used by itself or mixed with other elements medicinally for a very long time. Crush one of the flowers in your hand and it will smell a little like apples! Alone or mixed with other herbs, it can act as a mile sedative, aid in wound healing or even help relieve menstrual cramps for humans! Besides all that, it's a beautiful and cheerful flower. I think I like what you call them, though. Sunbursts. Yes. I do like that!"

"Cham-mo-mile." Pic pronounced slowly. "Yeah, that's okay, but I think I like the name Sunbursts better, too," Pic said thoughtfully. Then she ran to the next plant. "What about this one? I love the little red fruity things growing on it," Pic exclaimed, plucking the tiny fruit from the plant. She smelled it and was about to take a bite of it.

"Don't eat that!" Elswyth grabbed Pic's hand. *"That's called cayenne pepper. It's a wonderful spice for cooking, but it also has lots of important medicinal uses. I can show you all about it in the Little Book of Healing."*

"I'd love that. I want to learn about all of it, Elly!"

Elswyth spent the next hour explaining the medicinal properties of plants she recognized in the gardens. The more Pic heard, the more she wanted to know, and soon her journal was full of notes and plant sketches.

THIRTY-ONE

"*D*id you put those there, Pic?*" They had just returned to Elswyth's apartment after spending another afternoon in the gardens, and their textbooks had mysteriously made it to the table!

"No, I didn't. I thought yours was in your desk drawer and I'm pretty sure I'd left mine in my bedroom on the dresser!" Pic said, eyeing the books. "Well, that's not strange at all!"

Cicero shrugged. "Don't look at me. You know I could never lift those things!"

While they stared, both book covers opened, the leather creaking and the pages inside fluttering back and forth before they settled down. Everyone exchanged glances. "Nope. Not strange at all!" Pic repeated.

They hurried to the table, and Elswyth flipped through the pages of her book, her brows furrowed with curiosity. *"Hey look! The page for chapter two is blank. Nothing is showing up there."* She turned it around for Pic to see.

"Mine's the same. There is nothing after the first chapter." Pic flipped through more pages. "As a matter of fact, there is nothing in the rest of the book at all! Even the table of contents only lists chapter one." Both their tomes pulled back out of their hands, closed their own covers and wavered in midair before they set themselves down again in front of Elswyth and Pic, opened to chapter one.

Cicero hopped onto the table next to Elswyth's book and shrugged his shoulders. "I think it's telling you two it is time to study. And, really, ladies! Don't either of you listen? If you recall, Madam Teshka told you that your books won't allow you to skip ahead and you have to master each lesson in order." He shook his head at them. "Now, let's start The Five Tents of Majik," he said, proudly acting the part of their self-appointed teacher's assistant.

Elswyth looked down and nodded, ready to begin. *"You're right, Cis. I completely forgot all about that. Let's get to it, then, Pic!"*

The only sound in the room was their pens scratching in their notebooks as the two wrote the five tenets down multiple times to help cement the list in their minds. Cicero waited off to the side until they gave him the signal they were ready to be quizzed. Elswyth slid her book over to him while Pic closed hers and smiled, confident she was ready.

"Okay, Elly. What are the first three tenets of Majik?" Cicero asked from his perch.

Elswyth closed her eyes and recited. *"Number one: Majik is to be used to nurture and never to harm. The only exception is in a case of self-defense or in the defense of another living being. Number two: Majik can be used to assist in the practice of healing, but it should never be used to reverse the finality of death. And number three: Honor and respect the gift of your own Majik."* She sat back in her chair, smiled and crossed her arms.

"Perfect!" Cicero praised her while following along in the book. "And Pic? What are the last two of the five tenets?"

"That's easy! Number four: Honor and respect the gift of other's Majik. And number five is: Majik is never to be used as means for revenge. Doing so risks inviting Dark Majik into one's life."

"Word for word! Excellent, ladies!"

Pic then added, "Oh yes, and this is all from the 997th edition of The New Student's Handbook of Majik."

"Really now, Pic. I doubt the governess is going to ask if you know what edition your book is," Cicero chided.

"You never know, and I want to be prepared just in case I'm asked!"

"Next, you'll be memorizing the page numbers for each chapter," Cicero mumbled.

"I heard that," Pic said and reached up to pet his back feathers. Elswyth smiled at their banter.

Serious about his duty as tutor, Cicero turned to the next chapter. The page was blank. "Hm, it seems there must be more to do?" he said. "Since you both did so well giving me the five tenets in order, Pic, give me the third and first tenets. And no fair looking!" he said, as they both reach for their books.

"Hey! I only memorized them in order!" Pic whined.

"Me, too!" Elswyth said.

"You will need to know all this by rote," Cicero shrugged and pointed to the page with his beak. "Look here. There is still nothing in chapter two and your books will not let you go further until you truly know the tenets, backwards and forwards."

"Oh wow," Pic moaned and slumped in her chair.

"It's okay. We can do this, Pic," Elswyth said

For the next hour, the three worked together and finally felt they were ready to move forward, the material firmly planted in their minds. Even so, chapter two remained a blank page.

"Really?! We did as you asked!" Pic waved her hands at her book in frustration. Then, more words appeared below the list of tenets: Discuss the tenets together.

Not sure where to start, the three launched into a discussion of various scenarios about how one or more of the tenets would apply—or when they wouldn't. The conversation made them think more about each of the rules. After another hour, Pic was going to ask if they could finally move on when both their books turned to the next page and a new text appeared.

CHAPTER TWO. MAJIK VERSUS DARK MAJIK.

Finally, their books had deemed them worthy to move on! The only problem was that the chapter contained just two sentences.

MAJIK IS BORN OF THE LIGHT AND DARK MAJIK IS BORN OF THE DARK. DARK WILL ALWAYS BE DARK BUT LIGHT MAY BE A MATTER OF PERSPECTIVE.

"That's it? Two sentences? Well, that's simple enough to remember," Elswyth said, pushing the book back. *"But I don't understand how Light is a matter of perspective, though!"*

"Me either. I mean, stuff is either good or bad. Right?"

They both looked at Cicero for his input. "Don't ask me. I don't get it either," he offered and shrugged.

Even after memorizing the words, their books wouldn't allow them to progress any further and the pages that followed chapter two were still blank. They would have to wait until their lesson with Madam Teshka to learn more.

FROM THE 997TH EDITION OF THE NEW STUDENT'S HANDBOOK OF MAJIK

CHAPTER ONE. THE FIVE TENETS OF MAJIK.

TENET ONE: MAJIK IS TO BE USED TO NURTURE AND NEVER TO HARM. THE ONLY EXCEPTION IS IN A CASE OF SELF-DEFENSE OR IN THE DEFENSE OF ANOTHER LIVING BEING.

TENET TWO: MAJIK CAN BE USED TO ASSIST IN THE PRACTICE OF HEALING, BUT IT SHOULD NEVER BE USED TO REVERSE THE FINALITY OF DEATH.

TENET THREE: HONOR AND RESPECT THE GIFT OF YOUR OWN MAJIK.

TENET FOUR: HONOR AND RESPECT THE GIFT OF OTHER'S MAJIK.

TENET FIVE: MAJIK IS NEVER TO BE USED AS A MEANS FOR REVENGE. DOING SO RISKS INVITING DARK MAJIK INTO ONE'S LIFE.

CHAPTER TWO. MAJIK VERSUS DARK MAJIK.

MAJIK IS BORN OF THE LIGHT AND DARK MAJIK IS BORN OF THE DARK. DARK WILL ALWAYS BE DARK BUT LIGHT MAY BE A MATTER OF PERSPECTIVE.

THIRTY-TWO

Madam Teshka stood on the top step of the gazebo. "Good morning! I thought holding your first class here in the royal gardens might be conducive to learning. It is, after all, an exceptionally gorgeous day, and what better way to learn than in the middle of all this beauty?" she said, gesturing at the surrounding grandeur.

With her usual airy elegance, their governess drifted to a round table made of bent willow branches in the center of the gazebo and invited them to join her. Off to the side stood a small table set with tea and cookies, and Madam Teshka saw Elswyth and Pic eyeing the treats. "Ah no, my dears! Tea and sweets are for our break. Until then, we have much to discuss."

"Okay. I mean, yes, ma'am!" Pic replied, setting her textbook on the table.

"Yes, ma'am!" Elswyth echoed as she sat down with her own book.

"That doesn't include me, though. Right?" Cicero bobbed his head toward the tea service.

Madam Teshka smiled at him. "Ah, but yes, it does, my little assistant, since I will need your help and attention throughout the lessons."

"Oh then, of course! I'm honored to help! I'll gladly wait for a break in the schedule," he said, happy to be given an official position.

Madam Teshka rearranged her shawl, cleared her throat, and began. "Well then, first I need to ask you if you completed the assignment. Did you both read and memorize chapters one and two?"

Elswyth and Pic remembered that their teacher already knew the answer since she could read their thoughts while in class, but still answered they had.

"Lovely! This morning, we will go over what you read, and yes, I shall quiz you. Then, we'll discuss your Awakening, Elswyth. I want you to understand what happened and its importance, after which I will give you options for opening up further to your gift. Pic, the discussion will also be pertinent to you, since you're not that far away from your own Awakening. And, of course, Cicero, you need to pay attention, too. This is important for you to understand."

Reading Elswyth's fears, Madam Teshka reached over and put her hand on Elswyth's. "Don't worry, my dear. As I told you before, your gift, *your power*, will be for your good, as well as the good of others. You shall be the master of your Majik and you'll learn to honor and control it. It *shall not* control you. I promise."

Elswyth nodded her head, calmed by her teacher's touch, but still doubtful. Her Awakening brought back the terror and helplessness she felt as a child, but multiplied it tenfold. She didn't relish revisiting that experience.

Madam Teshka had them recite and write the five tenets not only as listed in their book, but in random order. Elswyth looked at Cicero, smiled, and gave him credit with a nod for making them practice so much, while Pic playfully stuck her tongue out at him. They reviewed the importance of following each tenet and how it could negatively affect one's Majik to not do so.

Then came chapter two. "And what did you ladies think about the next lesson in your book?" their governess asked, sitting back in her chair.

"I didn't understand it," Elswyth answered and Pic agreed. *"How can Light be a matter of perspective? Light is Light and Dark is Dark. I kind of thought that would be as straightforward as day versus night."*

"Indeed. So it would appear, wouldn't it? But is that always the case?" their teacher posited, sitting back in her chair.

"Well, it would be common sense, wouldn't it?"

"Good is good and bad is bad," Pic said.

"Ah, but as it is with many things in life, what you consider to be *good* may not always be so clear with Majik." Madam Teshka tilted her head to the side. She pointed one elegant finger in the air. "Ponder this. With great power, we must also exercise great discernment. We need to understand and honor, when possible, the Majik of others, because their definition of Light may differ slightly from ours. Even minor differences can cause everything from misunderstandings—to war. This is especially important for you, Elswyth, as you are royalty and you may someday be in a position of ruling between factions, be it for this kingdom, the human kingdom, or both."

Madam Teshka watched as Elswyth sat, absorbing her words. "I know you aren't yet comfortable with your new status as princess, Elswyth. Give it time. You've had a lot thrown at you and there will be even more you must learn. Please know that you have all you need already inside you. I promise." She met her student's eyes and smiled with encouragement.

"But right is right and—" Pic interrupted, before Elswyth could say anything more.

Their teacher put a hand up and continued. "Let me give you an example, ladies. Elswyth, humans teach their children that elves are evil, without ever really knowing any. So, a human might use their Majik to harm or even kill an elf, believing they are the enemy. In their eyes, they are following the second part of the first tenet: "The only exception is in a case of self-defense or in the defense of another living being". As far as their understanding allows, they'd be on the side of Light and ridding themselves, or their loved ones, of danger if they used their Majik to harm—or even kill—an elf. It would be the same if we are talking about elves against humans," she explained. "As you know, there are still some in this kingdom that believe all humans are evil."

Both Elswyth and Pic sat back in their chairs, considering their teacher's words. Then Pic spoke up, "But, I don't understand what we are supposed to do then? We can't let someone harm us, or someone else, just because they might think they're in the right!"

Madam Teshka nodded. "That is correct. But, perhaps, before things ever come to the point of tragedy, there could be a meeting of the minds." both girls objected, but their teacher raised a finger again. "True, that is not aways possible. Sadly, often it is not. But Majik should not be the first and only answer to conflict. You must learn to know when, and when not, to use your Majik. If possible, seek to use words, compassion, and compromise first. When that course of action is not open to you, and that will happen, ladies, then you must use your Majik to protect yourself or others."

"That makes sense, I guess. Not always easy but, it makes sense." Elswyth shifted in her seat.

"True. It may take effort to see things from someone else's perspective. But doing so, however, may at least change what could be a disastrous outcome for the better—for everyone." She let that sink in before continuing.

"One other thing you must understand," Madam Teshka added. "never—even when ultimate justice is your only option, never relish in causing pain, or ending the life of another being. If you do, you will risk becoming the very thing you hate and quite possibly, invite Dark Majik into your own life. Yes, always rejoice in justice. But also, be sorrowful for what that life could have been if things had been different. Grieve deeply, from your heart, for the lives to whom that individual caused harm and help them to recover, if it is in your power. But do not harden your spirit with callous disregard for life. That is a darkness that could poison your soul—irrevocably."

Both Elswyth and Pic considered their teacher's words, their mood then decidedly somber.

"That leaves little room for revenge or just even wishing someone ill, I suppose," Elswyth said, thinking of her mother.

Madam Teshka smiled with tenderness at Elswyth and patted her hand, realizing whom she was referring to. "There will be those in life that hurt us, and yes, that pain can be grievous and deeply wounding. Perhaps even crippling. Sometimes it is their own pain that drives them to do what they do.

Sometimes it is simply that they have given themselves over to Dark Majik, knowingly or unknowingly. Whatever the reasons, justice may not always be available to us. Yes, we should seek that justice when we can, but when it is not in our power to have it, sometimes the best we can do is to rid them from our lives. That is when we can heal. That healing may be a lifelong endeavor, but letting them continue to control your heart and mind is allowing them to have power over you."

"Another example of easier said than done," Elswyth replied, looking down at the table.

"Yes, it is, my dear. What counts is that you never stop trying to be the best you can be, despite what anyone ever says or has done to you. I believe you're doing that," she said. "I also want you to understand that you have a lot to offer this world, whether or not you believe it yet. Regardless of what anyone ever told you, you are worthy."

Pic offered her synopsis as she understood it. "So, the Light is when we use our Majik with the intent of the first tenet. For a higher good. But we also need to be open to understanding the Majik of others. To honor it like it said in tenet number four. Their definition of Light may come from a different perspective or situation than ours. But darkness is more clear-cut. It is the absence of understanding, selflessness, and hoping for the best for all living beings. We invite darkness when we act out of anger, vengeance, or fear. Is that right? "

"I believe you've summarized it well, Pic," the governess smiled. "Does anyone have questions?"

Cicero spoke up. "I get it. We must be responsible and exercise sound judgement when using our Majik. As Elswyth said, it isn't always easy, but I get it."

"No, it isn't easy, Cicero," Madam Teshka agreed. "And we don't always get it right, but we must at least do our best." Then she gestured to the books on the table. "Now, please look at the pages for chapter two again," she said, pointing to their open textbooks. The conversation they just had appeared written, verbatim, on their pages. "You now have all the notes you need for this chapter. Our next subject will be all about Awakenings. I believe for the moment, though," she said, rising from the table, "you all deserve a break. Let's have some tea and cookies and then afterwards, I think a stroll through the gardens would be in order."

And, of course, Cicero was first at the break table.

Madam Teshka watched the trio wander around the garden, laughing and talking, the heaviness of the last conversation put aside for the moment. She smiled brightly when they looked her way but, in her heart, she worried about what Elswyth would face soon. Dark days were on the horizon and what that meant and when that would happen, she wasn't sure. The Fates hadn't yet revealed that to her. But she could sense that Darkness was imminent. She hoped and prayed that she'd be able to prepare Elswyth with the courage and strength she would need.

THIRTY-THREE

"I trust everyone is suitably refreshed and ready to continue?" Madam Teshka rearranged her shawl and settled into her chair. "If you would be so kind to observe your textbooks, you'll see we're ready to move on to chapter three." She pointed to both books as they opened on their own.

Elswyth, Pic, and Cicero leaned in to read the heading on the page. Chapter Three. What to expect after your Awakening. Beginning the fullness of your Majik journey. Madam Teshka could sense Elswyth's nervous energy building as she read the words.

"Now, I would like to give you the basics first. As you've already learned, most often, an Awakening happens within the first 24 hours of your birthday. Elswyth, for you, being half human, it was on the eve of your eighteenth birthday. Pic, since you're full Elven, yours will not be until the eve of your twenty-first, which will be soon, so do pay attention."

Pic nodded at her teacher, eyes wide. "Yes, ma'am. I am."

Cicero cleared his throat and interrupted. "Madam Teshka, I've been wondering. What about me? Do complements have an Awakening? I don't recall that ever happening to me. As I remember it, one day, I was just a regular raven, flying about and doing, well, raven things. The next I simply woke up and became as I am now."

"Ah, what a wonderful question, my little assistant! Thank you for asking it. The Majik of a complement occurs without a formal Awakening, as you described happened with yourself. Not only that, but their Majik is unique and comes into being only when the Fates have determined there is an elf—or a human," she gestured to Elswyth, "who either needs or would benefit from the blessing of one. And, as I'm sure you've noticed, this blessing is not commonplace. Not everyone will have a pairing in their lives." She then spoke directly to Cicero, her tone serious. "A complement may be called upon for more than companionship. Situations may arise that require great sacrifice and bravery. The match of a complement and their human, or elf, is both lifelong and sacred, only ending upon death."

Elswyth reached over and brought Cicero to her chest. *"Do you hear that, my friend?"* She pet his back and he replied by nuzzling her under her chin.

"What about me?" Pic asked. "Can I pray to the Fates to send me a complement?"

"No, child," Madam Teshka answered. "They are a gift and given with a higher purpose in mind. Apparently, they have decided that, at least for the time being, you're not in need of one. That's not to say that wouldn't change in the future. Any further questions before we begin?"

"Not for me. Thanks for answering my question," Cicero said. "I'm ready to go on."

"Then, go on we shall," their governess said. "As I was saying, your Awakening happens on the eve of your birthday and it is a foretelling of what one of your strongest Majik gift or gifts will be. Elswyth," she paused and faced Elswyth, "Your Awakening told you that you can detect, see, and even connect with a Dark Majik presence. Very few can actually encounter such a being, especially as strong as the one you saw."

Elswyth's face turned ashen, and her eyes blinked. *"That's what I faced that night? An actual dark entity?! I thought it was just a horrible nightmare! What am I supposed to do with that? I was completely powerless, and it almost took me."* She jumped up from the table and paced. *"Madam Teshka, I mean*

143

no disrespect, but this is not a gift. It's a curse!" She looked at her governess. *"And I don't want this so-called gift!"*

Pic jumped up and held her friend in her arms. "Elly, we'll figure it out together. Right Cicero? Madam Teshka, what can we do? That was a horrible night!" Cicero flew up, lit on Elswyth's shoulder, and nestled close to her neck.

Madam Teshka rose from her chair and gently guided Elswyth back to her seat, sending soothing energy to her heart center as she helped her to sit back down. "Please take a deep breath, my dear, and listen to me," comforted her teacher. "Yes, it was a horrible experience. I don't deny that. But you are incorrect about one thing. You are not powerless against a Dark Majik being. Far from it. You just did not know what to do. Today, you will start learning how to shield yourself. That is a first step."

"I don't know about this. I'm terrified of it coming after me again!"

"I know you are, dear. And I shall be honest with you. It may or may not try again."

Elswyth's eyes grew large. *"You're not exactly instilling confidence in me right now,"* she said, feeling weary and scared.

"Just hear me out." Madam Teshka leaned over the table towards Elswyth. "It was, indeed, a very potent black entity. The only reason it came to you in the first place was because it sensed your immense power and it was terrified of it. It was afraid of your Majik. But it also knew you were young and inexperienced. It hoped to best you because of that. If you'd had even a little training, you would have recognized its fear and been able to banish it, just as I did for you."

"Then why didn't you warn me that could happen? I could have been prepared for it!"

"My dear, I've not encountered an Awakening as strong, and as frightening, as yours for hundreds of years. I've known very few elves, and never a human, who have your level of power or your particular gift. It is very rare. For most, their Awakening is a pleasant and exciting experience. For a few, it can be confusing, but soon understood. Whether the strength of your Majik is so strong because you're half human and half Elven royalty, I don't yet know. I've been consulting the Fates for answers. In the meantime, you must move forward to develop both your Majik and the ability to shield yourself."

Elswyth slumped in her chair and put her hands to her face. *"I guess I don't have any choice, do I?"*

Madam Teshka spoke softly, "You absolutely have a choice. You can give up, do nothing and live in fear, or you can grow strong and triumph. It is up to you. I know you have it in you and always have. You are so much more powerful than you know, and I am not just talking about the strength of your Majik." She put her finger under Elswyth's chin and lifted her face. "Please, allow me to help you. What do you say, my dear? Do you trust me?" Both Pic and Cicero let out an audible sigh as Elswyth nodded yes.

"Will I still have your protection, at least until I can do it myself?" Elswyth asked.

"Of course. This is how we will proceed. I shall gradually loosen my shield around you, but never without letting you know when I do it. I will venture, however, that your progress will surprise you! You won't need my protection for long." She clasped her delicate hands on the table. "And that goes for all of you! Now, let's work on some basic self-protection techniques! You'll have the weekend to practice what I show you and then we will begin afresh next week."

Madam Teshka turned to face Elswyth. "And, my dear, it is going to be especially important for you to practice this weekend in case you have any future encounters with Prince Terrick."

Elswyth looked surprised and glanced at Pic.

"I didn't tell her about it, Elly."

"Neither did I!" Cicero added when she looked his way.

Madam Teshka sat back in her chair; her hands folded in her lap. "Elswyth, remember that I can access your thoughts while you're learning to strengthen your abilities. I've been waiting for you to bring this up today, but since you chose not to, I feel it is important to discuss."

Elswyth slumped in her chair. *"I wanted to forget it and just avoid him."*

"I think you know that he's not going to leave you alone. Of course, by all means, try to avoid any interactions with him, but you cannot evade him forever, my dear." She reached out and took both Elswyth's hands in hers. "And, Elswyth, I believe what you witnessed in the hall that day was a Dark Majik entity attached to him. Your gift allowed you to see it, and that means he may be farther gone than I thought. So, it is even more imperative that you learn to shield yourself. So please, for your own safety, do come to me when anything happens in the future. It is important. Am I clear?"

"Yes, ma'am. I promise to come to you if anything else happens."

For the rest of the afternoon, under their teacher's guidance, they practiced bringing a protective shield up from their heart center. Even Cicero practiced along with them. By the end of the day, everyone was ready for a well-deserved rest.

THIRTY-FOUR

Elswyth sat at her table, their classes done for the day, while Cicero snoozed on his perch, dreaming about something that made him chuckle in his sleep. In two weeks, they'd only gotten four chapters further in their textbooks, and she was tired of studying. *"Thank goodness Madam Teshka said we could take a couple of days off. I need a break from classes. All day, every day, is exhausting."*

Pic laid sprawled upside down on a chair by the hearth, feet in the air, her braids hanging to the floor. "You said it! Who would have thought someone as sweet as Madam Teshka could be such a taskmaster? Still love her to death but, gosh, she's tough! Although I have to say, we've gotten pretty good at putting up our shields, at least. Don't you think? Madam Teshka said she might start relaxing her protection over us next week as a test. I'm kind of looking forward to that!"

"I'm not going to lie. That scares me. At least we haven't run into Prince Terrick since that first time in the hall. I have seen him on the balconies overlooking the gardens, though. He's been watching me from up there and I can feel his energy even from that far away." She shuddered and went to the window as Cicero woke up and yawned.

Pic joined Elswyth at the window and gazed down at the city below as she looked to be in deep thought for a few breaths. She turned and then tapped the side of her head. "You know what? We should get out of here and do something different. I was thinking—"

Cicero ruffled his feathers. "Oh no. I think I feel trouble coming!" he said, fully awake now.

Elswyth winked at him and turned back to Pic. *"What is it? We've already explored all we can in the castle."*

"We should go down to the bazaar in the city tomorrow. I could introduce you to some friends and there are street performers, import shops, clothiers, haberdashers, and more. It's so much fun and," she turned towards Cicero, "there are lots of places with wonderful things to eat, too!"

"Well, maybe that's not a half bad idea then." Elswyth could see he was all in now.

"Hm. That does sound like it could be fun and I have wondered what it's like in the city. Of course, we'd have to go with my guards. I'm kind of tired of them following us everywhere, though, because we can't do anything without them tagging along."

Cicero fluffed up his feathers. "Elly, that is for a reason. You know there are those that don't accept you here. At least not yet. You need the protection."

Elswyth sighed. *"I know. You're right. It's just so tiring to be followed everywhere I go. I miss being able to just go for a walk without babysitters."* She looked over at Pic staring out the window at the city below and swore she could hear the gears in her friend's head turning. She watched as a huge smile spread across Pic's face.

"I've got a brilliant idea!" Pic said with her usual enthusiastic flair.

"Okay. And?" Elswyth was intrigued. Pic always came up with fun adventures.

Pic laid out her plan to get them to the bazaar, free of any chaperones for the day. The more Elswyth heard, the more eager she became. They could get into a lot of trouble, but the idea of being free of her guard's scrutiny, even for a short while, was too enticing and worth the risk.

Cicero, however, listened to Pic's scheme with a healthy dose of anxiety.

The next day at noon, Pic wheeled a large tea service cart full of food to Elswyth's front door and instead of letting her walk in as she usually would, the two guards stationed outside Elswyth's rooms stopped her. "Sorry, Pic. We always have to check behind the linen curtain under the cart." The younger of the two said as he stepped in front of the door.

"Of course. It's fine. You're only doing your job," she said and pulled back the cloth. "I just have a couple of small food hampers under there. See? Princess Elswyth wanted to do some extra studying this afternoon, and I offered to make her a nice lunch so she has the energy to work hard on her lessons."

"Ah, I see. That's very nice of you, Miss," he said and waved her by.

"Thank you." She pulled two cookies from inside one of the baskets. "Here, I made extra cookies. Why don't you have a couple?"

"Thank you!" He popped one of the cookies into his mouth while the older guard gave him a disapproving glare.

She beamed her most innocent smile, pushed the cart past them, and opened the door. Once inside, she rushed to the table and set everything out. "Okay. We need to eat up and then get ready! I am so excited!"

Between bites, Cicero said, "I'm going on record that I still don't agree with this so-called adventure."

"Duly noted," Pic said, as she set a plate of food in front of him.

"Does that mean you don't want to go? It won't be as much fun without you. Please say you'll go, Cis!" Elswyth pleaded.

"Of course I'm going. Someone has to watch over you two!" He did not sound thrilled about the day.

As soon as they finished their meal, Pic reached under the cart, pulled out the little baskets, and removed two complete outfits from the first one. Much simpler than the more elaborate royal attire Elswyth had on, she chose the simpler of the two and returned the other set to the basket.

"I see your Majik can make small baskets hold more than lots of food!" Elswyth said, remembering the ride from the standing stones. Pic grinned proudly and reached into the second basket and pulled out a pair of sensible walking shoes that fit Elswyth perfectly.

Last came a large canvas bag. "For shopping!" Pic said, waving it around in the air.

Eslwyth ran to the bedroom, changed into her chosen dress, stepped into the shoes and checked herself in the mirror. *Not bad. This will work and be comfy, too,* she thought, satisfied, while twirling in front of her mirror. She went back out to the living room where Cicero was, once again, trying to convince Pic to change her mind about the plan. "How do I look, you two?"

Cicero muttered his approval, while Pic looked at her with an appraising eye. "Yes! You look perfect. But I think we need to do a little glamour work to finish this off!" She sat Elswyth at the table, waved her hands over her hair, and within seconds, she was no longer a redhead.

"Wow, Elly. You look so different with brown hair!" Cicero considered. "I wouldn't recognize you on the street." Then it hit him. "Oh, I get it!"

They stacked all the empty dishes back on top of the cart. "Okay. Let's go over the plan one more time. You two hide underneath and pull the linen curtain closed. Then I'll roll the cart out past the guards to the hall where," she paused and then leaned in close to whisper, "our secret entrance is located."

"I still don't know about this, Elly." Cicero said.

Pic rolled her eyes and sighed. "Cis, you worry way too much! Now, you two be sure to bring your shields up so they can't detect you and don't come out until I say it's okay. The guards will think you stayed in your apartment and they'll never know you're gone. We'll bring the cart back for dinner service and I can sneak you back in. Easy as pigeon pie!"

"Pigeon pie may be easy for you to make, Pic, but I've never had one turn out right yet!" Elswyth's palms were sweating and her stomach was doing flip-flops as she began having second thoughts about their plan. There was

no turning back now, though. She wanted to feel free again—even for just an afternoon. She hoped Pic was right and the guards wouldn't check under the cart when they returned. *"Let's do this before I lose my nerve!"*

Cicero gave one last word of warning. "Are you sure we should do this? What if we get caught?"

"Oh my gosh, Cis. Don't be such a spoilsport!" Pic said. "I'm sure we'll be okay. Besides, it's just this one time and who are we hurting anyway? We deserve some fun after all our hard work, don't we?"

Knowing he'd lost the argument, he grunted and lowered his head, resigned to their risky adventure. "Fine! Don't say I didn't warn you both. Let's go."

Elswyth climbed under the cart with Cicero, pulled the linen curtain closed, and Pic pushed the cart out the door. Since the guards had checked the cart going in, they didn't think to check it going out.

Their adventure began.

THIRTY-FIVE

"*A* *re we there yet? It's a tight fit under here.*" Elswyth thought to Pic from under the cart.

Pic pulled to a stop. "Yep. Come on out. It's safe now."

Elswyth tumbled onto the floor, stretched out the kinks in her arms and legs, as Cicero hopped out after her. She stood up, held her arm out for him, and saw the ten ornate gold framed, life-sized paintings of what she assumed were past Glenorim nobles, hung along one wall. The hall was dark, and it looked like elves hadn't used this area of the castle in a long time. Pic's shoes and the cart had left tracks on the dusty floor leading up to where they were standing.

"*Where is the door? I don't see it.*"

"It's a secret. Remember?" Pic said, waving her finger in the air. "It's right behind you. Look!" She stepped up to the nearest painting and pushed the right side of the frame. There was a muffled click, a rush of musty air from behind the artwork, and then it swung out on squeaky hinges. "Ta-da!" she cried. After pulling the door open, Pic brought the cart inside and motioned for Elswyth and Cicero to follow. "Mind the threshold," she said, pointing down and stepping over the lip of the opening in the wall.

Once they were inside, Pic pushed a button on the side of the tunnel wall and the frame-door closed, sealing them in darkness. Elswyth put out her palm and conjured up a ball of soft blue light, grateful for the chapter about luminosity in their Majik textbooks. *"Wow. It looks like no one's cleaned this place in a long time! And I mean a very, very long time."* The cobwebs and dust brought her back to the first night in Willow Grove. *"It needs sprucing up, doesn't it, Cis?"*

Cicero ignored her question, looked around, and shuddered. "Shouldn't we get going? This place is making me nervous and I really dislike enclosed spaces and low ceilings. It's not a very bird-friendly place," he said.

Pic acted as their tour guide while they made their way down the dark hallway, their lights bouncing off the ancient stone walls. "It may not look like it now, but this was actually used a lot back in the day. It's probably been more than a couple of hundred years, though. Maybe more! I was told it was once a main passageway to the city, but I'm not sure why no one uses it any longer."

"Well," Cicero interjected. "pretty sure the windowless and crumbling condition of the place has a lot to do with no one using it now. Not to mention, it's kind of creepy in here!" Elswyth secretly agreed with him as she wiped a spider web out of the way.

Pic rattled on, "So, Alma, one of the apprentice cooks, showed it to me years ago. She'd used the passageway to visit her family in the city. She's moved on to work somewhere in Glenorim since then so I've used it occasionally when I want to go to see Sweets and her family. There are other passages, actually there are lots, from what my dad told me but this is the only one I know about."

"Sweets? I like that name!" Cicero said.

"Who is Sweets?" Elswyth asked.

"Sweets and her daughter, Dilly, are two of my oldest and dearest friends. You'll love them! And Sweets' husband, Baylin, is a sergeant in the royal army." Pic stepped over a broken piece of stone that had fallen from the wall. "Anyway, Sweets owns a wonderful shop full of the best treats you've ever eaten and they make everything in their shop with dates! Sweet or savory, every bit of it is amazing." She stepped over a few more fallen rocks, pointing them out to Elswyth. "Oh, yes! We should also stop at Zingett's Imports & Antiques Emporium, where you can find trinkets and treasures from faraway places like Belnoir. That's where the queen's from. I've heard it's a beautiful land where artisans of every kind go to study their craft. It's also known for making the finest Majik swords. Soldiers here will save up a month's wages just to buy one!"

Pic's chatter helped take Elswyth's mind off feeling so enclosed with only their Majik to light the way. The hall finally ended at a doorway that led to a spiral stone staircase that disappeared down into the darkness below. Pic started down first, still chattering about all she wanted to show them at the bazaar, seemingly oblivious to the dark and slippery steps. Elswyth took a deep breath and followed close behind. Since there were no railings on the stairs, she hugged the wall and stayed as far from the edge as possible, the very thought of the probable depth of the drop making her queasy. Cicero moved to her shoulder closest to the wall, too.

"We don't have to go into the emporium, but I at least want to check out their shop windows. Oops! Watch out for the pebbles here on the steps—" Pic said, avoiding a small pile of gravel.

Elswyth felt the crunch under her shoes just before her feet slipped out from under her.

Her arms and legs flailed through the air, and her light went out. Time slowed as she somersaulted down the steps. She crashed into Pic, and they both plunged forward blindly as they tumbled over each other down the stairs in the pitch dark. Cicero cawed frantically somewhere above, his voice echoing against the unseen walls. Elswyth slammed down hard onto the stone; the air exploding from her lungs. She laid in the darkness, desperately trying to gulp air back into her body.

Her chest seized as she realized her arm and leg were dangling in nothingness over the rough edges of the steps. A stone broke loose somewhere and she could hear it as it bounced off the spiral stairway into the depths below—never hearing it land. She broke out into a cold sweat as she dragged herself from the edge an agonizing inch at a time, reaching for the safety of the walls.

Cicero's wings flapped somewhere overhead while he called for her. "Elly, please tell me you're there!"

The darkness brightened as Pic conjured her light again. "Are you all right, Elly? Talk to me!"

The glow helped Elswyth to see the wall, and she moved as close to it as she could, forcing her breathing back to a regular rhythm. Cicero landed next to her head on the step. "Are you okay? Did you break anything?" He turned angrily on Pic, "I told you this was a bad idea!"

Her breath crept back into her chest as Elswyth sat up and felt her arms and legs. *"Cis, I think I'm okay—just a little shaken up. I may have a lot of bruises later but, other than that, I don't think I broke anything. That was scary! Are you okay, Pic? I fell right into you!"*

"Yes, I think I am."

Cicero moved closer to Elswyth. "By the Fates, Elly! You almost gave me a heart attack! Please be careful. I thought I lost you just then!"

"Cis, really. I'm okay! We're all okay." She picked him up and hugged him, still trembling from the scare.

Pic sat on the step just below, her hand resting on Elswyth's knee, her face stricken as she looked up at her friend. "Oh my gosh, Elly. You scared me, too. We'll slow down a little and we should maybe watch better where we step."

"Good idea. Let's get moving. The sooner we get to the bottom, the better!" She held out her hand to bring up her own ball of light.

"I second that," Cicero said. "Let's get out of here!"

Their descent continued in silence, guided by the bluish glow of their Majik. There were more rocks and debris along the way, but they safely avoided any more accidents. Finally, they came to level ground again.

"We're almost there!" Pic announced as she skipped ahead down a hallway.

"Thank the Fates!" Elswyth breathed a sigh of relief when up ahead, she watched as a vertical crack of light appeared where Pic was opening a metal door, the sharp screech of rusty hinges reverberating against the tunnel walls.

"Hang on just a moment," Pic whispered as she peeked through a heavy veil of ivy that hung over the opening on the outside. "Okay. No one is around. Let's go!" And then she was out the door with Elswyth and Cicero close behind.

The older guard peeked around the corner of the gallery hall as the door behind the painting clicked shut. He rubbed the stubble on his chin and smirked. "So, Princess, looks like I got you!"

Turning on his heels, he walked back in the direction he came from.

Thirty-Six

T hey stepped out into the warm sunlight in an alley behind a building
painted with bright summer colors. Elswyth turned to look at where
they'd come from and couldn't see the doorway through the curtain of vines
hanging in front of it. Pic pulled her forward through the alley and into the
street, giddy with excitement.

"Elly! Look at all this!" Cicero said, his earlier reluctance to the plan apparently forgotten.

"I know, Cis! Wow!" Elswyth turned in a circle to take it all in. She looked
over at Pic, who was grinning ear tip to ear tip.

"I told you it's amazing! Let's go. There's lots to see."

Elswyth stared around her in wonder as they moved through the crowded
street. Elves of every size, shape, and age roamed the shops and booths that
lined both sides of the busy cobblestone roadway. She noticed, though, other
than one young elf couple holding a tiny baby, only a handful of very young
elves wandered the street. The village back home was teeming with children,
so the absence of Elven youngsters stood out for her.

The noise! She'd never heard such a cacophony in her life. Vendors called
out to elves passing by, hoping to lure them to their booths. Musicians sang
songs and played instruments she'd never heard or seen before. Shopkeepers

swept their front steps, chatting with their customers. Merchants led braying donkeys hitched to carts along the bumpy cobbles, the contents of those carts occasionally falling onto the street.

And color! Everywhere she looked, there was a riot of rich, sumptuous color, from the clothes the elves wore to the colorful buildings, to all the things being sold. "Pic. This is so—" Elswyth could not find the words and waved her hands in the air. Her earlier trepidation about coming down here completely forgotten as she smiled at Cicero, turning his head at everything around him.

Elswyth breathed in all the scents that floated in the air and tickled her nose. Some promised mouth-watering feasts while exotic perfumes danced in the air as elves passed her by. The fragrance of fresh-cut flowers made her smile as they passed the florist stalls.

Pic laughed. "I knew you would love it. Follow me. You haven't seen anything yet!"

Elswyth allowed Pic to pull her through the crowd a few blocks until she stopped in front of the most amazing shop she'd ever seen. A sign hung over the entry that read Zingett's Imports & Antiques Emporium in gold letters. Painted on the door was another sign that read A Compendium Of Treasures From Around The Known And Unknown World. The expansive paned windows ran the length of the storefront which took up the entire block. Displays of jewelry full of precious stones sparkled behind the glass. Swords and daggers engraved with mythical creatures hung in neat rows against a black velvet backdrop. Exotic robes, doublets, pants, and dresses hung on dress forms. Items of every description, from simple housewares to objects she wasn't even familiar with, filled the space in the windows.

Cicero landed on a planter box that ran the length of storefront and hopped back and forth as he looked through the glass. "Can you believe this? I've never seen so many sparkly things! Look at the golden toy merry-go-round. It actually spins and plays music." Elswyth had never seen him so captivated.

She watched Pic eyeing a beautiful wood and gold-trimmed box, with a small sign next to it that said it was a one-of-a-kind antique healer's case that included multiple vials and tools. It had a wide strap made of embroidered cloth and, according to the sign, the box even held secret compartments. She thought it would make a wonderful birthday gift for Pic.

Another display featured an assortment of silver healer's chatelaines that had small engraved vials and instruments dangling from them. *Another gift idea?* One of those chatelaines would be perfect for Agnes! There was a definite trip happening in the next couple of days.

Pic clapped her hands. "Okay, we need to get going so we can see more, and so I can introduce you to Sweets. Maybe on the way back we can go inside Zingett's. This place is one you have to keep coming back to. It's impossible to see everything in one visit!" Pic said and pulled Elswyth along again. Cicero was so entranced with the store, it took him a moment more to fly after them.

They wound their way through the crowd for a few more blocks, occasionally stopping at shops and booths to ogle or admire things along the way. Finally, Pic stopped in front of a small restaurant, painted in purple and white. The large sign across the top of the roof read, It's A Date Cafe.

"Did I forget to tell you that Sweets has a sense of humor? What a perfect name for their shop. Right? It's been a special place elves have gone to for first dates, marriage proposals, and anniversaries for the last two and a half centuries! Not only that, if someone gives you a bag of treats from her shop, count yourself lucky and loved!" Pic giggled, pointing to the sign. "Of course, we also come here just to have something good to eat, too. Let's go in."

THIRTY-SEVEN

There was no place like the It's A Date Cafe in the village near Willow Grove. Glass cases filled with delights of every kind, all made with dates, lined the walls. In the center of the shop, customers filled every one of the twenty cafe tables, their laughter, and friendly discussions added to the light-hearted and warm atmosphere. Cicero's body vibrated with excitement in her arms. "Oh, Elly. I think I've died and gone to be with the Fates! They have breakfast, lunch, dinner, *and dessert* all under one roof! We could rarely even get dates at all back home."

Someone shouted above the din from across the room. "It's our Pic!" Elswyth turned and saw a plump elf run from behind the counter to meet them at the door, her long, salt, and pepper braids bouncing against her broad back. "Oh, my dear Pic, it has been too long!" Pic disappeared in the fiercest hug Elswyth had ever seen.

"Sweets! You're crushing me!" Pic laughed with happy tears in her eyes.

"Oops! Sorry," Sweets said, chuckling and smoothing Pic's clothes as she let her go. "I always forget my own strength! What brings you down here today?"

"Well, Sweets, I brought some new friends with me. I've wanted to bring them to meet you for a while. Can they have a private tour of your kitchen? I'll make the introductions in the back." Pic nodded towards the kitchen door.

"Of course they can!" Sweets erupted into a full, hearty laugh that filled the room. "Follow me and I'll treat you to some of my very best delicacies! Dilly is going to be so happy to see you, Pic," she said as she herded them to the door in the back of the shop.

The kitchen was as much a delight as the front of the cafe. Brass pots simmered on an enormous stove and warm, yeasty aromas wafted from two large ovens. Baskets of dates sat everywhere on the counters and dried herbs hung from the ceiling. Neatly arranged boxes of fresh produce, tins of spices and sacks of flour lined the shelves and countertops. Across from the cooking area stood a slender young elf working at a counter, and Elswyth guessed she was close to her age. When the elf turned around, she dropped everything and ran to them, arms open wide.

"Our Pic!" she said happily in thought. Elswyth noticed the elf talked using her mind voice, just like she did.

"Dilly! Oh, it is so good to see you!" Pic squealed as they ran into each other's arms.

Sweets went to a cozy booth in the back of the kitchen and set out several dishes of food and a tea service, then waved them over. She was so big she couldn't fit in the booth and took a side chair at the end of the table.

"So, tell me, Pic, who are your two lovely friends?" Sweets asked and nodded at Elswyth and Cicero.

Pic sat up straight in her seat. "Now you'll understand why I wanted to make my introductions back here in the kitchen. Sweets, Dilly, meet Princess Elswyth and her esteemed complement, Cicero."

Both Sweets's and Dilly's eyes grew large as they jumped up from the table and curtsied. "It's our honor to have you here in our humble kitchen, Your Highness! We've heard all about you."

"Oh please, please sit. You're very kind and the honor is mine. Pic told me all about you and bragged about your cafe so I can't wait to try some of your

goodies!" She shifted in her seat, then asked, *"So, um, what have you heard about me?"*

"Oh, don't worry, Your Highness. It's all good things. Most of us are old-school elves and believe that believe a child is always a matter of joy and celebration here! You see, we aren't like humans. Elven children are rare," she said, turning to Dilly to squeeze her hand. "and so, for the royal family to be blessed by the Fates with a *granddaughter*, well, that is a wonder to be cherished. I must say though—" she sat back in her chair, rubbing her chin, "You don't look quite like what we thought you would, but you are as beautiful as I've heard tell!"

Pic waved her hand over Elswyth's hair, and it went back to red for just a moment. "Is this more what you were expecting?" She smiled at the nods she got from across the table. "We snuck out today to have a bit of fun, so I disguised her just a little. We've been studying our Majik lessons for two weeks straight and finally wanted a day off without Elly's guards following us around. I thought she would love to see the bazaar, but I especially wanted her to meet you two."

"Again, we're honored to have you here, Your Highness."

"Yes, Your Highness. So very honored!" Dilly said, passing a plate of date confections around.

"Thank you, Dilly." Elswyth nodded with a smile and turned to Cicero. *"Cis, we can take some home with us. There's no need to eat everything all at once!"* She laughed as he helped himself to seconds when the serving platter passed him.

Pic then lost her smile and turned to Sweets. "So, what's the news here in the city? What's been happening?" Elswyth sensed a change in Pic—a nervous expectation.

Sweets sighed, picked up a napkin and smoothed it over her lap before she answered. "I'm afraid there's been more trouble from Prince Terrick's followers down here in the city. They're spreading lies about the king and queen and pushing for a takeover of the throne—with Prince Terrick in power, of course. Elves like us are being bullied and intimidated more than ever. Their cowardly activity is still in the shadows mostly, but they're getting bolder and, I fear, their numbers are growing. My husband told me there are even elves loyal to Prince Terrick within the ranks of the army. He's very concerned about that." Sweets shook her head and brought her hand to her heart. "Two weeks ago, a group of them threw a rock through our window in the middle of the night. The note tied to it called us dirty halfling royalists." She held her head high. "We make no secret of defending King Garreth and Queen Araleia and will always do so."

Elswyth couldn't help asking, *"Halfling?"*

Cicero's head shot up, interested. "You?"

"Yes. I'm also a halfling, Princess. And I'm darn proud of who I am, too, just so you know. My father was human, and he is where I got my—roundness from," she said, winking and gesturing to her large middle. "You've probably noticed other elves, like me, who are not the usual tall and slender example of our species. Chances are, they have human blood somewhere in their past and carry that identity with pride."

"Honestly, since I've never known any elves personally, I just thought you were all as different from each other as we humans are."

Shifting in her chair, Sweets said, "We lived in Carthia until my father passed away a little over two hundred years ago. Then, Mother and I moved back here to Glenorim. Of course, then the Portal was closed not too many years later. It was a sad time all around."

"I didn't realize there were that many that mixed between the kingdoms." Elswyth could think of a few people back home who wouldn't be happy to hear this revelation. Hating and fearing the elves from the mountain was a given in Carthia.

"Oh my, yes. Love doesn't distinguish between Elven and human and, over the thousands of years our kingdoms were friendly with each other, many such unions happened. Of course, humans don't live as long as we do, so there were always bound to be sad goodbyes at some point. But the love was always worth it for them, as it was for my parents."

Cicero had been deep in thought during the conversation, then blurted, "Wait a second. That must mean there are still humans in Carthia who are—"

"Of course! There are halflings in your kingdom that are descended from elves. You may never know it to look at them now. I hear our pointed ear trait weakened in your world over time and it is no longer a thing with halflings there in Carthia. Either that, or there are Elven in Carthia that glamour their ears. Even so, Elven genes still carry other characteristics such as living a longer life than humans usually do. They may also have extraordinary Majik abilities, or any number of other things." She frowned and added. "After the portal was closed, there were many elves who stayed behind in Carthia. They most likely had to glamour their appearance, but they wanted to be with their loved ones. Others petitioned to return here for their own reasons. Either way, many families, and friends were torn apart, sadly."

"Wow! I am not the only one from Carthia?" Elswyth said, this revelation somehow making her feel more whole—less an outcast. She had always been the different one in the human world.

"No, you are not! And, and how wonderful is that!?" Sweets said, her palms up.

Pic reached out to Sweets. "I'm so sorry to hear about all the trouble. I've wondered if things were getting worse, but I had no idea Terrick's influence had become so strong in the city. My father said no one realized just how much the prince had been working to gather elves on his side until recently. It is frightening. Elly and I try to avoid Terrick as much as possible."

"That's true. We do, Sweets. And I am so sad to hear he has such a dark old on so many elves down here. I wish we could do something to help." Elswyth was angry on behalf of all the elves Terrick was hurting. She knew what it was like to feel helpless and bullied.

"Thank you. But I have to say, I am surprised you two have come to the bazaar without your guards. It really isn't safe, even with the glamour you did on the princess, Pic." Her brow crinkled with worry. "If any of those thugs even suspect you're from the castle, much less if they discover who you are, Your Highness, it could be dangerous. Very dangerous."

"I guess we have been a little reckless." Elswyth said, suddenly feeling vulnerable and irresponsible.

"I will not say I told you so!" Cicero muttered between nibbles.

"Maybe we should head back then," Elswyth looked at Pic.

Sweets nodded. "I think that would be for the best. But we are so very glad you came to see us!"

Dilly jumped up. *"Let me get you some treats to take back with you!"* After loading Pic's bag with goodies, Sweets, and Dilly made them promise to come back soon, but with royal guards, next time.

Elswyth and Pic held hands and pushed their way through the noisy tangle of elves in the street, trying to get back to the door of the castle passageway while Cicero flew up ahead, keeping them in sight. They'd only gone a few blocks from Sweets's shop when things took a turn. Someone grabbed them from behind by the shoulders. Hard. And whoever had them was not letting go. No matter how much they wiggled or tried to pull away, they couldn't get free.

"Help!" Pic began to hyperventilate. The elves passing by looked their way wide-eyed, but when they saw who was trying to restrain Elswyth and Pic, they put their heads down and hurried past.

Elswyth gulped a huge sob and tried to twist out of the grasp of her captor, fear turning her stomach to jelly. Nothing was working. *"Fates save us, Pic! It must be Terrick's followers! They found us!"* Icy panic squeezed her chest.

Cicero flew behind them, flapping and pecking at their captors. "Leave them alone or you'll answer to me!" he yelled above the noise of the bazaar. Elves in the surrounding throng did their best to get out of the way.

"Oh Elly! I'm so sorry I got you into this!" Pic wailed.

THIRTY-EIGHT

"Ow! Stop that, Cicero!" Elswyth heard someone yell behind her. Both she and Pic stopped struggling, froze and looked at each other.

Cicero landed on Elswyth's arm and shook his head. "Elly, you know when I said I wouldn't say I told you so? I lied. Um, you two should turn around. And—for the record—I told you so."

Both Elswyth and Pic slowly turned to face whoever had such a tight grip on them, then both their mouths dropped open.

"Um—Hi Dad?" Pic gave her father a sheepish grin.

Elswyth stared wide-eyed at her own father, her grin matching Pic's.

Prince Dayel and Caden stood before them, their shields up and glamoured to look like castle guards, their Majiks, however, still recognizable to the perpetrators. *No wonder no one stopped to help,* Elswyth thought. *They probably thought we were being arrested for shoplifting or something.* Her face burned with embarrassment.

"I think you two have some explaining to do," Caden said with raised eyebrows.

"Let's go," Prince Dayel said, rubbing his head where Cicero had pecked him.

Ratheus shuffled over next to Prince Dayel as Elswyth and Cicero sat across from them by the fireplace in his study. She dreaded this moment. She hated being a disappointment and her irresponsible decision to ditch her guards weighed on her conscience. *How could I have been so stupid?* She steeled herself for a much-deserved punishment.

Prince Dayel reached up to rub the back of his neck. "I guess we should talk about consequences for today?" He cleared his throat and sat forward in his chair. "Oh, Elswyth." He shook his head and took a deep breath. "I'm afraid I haven't had any practice being a father," he said.

"Wait, please." She stared at the floor, her hands clasped in her lap. *"Before you say anything, I want to apologize first. I wanted—needed—so badly to get out and do something fun, to feel normal, and I didn't think it through. We could have gotten into a lot of trouble. I understand that and it won't happen again. I promise."*

"Elswyth," he said. She raised her eyes to his. "I was going to say that I understand. You were torn from your home, dropped into a completely unfamiliar world and left Agnes behind. If she were here, she would no doubt talk you through this with care and understanding. That is all I want to do."

Elswyth's heart twisted at the mention of Agnes, and she reached over to hug Cicero close to her chest. He snuggled her back.

"Perhaps I should have been more sensitive, helped you through everything, Elswyth, so I am taking part in the blame. But, also, I wanted to tell you it appears you have a little more of me in you than I thought," he said with a faint smile.

"I do? How is that?" She searched his face, curious.

"Well, you apparently inherited a little of my impulsive side. If you recall, I once did something very reckless and irresponsible myself. Instead of going to my parents and asking for help or advice with what I wanted to do, I simply went off on my own. Because of that, my actions caused you a very hard start in life and I will always regret that. I'll never be able to make up for it. But I also want you to know that my mistake gave me—gave our family," he said and gestured to her, "you. And, of course, Agnes, and Cicero. For that at least, I will be forever grateful. I am not here to judge or punish you, Elswyth. If you're anything like me, you are punishing yourself enough at the moment."

Elswyth let out a breath. *"Thank you. And for the record, I think you're doing pretty good for first attempts at being a father. I think Agnes would approve. And,"* she said and paused, *"maybe, it is time to call me Elly."*

Her father turned his gaze to the flames in the fireplace, and when he looked back at her, she noticed his eyes were misty. "Well, then—Elly it is. Thank you. And when you're comfortable doing it, I'd be honored—that is, if you wanted to—for you to call me Father. There is no rush, of course! When, and if you're ready. Or never, if that's what you want. I don't want to pressure you," he said, rubbing the back of his neck.

Elswyth looked down at Cicero, and he nuzzled her arm in response. When she looked back at her father, she realized the awkward wall that had been between them was crumbling. She still wasn't sure if she was ready to call him father yet, but it felt more possible than it had before. Not knowing what to say, she changed the subject instead. *"By the way, how did you know we snuck out?"*

"Ah. One of your guards thought something was up and followed Pic. He came to me shortly after you went into the passageway. From there, Caden and I only had to go down to the bazaar and focus on your Majiks to find you."

"I guess that means we have to practice more with our shields?" she shrugged her shoulders and half-smiled.

Her father chuckled, but then said, "I will always be able to find your Majik, Elly. Shields or not. You're my daughter, and our Majiks will always be connected to each other's. No matter what, I will do my best to protect you, whatever the cost."

His words made her feel safe the way Agnes did when Elswyth awoke from a nightmare. *"Thank you. That means a lot."*

Then she remembered the conversation with Sweets about what had been going on in the city and relayed it to her father. *"I'm worried about them, about what's going on down there. Isn't there any way to help them?"*

"Yes, we're aware things are getting worse and we are trying to help where we can but, there are elves, both civilian and military, that Terrick's been able to manipulate." Her father shook his head, his jaw set.

"I don't understand. Why can't the elves see him for what he is? For being so manipulative?"

"One of his abilities, his strongest, is to reach into the hearts and minds of others and actually see their deepest desires or darkest fears. He exploits that for his own purposes by promising whatever it is they want or need. He never intends to follow through with the promises." Her father got up from his chair and stepped closer to the hearth. He stared into the fire before going on. "He could've used his Majik to help others heal or to teach or—in so many other ways. Instead, he's used his gift selfishly."

"Why hasn't he been stopped? Wasn't there something the family could do before this?"

"Father and mother have tried over the years. From early on, they gave him positions of responsibility. Tried to encourage him to use his talents and Majik for Light, for himself as well as for the good of the kingdom. They gave him every opportunity. It was never enough. He wanted the throne and the power behind it, but knew I was next in line, so that wasn't within his reach. Then he wanted our father to open the standing stones so he could invade Carthia."

Elswyth shuddered, her eyes wide. *"He wanted to occupy our kingdom? What about all the humans?"*

"Terrick's plan was to kill most of them, enslave the rest, and rule Carthia. Our father flatly refused and they haven't spoken since. Your uncle wants power and always has." He looked off into the distance. "Maybe we didn't want to believe he would truly go against the family—against our kingdom, but he has. His power has grown and now we're learning just how many are blindly following him." Elswyth could see his jaw clenching. "We know there will be a reckoning at some point; perhaps soon and it will be especially devastating to our mother. She had hoped he'd find his way. I think she still hopes for that, but as far as I can see, it's clear he made his choice. "

Elswyth sat still for a moment before speaking. It was time to tell her father about her encounter with Terrick. She should've brought it up sooner. *"There's something I need to tell you about Prince Terrick—"* Cicero looked up at her and tilted his head encouragingly. *"He and I ran into each other in the halls."*

"It's okay. I know all about it. Madam Teshka told me, and I was grateful she did. I've been waiting until you were ready to come to me about it. I understand if you may have been afraid to tell me."

She felt a surprising rush of relief at the whole incident finally being out in the open with her father. *"Oh, I wasn't afraid of you. I guess I just didn't want to be the reason for any more trouble. It's obvious there was enough stress in the family about him so I thought I could just avoid him. He's been keeping his distance, so there's that."*

"You are not, and never will be, a burden to me or your grandparents. Please believe me when I say that. Know you can always come to me. Okay?"

"Okay. Thank you."

"And as for him bothering you again, I told him in no uncertain terms, that he is to leave you alone. So let me know if anything else happens. Yes?"

"I will." She reached out to Cicero.

Then Dayel turned back towards her. "Anyway, Terrick is the last thing you need to concern yourself with at the moment. You have far more important things to worry about—like your classes, which are vital for you right now. You're also still adjusting to life here. Besides, there is something else I needed to discuss with you."

Elswyth felt her muscles tense and braced herself for whatever was coming. *"Oh, no. Did I do something else? I'm sorry!"*

THIRTY-NINE

D ayel chuckled and put his hands up. "No! You did nothing wrong. Don't worry. This is going to be something fun. We need to plan a birthday party for Pic."

Elswyth's shoulders dropped, and she sat forward while Cicero hopped onto the arm of the chair, all ears. *"Cis and I have been talking about that! Can we make it a surprise? And I want to invite lots of elves, including some of the kitchen staff. They've been good friends to her. Oh yes, and Sweets and Dilly need to be there. Can we invite the king and queen or is that not allowed? Madam Teshka needs an invite, too, of course!"*

Cicero finally spoke up now that the conversation had shifted to a happier subject, "Yes! We'll need lots of delicious food and drink, too!"

Ratheus, silent this whole time, even chimed in, "How about we bring in musicians so we can dance? After all, who doesn't love a spin around the ballroom?"

Elswyth tried to imagine the big, lumbering bear dancing gracefully across the floor, and inwardly chuckled.

Her father laughed and put his hands up again for everyone to slow down as he sat back in his chair. "Your grandmother has already told me she and your grandfather would like to attend. As a matter of fact, she suggested we use the reception terrace off the grand ballroom for the celebration. since it's more than big enough to hold a large party. We'll have plenty of room for guests, food, and," he turned to Ratheus, "of course, music, and dancing."

"That would be perfect! And it has a spectacular view. Oh, and there are actually some things I saw in Zingett's that would make perfect gifts for her. Could you and I go together?"

"That is a splendid idea! Let's plan to go down there together to do a little shopping and bring Caden along with us, too. Maybe we can even stop at It's A Date Cafe to offer a formal invitation to Sweets and Dilly."

"And get something to eat there?" Cicero asked.

"Yes, Cicero. We should plan to have lunch there!" Dayel said.

"This is going to be perfect!" Elswyth was already picturing the trip back down to the bazaar.

They discussed their big plans for the birthday party, with Dayel adding a few suggestions from the queen. It would be difficult to keep the party a secret from Pic, but it would be worth it. Since keeping secrets had never been easy for Cicero, Elswyth warned him to try extra hard to not ruin the surprise.

"One more thing, Elly," Dayel said as Elswyth and Cicero were leaving. "Ruby will deliver a letter from Agnes to your rooms right after dinner tonight. Just remember to burn it when you've read it, so that there is no way to trace it back to Agnes. She'll do the same on her end with your reply. It's for her safety and yours."

Getting a letter from Agnes was the best news of the day. *"I can't wait!"* She paused for a heartbeat and then added, *"Thank you, Father!"*

FORTY

Terrick kept the fireplace in his study roaring at all times now. *Why can't I ever get this blasted room warm enough?* He peered into the flames before he willed them higher, then turned his attention back to the elf sitting across the desk from him. Either the commander was too warm or he was very nervous. Terrick hoped it was both as he watched a bead of sweat dribble down the soldier's temple and down to his neck.

The leather in Terrick's chair creaked as he shifted forward. With his elbows rooted to his desktop, he steepled his fingers in front of him and narrowed his eyes at Colonel Rohne while the soldier sat ramrod straight, clutching a warm glass of Glenorim's royal aged nectar in his hands. "Relax, Rohne," Terrick said. His tone dripped with saccharine and he noticed Rohne shiver. "Enjoying your drink?"

"Yes, Your Highness. Very much. Thank you." The commander raised his glass with a stiff arm to Terrick, then took a sip.

"Good, I'm pleased. It is, after all, some of our finest reserve," Terrick said, knowing this royal treat would make the soldier feel both entitled and indebted. He peered at Rohne over the tips of his tented fingers. "Are you absolutely confident you will have enough of your ranks on my side in time to implement the plan? Time is growing short." Terrick crossed his arms and cocked his head.

"Yes, I believe we'll have more than enough when the time comes. Those that aren't yet loyal will be. I guarantee that!" He took another sip. "I will find ways to convince those that don't fall in line."

"And you're stressing they must appear to still be loyal to the king and queen? That is crucial."

"Yes, absolutely, Your Highness. I've been very clear with the troops." A knock at the door interrupted them.

Terrick called out, "Enter!" A soldier escorted the older guard from El-swyth's apartment into the study. "Ah, I've been waiting for you to return. So, what do you have to report?"

"Your Highness!" He bowed. "I did as you ordered and reported the princess—"

"WHAT did you just say to me?!" Terrick's eyes grew dark and his nostrils flared. He felt himself losing control as the dark tendrils returned, creeping up and around his feet and threatening to travel higher up his body. He squeezed his eyes shut and took a moment to breathe in and out, quelling his anger and forcing the blackness back into the cold stone tile beneath his chair. In control once again, he slowly opened his eyes and glared at the guard. "You know better than that! She is a *halfling* sham and not fit to be called *princess*," Terrick hissed. "I don't care what else you call her in my presence, but never, *never* call her that again! Is that clear?"

The guard stared straight ahead, his eyes bulging. "Yes, Your Highness. My apologies." His fists clenched so tightly by his side that his knuckles turned white and shook with the effort. His words came tumbling out. "The halfling, per your orders, after I reported her escape to you, I—I did as you ordered and reported her and Pic's absence to your brother. I told him they snuck past us and had gone out the old passageway to the city. Prince Dayel and his regent then went to the bazaar to retrieve them. It is my understanding both girls are being disciplined by their fathers as we speak." The soldier's face was covered in a sheen of sweat.

As always, Terrick relished seeing someone squirm in front of him, so he sat back in this chair and let the moment stretch out before saying anything. "Good. That is very good. Not a word of this to anyone, soldier. You're dismissed."

The guard let out a soft huff of air, bowed, and left.

Terrick looked at the commander, who wore a frown. "You look confused, Rohne."

"Yes, Your Highness. Begging your pardon, but we could have taken her easily down there at the bazaar. She would no longer be a problem."

"Ah, yes, we could have done that but then I would still have other problems to deal with, wouldn't I? My plans are bigger than just getting rid of her," Terrick said, a glint in his eye. "Yes, my plans are much bigger so, for now, I want her to live under the assumption that she is relatively safe. Make sure my followers understand they are not to touch her. She and everyone else in the family needs to be complacent until the time is right. When their day of reckoning comes, their shock will be, well, it will be even more delicious for me." His chuckle sounded like a rabid dog's growl.

Rohne looked down at his glass. "I understand, Your Highness." He took another swig of his drink.

"And remember, Colonel, you'll be amply rewarded for your service when I am crowned king. As promised, you will have the head seat on my war council. Patience. Just have patience and do what I say. Do I make myself clear?"

The nectar had made Rohne more relaxed, and he raised his glass again towards the prince with a smirk. "Completely, Your Highness. I am your humble servant."

Terrick didn't want Rohne to get too comfortable in his presence. "There is nothing humble about you, Rohne," he said. "Just remember, cross me and you will wish you'd never been born. That goes for you and all those you hold dear. Understood?"

Rohne stiffened in his chair, his chin held high. "Yes, Your Highness. I pledge my fealty to you and look forward to the day I can address you as Your Majesty!"

"Excellent. We're done for now. You're dismissed," he said, waving his hand.

Rohne looked longingly at his unfinished glass of nectar and set it down as he stood, then bowed and left the room.

Terrick pushed up from his chair and stepped over to his mirror, his grin spread from ear to ear as he admired his dark, handsome reflection. "I am so close. So close. Just a little more patience and everything I've wanted my entire life will rightfully be mine. All. Mine!"

He shivered and brought the flames in the fireplace even higher.

FORTY-ONE

E lswyth reread Agnes's letter aloud to Cicero and Pic, heartsick at its contents. She knew she was supposed to throw it in the fireplace, but couldn't bring herself to do it. Not just yet.

"Wow." Pic whispered. "She wants to help other young humans rediscover their Majik? That's really brave, Elly, but it seems kind of dangerous, too. Doesn't it?"

"It is. And I'm terrified for her."

Cicero spoke up. "I'm worried, too, but it sounds like she's being as careful as she can, Elly. And you know her. When Sarah told her that King Markan had executed her mother for secretly teaching Majik, well, like Agnes said, she couldn't sit by and do nothing. Majik is sacred to her, and it's important for her to be part of keeping it alive for humans."

"But why does it have to be her? Why can't it be someone else?"

Cicero shook his head. "Elly, you know you can't tell Agnes not to do something, especially if she feels strongly about it. And remember, her students would only be there at Willow Grove long enough to learn basics so they can go out and teach others. From what she said, there are now many others like her joining the movement. She isn't the only one."

"It's dangerous, Cis! If she's caught, Markan will have her executed!"

"Yes, I know. But, if no one steps up, then Majik will disappear from Carthia. Well, except for the king, of course," he spat the last sentence out. "He'll be the only one to hold that power, and then no human will be safe—ever. Markan has gotten away with his greed for too long and people are beginning to fight back."

"Then I should be there to help her, Cis, and instead, I'm here! What if something happens to her? I would never forgive myself! Sarah may have moved on, but now she's spreading word that she and Agnes will help anyone who wants to regain their Majik. How long will that stay a secret? Why couldn't she let someone else do this?" Elswyth burst into tears, tears born of anger, fear, desperation, and guilt. It was all bubbling up at once, and she didn't know how to contain it all.

Pic rushed to her side and reached out to hold her. "Elly, but what can you do? Agnes wants you here, strengthening your own abilities. She even said so in her letter! She wants you safe and—"

Elswyth shoved Pic away. *"You don't understand! Agnes is my mother, maybe not by blood, but we're still connected as family. She's always been my protector and has been there for me through everything, yet I sit here, surrounded by luxury and safety, while she's in danger."* Elswyth pushed back from the table. *"I think I've learned enough here. I should go back to Willow Grove. She shouldn't be doing this alone and my place is with Agnes!"*

Pic stepped back, hurt, tears welling in her eyes and her arms at her side.

Cicero fluffed his feathers and shook his head in anger. "Pic was only trying to help, Elly! You did not need to treat her that way!"

Pic's voice trembled as she spoke. "I grew up without a mother, Elly. She died in childbirth and I have always wondered what it would have been like if she were still here with me. I can't tell you how many times I've missed her and I never even knew her. Dad is wonderful and I love him, but I would give anything to still have my mother here. So, yes, I do understand how deeply important Agnes is to you. I really do."

Elswyth sniffled and looked up at Pic, instantly horrified at pushing her away. *"I'm so sorry, Pic! That was awful of me!"* She brought her hands to her face and squeezed her eyes shut. *"Please forgive me. I know you're only trying to help. It's just that I feel so helpless. And angry! How could I feel so angry?"*

"It—it's okay, Elly. I understand you're afraid for Agnes." She wiped away her own tears. "Really. You love her, and of course you want to help. She's family and since Agnes is your family, then she's mine, too. But I honestly don't think we are quite ready—"

Elswyth looked up at Pic. *"We?"*

"Well, you didn't think Cicero and I would let you go running off to save Agnes on your own, do you? Of course we'd want to help! Right, Cis?"

"Absolutely. You're not going anywhere without us!" He flew across the table to settle on her lap.

"But think about it, Elly," Pic said, sitting down in a chair next to Elswyth. "What kind of help would we be now, anyway? When we thought it was Terrick's followers that had grabbed us at the bazaar today, we were helpless! How could we help Agnes if we couldn't even help ourselves? We need to learn more. Get stronger. And maybe get a little smarter."

"I agree on the getting smarter part," Cicero said. Both Elswyth and Pic looked over at him, eyebrows raised. "What? I meant all of us!"

"Besides," Pic continued, "from all you and Cis have told me about Agnes, she's really smart and her Majik is powerful, even for a human so I think she'll manage fine without us until we can get better ourselves. Okay?"

Cicero nuzzled Elswyth. "Listen to her, Elly. Please don't go back down the mountain yet. Stay here and we'll do what we can to get ready. Maybe then your father will help, too."

Elswyth's shoulders dropped, and she sat back. *"Okay. I guess you're right. I'm so very sorry, Pic. It's just that I love her so much and the thought of losing her is—I can't imagine life without Agnes in it. If anything happens to her, I will blame myself for not being there to help."* Elswyth hiccuped with a final sob and she looked down at the letter clutched in her hand. *"Pic, I don't think I can throw Agnes's letter in the fire. Can you do it for me?"*

"Sure. We can all do it together and we'll ask the Fates to keep her safe."

They gathered in front of the fireplace and Elswyth gave the crumpled letter one last squeeze before she reluctantly handed it over. Pic took it, and reached out her hand toward the fire, commanding the flames to lower and the wood to cool. She then set the letter on the logs.

They bowed their heads as Pic offered her prayer. "Dearest Fates, we ask that you protect and guide our Agnes as she works to do right for others. Grant her wisdom and keep her Majik strong. And we ask the same for us so we can someday be there to help her. We offer our praise and honor to the Fates." Pic then reached out and ordered the flames to rise again until the letter turned to ashes.

Cicero broke the somber hush. "Well now, who would've thought that Pic would be the one with the level head?" he asked and tilted his head to Elswyth. He laughed and winked at Pic.

Elswyth hugged him and watched the flames for a moment longer, still focused on the few reaming bits of ash from the letter.

Determined to get back to lessons, they pulled out their textbooks and set them on the table.

"Okay, Textbook. Let's see what you have planned for us tomorrow?" Elswyth asked. Nothing happened. *"Hello? Did you not hear me? What are we going to be learning next?"* she asked again.

Finally, the books opened, and their pages began to flip back and forth until at last they fluttered to a stop. Elswyth and Pic leaned over to read the assignment and gasped in unison at the ominous title that appeared across the top of the page.

"Let me see!" said Cicero, pushing his way between the two of them on the table. "Oh. My. Stars! That looks dire."

"Yeah, it certainly does!" Elswyth said, and frowned.

USING MAJIK AS DEADLY FORCE. DEFENSIVE AND OFFEN-SIVE TACTICS & MANEUVERS.

As they watched, two more lines of text appeared beneath the title.

LIVE DEMONSTRATIONS AND TARGET PRACTICE TOMOR-ROW MORNING.

MEET MADAM TESHKA AT DAWN IN THE COURTYARD OUTSIDE THE STABLES FOR INSTRUCTION.

"Well, I for one am not looking forward to that lesson!" Cicero said, speaking Elswyth and Pic's thoughts out loud.

FORTY-TWO

E lswyth stood on the cobblestones with Cicero and Pic in the early
morning fog, and waited for Madam Teshka to arrive for their lesson.
She could just make out the fuzzy figures of her ever-present guards standing
on the steps on the far side of the courtyard.

Cicero hopped around on the ground, grumbling. "By the Fates! Even the
horses aren't awake yet! Why did we have to come out here at the crack of
dawn? I bet the stable hands are still asleep in their warm beds."

"Well, good morning, my little assistant. I've no doubts they are indeed still
snug under their blankets." They turned to see Madam Teshka as she floated
towards them through the mist.

"Oh!" Cicero cleared his throat. "Good morning, Madam Teshka!" Elswyth wiggled her eyebrows at him, suppressing a smile.

Their governess wasted no time with her usual pleasantries. "This is an
important day in your education. We are beginning class early, and in the
carriage house courtyard, because it is the safest place to practice. There is
less danger of anyone getting hurt out here, especially at this time in the
morning. Once you're better with your aim, we shall try different venues."
She paused and set her bag down beside her. Elswyth wondered if her teacher
ever went anywhere without that wonder-filled purse. "It is important you

understand today's lesson is to be taken very seriously. Although this is a chapter I would have preferred to do much later, it appears your books have deemed it essential to learn now, and it is always wise to heed your textbooks!"

"Yes, ma'am!" they all said in unison.

"Pic, even though you will not have complete power until your birthday in a few days, you will work along with Elswyth. I believe you will have sufficient strength to at least practice."

"Yes, ma'am!" Pic said, wringing her hands.

"Very good. And Cicero," she bent down to him and touched under his beak. "I want you to know that, as her complement, this is a sign you must now be even more diligent regarding Elswyth's safety. Perhaps keeping an extra eye out for Pic would be prudent as well."

Cicero nodded and puffed his chest out. "Of course I will. Gladly!"

Madam Teshka kept talking as she searched through her bag. "As I have already said, your textbooks would not have opened to this particular lesson if it were not of the utmost gravity."

Elswyth felt Pic's hand reach for hers.

"I'll be doing a demonstration and then you shall try the technique yourself." She furrowed her brow as she dug deeper into her bag, shuffling through whatever was in there. "Ah! Here they are. I knew I'd packed them," she said, pulling a stack of round wooden targets, each no bigger than her hand, from her bag. Madam Teshka moved to the far edge of the courtyard, set the targets against the balustrade, then came back to her students.

"Before we begin, you must understand one vital issue about using your Majik as a weapon. This is true whether you deploy it defensively or of-fensively since the same amount of power is expended. Every time you use your power with deadly force straight from your hands, it will drain your energy—and quickly. Of course, over time, practice will help to build your Majik muscles, as I like to say, but even when you are at your strongest, you will still have the same problem. For this reason, you must also begin instruction on swordsmanship soon."

Elswyth glanced at Pic, eyes wide. She didn't relish the idea of handling swords. She'd often cut herself by simply preparing meals, and Agnes was always warning her to be more careful with knives. How was she going to handle a blade meant for battle? *"But, Madam Teshka, why do we need to learn this? If our Majik can become more powerful with practice, why can't we just use that? We could—"* she shivered at what she would say next. *"We could just make each attack—count—with our Majik."* Both Pic and Cicero nodded earnestly in agreement.

"Another excellent question. You three do have the best queries." She leaned down and pulled a three-foot-long sword from her tote and held it up for them to see. Then she called the older of Elswyth's guards to join them. As he walked over, she explained, "If you release your Majik in large bursts from your hands, it will, as I mentioned, drain you in equally large doses almost immediately. However, a sword acts as a conduit and a regulator, if you will, of your power, and helps sustain your Majik much longer. Observe!"

She spun towards the guard and brandished her sword with such lightning-fast speed and agility that they all gasped—even the guard, his mouth wide open in shock. He drew his weapon and both their blades glowed as they faced each other. The students held their breath as their teacher grinned, ever so slightly, at her opponent. In a flash, Madam Teshka brought her rapier down hard, and a brilliant white light flashed between them with a resounding CRACK, when their blades met. Then it was over.

"Thank you, sir. You may return to your post." He walked back to his post, a scowl on his face. Turning back to her students, she said, "By using a weapon, I felt no diminishing of power. Does that help?"

"I think so?" Elswyth said. She actually didn't understand, but, as nervous as she was, she was still determined to learn whatever it took to prepare herself to go back and help Agnes.

Madam Teshka tilted her head and pointed her index finger in the air. "Let us, for the sake of argument, consider you, or someone you love, are surrounded by multiple assailants. You cannot use your Majik, without the aid of a weapon, against all of them at once. Not without dire consequences. A sword will give you an advantage if you learn to use it well."

Pic's brow furrowed. "But, Madam Teshka, what about the tenets? About never using our Majik to do harm? I know it says it's okay in self-defense or when defending someone else. I just don't know if I can do this and am not sure I could hurt someone or—worse."

"Ah, my dear Pic. You want to dedicate your life to healing, and I understand that. I do believe that is to be your calling and you must continue to learn all you can about that. But what if the moment comes when you had it in your power to protect someone you love from deadly harm? What if you had not prepared yourself, and so, could not help them? Of course, you may never have to use what you learn here. That is my hope for you. Using your Majik in this way is always a last resort but, it is still important to be prepared for all possibilities."

"Does every elf have to learn all this?" Pic asked.

"No, my dear. They do not, however it appears it is something you two are supposed to be learning now," she said, with some sadness.

"Madam Teshka," Elswyth said, a growing dread creeping into her chest. *"do you, and our textbooks, see a time when we will have to use what we're learning today? Is there something you're not telling us?"* Elswyth, Pic, and Cicero looked at their teacher expectantly.

Their governess carefully put her sword back in her bag, then folded her hands in front of her. "My dears, I've felt for some time there were dark days ahead for our kingdom. Very dark, indeed. Unfortunately, I wasn't sure when that would be and, to be honest, I still don't know. The Fates are not always as forthcoming with their messages as I would hope, but they have let me know we need to prepare. However, the fact your textbooks want this to be your lesson immediately tells me that the time may be sooner than I thought." She inclined her head towards them. "Now, we must get to the lesson." She reached out and set her hands on their shoulders.

FORTY-THREE

The demonstration rattled Elswyth, and she was even more convinced this was something she'd never be able to do. The blade
terrified her, and her breathing became erratic from the stress. Madam
Teshka read her anxiety, reached out to touch her arm, and sent calming
strength into her body. It helped, but only enough to gather courage to
ask the one question she'd been afraid to ask. *"You said you would start
relaxing your protection on us soon. When will that be?"*

"I was going to tell you at the end of today's class, but I plan to loosen
my shields on you all beginning today. It will only be a little at a time,
but it is time for you to begin standing under your own power."

Elswyth sighed and looked at Cicero and Pic. *"Well, this day just keeps
getting better."*

Madam Teshka smiled tenderly. "My dear, there may indeed be some
things I cannot see clearly yet. I will tell you if, and when, I learn more from
the Fates, but this I can see and tell you, Elswyth. You will be more than you
ever imagined—to yourself and to the kingdom." She clapped her hands and
turned toward the targets. "Now, you three stand behind me and I will show
you how to use your Majik straight from your hands. You need to experience

it before you learn to use a sword. There may be a time when this form of attack could be your only option, so it is best to be prepared."

Facing the balustrade, Madam Teshka raised her arm straight out and parallel to the ground, her palm facing the targets. "You must first brace your stance. Then, take a deep breath and, as you let it out, pull all your power from your heart center, sending it out through your hand. Remember, you must propel your Majik out harder than you ever have and do it with the intent to do damage. Like so—" A blinding blue-white stream of light shot from her palm and hit a target, blasting it into sawdust. Ozone hung heavy in the air. "Hm! I dare say I've still got it," she said to herself, and brushed her hands off.

Never dreaming their sweet teacher possessed that kind of deadly power, Elswyth stood staring with her eyes and mouth wide open. She had a newfound respect and awe for Madam Teshka. One look at Pic and Cicero confirmed they felt the same.

Knowing what they were thinking, Madam Teshka sniffed and placed her hands on her hips. "Never allow appearances to fool you, my dears. I may not be in my prime, but I am still not to be trifled with. Now, are you ready to try, ladies? Elswyth, you first," she said.

Elswyth stepped up and prepared to do as instructed. She eyed the fuzzy group of targets through the morning mist against the balustrade and thought, *How hard could this be? It looked easy enough when Madam Teshka did it.* She raised her hand, focused, chose a target, then recited to herself, *"Deep breath, pull power from heart center, breath out, then—"* She closed her eyes at the last second and let loose.

POP! SNAP! FIZZLE! PHHHHT! The release knocked her off her feet and sent her crashing backwards onto the cobblestones. Elswyth sat on the ground, dizzy, and looked towards her mark. She could tell, even through the fog, they were all intact. She looked up at Pic, who was trying, unsuccessfully, to stifle a giggle.

Cicero wasn't trying to hide anything at all. He was laughing out loud and only stopped long enough to say, "Elly, you just shot some itty-bitty fireworks

187

from your hand. Impressive party trick, but the only enemy that needs to fear you at the moment is a mosquito!" He erupted into fresh laughter and mimicked the sound of her attempt. "PHHHT! PHHHT!" That sent him rolling on the ground.

"What did I do wrong?" she asked, slowly getting up and smoothing her dress, her pride hurting more than her backside.

Madam Teshka shook a finger at Cicero. "Tut-tut! That is enough from you, please. We must support everyone's efforts here today." Even Madam Teshka was trying to suppress a grin, then composed herself. "Elswyth, I believe you failed to brace yourself, my dear. You also closed your eyes when they should, in fact, remain open. Shall we try again? You will only be able to do this a time or two more and then we must conserve your energy."

Letting out a frustrated sigh, but now determined to master the exercise, Elswyth faced the balustrade again and prepared herself a second time. She pushed her shoulders back, and recited to herself: *brace, breath, pull from heart, and then—*

"You can do it, Elly!" Cicero shouted.

Elswyth jumped in surprise, and her arm flailed through the air as a bright blue stream of light shot from her hand. Once again, she landed on the ground. The scent of ozone was stronger this time, but now she smelled something burning. Feeling the drain of energy, she looked towards the targets and saw she had hit none of them. Not a one!

"Cis! You startled me and I didn't hit anything again!"

"Sorry, Elly. I was just trying to be supportive." Cicero said, sheepishly.

Pic tapped Elswyth's shoulder and pointed towards the guards at the far wall. "Um, Elly. You actually did hit something."

Elswyth looked and gulped. The wall in between the two soldiers had a jagged, smoking gash up it and the older guard had some hair missing from the left side of his head. He stood at attention as he patted at the crispy stubble, which was still smoking. He did not look happy. The younger guard lay curled up on the ground, his head covered with his hands.

"Oh, no! By the Fates! I'm so sorry!" Everyone gawked at Elswyth's handi-work.

Madam Teshka broke the awkward silence. "All right, then. No one was hurt, thankfully. Well, not too bad, anyway." She nodded and gestured to the guards. "Perhaps it would be best if you two joined us over here and *behind* the princess. That may be, perhaps, a safer option." The younger of the two guards almost ran over, but the older one kept his military bearing, strode over to the group, and then stood at attention behind everyone with a scowl on his face.

"Would you like to try one more time, my dear? Do you think you have enough energy?" Madam Teshka asked with her hand on Elswyth's arm.

"Yes. I want to try again. I know I can do this!"

"Well, then you may proceed. Just slow down and concentrate. And no help from the choir, please," she said, turning to Cicero.

Determined, Elswyth faced the targets, but this time, took a few moments to fully engage in the moment. She shut out everything else around her and imagined protecting Agnes from Markan's soldiers. *Brace myself. Deep breath, pull from my heart center and send to my hand, focus on the target, and—*

CRACK! Ozone hung heavy in the air, and her target vaporized. Elswyth sat down hard on the ground, utterly drained but exhilarated.

"Bravo, my dear! I am impressed!" Madame Teshka said.

Pic knelt next to Elswyth and grabbed her around the shoulders. "Elly? Wow! You did it. Are you okay?" She paused and held her hand to Elswyth's cheek. "Um, you don't look so good."

Cicero hopped onto her lap and looked into her eyes. "Elly, you're really pale!"

"Pic! Cis! Did you see that? Madam Teshka, I did it!" She felt herself slumping into Pic's arms and then everything went black.

FORTY-FOUR

Elswyth awoke in her own bed as Cicero snored softly beside her on a pillow, the late afternoon sun shining through her window. She tried to stretch without disturbing him, but as soon as she moved, his head popped up, and he spoke Pic-style, barely taking a breath between sentences.

"Elly! Oh, it's so good to see you up! Madam Teshka said you'd be fine, but I was still worried. How are you feeling? You were out cold after you destroyed that target and, I have to say, that was some impressive work! And can you believe how fast Madam Teshka was with that sword? She sure can move for her age, can't she? Anyway, your guard, the older one that tattled on us, carried you up here—you know, the one whose hair you singed? Anyway, do you remember any of that? Madam Teshka told me to stay with you until you woke up—like I would leave your side! Ha! Did I tell you I was worried?"

She laid her hand on his back. *"Calm down, Cis. Everything is fine and I'm feeling fantastic, actually better than I could imagine after this morning. And no, I don't remember the guard carrying me up here but what I do remember was hitting the target and being shocked I did it—shocked at the power that came out of me. Madam Teshka was right because it was weird how right after that last blast left my hand, it felt like someone pulled a plug on me and every bit of energy just rushed out. I can understand why we need to get stronger but I'm still not looking forward to working with the swords."*

"Yeah, the part about the sword does sound intimidating. Sorry to say this, Elly, but I've never even trusted you with a butter knife, much less a sword!"

"Thanks for the vote of confidence!" She said and scratched his head. *"In truth, I don't trust myself with one either, Cis, so this will be interesting, to say the least."*

"You'll do okay. I'm just glad you're all right after this morning."

"Thanks." She sat up in the bed. *"Um, Cis? I need to share something about this morning with you. Don't look so worried. It's actually good. It's just that I've never felt as powerful as I did today. Not in my entire life have I felt I could speak up for myself—or that I even had a right to. Agnes always fought my battles when people teased or shunned me. The only reason villagers allowed me to work with her as a healer was because she refused to treat them unless they accepted me. The one and only time I stood up to Mother was that last day she came to the cottage. All those years growing up, I acted tough but, still, I never spoke up—even when Agnes taught me a way to communicate. Mostly I just took whatever happened, but what I'm beginning to understand is that I do have my own power. I'm still afraid to really open up to it, and am both excited and afraid of it, but I know it is there. I'm not saying I want to go around blasting anyone. It's not about that. The idea of hurting anybody is still hard to imagine but, just knowing I can protect myself, stand up for myself, or for someone else, is freeing."* Elswyth put her hands up and shrugged her shoulders. *"I'm rambling and I hope I'm making sense!"*

"Aw! You are making sense, Elly, and you'll never know how glad I am to hear you say all this. I've always hoped you would find your own strength and Agnes will be so proud of you when you tell her. And you will tell her someday soon!"

"Thanks. I think she'll be happy for me, too. Hey, wait! I completely forgot about Pic? Where is she?"

"After the guard brought you back to your room, Madam Teshka made her stay in the courtyard to practice hitting targets, too. From what I understand, she is resting in her own apartment now. I don't know how she did, though."

Right on cue, Elswyth heard the front door open and close. "Hellooo! Elly, are you up? Cis?"

Elswyth jumped up from her bed, with Cicero close behind, and went out to the front room. *"Pic! How did you do? Are you feeling okay? What a morning that was. Right?"*

Pic spread her arms wide and smiled. "I'm feeling fine now. You look like you're doing okay, too. More than all right, as a matter of fact, because you looked pretty iffy the last time I saw you. I've got to say it was a little scary when you passed out, but Cicero and I were told you'd be all right. By the way, did you see how fast Madam Teshka was when she used her sword against your guard? Wow! I never expected that from her and I will never think of her as our frail, old teacher again!"

"I said the same thing, Pic! She was amazing!" Cicero said.

"I'd be careful about calling her old and frail to her face or even thinking that about her! Remember she can hear our thoughts when we're in class." Elswyth said, laughing.

Pic chuckled and rolled her eyes. "Don't worry. I won't. So anyway, I sure didn't do anywhere near as well as you did, Elly. My attempts were more like *PHHT* and *SIZZLE!* I tried four times and never got it right." She laughed at herself. "There were a few sparks here and there, but that was about all. It still wore me out, and now I am so hungry."

"I'm ravenous. For once, it isn't Cis who is starving!"

"Hey! I'm right here, you know!" Cicero said.

Pic reached out to Cicero and pet his head. "Glad to hear it isn't just me, because I already ordered food."

Elswyth looked over at Cicero and they both said, "Of course you did!"

And then came the knock at the door and dinner was about to be served.

After another of Pic's hearty dinner menus, they sat in front of the fireplace, the day's excitement gone and contentment ruled the night. Pic usually dominated their evening discussions, so both Elswyth and Cicero noticed when she was uncharacteristically silent. *"Is everything all right, Pic? You haven't said a word since we ate. If you're worried about how you did this morning, it's just going to take some practice, and once you come into your full power, you'll get a lot better."*

"No. It's not that. Well, maybe it is a little, but mostly it's something else." She fidgeted with the button on her blouse.

"Pic, come on. What is it? You can tell us," Cicero said.

"Um, well, you know that tomorrow night will be my birthday eve and I was wondering if you two wouldn't mind me staying here overnight? I'm nervous about my Awakening and I don't want to be alone." She glanced up at Elswyth. "I know Madam Teshka said yours was unusual, but now I'm kind of nervous about what might happen." She looked back down, chewing on her lip. "I don't want to impose."

Elswyth tapped her cheek in mock concentration. *"Hm. I don't know. Cis, what do you think?"* She looked down at Cicero and wrinkled her nose, trying to hide a smile.

Cicero played along. "Well, I seem to recall we had other plans for tomorrow night, but I suppose we could change them if we really have to."

Elswyth leaned over and squeezed Pic's hands. *"Silly Pic! Of course you can stay here!"* she said. *"We'll make a night of it. How about you make us some of that frozen cream? That sounds like fun, doesn't it? And, really, I am sure everything will be fine. Wait and see!"*

Cicero fluffed up his feathers. "And besides, it will be fun to be together before your birthday par—" He cut himself off when Elswyth gave him a warning nudge. Pic looked at him.

"Cis! Careful. Don't spoil the surprise party for her!" Elswyth thought to Cicero's mind.

Cicero made a clumsy effort of backtracking. "Er. Um. You know, we want to spend your birthday day with you and it would be fun to start early and if you're here with us anyway, well, then we can start even earlier. And remember, we are going to have a birthday lunch with you on the terrace with your dad and Elswyth's father, too. So, ah, yes, stay with us tomorrow night," he said, stumbling through his words.

"Not the best way to back up the cart up to the donkey, but it will do!" Elswyth thought to him again.

Pic seemed too relieved to have noticed anything suspicious. "Oh great! Thank you! I will be happy to make some frozen cream and I've working on one with apples in it, so it will be a perfect time to try it out. Maybe I can make something for dinner, too. This will be fun! I can bring a deck of cards and maybe—"

Elswyth smiled and let her keep talking. She could tell Pic was still nervous but knew focusing on other things would help her stop worrying so much. She tucked Agnes's quilt in around her lap. The birthday plans were still on track and she imagined picking out the perfect gifts at Zingett's with Cicero, her father, and Caden in the morning. She couldn't wait to surprise Pic.

FORTY-FIVE

P ic felt less anxious about her impending Awakening tonight, but only a little. She tried to convince herself that Elly was right, and it would be okay, but just the same, she was grateful to be with friends. Pic reached for the decanter of nectar and topped off their glasses.

"Happy birthday eve, my friend!" Elswyth said, holding her glass high in the air.

"Yes! A very happy eve to you, Pic." Cicero said.

"Aw, thanks you two. And thanks again for letting me stay here tonight."

Cicero let out a loud burp. "Oh, excuse me! Pic, I've got to say you outdid yourself with the meal tonight! That was a lot of delicious food, even for me."

Pic blushed to the tips of her ears. "Thanks. I guess I always cook a lot more when I'm nervous."

The meal *was* fantastic, even if she did say so herself. She'd worked all day on it, but Elswyth and Cicero let her know the apple frozen cream was a crowning achievement, and she was still happy about it an hour after they finished the meal. They still had a tea service with small cakes and cookies left on the table, but decided to save it for later.

Elswyth and Cicero sat contented next to the fireplace but, Pic struggled to sit still more than five minutes at a time, unable to calm her frazzled nerves, her thoughts tumbling against each other in her head. *What if something scary happens tonight? What if nothing happens to me at all? Does that ever happen?* She kept trying to reassure herself, but with every twitch or itch, she wondered if it was the beginning of something, anything, happening. Too nervous to relax, she got up and rearranged the tea service on the table for the twelfth time that night.

"Pic, please come sit down. It's going to be fine." Elswyth said. *"Why don't you take out your card deck and we'll play a few rounds of Dragon's Heart! That should keep your mind off things."*

"I love that game!" Cicero said.

Pic plopped down on the chair again. "I don't think I can concentrate on a game. Sorry."

"That's okay. Why don't you tell me more about growing up here in the castle, then? You've never really said much about it."

Pic saw Cicero nod at Elswyth and knew they were just trying to get her to focus on something else. Okay then. Maybe that would help. "Well, it was actually kind of dull, I guess. Often lonely, too. Since I was the only elfling in the castle, there was no one to play with so, I mostly entertained myself. I had a nanny when I was really little. She was nice, but ancient, and I think I tired her out a lot because she used to tell me I talked too much. Can you imagine that?" She chuckled at herself.

"Imagine that!" Elswyth said and grinned.

"Of course, Dad was always great, when he was home. He had a lot of duties to attend to as Prince Dayel's, I mean, your father's regent. But when he was home, we would do things together. He'd take me to the bazaar, and we *always* spent holidays together. Winter solstice was my favorite and still is!" She smiled, looked off into space, all the yesterdays with her father vying for attention in her mind.

Pic looked back at Elswyth and Cicero. "You know, I never said anything to Dad, but I'd sometimes pretend Mom was still with us and imagined what our days would be like with her there. I'm pretty sure he did the same thing, but I've never asked him about it." When Pic paused, the only sounds in the room were the flames crackling and popping in the fireplace.

Pic stared at the fire. "One night, when I was around six years old, I walked into the living room and Dad was holding my mother's locket. He was crying, being really quiet, but I could see his tears and it frightened me, so I went to him and gave him a big hug. I told him I was sorry Momma was gone because of me. It was something I had often wondered about, you know? Like, was it my fault she died? Dad sat me on his knee, hugged me tight, and told me never to think like that again. He said she didn't die because of me and that, sometimes, mothers died when giving birth and it wasn't anyone's fault, most especially not mine. I needed to hear that because, until that moment, I'd believed it was my fault she was gone. It was an awful weight to carry as a kid, and my dad took that off my shoulders." Pic wiped a tear from her cheek.

Elswyth wiped her eyes. *"Did your dad tell you much about your mom? What she was like?"*

Pic sat up, and her smile returned. "Oh yes. He used to talk a lot about her. She liked to cook and make up recipes, so that must be where I got my love of cooking! Dad said they often had friends over for meals, and everyone loved the things she prepared. She was also brave, and kind, and very funny. Oh, and she loved animals! Her gift was being able to talk with wild creatures, and on the night of her Awakening, she could suddenly understand what the birds were saying outside her window. Isn't that amazing? She never had a complement, but with the ability to befriend all the *wild* animals, I guess she didn't need one. Dad said that when they used to go on outings in the woods on the mountain, the rabbits, and squirrels would tell her where to find the best mushrooms, nuts, and berries for her recipes." She smiled and settled into her chair. "Do you think it's strange to miss someone you've never met?"

"Not strange at all," Cicero said, as Elswyth nodded in agreement.

Pic's gaze returned to the flames again. "Once I asked Dad what Mom looked like. Again, I was pretty small at the time, but I still remember what he told me like it was yesterday. *Pic, my little love,* he said, *she was as beautiful as you are.* I'll never forget that." She shook her head and looked over at Elswyth and Cicero, their eyes glistening in the firelight. "Gosh. I didn't mean to go on so much about my mom. I haven't talked about her in such a long time."

"Your mother sounds wonderful, and we loved hearing about her. After all, she's part of who you are, which makes her important to us, so thank you for sharing her."

"She sounded like a very special elf, Pic," Cicero said and sniffled. Elswyth hugged him close.

"Thank you both for letting me share her with you." Pic took a deep breath, rubbed her hands together, and got up from her chair, feeling much better. "I think it's about time for tea and cakes. Anyone ready?"

"You know I won't say no!" Cicero said.

"How about I pour, and you serve the cakes? Okay?" Elswyth asked.

"Perfect! I hope you like the cakes. They're filled with berry jam!"

Mood lifted, they made their way to the table, laughing and chatting while Cicero flew to his perch, where he waited for his share of treats. Elswyth turned to watch him land, and inadvertently knocked two cups to the floor, where they shattered into pieces.

"Clumsy me! I'll get it," she said, and got down on her hands and knees to collect all the shards. She grabbed the first piece, and it cut a deep gash in her left index finger. *"OW!"*

"OW!" Pic felt the pain in her own finger, too, but when she looked at it, there was no visible wound. Why did she feel pain? *Okay. Um, that's weird,* she thought, and looked at Elswyth, who was holding her bloody finger up while trying to grab a napkin from the tabletop. Pic's right hand grew warm and tingled—and it began to glow. *Woah! What is happening? This just keeps getting more and more strange.* Her eyes grew wide and she suddenly, instinctively, grabbed a napkin, and knelt down next to her friend.

"Give me your hand, Elly!" Pic commanded.

Elswyth looked at Pic's hand, her eyes round with surprise. *"Pic! Your hand! It's glowing!"*

Without thinking, Pic took Elswyth's hand in hers and felt the tingling and warmth increase, somehow knowing she could send healing energy, her energy, into the wound. She watched as her light disappeared into Elswyth's finger, and then the tingling and warmth subsided. Using the napkin, she wiped the blood from Elswyth's hand and saw the gash had knitted itself together before their eyes, in seconds, leaving nothing left but a thin scar. Pic's own hand was then pain free.

Elswyth sat open-mouth for a moment. *"Pic? I—wow! First of all, thank you. Second, I don't think you have to worry about your Awakening any longer!"*

"That was amazing, Pic!" Cicero said, bending over the edge of that table.

"Um, thanks! I can't wait to talk to Madam Teshka about all this. And if I had the salve I recently learned about to put on the wound before it healed, there'd be no scar at all. Don't ask me how I know that!"

Pic sat back on the floor, a smile spreading across her face. "I think I'm ready for that cake now!"

FORTY-SIX

Samésh stood shivering in the glow of wall torches in front of the ancient door and pulled his collar tighter against the dank, chilly air. Somewhere in the darkness, he heard water dripping and rats squeaking. He checked for the hundredth time that he hadn't crushed the roses he held beneath the folds of his cloak. It was taking forever for someone to answer his knock, but finally, the little window at the top slid open, and a set of pale blue eyes under bushy gray brows looked out at him. The window snapped shut, and the heavy oak door creaked open.

"Nareed! My old friend," Even though Samésh kept his voice low, it bounced against the walls of the stone antechamber.

"Samésh! Hurry in, please!" Nareed quickly looked out into the hallway to make sure no one had seen them before closing them in, then turned and hugged Samésh tightly. "It's been a very long time, my friend! I wish we were meeting under happier circumstances!"

"So do I, and I understand you do this at risk to yourself and your wife, but I am ever so grateful to you for contacting me and sneaking me in to see Justa. Terrick wouldn't tell me where he'd taken her, or even if she was still—" He began to tear up and Nareed grasped him by the shoulders and ushered him to a long bench carved into the side of the stone wall.

"Courage, my friend. Let's sit here for a moment." He turned to face Samésh. "They only stationed me at this post the day before yesterday. Truth be told, until then I wasn't even aware this old section of the dungeons was still being used, and I didn't know Justa was here. You told me and Shara that she was visiting family, but when I discovered her in her cell, Justa told me that Terrick's men brought her here a couple of months ago so, I sent word to you right away. I must warn you, Samésh. She is doing poorly in the dampness and cold. Between that, and her Majik being taken away, she is weak and tired. I brought an extra blanket from home, and my Shara made her stew and fresh bread, so she is at least eating better the last couple of days."

"Again, Nareed, I can never thank you and your wife enough for your kindness!" Samésh said. He felt his heart crumbling into small pieces, as he imagined his beloved down here all this time, but tried to pull himself together. "Yes, I'm *very* grateful, and I'm sure Justa is, too." He pulled the bouquet from under his cloak. "Look. I brought her some of her favorite flowers from the gardens. Purple roses." His hands shook. "Oh, Nareed. Terrick has to let her go soon!"

Nareed hung his head, then looked up into his friend's eyes. "We've known each other far too long for me to lie to you. I don't believe elves sent this far down in the dungeons receive pardon or—or release. I believe it's Terrick's intention to forget them until—" His voice trailed off.

"No. I will not accept that outcome. Take me to her. Now!" Samésh stood and made for the dark hallway beyond them. Nareed hesitated and looked at his friend with concern. "Please, Nareed. I need to see my Justa."

"Of course. This way."

Nothing could have prepared Samésh for the walk down the corridor, every step a hopeless echo that bounced off the low barreled ceilings, the air stale and oppressive. The only light came from small flickering torches mounted between the cells along the wall. Spaced evenly on the floor, between the cells, were holes just big enough for an elf to fit through, the openings covered with padlocked, barred lids. It was too terrifying a thought to see into them, so he avoided looking down. He glanced furtively into the dark prison cells as they walked past. The elves inside sat unmoving, hunched over their beds, and if they looked out at them at all, they did so with empty, haunted eyes. He noticed fresh blankets on some cots and knew his friend was most likely responsible for that. This could not be where his beautiful Justa was. She was made for sunshine and color, not this shadow-filled, gray place.

Nareed stopped. "This next one on the right is hers," he whispered and squeezed Samésh's shoulders. "I will give you some time to yourselves and be back in a short while."

"I am forever indebted to you," Samésh said, grasping his friend's hand.

Nareed went to the cell and took out his keys. "Hello, Justa. I've got someone here to see you," he said kindly.

"To see me? Is it my Samésh? Please tell me it's him!" Samésh didn't recognize the voice. *That can't be her! Her voice was always filled with strength and joy, while this one sounded thin and tired. This must be a mistake!*

He stepped into view at her barred door, and Justa brought her hands to her mouth as tears ran down her cheeks. She tried to stand, but only made it a short way before sitting back down again. "Oh, my dear husband! Fates be praised. I have missed you so much!"

The moment he entered the cell, he felt his Majik sucked from his body, a terrifying sensation that left him weak and disoriented. *No wonder I haven't been able to find her or detect her Majik anywhere. They've taken it from her!* he thought angrily. Justa reached out to him, and he ran to her cot, burying his face in her shoulder. He wasn't sure how long they stayed locked in each other's arms, but it felt so good to hold her again. Finally, he pulled back and held her face in his shaking hands.

"I've missed you, too, my flower." His heart broke to see her now, so pale and thin, her usual bright energy dimmed beyond recognition. "Nareed told me his wife brought you some food and a blanket." She gave him a weak smile and held up the quilt to show him. "I'm glad. Oh, Justa. I didn't know where you were and no matter how many times I asked, Prince Terrick refused to tell me. I looked everywhere for you but, with your Majik being taken, I couldn't sense you at all!" He didn't tell her about the prince's threats to end her life. He pulled out the flowers, now slightly crushed from their hug, and put them in her hands.

"Oh! Purple roses! My favorite! Thank you, Love. They're beautiful. Are the gardens doing well? Is anyone tending the plants? I so miss being there with all the flowers." She brought her face close to the delicate petals, closed her eyes, and breathed in their scent, then started coughing. Samésh reached for the nearby glass of water, realizing that Nareed most likely had made sure her water was fresh, too.

"Oh yes, the other cultivators are tending to the garden, but it certainly isn't the same care you give. The queen said she misses you. I told her you're visiting family, so Terrick wouldn't retaliate and hurt you or—" He couldn't finish the thought. "He hasn't summoned me to his office in weeks, though. Maybe he no longer needs me and will set you free."

Justa placed the roses in a water pitcher next to the bed and admired them. A few petals fell onto the tabletop and her eyes trailed their descent. When she turned back, she took his hands in hers and he was shocked at how cold and thin they felt to him. "Samésh, I don't want you to get your hopes up. At night we prisoners talk and there are others, like me, who are pawns of Terrick's. No one leaves here, Samésh. At least not alive. I've not been well recently, and I'm only getting worse, so I don't know how much longer I will—"

"Don't say it! Now that I've found you, I'll find a way to rescue you. Perhaps Nareed can help me sneak you out of here and we can go north to Belnoir. The queen's people will give us sanctuary!" His shoulders shook as he fought to keep his composure. "This is not fair, Justa! You've done nothing wrong."

Justa shook her head. "Oh, my dear husband. Nareed, and Shara would be in danger if Terrick ever found out they helped me to escape. Trust me when I say his men are everywhere and he would find out. I cannot be responsible for anyone getting hurt, or worse, on my account." She shivered, and he pulled the blanket around her shoulders. "I don't know how much time we have together today, so please listen to what I have to tell you." She reached up to stroke the side of his face, and he leaned into her hand. "There have been more elves sent down here in the past two weeks and they are kin or friend to soldiers or servants who are secretly being threatened, just as you have been. This dungeon was officially closed at least three hundred years ago, so no one knows we're here!"

She straightened as much as she could and looked into his eyes. He could feel the love in her gaze and his heart twisted in his chest. "Samésh, I want you to resist. I want you to be brave and go to the king and not worry about me. Terrick must be stopped before it is too late, and I fear it already is."

"No! I can't do that. I'll lose you. If I go to the king, Terrick said he will kill you and I cannot let that happen! There has to be another way." He could no longer pretend to be strong and wept openly.

"Oh, my Love, you must do this. It's the right thing to do. You and I—we've had a wonderful life together, but now we must do what needs to be done for Glenorim," Justa said, and then coughed even harder than before.

Samésh folded her in his arms until the spell passed. "Here, drink a little more water, my dear." He waited until she had a few sips, then held her close again. "I'll do as you ask and go to the king, my brave wife, but first I *will* get you out of this dark hole. I don't know how, but we will be together again! That is a promise." Justa relaxed into his arms, and they wept together.

Nareed cleared his throat at the doorway. "I'm sorry, my friends, but it's time for you to go, Samésh. There will be another guard relieving me of duty in twenty minutes, and I don't know yet if we can trust him. I'll be back tomorrow for my shift if you want to return then."

Samésh reluctantly stood up, but it took every fiber of his being to let his wife go. He stepped outside the cell and his Majik slammed back into his body, making him hold on to the bars to steady himself. "I will be back for you, my flower." He turned to Nareed. "Please, please take care of her for me."

His friend nodded solemnly. "You know I will. And we must talk more. Be here tomorrow at the same time."

Nareed's face looked pained as he turned the key in the lock and Samésh gazed at Justa one last time.

As he started down the hall, she called out to him, "Remember what I told you, Love!"

As he walked back up the corridor, he could hear her coughing again.

FORTY-SEVEN

Elswyth opened the doors to the grand ballroom and stepped in with Pic
while Cicero flew in behind them, cawed for all he was worth, the sound
ricocheting everywhere off the vaulted ceilings and tiled floors. Both Pic and
Elswyth jumped and covered the sides of their heads against the onslaught to
their eardrums.

"Cis! Did you really have to do that?" Elswyth gave him a side wink when
she was sure Pic wasn't looking.

"Wow, Cis, you just about scared the freckles off my face! Give us a little
warning next time, why don't you?" Pic said with a laugh.

"Sorry. I've always wanted to do that in here, you know, the acoustics and
all that. This place is so huge and since no one is around, I couldn't help
myself."

"It's okay. A little scare once in a while is good for the blood. Right?
Anyway, Dad and Prince Dayel are waiting outside for our lunch, so let's just
get out there. I'm ready to eat. I've been looking forward to my birthday lunch
all morning and the weather couldn't be more beautiful for an outside meal.
Thanks for setting this up, you two."

Elswyth reached the terrace door, opened it and turned to Pic before going
through. *"Birthday girls first!"* she said and waved Pic ahead of her.

"Surprise!" Applause erupted as Pic stood frozen in the doorway, staring at everyone gathered in front of her on the expansive balcony terrace. Every elf she knew was in attendance—from her father, to the royal family, to the librarians, to the kitchen staff, and Madam Teshka who stood next to the door, a warm smile on her face. There was a band getting ready to play, and streamers strung between pillars, moving in a soft, Majik-conjured breeze.

Before she even saw her coming, Dilly ran up and squeezed Pic in a tight hug. *"Our Pic! Oh, happy birthday! Mom and I were so excited to get the invite for today! We have a gift for you on the table over there. And guess what? I invented a new date candy and named it after you. I call it a Little Pic. Among other ingredients, it's made with dates (of course), pecans and white chocolate. They are sweet and a little nutty—like you!"* Dilly said and blushed deeply. *"The white chocolate is for your white hair. And in honor of winter solstice being your favorite holiday, that's the only time I'll put them in the shop. Of course, I'll make them for you any time! I brought a box for you today and I hope you like them."* Dilly stepped back, her smile reaching from ear to ear.

"That sounds wonderful and thank you, Dilly! I can't wait to try some." Sweets was next in line with her usual even bigger, all-encompassing embrace.

Pic's eyes teared up as she looked out at the crowd. "Wow, thank you, everyone, for being here and making this the best birthday ever!" The band started their first song while Elswyth steered her through the crowd, stopping for hugs and congratulations along the way. Finally, Pic made it to her father, who stood smiling at her next to a table piled high with birthday presents.

"Happy birthday, Pic. Your mother would be so very proud of the elf you've become. I know I am!" Caden wrapped his arms around his daughter and they stood together, enjoying the laughter and dancing around them. He stepped back and waved his hand across the terrace. "So, are you surprised?"

"I honestly had no idea, Dad! This is wonderful, and I can't believe someone didn't slip and say something, especially Cicero. Never in a million years did I expect all this. Oh, wait a second. I think I just figured out why Cis made all that noise coming into the ballroom. Was it so he could warn everyone I was coming?" Caden nodded and laughed.

"How about we go over to our table and you can open the gifts from us? You can open these a little later in the party?" When they got to the table where the royal family sat, King Garreth, Queen Araleia, and Prince Dayle stood up with Elswyth and applauded while Cicero hopped back and forth on a perch. There was a silver cart nearby with gifts.

King Garreth was the first to begin. "Dearest Pic! We're honored to be here for your special day and I hear congratulations are in order for your Awakening, too. It sounds like a very special gift indeed. Here's to a very happy birthday!" He raised his glass and everyone followed his lead with a cheer!

The queen walked around the table, stood in front of Pic and held her hands over her heart. "Oh, my dear. I remember when you were just a wee elfling. I must ask you to forgive me in advance because it will be difficult for me not to think of you as our *little Pic* any more. Ah, but how time does slip by us," she said, shaking her head and beaming at Pic. "You've grown to be such a beautiful and talented young elf and we are all so proud of you! Happy birthday, dear. I hope you enjoy our gift to you," she said as she handed Pic a stunning wooden box that contained a gold necklace with a portal stone set in its pendant. "As a healer, you may need to go through the portal to collect plants and herbs from the mountain. You will need your own stone! Be sure to wear it close to your heart."

"Thank you so much, Your Majesties! I will treasure this and promise to use it well." Pic put the necklace on and tucked it in her blouse.

Caden stepped up and handed her a large package wrapped in brightly colored cloth and ribbons. "This should help you get started on your journey as a healer, Pic! Happy birthday to the very best daughter a father could ever want."

She made quick work of unwrapping the bundle, and when she saw what was inside, gasped and looked up at her father, excitement written all over her face. "It's the healer's cloak I saw in the window at Zingett's! Wow! Look at all the pockets inside! Oh my gosh, this is wonderful! Thanks, Dad!" She immediately draped it over her shoulders and modeled it for everyone to see, twirling around in the floor length, velvet hooded cloak.

"You're welcome," he said, his daughter's joy making him laugh. "In case you didn't know, it's infused with Majik that repels rain, cold, and heat so, no matter what the weather, you'll always be comfortable. And all those pockets inside will work the same way as when you put big things in your little baskets, storing a lot."

"I can't wait to fill it!"

Prince Dayle spoke up next. "Pic, I've known you since the day you were born and you've always been a bright light to us all. I have fond memories of you just yea-high, bringing us your first culinary experiments."

Pic interrupted, "And as I recall, many of them were failed experiments, too! But you ate them anyway!"

"Ha ha! Yes, you're right about that. Many of them didn't quite turn out, but we still ate what you brought us. You were always so eager to learn, to create, and to grow, so how could we not have encouraged you? You're a marvel, Pic, and we wish you the very best for today and all your days to come!" He turned to Elswyth. "Elly, Cicero and I have your last gift for you."

Elswyth stepped up and smiled. *"Pic, I didn't grow up with friends my age and it was something I always longed for—and then I met you. But in you, I have more than a friend. You've become like a sister and I thank the Fates every day that you're in my life."* She looked over at Cicero, and he flew to her arm. *"We are both thankful to have you in our lives. Happy birthday!"* Elswyth wheeled the cart with a final gift for Pic. There was a large rectangular shaped box draped in purple velvet sitting in the center.

"Is that the—?"

"Open it and see!" Cicero said.

She pulled the drape off ever so slowly, gasping when she saw the antique healer's box, its gold fittings sparkling in the sunshine and the rich stain of the wood, that invited her to run her hand along the grain. She looked back and forth between Elswyth, Prince Dayel, and Cicero. "Thank you! Thank you so much. This is wonderful!"

"Open it up. There's something else inside!" Elswyth said.

Everyone around the table stilled while Pic lifted the lid and, there amidst all the bottles and tools, another gift, wrapped in green silk, sat nestled at the bottom of the box. She unwrapped it, clutched the gift to her chest, and looked up at Elswyth with tears in her eyes. "Elly! This is your Little Book Of Healing. But Agnes gave this to you! Are you sure you want me to have it?"

"Yes, I am absolutely sure. There were many healers that had that book before Agnes did, Pic, and then she handed it down to me. When she did, she told me that someday I must share it with another apprentice healer, someone whose passion it is to help others and make the world a better place. I know she would agree that should be you. Happy birthday!"

Pic flew into Elswyth's arms. "Thank you so much, my friend. I will treasure this and I promise to do the same with this precious book someday!" She stepped back and faced everyone. "Oh, my gosh. Thank you, everyone. I—I can't believe it, but I am at a loss for words!" Pic choked out.

"We can't believe it either, Pic." Cicero said and everyone laughed. "Now, let's say we all eat!"

The party had been going on for hours when Elswyth slipped off to a corner near the ballroom doors to catch her breath. She watched Ratheus on the dance floor and had to admit that, for such a big, lumbering giant, he was a fairly graceful dancer, as bears go. Cicero even appeared to enjoy the music, bouncing and hopping to the rhythm on his perch. Everyone danced, ate and laughed together. The party was a success!

Elswyth froze. She bolstered her shields as the hair at the back of her neck stood on end. Her blood chilled, and it became hard to breathe as she sensed darkness creeping up from behind. It was a darkness she immediately recognized. Terrick! Slowly, she turned around as he stepped out from the ballroom doors, his black eyes boring through her. Despite the warm day, he was covered in a long, black fur cloak.

"What are you doing here? You're supposed to leave me alone, so just—go away," she said, trying to sound braver than she felt, her newfound sense of strength quickly evaporating in his presence.

Ignoring her comment, Terrick crossed his arms over his chest and looked her up and down. Then, to her surprise, he laughed, a horrible, icy chuckle that went straight through her bones. "Feeling a little full of yourself, are we halfling? Just because you did so well in your little—lesson—doesn't mean you're a match for me. You never will be." His grin spread across his face. "The day will come when you'll find that out."

How did he find out about my lesson? Her resolve crumbled further. *"I said leave or I'll—"* She clenched her fist while watching the dark tendrils as they crept out from his collar. His Majik felt stronger now. Darker, if that was possible, and he felt more in control.

"Or you'll what? Call your loving father? Spare me, human brat! Do you actually think I fear him?" he said. "That weakling doesn't deserve a seat on the throne and could never rule the kingdom with the same power I can." One eyebrow arched high, and he waved a dismissive hand towards the elves celebrating on the terrace, who were unaware of their conversation. "Go back to your friends and enjoy your time with them. I won't stop you. As a matter of fact, I will not be bothering you at all, going forward, but know that I'll be watching you, halfling." A corner of his mouth moved up in a jagged sneer and she shivered.

"Terrick! What are you doing here?" Prince Dayel growled from behind Elswyth. She hadn't seen him coming, but was relieved he was there. Her father reached a protective arm around her shoulders and pulled her close. "You weren't invited, Brother, and you need to leave. Now."

"Don't worry. I only stopped by to see what all the—frivolity—was about and had no intention of partaking in the festivities." He gave them each a cool stare and a toothy grin. "I will leave you to your merrymaking, then." He turned in a swirl of dark fur and walked back inside, disappearing into the shadows of the ballroom. Elswyth felt the dark energy follow him and she could finally breathe again.

Her father turned to Elswyth. "Are you all right? Did he threaten you?" He asked, his jaw clenched and his eyebrows raised in worry.

"I—I'm okay, Father, really. I think I was just in the wrong place when he came to see what was going on. He said nothing he hadn't said before, except he knew how my lesson in the courtyard went. Please, say nothing to Pic or Cicero, at least for today. I don't want this to spoil her birthday." Again, she tried to sound stronger than she felt at the moment, but she was shaking inside.

Her father looked back in the direction Terrick had gone and steered Elswyth back to the party. "I think I'm going to switch your guard detail, Elly. Just to be safe. Aside from Madam Teshka, they're the only ones that knew about that lesson." Then, more to himself than to her, "Terrick is getting bolder and I am afraid his influence over some elves in the kingdom has become a real danger. We've been blind to his actions for too long and I need to speak to mother and father."

Elswyth joined everyone back at the royal table. But in the back of her mind, she heard Terrick's words echoing in her mind:

"...Know that I'll be watching you, halfling."

FORTY-EIGHT

T he next morning, two new guards waited outside Elswyth's door
when she, Pic, and Cicero left for the training arena, and they
followed the students as they made their way to their first lesson in
swordsmanship. Elswyth knew Pic was on edge and wanted to help. *"Are
you doing okay, Pic?"*

"Madam Teshka said we'd be using wooden swords this morning. At
least that sounds a little less scary than the real ones," Pic said as she bit
her lip.

*"I suppose. But remember, we'll be switching to the real thing by the end
of the day."*

Pic responded with a heavy groan.

Cicero tried to insert a joke into the conversation. "I feel like I should
do an inventory of both of your fingers and toes before class."

"Not funny, Cis!" Elswyth nodded at Pic, who gasped and clutched her
chest.

"Pic, I am not as worried about you," he said. "It's you I was really
talking about, Elly. And I was only half joking because you aren't exactly
known for your finesse with blades. I never thought I would see the day
you'd have a sword in your hand."

"That makes two of us!" She tried to remind herself that all this training would help her defend Agnes someday soon, but the butterflies in her stomach were multiplying.

"Make that three of us!" Pic said, wringing her hands. "I tried to memorize the beginning notes and techniques our textbooks listed last night, but I've already forgotten all of it."

Cicero began reciting, "Number one: Be aware at all times. Number two: Playing fair is for board games, not sword fights. Number three: Stay calm and in control of your emotions. Number 4: Don't be predictable!"

"Now you're just showing off!" Elswyth rolled her eyes.

He cleared his throat and continued, "And beginning techniques are as follows: slash, thrust, chop, parry, block, and deflect!" he said.

"Like I said—show off!" Elswyth laughed, but appreciated the reminders. She looked at Pic and felt bad for her friend's obvious show of nerves and decided she'd try to be brave for them both today. *"Don't worry, we'll do okay, Pic. Once we've practiced enough, we'll be old pros! Right?"*

Pic groaned again in response.

The enormous oval enclosure was full of soldiers, male and female, practicing various forms of engagement, from hand-to hand combat, to sword fighting, to archers shooting at targets. Arched doorways under covered colosseum seating surrounded the immense perimeter, and Elswyth couldn't help but wonder if Terrick was up there somewhere, watching from behind a column. She shivered involuntarily. Dust covered every surface from all the activity, and she was glad their textbooks warned them to dress in tunics and pants. *This place must be a muddy mess on rainy days,* she thought.

A booming voice startled them. "Good morning, Your Highness. And to you, Miss Pic! I am Colonel Willen." They turned to see a smiling older elf in a dusty combat uniform. Despite his age, he was obviously more than capable of handling himself in a battle, or so the imposing muscles under his leather vest hinted. If it weren't for the fact he had a warm smile, it would've been easy to see how he could strike fear in an enemy's heart. "Are you ready for your first lesson?" His braided white beard wiggled when he spoke.

Elswyth and Pic stared up at him and simply nodded.

"Yes, they are!" Cicero answered for them.

"Dragons got your tongues, ladies? I asked YOU if you were ready for your lesson, not your dark friend here." He was still smiling, but firm.

"Yes, sir!" both Elswyth and Pic answered.

"This way, please." He did an about-face, and they sprinted to keep up with him as he led the way through several groups of fighting soldiers, occasionally jumping out of harm's way from errant fists or sword blades. The colonel stopped in front of a long double rack of swords, their metal gleaming in the morning light. Off to the side was a barrel filled with wooden imitations of the shiny metal ones. "Here we are. Your guards can stand at the far end of the rack there, and I suggest you, Raven, light there on that post. It would be safer for you."

"It's Cicero, if you don't mind," Cicero said, a little testy.

"My apologies—Cicero," Willen said, bowing, then gestured to the racks. "Please wait here for your teacher. He's due to arrive momentarily."

Before they could say or do anything else, the colonel strode through the crowd and disappeared. Elswyth glanced at Pic and watched her fold her arms tight across her chest, looking dumbstruck at the surrounding melee. It was obvious her friend was growing increasingly nervous, and she didn't know how to help her calm down. *"Pic—"* she started to say.

"Will you look who's here? It's our Pic and her friends!" said a voice behind them. All three turned and Pic's face lit up with a broad smile, her nervousness seemingly forgotten in an instant.

"Baylin! Oh, am I happy to see you! Are you going to be our teacher today? Please tell me you are. Elly, this is Baylin, Sweets's husband and Dilly's dad!" She ran to Baylin and wrapped him in a tight hug. His full laughter and deep voice fit his rugged figure, and Elswyth could picture him and Sweets together. His Majik was just as kind as his wife's, but powerful, and she instantly liked him.

"That I am, Pic! Madam Teshka asked if I could conduct your lessons. She said you were pretty nervous and thought that, perhaps if I were your instructor, it would help you feel less anxious. Of course, I couldn't say no! And Princess Elswyth," he said, bowing to her, " it is a pleasure to finally meet you and I'm honored to act as your trainer, as well." He didn't forget to include Cicero in the pleasantries, which ingratiated him to Elswyth even more. "Cicero, I've heard a lot about you and it is great to finally meet you!"

"Likewise, Sergeant Baylin!" Cicero said.

"I'm happy to meet you, Baylin, and looking forward to our classes."

"Well then, why don't we st—"

Two soldiers jogged by and one of them rammed his shoulder into Baylin's, the shove obviously intentional. The two elves, who Baylin recognized, turned to look at him. One smirked and crossed his arms, while the other giggled stupidly and stood behind his friend. "Hey! Watch where you're going, halfling lover!" the soldier said, his face twisted in disgust.

Elswyth's guards immediately stepped in front of her, their hands ready at their weapons. Soldiers practicing close enough to hear the slur stopped their drills and stepped to Baylin's side, hands on their hilts and jaws set, staring down the offenders. Elswyth reached for Pic's hand and they both froze in place, not daring to move. She heard Cicero's wings flap behind her and sent a silent plea to him not to do or say anything.

"You have a problem with me, Rayel?" Baylin's measured and slow words sent a shiver down Elswyth's spine. The friendly sparkle that lit his eyes moments ago was now a smoldering flame.

Rayel spat on the ground. "With you? No. Only with your halfling wife. And that!" he said and pointed to Elswyth with disdain. "Oh wait. I guess that means I *do* have a problem with you, don't I?" Without taking his eyes off Baylin, he addressed the soldier behind him. "What do you say, Kel? Do you have a problem with the sergeant?"

"Yeah. I do." Kel snorted a laugh, but stayed behind Rayel.

Cicero cawed and flew to Elswyth's arm. His feathers quivered in agitation and he looked ready to take off after the two offenders. *"Steady, Cis. Please, just stay with me and let Baylin handle this,"* she sent the thought to him.

More soldiers were paying attention and stepped closer to Baylin in support, while several others joined Elswyth's guards and surrounded her protectively. Still, there were others that hung back, seeming to wait to see what happened next. Elswyth searched those faces and saw a few looking her way with unfriendly, narrowed eyes. It became increasingly quiet as more soldiers stopped what they were doing and watched the tense interchange. Elswyth watched Baylin's jaw muscles grind and his face turn red, as he moved closer to her and put his hand on the hilt of his sword.

Baylin's voice was now a low growl. "Not only do you insult my wife, whose hem you are not worthy to touch, but now you're insulting Her Highness. I believe an apology is in order and then I think you need to leave before I have to teach you a lesson in respect. And you know from experience, Rayel, that I am more than capable of besting you in a fight, you disloyal worm." Rayel flinched but held his ground. Kel made a small step back, glancing at the other elves around him.

Elswyth held her breath. Baylin, the kind husband of their friend Sweets, was wonderful, and she had felt comfortable with him a few moments ago. But now, she saw that Baylin the soldier was no one to be trifled with and she shivered at his power, glad he was on her, Cicero's, and Pic's side.

By now, the entire arena stood glued to the interchange. Everyone waited for someone to say or do something that would light the fuse to the bomb of anger and tension hanging in the air. Baylin looked ready to pounce, as did those standing around him. Rayel and Kel backed away, grinning nervously the entire time.

"I don't apologize to halflings. But I will leave—for now."

"Rayel! I demand you apologize!" Baylin said, raising his voice.

"That's enough!" Colonel Willen said, as he walked up behind the perpetrators. "You two. Out! And I want you in my office in an hour!" Rayel and his cohort didn't move. "NOW!" Willen shouted.

Rayel gave Baylin one last glare. "Yes, sir, Colonel." He turned on his heel and snapped his fingers at his friend. "Let's go, Kel." he said and stomped away, Kel close on his heels like an obedient puppy.

"Everyone else, carry on!" ordered Willen. One by one, the crowd dispersed, some of them patting Baylin's back as they left. Those that surrounded Elswyth bowed before returning to their practice.

The soldiers in the crowd that were staring down Elswyth were the last to resume their activities. She felt their intense scrutiny, and it chilled her. Their dark Majik may have been far weaker than Terrick's, but she was sure of their connection to him just the same. *Even when Terrick wasn't near—he was!*

Baylin cleared his throat, his face still red. "I am sincerely sorry you had to witness that, Your Highness. You, too, Pic. It was entirely uncalled for. Those two don't have a spine between them and have been troublemakers since they were elflings." He shook his head sadly.

"You have nothing to apologize for, Baylin. Thank you for your loyalty and for defending me."

"Wow, Baylin, That—that was scary!" Pic's voice shook.

Elswyth looked down at Cicero and stroked his back, trying to smooth his still ruffled feathers. He was uncharacteristically quiet. *"Cis,"* she thought to him. *"Are you all right?"*

"Yeah, fine," he said in a low voice.

She could tell he was anything but fine, though, and gave him a gentle squeeze; determined to talk to him later.

Baylin shuffled his foot in the dirt and cleared his throat. "By the way. Please don't mention what happened today to Sweets. It will only upset and worry her. Okay?"

"Not a word, Baylin. We promise," Pic said. Elswyth and Cicero agreed.

He inhaled a large dose of the dusty air, and the twinkle in his eyes returned. "Thank you! Now, what do you say we teach you ladies some swordsmanship?" He slapped his knee and chuckled.

Elswyth glanced at the soldiers resuming their exercises in the dusty arena and vowed she'd work as hard as they were. She was more determined than ever to learn to defend herself and Agnes. *"Okay. Let's get this started!"*

She smiled at Baylin and pulled two wooden swords from the barrel—one for her and one for Pic.

FORTY-NINE

The door to the Colonel's office opened, and Rayel and Kel entered, cracking jokes about the incident in the arena. Terrick watched them freeze, the color draining from their faces, when they saw him sitting at the colonel's desk. "Don't be shy. Come in and close the door behind you," Terrick said.

"What is wrong with you two? Bow to your prince!" Willen barked from the side of the room.

They bowed, and Rayel said. "Your Highness! We didn't realize you would be here." Kel could only manage a nervous squeak. They stood at attention and looked sidelong at Willen, whose expression was grim.

Terrick inhaled a slow, deliberate breath, sat back in the chair, and stared at them, letting the seconds stretch into a painfully long minute. "I heard a nasty rumor that there was a bit of a commotion in the practice yard today." Neither soldier said anything. "Well? What do you have to say? Surely you know I have more important things to deal with than your stupidity?" He could feel the tendrils licking at his heels as he worked to keep his anger from taking control. *Does no one keep their fireplaces going in this blasted castle?* he wondered and pulled his fur collar closer to his chin. "Nothing to say for yourselves?"

"I—er—we were standing up for Elven purity, Your Highness! The halfling was in the yard for training. We thought—"

"Ah! But you didn't think, did you?" Terrick stood up in a slow, deliberate rise from behind the desk and made his way in front of the now trembling soldiers. "Willen, what was that order I gave regarding the royal family and the halfling?" he asked, beginning to circle the two elves. "It seems these two need a reminder." He came back around to face them, his dark eyes boring into theirs.

Willen recited the order. "No one is to bother, molest, or in any way harm members of the royal family, to include the halfling, without Prince Terrick's express orders. The family is to believe there is no threat to them until the prince decides otherwise."

"Why, I do believe that is correct. Thank you, Colonel." He said with feigned lightheartedness, his eyes never leaving Rayel and Kel. "Hm. And how do you propose I handle this insubordination, Willen? Surely there must be consequences for their inability to follow orders?"

"Your Highness, perhaps some time in the dungeon would be in order before they return to duty?"

"That is, indeed, one possibility, I suppose." Pulling his coat tighter across his chest, he returned to the desk and sat. "Of course, there is also the added inconvenience they caused me of coming up here to handle this—little problem. Not a good move on your parts, no matter how we look at this. Isn't that right, elflings?" Terrick leaned forward and tented his fingers on the desk. "I just may have to consider your disobedience as treasonous. That, of course, would call for a heavier sentence."

"We're very sorry, Your Highness. It won't happen again!" Rayel's earlier bravado in the arena now reduced to a whimper.

"You should be sorry. That being said, I think you're about to be even more so" Terrick set his hands flat on the desk, smiled, then mentally reached into Rayel's mind and watched with glee as the soldier swayed under the intrusion. Tears ran down the Rayel's face as he looked back at the prince, clutching his head in pain. Kel backed away, shaking. "Hold still, Rayel! I'm just accessing

221

that small mind of yours to see what I can find—" Terrick put his hands together and his eyes lit up. "Ah! I think I found just what I needed!" Rayel slumped to his knees, mercifully released.

Terrick laughed his mad dog growl. "Yes. Exactly the thing I was looking for! So, you're afraid of dark, cramped spaces, are you? I see Daddy locked you in the cistern when you were a naughty wee elf, and it appears you were naughty quite often. Perhaps something along those lines would be a fitting punishment for today's infraction." He turned to Willen. "What say you, Colonel?"

Willen shifted on his feet, his brow furrowed. "Whatever you decide, Your Highness."

"Yes. I think that's what we'll do. You can place the restraints on his wrists now," he said to Willen with a dismissive wave of his hand. Then he turned his attention to the now prisoner Rayel and spoke in a matter-of-fact tone. "There are—special—cells in the old dungeons that are just big enough to stand up in, if you like low ceilings. I've heard tell there could be rats, too, but I cannot figure out how they get into such a small space. No windows either, I'm afraid. Not the best of accommodations, but, well, that's what you get for disobeying my orders, you know."

Willen avoided Rayel's eyes as he placed the energy-sucking manacles on his wrists. "How long should we leave him down there before bringing him back up, Your Highness?"

"Oh, my. Did I say we'd be bringing him back up? No, my dear colonel. He will remain down there indefinitely. I cannot abide disobedience," he said with a slash of a grin.

Rayel broke out in a sweat as his eyes bugged out. He looked frantically between the colonel and Terrick. "Your Highness. No! Please!" Rayel said, his manacled hands stretched forward. By now, he was weeping uncontrollably. Then he swung his arms toward his friend. "Wait, what about Kel? He was there, too!"

Kel looked horrified and shrunk back against the wall.

"Ah, yes! Loyal friends to the end, I see, soldier. What should I do with Kel? Hm?" He turned his attention to the quivering elf while tapping his chin thoughtfully. "Lucky him. He will serve as a witness to what happens when my orders are ignored. You, Kel, will inform the others of what has befallen your friend here. I think that should stop anyone else from, well, misbehaving. Yes, Kel?"

"Yes, Your Highness. Absolutely! Thank you, Your Highness!" Kel squeaked, falling to his knees.

Rayel looked incredulous. "But that's not fair! He was out there with me and—"

"QUIET!" Terrick shouted and waved a hand at Rayel's face. The young elf's mouth moved, but no sound came out.

"You've made me very angry, Rayel, and I don't like to be angry!" Terrick could feel the tendrils climbing up his legs, and he struggled to regain control of his emotions. He closed his eyes and took his usual deep, calming breaths, sending the fury back into the ground. When he opened his eyes, Willen, Rayel, and Kel were staring at him.

"Take care of this traitor, Willen. Oh, and be sure to strike his name from the rosters." He started out of the room, but looked back over his shoulder in the doorway. "Don't bother me for the rest of the day. I've got work to do in my office." *My warm office,* he thought. "And for the love of the Fates. Get some heat in here!" He walked out the door, his fur coat billowing behind him.

FIFTY

After four and a half weeks of daily, early morning swordsmanship classes (and still more to go, according to Baylin), Elswyth was grateful for her friend's healing abilities. Each afternoon, before they reported to Madam Teshka's classes, Pic tended to any bruises, abrasions, cuts, and sore muscles they got in the arena and she was quickly making a name for herself as a gifted healer in the castle, as well. Elves from the kitchens to the court sought her out and the king and queen made a point of complimenting her on her talents. Healing was what Pic felt led to do, and Elswyth was happy for her.

Although Elswyth's first few days of handling a real sword were rocky, she surprised herself by how fast she became comfortable wielding the long blade. Even Cicero praised her progress. At first, she gave the credit to Baylin's patient instruction and told him as much, but he assured her that her progress was all due to her drive and commitment to learning the art. If only Agnes was there to share in her accomplishments.

Aside from missing Agnes, there was something else on her mind. Ever since the confrontation that first day in the arena, Cicero hadn't been his usual chipper self. She tried to coax him into talking, gave him hugs, food, and trips to the gardens. Nothing worked. In the past, he may have occasionally sulked about something for a few hours, but this was bigger. It had been weeks this time, and he still wasn't telling her what the problem was. Had she done something that day to make him angry? Had she hurt his feelings somehow? She missed her sometimes bossy, chatty Cis.

As a welcome change of pace, Elswyth, Pic, and Cicero were invited to lunch with her grandmother and Madam Teshka on the terrace. She hoped that would cheer him up.

"Good afternoon, ladies," Madam Teshka said as they walked out onto the terrace. A colorful canopy covered a table full of teas, sandwiches, and desserts. Elswyth could even see some of Dilly's Little Pics on a crystal dish.

"Hello!" the queen said, getting up from the table to distribute hugs. "Because of your busy schedules, I've seen very little of you all over the past few weeks, so we thought a nice break was in order. Madam Teshka has been keeping me apprised of your lessons and, I must say, I'm impressed with how well you've each been doing. And you, dear Cicero, we also haven't had time to catch up as of late! I've missed chatting with you, as well!" She offered her arm to Cicero. He hesitated, but then hopped from Elswyth to the queen, and then she set him on a perch next to her seat at the table. Everyone took their seats.

"I missed visiting with you, too, Your Majesty!" he said, bowing.

Madam Teshka's expressions were often stoic, and it was difficult to tell what she was thinking. Today, however, even her eyes were smiling! Something was up and Elswyth was curious. They all chatted and laughed for the better part of an hour and the suspense was getting to Elswyth. Maybe this really was just a nice get-together and nothing was amiss. She kept stealing glances at Madam Teshka, who only smiled back.

After servants cleared away the empty plates and refilled the teapot, her grandmother folded her hands in her lap. "Elly, are you curious about your Belnoir Elven heritage? Would you like to learn a little about that?"

"Yes! I'd love to." Elswyth had to admit she'd wondered about it, but it never seemed to be a good time to ask with her busy schedule. For most of her life, all she knew of her family history was that she had a mother who didn't want her. Her family had begun and ended with Agnes, so this was exciting. Even Cicero appeared to be paying attention.

"To begin with," her grandmother said and reached up to touch her long hair, "our red hair, yours and mine, is uniquely Belnoirian. Almost every elf there has it, unless they are of mixed heritage. So, if you see an elf with hair like ours, they most likely have Belnoirian blood."

Elswyth reached up to touch her own curls and smiled in wonder as she imagined a world of elves that looked like her, rounded ears notwithstanding. *"Really? I want to see Belnoir someday!"* She felt her world had expanded beyond what she had ever imagined.

"And then there are our many talented artisans," the queen went on, "You saw much of their work at Zingett's. Belnoirian artists export their work, in all its forms, to many kingdoms and it's highly sought after. It is their sword-making, however, that is especially admired. The artists that create them are gifted with the ability to imbue a powerful channeling Majik into the engraving on the metal. Their blades can dissipate powerful energy blows better than any other. And it's not just the exalted Belnoirian warriors that use the swords. Soldiers around the world have coveted and used them for centuries."

"I did see the swords at Zingett's, but had no idea they held such power. I just thought they were beautiful. Right, Cis?" Elswyth tried to engage him in the conversation.

"Um, yes. That's interesting." He said without enthusiasm. Madam Teshka raised an eyebrow at him.

"So, Elly. In light of that, I have a surprise for you." The queen clapped her hands and called out, "Samésh! Could you bring the cart out now?" He pushed the trolley up to the table next to her chair, bowed and stepped back.

Elswyth noticed the queen's eyebrows briefly drawing together in concern when she looked at Samésh. He didn't look up at anyone and kept his eyes focused on the gift on the cart. *He seems off somehow—tired? Stressed?* Elswyth thought. His Majik was still hard to read, but she did like him and hoped he was okay. Then Elswyth's eyes locked onto the long wooden box, its gold hinges gleaming in the sunshine, and she forgot about Samésh standing there.

"Go on, Elly. Open it, dear." Her grandmother urged.

All eyes were on Elswyth, and everyone held their breath as they waited for her to move. She reached out and lifted the lid.

"Oh, my gosh! It's—it's beautiful!" she said. She picked up the finely tooled leather scabbard and admired the gold and silver fittings, then slowly pulled out the sword and gasped. The blade was engraved with willow trees swaying in the breeze. The golden guard and grip were fashioned into woven willow branches, and a sitting raven adorned its pommel. It was an incredible piece of art. *"I can't believe this is mine. Thank you, Grandmother! I will treasure this always."*

Elswyth had envied the beautiful sword Pic's father gave her yesterday. It was engraved with wild animals in honor of her mother, with a guard made to look like an oak tree. Prince Dayel told Elswyth he'd take her to Zingett's soon to pick out a sword, but she was now almost positive he knew the queen was going to be giving her this one. One look at Pic's smiling face told that her friend knew about it, too. *That elf can sure keep a secret,* she thought.

The queen's laughter was bright and airy. "You're welcome, Elly. I had it designed just for you. I wanted to reward you for your hard work and give you something that would remind you of your rich heritage, one that included your Elven side while still giving homage to where you came from. You remind me of myself when I first began my training. I took to it as quickly as you are, too. My mother gave me my first blade and I still have it." Everyone at the table applauded, but Elswyth noticed Cicero put his head down.

Reaching over to pet him, the queen continued. "We have something else we need to discuss. Madam Teshka informed me there is a situation that needs to be remedied. Cicero, as you know, it's possible to hide your thoughts from the rest of us, but you cannot do that with your teacher." She inclined her head at Madam Teshka, who nodded back. "And so, my intrepid friend of the court, it's come to my attention that, since Elly began her sword training, you've felt you are, let's just say, no longer essential."

Cicero sighed and tucked his head further into his chest. "Yes, Your Majesty. What good am I to Elly now that she is better able to stand up for herself?"

"Cis, I still need—" Elswyth tried to interrupt.

He shook his head and opened a wing out to her. "Be honest, Elly. What could a mere raven have done that day in the arena that would have helped to diffuse the situation? Yes, I was angry and ready to fight, but I also feared that whatever I did would not be enough to help you. I've never been afraid of that before. Not like that."

The queen tilted her head at him. "Surely, you know, my dear Cicero, that bravery means taking action, even in the face of fear. All wise and valiant knights feel fear and you were ready to defend the princess, to defend your friends, and that was courageous."

"But—" he began.

"Cis! No! Why didn't you tell me that's how you were feeling?" Elswyth got up to stand next to his perch. *"You are always there to help and advise me. I know sometimes I don't listen to that advice, and I should. I promise I will from now on,"* she said and offered her arm to him. *"You're courageous, intelligent, and the most loyal of friends. I can't imagine life without you."*

He hopped onto her arm. "Elly, I've been so proud of your newfound strength, but just figured that, well, you wouldn't need me anymore. When I saw all those soldiers in the arena, each one more than capable of defending themselves, I knew you'd be like them. Strong, confident, and fearless. There was probably going to be little need for me, so I've been wondering if I should go back to Willow Grove. But then if I did, I would miss you."

"Oh, my silly friend! I thought we settled this when we got here. You aren't going anywhere! Do you understand that? I still need you and always will." Elswyth scooped him close to her chest.

"I'm going to remind you that you said you'd listen to me more!" he said, chuckling.

"I promise I will!"

"Hey Cis. Just so you know, she isn't crossing her fingers behind her back, so she's serious! But in case she forgets, I'll remind her, too, if the need arises!" Pic said. Everyone laughed, and the mood lifted.

Araleia sat back in her chair and smiled. "Now that we have settled that issue, there is one last item on our agenda, and it is a matter of preeminent importance." She nodded at the governess. "If you please, Madam Teshka?"

"Of course, Your Majesty." Madam Teshka pulled her brocade bag onto her lap, retrieved a small jade box from its depths, and handed it to the queen.

"Thank you," Araleia said, then held the box up and opened the lid so everyone could see what was inside. There, resting on a cushion of purple velvet, was a small gold band with a green portal stone embedded in it. The queen stood and held the band up for everyone to see. "Cicero, please return to your perch." It was a royal command, not a request, and he hopped over and faced her. He looked to Elswyth for a clue about what the queen was going to do, but she shrugged her shoulders.

"Your Majesty?" he asked.

She put her tip of her finger on his beak to hush him. Then, using her Majik, the band opened in her hand and she attached it to his leg. It glowed a bright green, sealed itself closed, and then its light dimmed. "Cicero, this band is officially sealed with my Majik and cannot be removed unless it is by your choice. Now, will you please bow?"

Touching the top of his head with her hand, the queen continued in a solemn tone Elswyth only heard her grandmother use in court, "Cicero, Royal Complement of Princess Elswyth and friend to the court; time and again, you have proven yourself to be loyal and brave. You are always more than willing to step up and fulfil whatever duty has been asked of you. Whether it be protector, guide, advisor," she nodded at Madam Teshka, "or even teaching assistant, you are ready to serve. In recognition of all that, Cicero, it is my honor as queen of this kingdom, to bestow upon you the position of Knight of Glenorim, with all the honors and privileges that come with the title." She paused, held her hand over his head, then continued, "And so, let it be known that, with this portal band, I hereby knight thee Sir Cicero the Brave of the Royal House of Glenorim. Rise, Sir Cicero, and be recognized."

Everyone cheered as Cicero looked down at the adornment, turning his leg every which way to admire it. *"Good to have you back, Cis! Or should I say, Sir Cis?"* Elswyth beamed at him, proud and happy.

"Good to be back, Elly!" He puffed his chest out. "Oh, my gosh! Look at me! I'm a knight! Won't Agnes be surprised when she finds out?"

"I don't think she'll be at all surprised, Cis. I'm not!"

"Just great. Now your head will be even bigger!" Pic said and hugged him.

"Hey!" Cicero struggled in her arms, chuckling. "What have I said about squishing me?"

"Just glad to have you back with us, Cis!" she said.

Sitting back in her chair, Elswyth felt a weight lifted off her shoulders. Things going well for her, Pic, and now Cis. Best of all, Terrick and his followers had backed off. All was right with the world, for now.

Samésh wheeled the empty cart away, leaving everyone at the festivities. It pained his heart to see the look of concern in the queen's eyes, and he knew he looked as exhausted as he felt. The king and queen had always treated him and Justa well, and keeping everything from them was tearing him apart. *I'm so sorry, Your Majesties.*

There was no time to think about any of that now. His wife, his best friend in all the world, was the most important thing on his mind and he needed to hurry if he was going to see her again tonight. With Nareed and Shara's help, Justa had rallied over the last month but, her health was failing again, and he was desperate to find a way to get her out of the dungeon. Nareed said he might have a solution. Samésh hoped so.

When he knew she was safe, he'd go to his king, no matter the consequences.

FIFTY-ONE

T he tea service had long been cleared, and the queen walked Elswyth and Cicero off the terrace in the late afternoon sun. Madam Teshka left with Pic two hours earlier because she said she wanted to show Pic some ancient manuscripts on Elven medicine, but Elswyth suspected the real reason they left was so she could hear more stories about Belnoir from her grandmother. She was already thinking about all the things she'd tell Agnes.

Before they'd made it to the ballroom door, Lieutenant Colonel Rohne stepped out and bowed. "Excuse the interruption, Your Majesty, but you're needed in the throne room." His eyes flicked to Elswyth, and she cringed inwardly at his hard stare.

"Thank you, Colonel Rohne. Please tell the king we're on our way," she said.

Rohne looked pointedly at Elswyth and Cicero. "Begging your pardon, Ma'am, but all of you? I believe it is an urgent matter of security and—"

Queen Araleia stiffened. "Rohne, I don't believe I stuttered. It's time for Princess Elswyth to be included in matters of the kingdom. As for *Sir* Cicero," she said, gesturing towards him, " he is both the complement to the princess and a knighted member of the court, and it is imperative he be included as well. I say again, inform King Garreth *we* will be there directly."

His nostrils flared, and he flushed red from the neck up. "As you wish, Your Majesty." He offered a curt bow, turned on his heels, and left.

Elswyth looked at this elf, her grandmother, and marveled. For someone who could be so kind, gentle, and compassionate, she could also wield power and authority with grace. No wonder her subjects loved her.

"Grandmother, are you sure? Cis and I can go back to our apartment if you need us to."

"Elly, Madam Teshka and I have agreed it's time for you to learn more about the workings of the court. That goes for you, too, Cicero. Besides, if this is truly an urgent matter for the kingdom, all members of the royal family must know about it. That includes you," she said, smiling. "Let's go." She hooked her arm through Elswyth's as Cicero flew overhead, still admiring his band.

The doors opened to the chamber packed with military, royal advisors, and high-ranking officials; frenetic energy from the dense mix of heightened emotions bombarded Elswyth's senses, and she paused at the door. A thick stew of fear, worry, and anger boiled over in the crowd as everyone tried to talk over each other, so she strengthened her shields against the onslaught to her senses. *By the Fates! What has happened?* Elswyth couldn't see a way through the crowd until someone noticed them and called out above the frantic voices, "Make way for Her Majesty, Queen Araleia, and Her Highness, Princess Elswyth!"

The crowd went silent and parted, opening a path to the low dais where her grandfather stood with her father, Ratheus—and Terrick! *Of course he would be there,* she thought. *Her grandmother had just told her that if there was a threat to the kingdom, the entire royal family was expected to be in attendance.* Still, her gut clenched into a tight ball as she watched him.

Something strange was going on with Terrick. *Could no one else see it?* The panic everyone else in the room displayed was absent in Terrick, his demeanor calm and measured. While the king, her father, and Ratheus were in deep discussion, Terrick focused on the crowd, the barest shadow of a sinister smile on his lips, until the moment he locked narrowed eyes on her, and his smile grew wider. The black tendrils slithered from his collar and crept up the base of his skull, sending a blade of icy fear down her spine, but she stood firm. Then, as if she meant nothing to him, he raised an eyebrow at her and returned his attention to the others in the room.

Cicero nudged Elswyth's shoulder, abruptly pulling her attention back to her surroundings as she followed her grandmother down the aisle to the front of the room. All eyes were on the queen; the room reduced to a hush as they made their way to the dais. Elswyth did her best to emulate her grandmother's poise and calm as they got close to the thrones.

Her stomach was churning, so she looked to her grandmother for reassurance, but it was her queen who put a steady hand up and gestured toward a space next to her royal seat. "Elly, if you two would stand here to my left," she directed quietly as she took her seat on the right of the stage. The king sat on the throne next to her, and Dayel and Terrick stood to his right while every elf in the room focused on their queen. Still composed and regal, Araleia looked at the king and raised her eyebrows in question. "Your Majesty? What has happened?"

"Your Majesty," the king answered, his voice low. He looked his wife in the eyes and Elswyth saw a tenderness there, but also worry. "We've received intelligence that the Kratens are preparing to invade Belnoir."

Elswyth's breath caught in her throat, in disbelief what she'd just heard. Everyone, whether human or fae, knew about the trolls in the barren kingdom of Kraten. Hundreds of years ago, Elven and human allies had joined forces and banished the bloodthirsty Kratens behind walls sealed by Majik in their territory far north of here. Someone—or something—must have broken through the walls that kept them in. No wonder everyone had focused on the queen. Belnoir, the queen's homeland and an ally, lay directly south of the threat. Belnoirian warriors were renowned across the globe, but even so, the trolls would attempt to leave her homeland in ashes, killing as many elves as they could. When they were done with Belnoir, if no one stopped them, they'd continue south to Glenorim and beyond. They needed to send soldiers north to aid their ally, the queen's homeland, and do it right away.

Elswyth glanced at Terrick on the other side of the stage and wondered if he could have been responsible for freeing the Kratens. *No. Even he would not do something so heinous. Or would he??* His Majik, hidden behind a mask of stone-cold darkness, was unreadable to her. The tendrils, however, still writhed like thin black snakes surrounding his head.

The single outward appearance of distress Elswyth saw from her grandmother was her grip tightening on the arm of her throne. Only seconds passed before the queen asked, her head held high, "And when do we send our army north?"

"We were waiting for you before we moved to the war room. But our military leaders have already said they can leave the moment we give the order," Garreth replied.

"Then what are we waiting for?" Her tone was all business. She rose from her seat, motioned for Elswyth and Cicero to follow the royal family. A select group of others trailed behind them to a door on the right of the dais.

Elswyth stole a glance at Terrick again as he walked with the family, the black tendrils still writhing from his collar—and his smile had returned! As soon as the discussions in the war room concluded, she would tell her father what she saw.

FIFTY-TWO

An enormous rectangular table with a three-dimensional map covering every inch of its top stood in the center of the war room. Elswyth marveled at the perfect miniature reproduction of known countries, topographies, kingdoms, and bodies of water of their world. If it hadn't been for the reason they were all gathered, Elswyth and Pic would have spent time just to appreciate the pure art of it.

The last court official to enter the room closed the double doors, secured the lock, and then everyone in the room turned their attention to the king and queen. At least the energy in here wasn't as frenetic as in the throne room, but the tension was still as thick as mud, so Elswyth kept her shields up, stood tall, and did her best to mirror her grandmother's grace and control.

King Garreth cleared his throat and gave a slight nod to the group assembled around the table. "Esteemed military leaders and governing members of the court, I thank you for coming so quickly," he said. "I will not mince words. We don't yet know exactly how it happened, but our intelligence has informed me that the rumors are true, the Kratens have somehow broken through the Majik seal on their wall." Agitated murmurs erupted around the table and the king held up his hand to silence the room. "Today, we call on our military to defend our ally, the queen's homeland. This will ultimately protect our beloved Glenorim, as well as our allies if we, together with the Belnoirian and Kerridin armies, can stop them." He lowered his voice. "I regret to say that many will be asked to make the ultimate sacrifice," He let that sink in to everyone standing there.

He then addressed an elf standing at the side of the room. "Jarrin, I am sending you west to Kerridin, as royal courier, with this missive. This is to be given directly to King Soral. Because the king has been ailing, he will need to send his son to assist in the resealing of the Kraten wall once we push the trolls back. Considering the threat is ultimately to all our kingdoms, I have no doubt they will want to send troops. You'll need to leave immediately, and I've ordered the livery to prepare a horse and supplies for you. Your haste in this matter is obviously crucial!"

A servant handed Jarrin the flat, leather-bound package. "It is my honor to serve; Your Majesty and I will go at once. May the Fates protect us." He bowed and turned to leave.

"Wait, Jarrin," the queen said. The messenger turned back and faced her. "I've taken the liberty of sending for your wife so you can say goodbye and she's waiting for you in the hall. Please know that she will be looked after until your return. I understand the elfling she's carrying will be a male. Congratulations!" She indicated a side door and gave him a kind smile.

"Thank you, Your Majesty," Jarrin said, bowing deeply to Araleia.

She bowed her head in reply to him. "May the Fates grant you a swift and safe journey, Jarrin. Go with Glenorim's, and my, gratitude." The courier closed the door and everyone's attention was, once again, on their king and queen.

Garreth continued. "First, we do not intend to leave Glenorim vulnerable. Colonel Rohne and his contingent will stay here to defend us. Colonel Willen, mobilize your battalion, effective immediately, and let them know they'll be leaving at dawn. And, as I understand it, Willen, you've also had volunteers willing to do their part. Please extend my, and the queen's, gratitude to all your elves willing to serve on this campaign."

"Yes, Your Majesty. I will do as you ask." Willen said.

Garreth turned back to address everyone else in the room. "With our combined armies pushing the Kratens back, the queen and I have every confidence we can squash this offensive. But we need to act right away. We will reconvene here in an hour to cover logistics. In the meantime," he said, shaking his head sadly. "I will also send out a decree that our kingdom is at war. Our citizens should prepare, just in case the armies are not successful. That is all for now. See everyone here in an hour."

The room emptied in a solemn and orderly fashion, the tension still thick. When the last elf closed the door behind them, Cicero moved from a perch he'd been on and settled on Elswyth's arm. "Well, this has been an eventful day," Cicero said, shaking his head.

Ratheus ambled over and sat up on his hindquarters next to Elswyth and Cicero. "Well, Cicero, I hear congratulations are in order, my friend! *Sir* Cicero. Yes, I like the sound of that," he rumbled.

"Thanks, Rathe!" Cicero stood even higher and showed the bear the gold band on his leg.

Elswyth smiled at the two. *"So it's Rathe now, is it?"* she asked.

If Elswyth and Cicero didn't know him so well, they would have thought the bear's chuckle was a growl. "Oh yes, Your Highness," Ratheus said. "Cis and I have become the best of buddies now!" Cicero flew back to his perch, and Ratheus followed him. The two of them were chatting together when her father put his hand on her shoulder. "Are you okay, Elly?" he asked quietly.

"Yes. No. Well—I'm not sure, actually," she said. "You know that new-found courage I had? Not sure where it went but, I have to admit I'm kind of scared."

"Then you aren't alone. We all are, but it will be okay. Between ours and the allied armies, I have every confidence those trolls will run back to Kraten with their boney tails between their legs. Mark my words. And by the way, you handled yourself beautifully today and I'm proud of you. And I must say that your new sword looks very smart on you!"

Elswyth felt her face blush. "Thank you, Father. The sword was such a big surprise! Will you have to go with the soldiers to Belnoir?"

"Not yet. In two days, I'll go north and meet up with the Kerridin prince and his army. When we push the trolls back into Kraten, the prince and I will seal the gate again with our Majiks. At least that's the plan for now. Please try not to worry, Elly. If our intelligence is correct, and we act quickly, we have time to ward off the attack on Belnoir."

Elswyth shifted on her feet. "Father, there's something else. When I saw Terrick in the throne room earlier, no one seemed to notice, but something was going on with him. It was almost like he was, I don't know, somehow connecting with everyone in the room. It felt wrong, but I can't tell you why." She let out a frustrated sigh. "His tendrils were showing, and he was smiling! It wasn't a good kind of smile, either."

Dayel's brows knitted together and looked over at his brother, who seemed intent on their parent's conversation over the map. "Thank you for telling me, Elly. I'll watch him, but I also need to concentrate on what's going on. I have to admit, I was surprised he even showed up at court today. He's been staying away for over a month and it's been much less stressful with him not being around lately."

Elswyth turned her head to look at Terrick. "I'm worried and I can't put my finger on what I sense with him. It almost felt like his Majik was affecting everyone there, but I can't prove it, or even say that's what was happening for sure. This feels important. Sorry. Everything is still so new to me and his shields are so powerful," she said.

He gave her shoulder a squeeze. "We'll figure it out. I promise. I don't think he's going to try anything during an emergency like this so, for now, I need to help with the final plans. We'll talk later. Okay?"

"Sure. That sounds good. I understand. This is more important for now." She moved closer to the table to hear what they were discussing, Cicero and Ratheus joining her. But Terrick's behavior in the throne room was crowding out all other thoughts, as she wondered, again, if he had a hand in releasing their most feared enemy. She wished she understood more of what her Majik was trying to tell her.

"Elly," Cicero whispered. "Where did Terrick go?"

She looked up and saw he was no longer in the room.

FIFTY-THREE

Checking to see he was alone, Samésh stood in a pool of pale-yellow light from the sconce on the stone wall, and faced the now-familiar, ancient oak door, then knocked. The wait was agonizing and long, but finally, when the small slot at the top slid open, the eyes he expected to see were different—and they were not friendly. *That's not Nareed!*

"What do yer want?" a gravelly voice barked.

"I came to see my wife, please. She is a prisoner here and her name is—"

"Don't care what her name is! Go away. No visitors allowed!" The opening snapped shut.

His shoulders fell, and he stared at the door, incredulous. *What do I do now? I need to see Justa!* He knocked again, but harder, and took the fresh bouquet of roses out from under his cloak, gripping their stems tight in his fist.

The slot slid open again. "I said no visitors! Go. Away!"

"Wait! Please!" The beady, ice-blue eyes squinted and hesitated, so Samésh kept talking. "Please. I have coins and can pay and—" The eyebrows in the opening shot up and Samésh heard a loud snort. He held the flowers up high so the eyes could see he wasn't carrying a weapon, then Samésh pled his case. "See? I don't want to start trouble. I would simply like to give my wife some flowers. She was—is one of the cultivators in the royal gardens, and it would mean so much if you could let me in to see her."

"Ya got coin, ya say?"

Samésh dug into his pocket and pulled out four gold pieces and held them up to the slot for the eyes to see. "Will this do? It's all I have with me."

The eyes grumbled something unintelligible, and the opening snapped shut again. Seconds later, the lock clicked, and the door swung open. A gnarled and dirty halfling stood in the doorway, his palm stretched out towards Samésh. He wore an official prison guard uniform, but it was ill-fitting and looked like it hadn't been cleaned in a long time, a very long time. "Gimme the coins and I'll let ya in to see her."

"Wait! I'll give you *one* now. Let me see her and then I'll give you the other three afterwards." Samésh held a coin up at the guard's eye level and returned the other three to his pocket, making sure they clinked against each other for emphasis.

The guard scratched his scraggly, dirty face, eyed the coin, and seemed to consider the proposition. "All right. Hurry up with yerself, then. Git in!" Before Samésh had even stepped over the threshold, the guard snatched the gold from his hand. He saw the blanket Nareed gave Justa spread out on the stone bench, leftover food, and trash strewn across it. "What are ya looking at? I gotta right to keep warm, ain't I? It gets cold down here! If ya got a problem with that, ya can just leave, but I keep the coin!" He pointed back at the door while digging around in his ear with the long nail on his pinky.

"No. It's fine," Samésh said, seething inside. *How dare this filthy elf take her blanket!* He would deal with this imp after he found a way to get Justa out, and he was so close to doing that. In the meantime, he didn't want to do anything to give the guard a reason to hurt her. Nareed had sent word he was going to help him get her out tonight and said he had a plan, but where was he? Samésh decided to see if the guard knew anything. "I haven't seen you stationed down here before. How come you're here and the other guard is gone?"

The elf stuck his chest out and tucked his thumbs in the sides of his vest. "I guess ya could say they promoted me. They even gave me this here official uniform!" He turned in a circle to model it for Samésh. "Used to be I cleaned the dungeon toilets. Dirty job, that is, and I been doing it for nye on—" he tried counting on his fingers but lost track. "well, anyway, it was a long time. Ya see, back a while ago, I got nabbed trying to nick some food from one of Terrick's guards. I was hungry, and I gotta say he didn't look like he would have missed it, but he got really angry, so it was the toilets for me. Could have been a lot worse, I guess." He turned and waved a dirty finger at Samésh. "I wouldn't recommend stealin' from a guard if'n I was you. Ya might end up in the toilets like I did," he said, and started picking his nose.

Samésh was fairly certain that the other reason this elf was here was because no one else wanted the job. As impatient as he was to see Justa, he desperately needed to find out where Nareed was. "Um—thanks for the warning and congratulations on your promotion, then."

"Yeah. This is much more fun," the guard said. He pulled his finger out of his nose and popped it into his mouth.

Barely hiding his disgust, Samésh asked, "So what happened to the guard that's usually here?"

"Oh, him? Ain't quite sure. I was just told that from now on I'd be working in this dungeon and they didn't get no argument from me. Anything was better than what I was doing." He grunted and scratched under his armpit. "So, ya want to see yer wife or what?" he said and eyed Samésh's pocket. "I got an important job to do, ya know. Ain't got time to chitchat with ya."

"Yes, please take me to her." He would look for Nareed after he saw Justa.

The guard picked up the blanket, shook off the trash, and wrapped it around his dirty shoulders. "All right. Let's get going then. Follow me."

No matter how many times Samésh walked down the dank corridor, it was as depressing and frightening as the first time. He passed one of the barred holes in the floor, saw a pair of hands clutching the bars from below, and heard someone weeping in the darkness of the narrow pit. "Please let me out! I promise I won't disobey any more orders! PLEASE!" Then the poor trapped creature let out a maniacal cackle, babbled something about someone else who needed to be punished, then continued to weep. Samésh hurried by without looking down.

"Here ya go," the guard said, nodding into Justa's cell. "I'll be back in a few minutes." He unlocked the door and Samésh crossed the threshold, prepared for the sensation of his Majik being drained as he stepped in. His wife was sitting on her bench, visibly shivering. She reached up to him and gave him a wan smile as he entered.

"Love! I'm so happy to see you again!" she said.

Samésh took off his cloak and placed it around her shoulders. He looked for something to put her flowers in, but the pitcher and glass were gone. His anger was growing hotter. "He took your blanket *and* your pitcher of water?"

"Yes, and the stew that Shara sent for me. I'm pretty sure he ate it, but I haven't had much of an appetite lately, anyway." She sighed and touched his cheek. "Did you speak with Nareed? He told me a couple of days ago he may have a plan to get me out without bringing suspicion to him and Shara."

He had to compose himself before he spoke. Because of Nareed, at least she'd had hot food and warmth, but now all that had been taken away, and he wasn't sure how long she could cope. "I'm going to talk to him tonight after my visit with you. I don't know why he isn't here. That other guard is taking his place for now so I'll find him as soon as I leave."

She folded her hands in her lap. "Samésh, I keep asking you to go to the king. I don't want you to wait for Nareed. It's been far too long and we have the power to make a difference now, if it's not too late. Please!" He looked away, but she gently reached up and turned his face to hers. "My dearest, you're the only one who's been able to visit down here so the other prisoners can't ask their loved ones to do this for the kingdom. I'm begging you, Samésh, be brave and go to the king. Do it for me." Justa trembled and huddled further under his cape.

A tear escaped his eye as he pulled her to his chest. "Give me tonight, Justa. Let me find Nareed and see what he says. I have to at least try. Then I promise you, I'll go to the king."

She sighed and sunk into his arms. Then, the cough he thought was getting better returned, only far worse, and she covered her mouth with the cloak. Even in the darkness of her cell, he could see several spots of blood left on the fabric, and it startled him. "I don't have the energy to argue, Samésh. Tonight then," she said. "But if he can't help us by tomorrow, then you have to go to King Garreth. Give me your word."

His emotions tightened his throat, and he couldn't speak. He could only nod his head against her cheek.

Samésh reluctantly stood and called for the guard. Once he was back in the corridor, he asked, "Where can I get my wife a clean pitcher of water and a glass?" He would bring it to her himself and had no intention of letting that elf touch anything close to Justa, not with those filthy hands.

"It will cost you extra!" the halfling said. He leaned in closer and pointed to Samésh's pocket.

"Just show me where the water is," he said, quickly losing his temper. "Then we'll talk!"

Before he left her, he made sure Justa drank fresh water and tucked her comfortably in his cloak. "I will see you tomorrow, my flower!"

She looked up at him and simply smiled, but her eyes told him she loved him back.

The guard held his hand out as they stood by the open dungeon door. "Well? What about them other three coins?"

Samésh watched as a flea scurried across the elf's forehead and disappeared under the oily hairline. His skin crawled just being in the presence of the loathsome creature. "Before I give them to you, you must promise to leave my cloak with her. And her water, don't touch her water. As a matter of fact, just leave her alone until I come back."

The guard wiggled the fingers of his boney outstretched hand. "What's it worth to ya?"

"I can bring you more coins tomorrow, *if, and only if,* I find you've done as I asked."

"Deal," the guard said quickly, his eyes alight at the prospect of more coins. He pulled his hand in and reached back to scratch his backside before extending it again.

Loathe to touch any part of the nasty elf, Samésh dropped the coins from several inches high into the dirty palm, but even then, he felt soiled. "I'll be back tomorrow, first thing. See that you treat her well!"

"Yeah. Yeah. No problem. Tomorrow then," he said, fingering the coins gleefully in his grubby hands. "I got important work to do here so, git out!"

Samésh turned and headed out the door, intent on finding Nareed.

FIFTY-FOUR

"Nareed's not here, Samésh. I'm so sorry. He volunteered to go back on active duty as a quartermaster hours ago. And at his age!" Shara said, wringing her hands. Her face was blotchy and red, her eyes swollen from crying. "He's doing supply inventories and won't be back until very late tonight—to say goodbye."

"Goodbye? Active duty? I don't understand."

"It's all very sudden. I only know that the Kratens have escaped their barriers and are heading south. Our army will probably leave at first light." She sniffled and blew her nose into an embroidered hanky. "Oh, where are my manners? I'm so sorry, my head is all over the place. Come in, Samésh. I'll make a pot of tea." Still sniffling, she opened the door to their apartment wider and motioned him in.

"No thank you, Shara. I was down in the—" he stopped himself, not sure of who might be listening in the corridor, then he stared at her, his eyes wide. "Did you say the Kratens? This is the first I heard about all this. Nareed was going to help me with something." Surely, she had gotten it wrong. The Kratens? That can't be correct! Should he ask Shara if Nareed told her about helping Justa escape, or would that endanger her? If something happened to her because of that, Justa would never forgive him—or herself. He fumbled with a button on his vest and turned to leave, not willing to put her at risk, and decided he would look for Nareed himself.

She brought her hand to her cheek and gasped. "Oh, no! Where is my head? Nareed left something for you, said you would probably come by for it. Wait here, Samésh!" She disappeared inside, came back out within a couple of minutes, and handed him a folded, sealed note. "Here you go," she said and leaned in close to whisper. "Please take care and may the Fates travel with you both. Be sure to give her my love, Samésh, and I hope Nareed and I will see you both again someday." She leaned back against her door, dabbing her eyes with her handkerchief.

She knows! Bless her courage, she knows, he thought. "Thank you. Thank you very much, Shara!" Samésh felt a rush of hope and, with trembling hands, tucked the paper into his vest pocket.

To keep the charade going, Shara said loud enough for any passerby to hear, "Oh, and do say hello to Justa when she comes back from visiting family. It's been far too long since she and I got together for a chat. Will you do that?" She tried to smile, but he could tell she was on the verge of crying afresh.

"I will. And don't worry. I'm sure Nareed will be home, safe, and sound, in no time!" He patted her hand and turned to go. As soon as the door closed, he could hear her weeping inside. His heart pained for his friends, but he had to stay focused on getting home and reading the note.

He made his way to his apartment and, after locking the front door behind him, lit the lamp at his table and sat down, his hands shaking as he took the note from his pocket and unfolded it. Nareed's neat handwriting spread across the page and gave him hope. *Please let this be our answer,* he prayed.

SAMÉSH, I'M SORRY I COULDN'T BE THERE TO MEET YOU, BUT I'VE ARRANGED FOR SOMEONE TO HELP YOU AND JUSTA. ARTHID IS THE SON OF ONE OF THE GUARDS IN THE OLD DUNGEON AND HE SAID HE WOULD HELP GET JUSTA OUT. HE WILL DEMAND PAYMENT OF FIFTY GOLD PIECES, BUT AT LEAST HE'S WILLING TO DO THIS. I'M HOPING WE CAN TRUST HIM, BUT I HAVE TO ADMIT, I'M NOT COMPLETELY SURE. AT THIS POINT, IT IS THE BEST, RATHER, THE

ONLY OPTION WE HAVE WITH JUSTA'S HEALTH FAILING. MEET HIM IN THE DUNGEON AT ELEVEN TOMORROW. HE'LL BE EXPECTING YOU. ONCE SHE IS FREE, USE ONE OF THE OLD CASTLE PASSAGES TO GET TO SOMEONE YOU TRUST IN THE CITY. MAY THE FATES BE WITH YOU BOTH. MAY THE FATES BE WITH US ALL. YOUR FRIEND, NAREED.

"Tomorrow then, my flower. We will be free of this nightmare tomorrow," he said aloud. He lit a fire in the fireplace and watched the flames devour the letter. There would be no sleep tonight.

The sun hadn't made it to the crest of the horizon yet, but Samésh rose from his bed and got dressed, anyway. He'd spent the night staring at the shadows on his ceiling, his thoughts competing against each other in his brain. Freeing Justa was the most important task he had right now, and he thought of a few elves in the city that might be willing to take her in. Would they be too afraid to help? And what if the Kratens made it to Glenorim? How would he protect her then? It was too terrifying to dwell on. Of course, once he got her to safety, he'd have to talk to his king, the elf who'd trusted him for so many years. Samésh would have to admit he'd kept Terrick's activities secret all this time, but he was ready to take any punishment he might be due. He broke out in a nervous sweat for the umpteenth time since coming home last night.

How many times had he counted the coins to make sure he had the required fifty? *No matter. Just count them again. It doesn't hurt to be certain;* he thought. Then he gathered an extra set of his clothes, a hat for Justa to wear as a disguise, and stuffed them in a satchel. No one would recognize her that way. Adding the rest of their coins to his satchel to take with them for later, he pulled up the hood on his coat and looked around their apartment. It pained him to think they may never come back.

Since he had time, he planned to stop at the royal gardens first to get a single purple rose for Justa. A whole bouquet would be too bulky to hide under her cloak, but a single flower would be easy enough to conceal. Most importantly, it would make her happy. Being a royal cultivator in the gardens had always given her purpose. After all, she'd worked there for over a hundred years and he knew how much she was going to miss it.

And what about this business with the Kratens? He needed to find out more. Maybe he could volunteer to fight once he got Justa to safety. Unlocking his door, he stepped out into the corridor.

Everywhere he went, the crowded halls were filled with mayhem. So many soldiers, each one with a bulging rucksack strapped over their purple and gold uniform, their scabbards hung from gold-buckled baldrics on their waists. Loved ones followed alongside them, many of their faces lined with worry. He stopped at one of the corridor windows overlooking the city below, saw the shops lit up in the dim early morning light and citizens who carried lanterns along the cobbles. Even more soldiers headed out along the street below, many on foot, some rode horses and still others drove wagons filled with food and supplies for what lay ahead. Samésh was too high up to see their faces, but it wasn't hard to recognize the worry in the crowd. Handkerchiefs went to weeping faces and elves leaned on one another as they watched their soldiers march out of the city. Many citizens waved their Glenorim purple and gold pennants above their heads.

All the soldiers were heading in one direction: north. That was the way to the road through the Pinnacle Mountains leading to Belnoir.

"Excuse me!" Samésh said above the din as he tapped an ancient elf passing by. "Could you tell me what's happening, sir? Do we know if the Kratens have reached Belnoir yet?"

The old elf shrugged his shoulders and jiggled a gnarled wooded cane at him. "Don't exactly know details, elfling! There are rumors flying everywhere. The beginning and end of it is that we're at war. Kratens! Can you imagine? And after all this time? The soldiers are leaving to defend Belnoir. Hopefully, they can stop them up there, if they haven't already missed their chance!" Samésh could barely hear him over the cacophony bouncing off the arched ceilings.

Not that he hadn't believed Shara, but now it was truly real. Frighteningly, real! Until then, he'd focused all his thoughts on Justa. They still were, except now Samésh had to find a place where she'd be safe from two threats: Terrick, and now, war, if it came to Glenorim. He set his jaw and pushed his way through the throng to the gardens.

FIFTY-FIVE

The oak door to the old dungeon was open! Samésh crept up to the door and peeked around the edge. The guard from last night wasn't there, but sitting on the stone bench was a young halfling, his feet propped up on an old barrel, eating a packed lunch. The ring of cell keys sat next to his basket of food.

As he stepped into the antechamber, the halfling looked up at him and smiled. "Ah. You must be Samésh. Yes? Name's Arthid," he said as he brushed his long, blond bangs out of his eyes. "So then, did you bring the coins? Not to rush you, but Prince Terrick might need me soon, so I shouldn't be down here too long. Besides, I'm sure you would agree, this is not one of the most pleasant of places to meet and I'd prefer not to linger here longer than necessary."

"Yes. I—I'm Samésh. Did you say Prince Terrick? Why would Prince Terrick need you?" *Was this a trap?* Samésh's stomach clenched, and his eyes darted around the room to make sure they were alone.

"Don't worry, he's not here. I work for him and I'm kind of an elf-of-all-trades, you might say, so I do odd jobs for him. There are several of us halflings that work for him, if you're interested," he said, while he waved a chicken leg in the air. Arthid noticed Samésh's mouth hung open in shock, so he rushed to add, "Oh, hey! He's not the villain so many have made him out to be, you know. He's promised us halflings that life would be better under him. Sure, he can be a little harsh sometimes, but *I've* never actually seen him *hurt* anyone. Okay, maybe only those that deserved it—like probably all the elves down here. Well, except for whoever it was you came here for, I'm sure." He took a large bite of the chicken leg, then spoke with his mouth full. "Sorry. I'm really hungry. I missed breakfast so I could get down here on time! Anyway," he said after swallowing, "the rest of the prisoners must have done some pretty awful things to get sent down here. Uh, so tell me again. Who was it you came for?"

"It is my wife and, yes, she is innocent! So, why are you doing this for me, then? Aren't you afraid of getting into trouble? What if Terrick finds out?"

Arthid tossed the last of the drumstick on the floor and licked his fingers clean, then brushed his bangs out of the way again and pulled out another piece of chicken from his basket. "I just figured this would be a quick way to get some extra gold in my pockets, you know? And who's going to tell Terrick? Don't imagine you will!" he said, winking.

"But your father is a good friend of Nareed. What does he think of you working for Terrick?"

"Ah, yes. Nareed. My father's friend. They are two of a kind, they are," he said, wiping his mouth with a napkin he'd pulled from his basket. "Dad asked if I'd be willing to help you out since he'd be gone. So, I went back to Nareed and told him I'd be happy to, for a price. And, since you mentioned it, good old Dad doesn't know I've been working for Terrick, he wouldn't approve or understand so I would appreciate it if you kept that under your hat. We're on opposite sides of the table, if you catch my meaning." He bit more meat off the chicken leg as he looked at Samésh, his eyes narrowed. "Hey! You judging me or what?"

"No! I'm—um—still wondering why you are working for Terrick. He is not a fan of halflings, you know."

The last of the second drumstick then ended up on the floor. "That's all rumors and lies. I'm telling you; he loves us. We are an important part of

Glenorim and contribute a lot," he said, and flicked his head to move the offending bangs out of the way again. "Of course, there are some elves who don't think we're worth their while, but he knows we are." He lowered his voice, his hand to the side of his mouth. "You mark my words. Someday, when he's crowned king, it's going to be all honey and smiles for everyone! You'll see." He pulled an apple from his basket. "I got an extra one. You want it?"

"No, thank you." Samésh needed to change the subject. "Where are the regular guards? Are they coming back soon? I need to know if I have time to sneak Justa out of the halls."

"I volunteered to work a short shift here today so I could help you out. Everyone else is either marching north or in important meetings with Colonel Rohne. The soldiers in the castle are on standby until further notice. As for the guards, you're in luck. I know they have no plans to send anyone down here until later tonight. I was told there were too many things going on so this place is a low priority for now." He took another bite of his apple, then started packing everything up. "So—the money?"

"Yes, of course! Here are your coins. I can wait for you to count them, if you want." He handed over a leather bag with the money.

"Nah. You have an honest face. Besides, if you're a friend of my dad's friend, then you must be okay. Here are the keys to the cells. I don't know which one fits her door, so you'll just have to try them all until you find one that works. To be honest, I couldn't even go into the corridor to check what keys go to which door. Too depressing down there, you know! Anyway, when you leave, just hang them up on this hook and close this door behind you. Okay? And we never met. Got that?"

"Of course."

The halfling started out the door, turned back, and brushed his bangs out of his eyes. "And, hey. Long live King Terrick. Right?" he said, giving Samésh a thumbs up. After checking both ways in the outer hall, he slipped out and was gone.

Samésh snatched up the keys and wept with relief as he ran down the passageway, feeling lighter than he had in months, laughing out loud as he made his way. *We'll go to our old friends, Roil and his brother Emale, in the city because I'm sure they will hide Justa, then I'll go to the king. After that, I can nurse Justa back to health and once she is strong again, we can make our way to Belnoir. It will be exactly what she needs. Yes! That's what we'll do. We'll miss Glenorim, of course, especially the royal family. They've been so good to us, but they will understand.* His thoughts danced with the possibilities of the bright future ahead, and his steps sped up as he got closer to her cell. *Maybe we'll plant a garden together in our new home. Not just flowers! No! We will have fruits and vegetables too. We might even open a booth in the Belnoir bazaar, and elves would come to buy our flowers and produce. We're were going to be so happy!* Before he stepped in front of Justa's bars, he took the rose from inside his coat, held it out, and called out to her. "Justa, my love. I've come to take you—"

Her cell was empty, the door ajar. "Justa?" Her name echoed against the walls of her cell and he began to tremble, his heart coming to a crashing halt. He pushed the door open and the screech of the hinges echoed painfully off the walls. She was gone. He was too late! Even the cloak he'd given her was nowhere to be seen, as if she'd never been there. "JUSTA?" he sobbed. The rose dropped from his hand and he crumbled to the floor.

He heard a gentle voice from the next cell. "I'm so sorry. Justa passed in the middle of the night. The guard found her and took her away, but we don't know where they—took her body." Her voice trailed off.

A growing red rage replaced his tears as he stood, braced himself against the wall, and looked down at the keys in his hand. Stepping up to the next cell, he saw the halfling that had just spoken to him, tried a couple of keys in her lock, found the right one, and opened the rust-ladened door. "You're free," he croaked. "There is no guard and won't be for a while. Make your way to one of the old passageways to the city and find a hiding place. Perhaps there is someone you know?"

She stepped out, her Majik having rushed back into her body, and she hugged him fiercely. "Thank you, Samésh! Justa was a wonderful elf, and she and I talked together all the time. She—she spoke of you often and loved you so much."

Samésh didn't trust his voice to answer her. If he tried to talk, he feared he might just fall apart. Utterly apart. He looked at the other cells in the corridor and made a decision. Justa's death, her *life*, would count for something right now; he would help the rest of the prisoners escape and get to some place safe in the city and do that in her name. Then he'd go to the king. He looked at the halfling and nodded to the other cells as he held the keys up, still not able to trust his voice.

She nodded back, and then gently took the keys from his hand. "I will take half and you take the rest. We'll let everyone out together. There is also an unfortunate soul locked in a hole in the hall floor I'd like to set free."

Samésh nodded and sighed his assent. Before he turned to unlock more doors, he looked back at the single purple rose lying crushed on the dirty stone floor.

FIFTY-SIX

G lenorim was silent. A heavy blanket of fear and uncertainty covered the mountain that night. No one walked the castle halls, the
streets of the city were empty, and the soldiers were long gone, their
absence deeply felt in every corner of the kingdom. From the castle above
to the city below, elves sat inside their homes and apartments, huddled
near each other around their hearths for comfort and courage. However,
one elf was not afraid, nor worried about a friend or family member.

Terrick stood looking out through the towering window in his study,
enjoying the view for the first time in a very long while. "I'm so close now
I can almost *taste* the sweet nectar of success, Rohne! By tomorrow night
you will finally address me as Your Majesty." He closed his eyes and let
that sink in. *By the Fates, it felt good to say it,* he thought. The tendrils
were writhing all over his body now, but he didn't care. He finally had
control.

"Yes, Your Highness. I look forward to the moment we can say that!"
Rohne sat in front of Terrick's desk and swirled his glass of nectar. The
tendrils, not visible to anyone but Terrick—and the princess—reached
out to Rohne, teasingly close enough to touch his face.

Terrick glared at Rohne. "Did you take care of Jarrin?"

"Yes, we dispatched him just after he entered the western passage. We destroyed the package, and the horse was taken care of as well. So, King Garreth's missive to Kerridin is no longer an issue. By the time anyone asks about Jarrin, it won't matter."

"Excellent. That courier was something I wasn't expecting to deal with. Is everything else in order? The banners? Are they ready to be hung?"

"Everything is prepared and ready for your orders."

"Good. Good." Terrick nodded his head slowly as he smiled at the view outside. "We'll begin separating halflings within a few days. Make sure they're treated well until then. Understood? I don't want a repeat of—whatever his name was."

"Rayel, Your Highness. It was Rayel."

"Yes, him. I don't want a repeat of that incident. The halflings must believe they are protected, until they're not, of course. That reminds me, make sure there is room for them in the dungeons once I am king. If you have to, you can release any pure Elven prisoners to make room, regardless of why there were down there to begin with." He turned to look at Rohne, his jaw set, and eyebrow raised. "Am I clear?"

"Absolutely clear, Your Highness." Rohne stiffened under Terrick's hard gaze and set his glass on the desk.

"Good. And, most importantly, the nectar? Is it ready?"

"I oversaw that task myself."

Terrick rubbed his hands together and moved to sit at his desk. "Everything is falling into place! By the time Colonel Willen finds out I've sent them to chase imaginary dragons, that the Kratens are still safely behind their wall, the throne will be mine and they'll have no choice but to fall in line under my rule." This time, he shivered with delight, and not just from being cold.

"And, Rohne, your soldiers will have earned a time of celebration for their loyalty. Remember, though. Only pure elves may take part. No halflings! Your soldiers can use the throne room for their festivities. First, move the king's throne, my throne tomorrow afternoon, and put it on the dais in the ballroom since I'll be using that room in the future. I need a grander space to rule from."

"Of course, Your Highness. I will see to moving the throne myself. And I know the soldiers will appreciate your benevolence where the party is concerned. Thank you, Your Highness!"

"You're dismissed. I have a lot to do tonight." Terrick said abruptly. The door opened, but Terrick noticed Rohne looking down at his unfinished glass. "Oh, by the Fates, Rohne!" he said with annoyance. "Take it with you if you have to."

"Thank you, Your Highness," He swept the glass up, bowed, and left.

Terrick pulled out the center drawer of his desk and removed a small, round obsidian box inlaid with silver and rubies. His hands shook with glee as he opened it. Inside was a tiny red pill. "I've been waiting to use you for some time, my little friend."

He picked it up and admired its glossy surface as it reflected the flames from the fireplace. Then he reverently placed it on his tongue, closed his mouth, and then his eyes. For just a few breaths, he savored the sensation of it in his mouth and then took a long drink of warm nectar to wash it down his throat. The tendrils writhed even further out from his body, dancing in the air around the room.

"I'm ready," he said.

PART THREE

J. A. FAGAN

Fifty-Seven

King Garreth listened to all Samésh had to say, sat back in his chair, his heart heavy in his chest and looked at the elf standing before him—this elf who'd been a loyal servant to the family long before Araleia and he wed so many years ago. Samésh and Justa had been dear to them, and now this. He looked at their beloved servant before him and hung his head, trying to find words to express what he felt. Nothing seemed to fit the gravity of the sorrow of the moment. "I'm so sorry, Samésh," the king finally said.

Samésh looked up, eyes blinking and mouth open wide in surprise. *"You're* sorry, Your Majesty? No, no. Did you not understand what I just told you? I am at fault. I should have said something to you long ago when Prince Terrick took my Justa."

Garreth put his hand up. "Please, sit, Samésh." He motioned to the chair across from him, feeling more weary than he had his entire life.

"Y—yes, Your Majesty." Samésh sat at the edge of the seat, his back ramrod straight.

Garreth clasped his hands together and looked Samésh in the eyes. "I understood everything you said, my dear Samésh. And yes, you should have come to me, but the bigger failure is still mine. So, again, from the depths of my heart, I am sorry. For years, we tried to guide Terrick toward a different path, offered him opportunities and education, tried to give him something that fed him heart and soul hoping it would make a difference. We forgave him repeatedly for small things, not realizing those small things would multiply into bigger, more dangerous problems. Instead of dealing with him more forcefully, we've been in denial, and thought that we could handle him. Then, I am ashamed to admit, we, or rather, I, tried simply ignoring him. Never did we dream things could ever reach this level. We were wrong. So wrong."

Garreth shook his head slowly and worked to control the trembling in his voice. "Terrick wanted more than anyone could give him, and the farther our relationship stretched apart from each other, the more blind we were to his greed and what he was doing. Because of that, you, Justa, and others, have paid dearly. I vow, Samésh, that Terrick will pay."

The sun shone through the window with a happy late morning light out of place with the dark moment. Garreth looked out at the blue sky, then back at Samésh. His heart hurt for everything this good-hearted elf had suffered because he, as a father and king, allowed it all to go too far. He was complicit in the pain Terrick had caused so many.

"Samésh, Dayel and I were already planning to send Terrick to the prison vaults on Kyper Island. His Majik will be stripped and it is going to happen—too late, but it is going to happen. I know it's too much to ask, but, as your king, I ask your forgiveness."

"Oh, Your Majesty! I don't deserve your apology," Samésh wept, his head in his hands. He composed himself and stood up, head held high. "I take responsibility because Justa asked me repeatedly to come to you. She didn't care about herself and it was always about others and the good of the kingdom."

The guard outside the study knocked at the door, and Garreth gestured to the back of the room. "Step into the servant's door so you won't be seen, Samésh." When he was alone, he called out, "Enter!"

The soldier stepped just inside the door and bowed. "Sorry to disturb you, Your Majesty. Prince Terrick requests an audience with you. He said he has urgent information about the Kratens."

"Tell him I will see him in ten minutes." Garreth said, his jaw clenched at the thought of his traitorous, cruel son being here.

The guard nodded and left, and Samésh returned to the study.

"Samésh, I want you to go back through the servant's door. Since you came in that way, no one knows you're here and you'll be safe. Stay close enough on the other side so you can hear our discussion, but don't come back in here until I call you back. I'm going to see what Terrick has to say, and I need you to be my second set of ears while he and I talk. Understand?"

"Yes, Your Majesty," he answered, his shoulders back.

"Good. I won't divulge anything you've said to me this morning, at least not yet. Later today, though, you and I will meet with the queen, Prince Dayel, and Princess Elswyth. You can help us decide how we proceed." He put a firm hand on Samésh's shoulder. "You are now covered by my shields and no one, including Terrick, will sense your presence."

Samésh had just made it behind the servant's door when he heard Terrick enter the king's study.

"Really, *Father*! You made me wait?" Terrick pulled his fur collar tighter around his neck. "And I have to say, it's freezing in here." He stepped to the fireplace, raised the flames with a wave of his hand, then sauntered to the desk to sit opposite his father.

"Terrick," Garreth said, acknowledging him from his desk chair. "I was in the middle of something and didn't want to be interrupted. You have some news about the Kratens?"

Terrick narrowed his eyes, looked around the room, and sat forward in his seat. "In the middle of something with whom? Is someone else here? Your guard said you were alone."

Garreth tried to keep his voice neutral and ignored the questions. If Terrick did, indeed, have vital information about the trolls, he needed to know what he had. It could mean life for death for his soldiers and for those of Belnoir and Kerridin. The sooner he could get Terrick to talk, the sooner he was out of his office. "My guard said you had important information? Is this something we need to send to the troops before they get to Belnoir? If it is, then let's hear it so I can send a courier to them. I'm sure you know how busy it's been and I haven't slept in twenty-four hours. It looks like I won't be resting anytime soon, either, so please just tell me what you know."

"Well," Terrick began. "I can see that, once again, you don't have time for me. As for the news, it might be nothing at all, actually, but I thought you should still know. Now that I think about it, it's probably nothing."

"Terrick! I am not in the mood for games, especially when we're talking about the lives of our armies! Do you have something to tell me or not?" Garreth clenched his jaw to stem his temper.

Terrick got up and drifted to the credenza next to his father's desk, and poured two short glasses of his private nectar from the decanter. "We should first toast our troops, don't you think?" he said casually. "After all, it is our tradition to do so when we send them out to war. Everything went so quickly yesterday that we didn't have a chance to do that." He handed one glass to his father and raised his own, wearing the barest semblance of a sincere smile.

Garreth took the glass but set it down on the desk. "I don't have time to drink with you. Besides, I would rather we toast them when they arrive home triumphant. In order to make sure that happens, I need to finish my work and you need to tell me what you know. Now!"

His glass still raised, Terrick tilted his head at his father. "Come on, Father. One drink and I will tell you what I know."

Garreth stood up from his seat and glared at his son. "Fine!" He picked up his glass, downed the nectar in one swallow, and slammed it back down on the desk. *Whatever it takes to get the information and get him out of here,* he thought. His anger was getting the best of him, so he took a deep breath and composed himself. "Happy? Now what is it you wanted to tell me? No more games!"

"As a matter of fact, I am happy—now. But you seem in a hurry to get rid of me. I think I'll stay a few minutes more, if that is all right with you. By the way, that drink should have been savored and not gulped." Terrick said, pointing to Garreth's glass. He sipped the rest of his nectar and slowly set his glass next to his father's, keeping eye contact as he did it. Once again, he smiled." I came to you today because I think I should be more involved with this campaign. I thought we could discuss strategies together."

"Why now, Terrick? You've not been interested in matters of the kingdom for years! So why now?"

Terrick shrugged his shoulders. "I'm interested today."

Garreth felt lightheaded and sat back down in his chair. He cleared his throat, and the dizziness passed.

"Are you all right, Father? You look a little pale. Can I get you some more nectar?" Terrick tilted his head and put on a less-than-convincing act of caring. He reached for his father's glass.

"I'm fine." Garreth covered his glass with his hand. "As I told you, I've just been awake for a long time and need some rest. Now, just tell me what it is you came to say!" Garreth said, his fists clenched on his desk. Another wave of vertigo, stronger this time, hit him, and he grabbed onto the arms of his chair to steady himself. *I must be more tired than I thought,* he mused. "By the Fates! Just tell me, son. Are the soldiers' lives in jeopardy?"

Terrick crossed his arms, looked down at his father, and shook his head. "No. Their lives aren't." Then a dark sneer crept across his face. "But yours is."

The king looked down at his glass, and then at Terrick's, reality crashing in on him. "You—poisoned me? Your own father? But, how? We both drank from that same decanter!"

Terrick took a moment to smooth back a loose hair from his temple. "I took the antidote last night, its potency good for quite some time, you see. I arranged to have your nectar especially prepared and delivered here last night while you were in the war room." He let out his mad dog growl of a chuckle. "I am finally going to have what I want, Father. The throne!"

Garreth felt his arms and legs going numb and heavy. His thoughts were becoming hard to organize, and it was getting harder to speak above a whisper, so he couldn't call for help. "Why, Son? Your mother and I tried to give you every opportunity. Wait!" Panic pushed through the thickening fog in his brain. "What have you done to your mother? Have you hurt her? What about Dayel and Elswyth?" Somewhere in the back of his mind, he remembered Samésh was listening. At least he hoped he was. "*If you can hear my thoughts, Samésh, stay where you are! I will continue to shield you as long as I can.*"

"Mother?" Terrick asked. "Oh, she'll be fine. I won't—I can't hurt her." For the briefest of moments, Terrick's face softened at the mention of his mother, and then his features hardened. "However, she *will* have a permanent home in the tower after today. It's where she will live out her days. Don't worry. I'll make sure she has everything she needs, except her freedom, of course. And as for Dayel and the halfling they will be blamed for your murder and executed. So, I guess by now you've figured out who will be left to rule, haven't you, Father dear? Me. I will be king! Finally. I. Will. Be. King!" He pounded his chest with his fist for emphasis. "I'll have what I am due! And fear not," he said dramatically, "I promise I will be the king Glenorim needs, a king with a firmer hand, one that will make Glenorim pure Elven again. Oh, and then I plan to conquer the humans."

Terrick stepped close to the desk, leaned over and braced himself on his fists. "And Father, you know that information I needed to tell you about the Kratens? There are no Kratens on their way to Belnoir." Terrick cackled as if he had just told a joke. He watched Garreth's confused expression with apparent joy. "Their wall is as secure as it ever was. You see, I needed to get as many of your loyalist soldiers out of Glenorim for all this to work. I simply had one of my men infiltrate your intelligence team and plant the lie. He was very convincing. Wouldn't you agree? Then I simply entered the minds of your court officials and war cabinet to make sure they believed the threat was real. And would you believe it? They feasted on their fears! I've gotten very good at convincing elves to believe their worst scenarios. It is a handy ability, as it turns out."

Terrick tapped his temple lightly. "Oh, and I almost forgot! What's his name? The one you sent as a messenger?"

"Jarrin," Garreth said weakly. He closed his eyes, guessing at what Terrick was going to say.

"Ah, yes. Him. Your dispatch to the king of Kerridin never made it, Father. Actually, neither did Jarrin. Or his horse, for that matter."

"He and his wife were expecting their first elfling!"

"Well, she can take comfort in knowing it will live in a pure Elven kingdom, then," Terrick replied, nonplused.

Garreth trembled and tried to point at Terrick, but his hand only dropped to his lap. "When the army comes back from Belnoir, they will throw you from the throne. You will not be king!" A small bit of drool dribbled from his mouth. His time was running out, and he knew it.

"I beg to differ, Father. Remember, I said they will be told that Dayel and the halfling conspired to murder you. Only you and I know that's not true, of course. And when you're gone, which I imagine shouldn't be too long by the looks of you, they will have to bow to me as heir to the throne."

The struggle to talk was getting more difficult, but Garreth still tried, his speech slurring. "Why? We tried to give you everything you ever needed, both you and your brother."

Terrick's eyes flared. "Don't talk to me about my innocent, favored brother! He could do no wrong! It all came easy to him, didn't it? He was the dutiful son who excelled at all he did. Damn the Fates, everyone loved him. I loved him—until I felt less than him. And then he sired a halfling and brought her here—*with no consequences*! I hate him!"

Garreth shook his head, the effort making him dizzy again. "You were loved, too. If ever there was a time you did not feel that—then I am sorry. But we loved you. I loved you." Garreth's vision was tunneling. "Please don't harm your mother," he whispered, tears in his eyes. "Please don't hurt any of them." He sighed deeply, tears running down his face. "I'm sorry, we failed you, son. I'm sorry I failed you."

Terrick looked uncomfortable and hesitated, then turned away. "I don't need to hear any more. I'll leave you to your last moments. As soon as someone finds you later, I'm assuming it will be Mother, then my reign will begin. Goodbye, *Father.*" Terrick turned and paused at the door, his back to his father. He reached into his coat and pulled out a leather pouch and dropped it on the floor. Then he opened the door and left the room.

Garreth could hear Terrick talking with the guard outside his open door. "My father isn't to be disturbed. He said he has a lot of work to do and doesn't want to be bothered until dinner." The door then clicked shut.

Samésh burst from the servant's door and knelt next to his king. "No! No! Please, no!" he wept, his floppy ears trembled with every sob. He took the king's hand in his own. "I'm so, so sorry, Your Majesty!"

Garreth seemed desperate to speak, but could barely manage above a whisper. Still holding his beloved king's hand, Samésh leaned his ear close to Garreth's lips so he could hear his faint words. When his king stopped talking, or at least when it appeared he could no longer manage it, Samésh sat back and spoke tenderly. "Yes! I promise, Your Majesty. I will do everything you ask," he said.

Looking into his servant's eyes, Garreth tried to speak one last time, "Thank you, faithful Samésh. May the Fates—" His words stopped and the light in his eyes began to fade.

Samésh smiled at him through his tears and he tightened his grip on Garreth's hand. "Thank you, Your Majesty. It has been my honor to serve you. May the Fates welcome you home." Samésh kept eye contact as he felt the king's protective shield slowly evaporate. Then he couldn't feel it all. He let go of Garreth's hand, gently closed his eyelids, and bowed his head.

The king was dead.

FIFTY-EIGHT

S weets's kitchen had become a welcome respite for Elswyth, especially after all that had happened in the last twenty-four hours. Everyone in Glenorim was on edge since the soldiers left yesterday morning and afraid of what could happen with the Kratens. So many had to say goodbye to a loved one who marched north with the army.

Elswyth had glamoured her hair a dark brown, and completed her disguise to include pointed ears. Pic helped Cicero with a new look, but he, however, wasn't happy because Pic had insisted he go as a parrot for a change. In the end, he relented and agreed to the look, but made it clear he preferred his usual boring black. Elswyth's only guard, Lieutenant Kara, even changed her look to be on the safe side. Her other guard went north with the army yesterday, and they had not assigned another soldier to replace him yet.

"Are you sure you wouldn't all like to stay for dinner?" Sweets asked, then added in her best tempting tone, "We're having goat cheese stuffed dates, baked yams and a salad. Of course, your guard is more than welcome, too. We've got plenty for everyone," she smiled at Lieutenant Kara, standing off to the side.

Elswyth considered the offer, but decided against it. *"As much as I'd loved to, and I know Cis would, we should go back to the castle. With everything that's going on, my place is with my grandparents and father tonight."* It still sounded strange to say that she was part of the royal family. She'd always imagined her life centered on their safe little cottage in Willow Grove with Agnes and Cicero. It was a cocoon that separated her from the cruelty of the world where she had no battles to fight—because Agnes fought her battles for her. But so much had changed. *"Pic, why don't you stay here for the night? I really don't mind. After all, I won't be able to spend much time with you anyway until we know more about what's going on in Belnoir."*

Dilly perked up and folded her hands together. *"Oh, please do, Pic!"* Dilly said. *"We'd love the company right now. Wouldn't we mother? Besides, elves are staying close to home, so there aren't as many customers and we're going to close early."* Her eyes pleaded with Pic.

"We would love you to stay," Sweets said.

Pic glanced at Elswyth with raised eyebrows. "Are you sure you don't need me?"

Elswyth shook her head. *"You should stay, Pic. I'm sure they're worried about Baylin. I know you are, too, so it would be good for you all to be together. Cis and I will be fine. We'll keep our glamour on until we get back up to the castle, and we'll have Lieutenant Kara with us. I'll see you sometime tomorrow."*

"Okay. I'd love to stay tonight then!" Pic said. Sweets and Dilly broke out into relieved smiles.

Screams and crying erupted from the restaurant, and everyone jumped in shock.

"By the Fates! What is going on out there?" Sweets asked.

They sprang from the table and exchanged frightened looks. Had something happened to their soldiers? Had the Kratens invaded Glenorim? Elswyth's guard immediately stepped in front of her, and Cicero flew to her arm as they ran out to the cafe dining room.

It was pandemonium in the cafe as elves shoved tables, chairs, and each other, in a rush to get out the door. They were shouting something about banners hanging from the castle walls. Once outside in the street, the hysteria was worse as everyone pointed excitedly up at the castle. Some wept or screamed, a few had even fainted on the cobbles. Elswyth's guard stood next to her, staring upwards, her jaw set and fist clenched, white-knuckled, around the hilt of her sword. Sweets knelt on the ground, her hand covering her mouth and her eyes staring upwards.

"Pic! What is happening? Please tell me what's wrong?" Elswyth thought to her, panicked and clutching Cicero. Pic only stared up at the castle with everyone else and shook her head.

Almost every window in the castle had a long purple and gold banner hanging from it. They were the court colors and Elswyth had seen them before, but each of these had an added black stripe across the golden wyvern. She grabbed Pic's arm. *"PIC! Please! What's happened? What do the banners mean?"* But in her terrified heart, she knew—and she just couldn't bring herself to say the words.

Pic turned to Elswyth, her face pale. "It's your grandfather, Elly. King Garreth. He—he's dead. The single black band on a banner means the king has died."

Elswyth snapped her hand from Pic's arm as if she'd been burned. *"What? That can't be! How? He was fine earlier. Cis! We have to get back up there!"*

Cicero's colorful feathers puffed out, and he shook in her arms. "Yes, we do! We need to find out what's happened and get to the queen, Elly. She must be devastated! And your father, he's going to need us!" He had to shout over the cries of the surrounding crowd.

Elswyth took a step forward, but Lieutenant Kara put a light hand on her shoulder and pointed ahead. "There are soldiers coming, Your Highness," she said into Elswyth's ear. "Maybe they can give us some answers so let's see what they have to say." She stepped in front of Elswyth and Cicero, blocking them from the oncoming soldier's view. "Sergeant! I am Lieutenant Kara. What's happened?" she demanded.

"I would think it obvious, Lieutenant," the sergeant answered as he pointed at the banners above, his rude attitude not hard to miss.

"Mind who you're talking, Sergeant! *How* was the king killed?"

The sergeant snapped to attention. "Yes, Lieutenant. Begging your pardon. He was poisoned."

"Poisoned? Do they know who did it? When did this happen?" the lieutenant asked. Without looking back, she sent thoughts to both Elswyth and Cicero, *"Steady, Your Highness. Stay behind me. And whatever you do, be sure you and Sir Cicero keep your shields up."*

The sergeant continued, the elves nearby now paying attention. "The way I was told, Her Majesty went to fetch the king for dinner and found him dead in his study. She was so overcome that a court healer had to tend to her. Anyway, it appears to be the work of Prince Dayel's halfling daughter. Stands to reason that as a healer it would be her, since she is familiar with poisons and all. And, between you and me, it seems like something a halfling would stoop to! You can't trust 'em. Besides, one of my elves found what looks to be her healer's pouch on the floor in the king's study. She must have dropped it."

Elswyth's skin crawled with the realization that someone had to have taken that from her apartment while she was out. She hadn't even noticed it missing. Cicero growled under his breath.

The sergeant scratched his head. "We think maybe she somehow tricked or drugged his guards to gain access to the room because they don't remember seeing her. Wouldn't put it past her. Prince Dayel and his regent are already in the dungeon, and the queen is locked in the tower. We haven't found the prince's complement yet, but he isn't our priority. We're focusing on the halfling princess right now."

"Why were the prince and queen imprisoned? Surely Prince Terrick doesn't believe they had anything to do with this?" the lieutenant asked.

"It's *King* Terrick now, Lieutenant, and he declared the queen and prince complicit in the king's death," he said, shrugging his shoulders. "So, there you have it."

"This is terrible!"

The sergeant snorted. "Well, the halfling is his daughter and he brought her here. From what I've been told, the queen knew about her, too." He pointed to one of his soldiers hammering a poster to the wall. "My elves are posting these wanted placards about the princess. She wasn't in the castle when we searched, but we understand she and her complement spend a lot of time in the city. They've got to be around here somewhere. Tell everyone to keep an eye out and let us know if you see her—or her mangy crow, for that matter."

Elswyth felt Cicero stiffen in her arms. "That ignorant peon! I am a RAVEN, not a crow! And I am most certainly not mangy!" Cicero hissed. She put her hand on his back to calm him.

"Shush, Cis. You're glamoured as a parrot for now, so they won't recognize you. Please keep quiet. We can't call attention to ourselves," she pleaded.

Before she could stop him, he took off, hovered just over the sergeant's head, and squawked like the parrot he was supposed to be. "Awk! Ugly, stupid elf. Really ugly, stupid elf! Awk!" Then he flew up to the roof of It's A Date Cafe.

The sergeant scowled up at Cicero. "I hate birds!" he said under his breath and turned to leave. "We have to get moving. There are a lot of these posters to put up. Remember, if you see her, tell us!"

"Yes, of course. We will," the lieutenant said. She watched the sergeant stomp down the street with his soldiers. The crowd pressed in close to the poster to read it and disbelief, anger, and confusion spread like a wildfire through the mob. Lieutenant Kara turned and herded Elswyth, Pic, Sweets, and Dilly back into the restaurant. Cicero flew in before they locked the door behind them.

Once inside, the stillness in the cafe was deafening, and everyone stood in stunned in the silence. Tables and chairs were helter-skelter across the dining room floor, and plates and cups lay broken or turned upside down everywhere. Discarded and crumpled napkins soaked up liquid and food. Dilly started picking up chairs, tears running down her face. Pic went to her, held her, and helped her to sit down, and Sweets joined them. Everyone stared into space with shocked, blank looks on their faces while the lieutenant walked around the dining room, making sure windows were locked and shades were lowered.

Elswyth wanted nothing more than to weep, to give in to fear, to anger, especially anger. Instead, from somewhere deep inside, she felt strength boiling up as she reached into the folds of her cloak to feel the hilt of her sword, and tightened her grip on it. *"This was Terrick's doing,"* she said to Cicero, seething. *"And I will not let him get away with this. I will not cower any longer."*

Fifty-Nine

Elswyth felt as if she was moving through a fog and detached from reality. Her grandfather was dead? Her father and grandmother imprisoned? How could this be real? She looked around the restaurant at everyone's shocked faces, the aftermath of the chaos in the room, and wasn't sure what to say or what to do. How was she ever going to help her father and grandmother?

Still teary eyed, but ever the mother, Sweets stood up and announced that everyone needed to eat—and right now. Sweets reminded Elswyth of Agnes at the moment because, whatever the trouble, Agnes's way of getting her head straight was to cook and there was no arguing with her. She cooked, and you ate.

When the objections started around the room, Sweets simply herded them all into the kitchen, and gave everyone, even the lieutenant, a hug. "All right, we've had terrible news today. The very worst," she said, choking up and dried her eyes with her apron. "But we can't just sit here doing nothing! We have to figure out what to do next and we are going to do that on a full stomach," she announced. "Besides, busy hands help make for a clear mind, so let's get on with it." Everyone was assigned a station and a task, and soon dinner was on its way.

"Sweets, how is a full stomach going to help?" Pic asked, holding up a yam.

"Well, it can't hurt. Can it?" Sweets answered firmly. "Now, you just get to scrubbing, Pic." Her tone was loving, but Sweets meant business, so Pic started cleaning the potatoes in earnest.

At least it's doing something, Elswyth thought. As Sweets had said, the work helped to clear her mind at least a little.

They ate their meal in silence, each of them focused on their plates. After dinner, Sweets once again gave everyone a task, and they cleaned up the dishes, pots, and pans. Dilly set a kettle on the stove as the last clean plate was put back on the shelf.

The mood around the table was somber as Elswyth watched Lieutenant Kara stationed near the door to the cafe. *"Lieutenant, what can we do?"* she asked. *"Is there any way to get to my father and grandmother? I have to do something!"* Everyone looked expectantly at the guard.

"Your Highness," she said, shaking her head slowly. "My primary duty right now is to keep you safe. Not only do I know you would never have done this horrible act of treason, but you were nowhere near the king today. You were with me and everyone else here. We have to find someone we trust to get to the truth, but if you go anywhere near the castle right now, if you're caught, Terrick will throw you in the dungeon, and if that happens, there will be no chance to prove yourself. If we want to help the queen and Prince Dayel—and if I am to keep you safe—we need time to figure out what to do and who to trust. So, my priority is to get you to a safe place. Then we can move forward."

"But how long will I have to hide? They need me now!"

Cicero spoke up. "Elly, Lieutenant Kara is right. We can't just go running back to the castle!"

Pic nodded. "They're right, Elly. As much as we all want to help, you getting thrown into the dungeon, too, would get us nowhere."

Sweets and Dilly looked at each other and said together, "We have the perfect place to hide you!"

Lieutenant Kara stepped next to the table. "Where?"

BANG! BANG! BANG! The noise jolted everyone from their seats. Lieutenant Kara quickly peeked out into the restaurant. "Soldiers are breaking down your front door, Sweets!"

Running for the cafe dining room, Sweets called back to Dilly, "You know what to do, Dilly! Hurry! I don't know if I can hold them off!" She ran out to the cafe just as the front door frame exploded into hundreds of pieces. The door slammed to the floor only inches from her feet, barely missing her as she stumbled backwards. When the dust cleared, she saw an angry soldier outside holding a battering ram, then the sergeant they saw earlier stepped into the restaurant, grinding his teeth, his veins pulsing in his forehead.

"We have reason to believe the halfling princess is here!" he barked.

Sweets shook her head. "There is no one here but my daughter, Dilly, and me!"

"You're lying! I have it on good advice the princess comes here to visit. Since we can't find her anywhere else, I think she is hiding out in your establishment," he said, jabbing his finger into her shoulder. "As a matter of fact, I'd be willing to bet your worthless halfling skin she is! You would be guilty of treason if we find her, you know." His eyes roamed around the room.

"I promise you she isn't here!" Sweets stuck out her chin and tried to stop herself from trembling. "Wait a moment! I remember you. Aren't you Fareth? You proposed to your wife right here in our restaurant. What was her name?" She tapped her forehead, trying to remember. "Larna! That's her name! It was such a lovely proposal, too! You asked me to arrange for a troubadour to sing for her and I gave you an extra box of candy to take home with you. Don't you remember?"

A moment of recognition passed over his face, but as quickly as it appeared, it was gone. "Quiet! That's enough out of you! Hold her here, soldier. See that this halfling stays put." The sergeant pushed past Sweets as a soldier slapped a set of cuffs on her wrists, her Majik sapped from her body. She could hear the rest of the soldiers ransacking the kitchen and then someone shouted, "Check that door back there, elves!" They were invading her apartment behind the kitchen.

"Dilly? Baby, are you okay?" She called out to her daughter, panicking. "Please don't hurt my daughter!" she cried. "Dilly!"

Dilly sent the thought to her mother, *"Mom! Mom, I'm fine. They are breaking everything in here, though. They're looking for Elly. I got them safely away just in time."* Sweets could hear more things breaking and crashing in the kitchen and then, *"OW! Stop! You're hurting me!"*

"Dilly? Dilly? I swear, by the Fates, if you've harmed my daughter—"

The sergeant came back out to the restaurant with his soldiers, two of them flanking Dilly, gripping her arms tight and her wrists cuffed. "Well, they aren't here." He said grumbling. "But they could show up, so I am going to leave some of you miserable elves here overnight," he growled. He pointed at Sweets and Dilly. "Say goodbye to your place. You two are coming with us."

"But—but why? You didn't find them!" Sweets said.

"Well, we were going to be rounding up halflings soon, anyway, so why not start a little early with you two!" He grinned at her.

"I don't understand. What have we done?" She looked at Dilly's stricken face and her heart twisted with fear for her daughter. "At least let her stay!"

"What do you mean, what have you done? You're halflings. That's enough. King Terrick is going to order *all* halflings rounded up, but I wouldn't worry too much about the dungeons if I were you," he said. "You both got cooking skills, so you'll probably get work in his kitchens—if you're lucky." He smirked, his face an ugly mask of prejudice. "Take them away. These two won't be using their kitchen anymore." Then he pointed out several soldiers. "You three. Stay here in case the princess shows up. And before you ask, yes, you can eat or drink whatever you find, but stay sober and vigilant! "

The soldiers shoved Sweets and Dilly out into the dark street. With each building they passed along the cobblestones, window shades went down and shutters snapped shut.

SIXTY

Elswyth, Cicero, Pic, and Lieutenant Kara stood below the kitchen in the dark, shields raised, fearing if they used their Majik's glow, they would be visible through the floorboards above. Pic sniffled in the dark when the soldiers kidnapped Sweets and Dilly, and Elswyth tried to send her encouragement. *"We'll find them, Pic. We'll find them and get them to safety. I promise!"* She didn't know if she could actually keep that promise, but she was going to do everything in her power to do just that.

Heavy boots stomped around in the kitchen overhead as the three soldiers raided the shelves for food and drink. "Aha! Look what I found! Nectar!" soldier one said.

"Now you're talking! Hey, that's the good stuff, too! You know, that apartment looked pretty comfortable. Why don't we take the food and nectar in there and have us a feast? We've worked hard all afternoon looking for that stupid halfling," soldier two replied.

"You're right. We deserve some rest and relaxation!"

Soldier three sounded young and his voice shook. "Um. I don't know about this. The sergeant said we should be watching for the princess and if he finds out we're drinking on the job, we could get in trouble!"

"Come on, young 'un. How is he gonna find out? You gonna tell him?" soldier one asked. "I wouldn't do that if I were you." That last remark sounded like a warning.

"Don't be a whiny elfling. Grab that other bottle and let's go," soldier two said. Their steps moved across the floor as the soldiers took their stash into the apartment. The door closed and everyone below let out a cautious sigh of relief.

Finally safe to use their Majik to light the space, Elswyth brought her palm up first, keeping her light just bright enough to see in front of her, where she saw Cicero back in his raven form. Pic and Lieutenant Kara lit their Majiks as well, revealing they were in a large storage area under the kitchen. Shelves lined the walls with jars of canned fruits, bags of flour, baskets with onions, and boxes full of potatoes. Spices and oils from far-away lands, some in fancy, exotic bottles, sat in neat rows. When Dilly sent them down there, she'd had just enough time to glamour the trap door to appear as regular floor boards, so from the kitchen above, no one would know there was anything below them.

"Pic, did you know this was down here?" Cicero asked, keeping his voice low.

"Yes, I've forgotten all about it, though. Dilly and I used to play down here when we were elflings, but that was a long time ago."

"Well, we can't stay down here forever, and the streets are going to be crawling with Terrick's soldiers. We've got to think of something." Elswyth said. She walked around just to keep moving and organize her thoughts, but stopped short at the far end of the long room. *"Hey! Could you two bring your lights back here? I found a door behind this shelf unit! Help me get all this out of the way."* She started moving things off to one side.

Pic shook her head and stepped back. "Elly, I remember that door and we can't get out that way. Sweets used to warn us to stay away from it when we were little. It's sealed with Majik all around the edges, but more importantly, it has all those iron bars mounted across the front of it! The shelves were moved there so no one can get close to the iron. We're going to have to wait until the soldiers leave, then go back up and out through the restaurant."

Elswyth moved close to the door and saw that the stone wall had literally grown over the wooden edges of the door and she realized someone had used powerful Majik to seal it that way. More importantly, ten heavy, rusted iron bars mounted horizontally across the front of the door, their ends disappearing into the rock, barred the way through to the wood. No elf could touch iron. It was poisonous to them.

Elswyth considered her options. *I've touched iron plenty of times back home. That was before my Awakening, though. Would it make a difference? Did that make my Elven half susceptible to iron now? There's only one way to find out. Besides, what do I have to lose at this point?* Elswyth reached out and grabbed a bar.

Pic gasped and whispered, "Elly, no!"

Cicero flew over to land next to her. "Elly?"

Lieutenant Kara rushed to grab her arm—too late.

Elswyth's hand firmly gripped the bar and everyone collectively held their breath, waiting to see if the metal had any effect on her. She turned halfway around, her hand still wrapped around the rusted metal, then smiled. *"I'm okay! Look! The iron doesn't affect me. I can get us out of here!"*

The lieutenant breathed out a long sigh of relief. "Your Highness. I ask you, please warn me the next time you plan to do something dangerous!"

"Would you have tried to stop me?" When she didn't get an answer, she said, *"That's what I thought. Back up, everyone, I'm going to melt the ends of the bars and remove them. Then we can cut an opening in the wood and get out of here."*

"But we don't know what's behind that door! It was probably sealed for a reason." Cicero said.

"Right now, I'd rather take my chances with what's beyond that door than go back upstairs. At least this way, we have a chance of getting away and fighting Terrick. Pic, you once told me the mountain is laced with tunnels. Maybe this will lead us someplace safe for now. I'm willing to take that chance. Anyone else

feel the same way?" When she got no objections, she turned back to the door and stepped back.

Reaching her palm out, she sent a focused, narrow stream of energy to one side of each of the lower five bars until they melted and separated from the rock. She cooled them with Majik and then moved sacks of grain below them on the floor. Then she heated the other end of the bars until they began to melt and drop, one by one, quietly onto the sacks. Once the iron pieces were safely off to the side, she turned to the wooden door, ready to cut a hole through it, but using raw Majik on the iron bars had sapped some of her energy, and she had to lean against the wall to recover.

"I'll do this part, Elly," Pic whispered next to her.

The Lieutenant guided Elswyth off to one side while they watched Pic use her energy to cut away the lower boards in the door. "Your Highness, it was incredibly brave to grab the iron, but it could have gone the other way. Halflings here are just as susceptible to iron's poison as full-bloods. I don't know why you weren't affected. Perhaps living so long with the humans made you immune? Either way, I just wanted you to know that I am proud to serve you."

"Thank you, Lieutenant. I am honored to have you by my side. Our side."

Since removing the wood was quick work, Pic only needed a few moments to recover her energy and there was now a way of escape. As quietly as they could, they cleaned up any mess they had made, and Elswyth hid the iron bars under the sacks in a corner. Then they pulled the shelves close to the opening.

Lieutenant Kara crawled in through the hole they made to see what the tunnel was like. She came back out to report. "Well, I know why the entrance was sealed. The rock walls are being held up by beams, but only just! There is crumbling rock everywhere and some beams are down on the ground. It looks to be a very old tunnel. The ceilings are also pretty low, so we'll have to be cautious." She shrugged her shoulders. "It's either the tunnel, or Terrick's soldiers in the streets. I think if we're quiet and careful, this is the only way to go. Everyone good with that?"

Cicero groaned. "Of course, it's ancient and dangerous. We couldn't possibly have discovered a brand new, well-lit tunnel, could we?"

"I say, let's go!" Pic said as she stepped closer to the opening.

Cicero shook his head. "Pic, what is it with you and your obsession to happily plunge headlong into scary passageways?"

Pic put her arm out for him to land on and grinned. "My dear Sir Cicero. I'm not afraid because you're here with me."

Cicero hopped on her forearm and cocked his head at her. "As Agnes once told me, flattery will get you nowhere." But he chuckled anyway.

Elswyth drew her sword and stepped forward, ready to crouch into the hole, but her guard put a hand out to block her. "Me first, Your Highness. And, Pic? I suggest you pull the shelves in front of the hole when you exit. It will at least hide what we've done here in case someone discovers the storage room later," Lieutenant Kara said.

"Good idea. I'll take care of it!" Pic pulled the shelves snug against the wall after she went in.

The storage room was once again dark and still. The only living thing left was a lone mouse that scurried across the floor.

Elswyth discovered they had to duck more than expected once inside. Not only were the ceilings low, but the many heavy, wooden beams holding up the stone ceiling looked rotted and cracked, a breath away from collapsing on their heads. The blue light of their Majiks cast sharp, angry shadows on the jagged, crumbling walls, and every few feet, they encountered piles of rock that had slipped off the sides of the tunnel. With each step, gravel crunched beneath their feet and Elswyth hoped, besides everything else, the sound wasn't traveling to unseen vents or doorways, giving them away. Her senses were on high alert, her sword, like her guard's, drawn and ready. She looked down at Cicero, who hopped along on the ground between her and the lieutenant ahead.

"How are you doing, my brave, Sir Cis?" Elswyth asked.

"I'll just be glad when we're out of this blasted, not bird-friendly, tunnel!" His voice was barely above a whisper.

The ground trembled, the walls cracked, and the wooden beams above them groaned. Falling rocks from somewhere in the tunnel echoed against the walls. Everyone froze and covered their heads as they looked up, expecting the worst.

When the quakes and echoes died away, they moved forward, this time even more cautiously than before. Elswyth's back was cramping from walking hunched over and it didn't help that every few minutes, they could hear more stones falling from the walls and ceilings. She had to constantly remind herself to breathe normally, but claustrophobia was threatening to suffocate her.

Lieutenant Kara's hand shot up, and they stopped, rooted to the ground. She looked over her shoulder, put her hand to her ear and sent the thought to them, *"Shh! I hear voices that don't sound too far ahead. I'm going to go see what I can find out."*

Cicero hopped past her. "I'll go! I'm small and don't make as much noise as you do on the gravel," he said. Then he disappeared into the darkness ahead. No one moved, waiting—then they heard Cicero cry out.

"By the Fates! I don't believe it!" Cicero's voice echoed from somewhere up ahead.

Elswyth ran past her guard. *"Cis! What's happened?"* Holding her sword straight out in front of her and still crouched low, she ran ahead as fast as she could. *"Cis! I'm coming!"* She could hear Pic and Kara running behind her, but something else began to drum out the sound of their steps.

"Stop! You're crushing me!" Cicero's words bounced off the walls just loud enough to be heard over the rumbling in the tunnel.

Chunks of rock, big and small, began falling off the walls and ceiling, the shaking gravel floor making it harder to run. Elswyth looked over her shoulder, torn between helping everyone behind her or Cicero. As she rushed around a corner, she saw a light coming from a doorway ahead and she pushed herself to run faster, just missing a beam that crashed to the ground.

"Run!" Lieutenant Kara yelled.

"Go, Elly! We're right behind you!" Pic cried out. The closer Elswyth got, the faster her heart beat. *Please let me get there in time! Please let us all get out of here!* A rock shard fell from the ceiling, hit her forehead and blood dripped down her temple. Her lungs hurt from sucking in all the gritty dust in the tunnel, but she pushed herself to speed up.

Elswyth burst through the door, stopped, and stared. *"Cis?"* Before she could utter another word, she landed hard on the ground as Pic and the lieutenant tumbled in on top of her. Behind them, the ceiling in the tunnel was collapsing, sending a cloud of dust and grit into the room they were in. Lieutenant Kara jumped up and shut the door just as rock and debris slammed against it. And then—silence.

Pic and Elswyth lay in a tangle on the ground, stunned and swatting dust from their faces and clothes. The lieutenant leaned against the back of the door, looked around the room, and then smiled. They were in a large, round space, the stuccoed walls painted with a floor to ceiling faded fresco that stretched the entire circumference. The artwork looked ancient and depicted elves and humans trading goods, its paint peeling off in places. Six lanterns hung from the ceiling, all brightly lit by Majik. Evenly space along the walls were wooden doors, some opened and some closed, each with a unique symbol carved into its surface. What caught their attention, though, was in the middle of the room.

Samésh was standing on a stack of books, dumbstruck and staring at them, as he leaned over a massive wooden table piled high with scrolls, paper, books, pens, and bottles of ink. Ratheus was on the other side of the table—hugging Cicero.

"Are you all right? Hey, look who's here," Cicero said, his wing on the bear's shoulder.

SIXTY-ONE

Elswyth got up, adjusted her dress and sword, then touched her forehead where the rock had hit her, wincing in pain. As she pulled her hand away from her head, blood dripped from her fingertip. Pic rushed over, retrieved a handkerchief from her cloak and pressed it against the cut to stop the bleeding. While Pic's healing glow ministered to the wound, Elswyth put her hands on her hips and eyed Cicero.

"Cis! I thought you were in trouble! I almost broke my neck getting here!" While her heart was still pounding in her chest, she was relieved to see him safe. *"We almost died in there! Ow!"* She flinched as Pic added an ointment to her head.

Pic patted Elswyth's shoulder. "Almost done, Elly. The ointment will keep you from getting a scar. Just need to add the energy to it now and you'll be fine."

Cicero lowered his head. "Sorry, Elly. Are you all right? But look who's here! It's Samésh and Rathe! They have maps of the castle and underground passages and, even better, Samésh said he has a plan!" Cicero said. Ratheus raised one of his huge paws in greeting, while Samésh bowed to Elswyth.

Still brushing the dirt from the tunnel off their clothes, Elswyth, Pic, and Lieutenant Kara moved to the large round table, piles of maps, parchments, and books spread across its surface. *"A plan? Where did all this come from? How did you two get here? And where exactly is here?"* Elswyth asked.

Samésh spoke up first, "I was with his Majesty when he died and—" His voice cracked and he looked down at the table, unable to go on.

Ratheus shuffled from the opposite side of the table, closer to Samésh, and laid one of his enormous paws on his shoulder. "It's okay. Take your time," Ratheus said, his voice rumbled kindly. "Just tell them what you told me and then we can all work together on this—for His Majesty, the queen, and Prince Dayel."

Samésh straightened and smiled at Ratheus. "Thank you, friend. I'm all right now," he said. Then he recounted it all to them: Terrick kidnapping Justa, her death, the exchange between Garreth and Terrick in his study, Terrick admitting there was no threat from the Kratens, and finally, Terrick poisoning his own father. He told them everything. "Before he died, the king gave me instructions to carry out and now that you're all here, you can help."

Elswyth stood, processing all she had just heard, her fury matched by a fierce determination to find Terrick and make him pay, to defend her new family, her second home here in Glenorim, and, now that she knew Terrick's plans beyond Glenorim, to defend her human home. She wanted justice for everyone he'd harmed or planned to and was tired of tyrants that belittled others and stole peace from the world.

"Elly? Are you okay?" Cicero asked.

Pic moved next to Elswyth and only had to look in her eyes to see the fire behind them. "We are in this together, Elly. Let's hear what else Samésh has to say."

Under Ratheus's direction, they began to arrange everything on the table in piles. "As soon as we get all this in order," Samésh said. "I'll be better able to see exactly what it is the king asked me to do."

"Samésh, how did you get all this down here? Did you know about all these tunnels?"

"Ratheus and I got everything down here together. He's the curator of your father's study. All those historical maps, books, and research papers?

They're catalogued and organized by him." He inclined his head at Ratheus. "Thankfully, he is a meticulous keeper of all that knowledge! I believe we got all we needed and then some. It took us a quite few trips, and we had to dodge a lot of Terrick's elves, but we were able to do as the king asked and got everything down here."

Elswyth's mouth hung open. *"You're the one who takes care of all that in my father's study? I'm impressed, Ratheus! Cis, why didn't you tell me that?"*

"Because you didn't ask?" He shrugged his wings. "Rathe is a pretty smart bear, Elly!"

"Apparently so!"

Ratheus laughed. "Don't act so surprised! Prince Dayel and I share a passion for history. I've been the curator of the collection for a long time. King Garreth had it for many years and gifted it to Dayel on his sixteenth birthday."

"Sorry! I didn't mean to insult you! It's just that you're always so reserved. Well, except, of course, on the dance floor. You're obviously a complement of many talents."

"Ah, yes. My second passion. Dancing!" he said, his back end swaying.

Samésh stood back from the table and spread his hands out over the neat piles. "I think I have everything here we need. First things first, King Garreth told me to find Ratheus because he'd know all about the tunnels and caverns and be able to tell me the safest places for everyone to hide down here. Then he wanted us to gather as many maps and scrolls as we could because we would need them for the plan to work." He pointed to several stacks of book off to the side of the table. "Those books cover the history of the kingdom and we won't need them."

"Couldn't you have left them? That must have taken precious time!" Elswyth asked.

Samésh placed his hand on a stack. "King Garreth said it was vital that I rescued these. He was afraid Terrick might destroy them. He wanted this done, and so I did as he asked."

Elswyth felt a growing respect for how this elf, who she had once thought of as meek and subservient, was now taking charge. Her grandfather would be so very proud of him.

"Once we gathered everything," he continued, looking at Elswyth, "I was supposed to find you, your father and grandmother, tell them what happened, and get you all down here to safety." He shook his head, his brows furrowed. "By the time Ratheus and I finished collecting all we needed, though, the queen and prince had already been arrested and we couldn't find you." He sighed, unrolled a large parchment, and pointed to the center of an intricate map. "This is where we are right now. It's one of many hubs that connect the tunnels under Glenorim and the mountain. See the symbols on the map key? They correspond to the ones you see on the doors. They mark the way to specific locations inside and outside the kingdom. Some of these tunnels have long since collapsed or are simply now forgotten and most of the older, more dangerous ones were sealed for safety reasons. Even the newer ones are over three thousand years old. Most elves don't even know about them anymore. I will caution you now," he looked up at everyone, his face stern, "without these maps, you could get lost in a maze of passageways."

"How does all that help, Samésh?" Elswyth was impatient to do something. Anything.

"I'm getting there, Your Highness," he answered with respect. "Your grandfather had a plan to defeat Terrick. Now that Her Majesty and Prince Dayel are in the dungeon, plans have changed. Ratheus and I were determined to carry on as best we could on our own, but now that you're here, it looks like it's up to all of us."

"We're ready, Samésh," Elswyth said. *"Just tell us what you need us to do."*

Everyone in the room crowded closer to the table.

SIXTY-TWO

E lswyth and Cicero had traveled for close to an hour through the dark tunnels, but according to the small map she'd copied in the hub, they were still on the right path. Many of the symbols painted on the walls had long since faded, so they counted the doors and forks along the way, compared them to their map, and double-checked their every step. The ceilings in this tunnel were also higher than the one from Sweets's storage basement, and the smooth, white tile on the walls reflected her light better, making it easier to see. All the twists and turns made it obvious, though, how someone could get lost, perhaps forever, by making a wrong turn. She was grateful for the map.

"How much longer do you think we need to go, Elly?" Cicero asked, hopping alongside her.

"Not much farther, I think," she said, holding the map up to her light again. "Cis, are you sure you want to do this? You know I'm going to worry about you."

"Yes, Elly. I have to do this and I'll be worried about you, too, you know. What you're doing is going to be more dangerous. Helping to hide halflings is a big job, even with three of you! I swear, if anything happens to you because of Terrick—" His voice rose with anger and he fluffed up his feathers

290

in agitation. Once he calmed down, he looked up at her. "You've come so far, Elly. From a mouse to a lioness! I'm so proud of you and I just want you to know that before I go."

"Thanks, Cis" Elswyth said. She didn't feel like a lioness, but she would take all the encouragement she could get.

Further down the passageway, the tunnel finally ended at a large, round wooden door in the wall. *"We're here! This is the door on the map, Cis!"* Elswyth set their map on the floor next to the wall and pulled on the handle. Nothing happened, so she placed her foot against the wall for leverage and pulled harder until it finally gave way, a little at a time, with a lot of dirt and pebbles raining down on them from outside. Once the dust settled, she could see out at the starlit night sky. She poked her head out the door, but the sheer drop to the bottom of the mountain made her retreat so fast she fell backwards onto the stone floor. *"This is definitely it,"* she said, brushing herself off. *"It's usually a two-day walk to Belnoir, Cis. Flying is obviously going to be faster, but I know you. You're going to fly without stopping. Don't push yourself to exhaustion. If you need to rest, please do, even if it's for a short time. Promise me. "*

Cicero hopped up on the threshold, looked out, and then turned back to Elswyth. "You're right. I do plan to fly until I reach them, Elly. Don't worry. I'll bring back both ours and the Belnoir army. Trust me."

She touched his gold band and smiled through her tears. *"I know you will, Sir Cicero The Brave Of The Royal House Of Glenorim. You know what? They are going to sing songs about you someday!"* She winked and tried to laugh a little.

"They better! And I'll deserve every one of those notes they sing," he said jokingly. He cleared his throat and glanced outside again. "Well, I guess I should go. Please be careful, Elly. I love you." His voice cracked as he turned and flew north into the moonlight.

Elswyth watched him grow smaller and smaller in the night sky. *"I love you, too, Cis. "*

As she reached over to shut the door, her map, still lying on the floor next to her, lifted in a swirling breeze that came through the doorway. She grabbed for it and missed, almost tumbling out and down the mountainside.

Elswyth watched in horror as the precious piece of parchment floated up and out beyond her reach.

Like Cis, it, too, disappeared into the night.

Lieutenant Kara and Ratheus made their way through a network of tunnels that led westward. They constantly had to consult their own hand-drawn map to keep from getting lost in the maze of passages, doorways, and steps built into the stone. Twice, piles of floor-to-ceiling rocks, that were once entryways, blocked their path, and they had to find other routes. Their progress had proven to be slower than they'd expected, which made them anxious about their mission.

Two and a half hours into their trek, they came upon a fork in the passageway. "Ratheus, this isn't on the map and I'm pretty sure we're lost," the lieutenant said. She acted calm, but Ratheus could hear the worry in her voice.

"Let me see that." Ratheus reached out for the map, studied it, and looked around at their surroundings. "Wait here. I'll be right back." He lumbered into the first tunnel, scratching the walls with his sharp claws and sniffing the air as he went. He disappeared into the inky black darkness of the tunnel.

Minutes passed. "Ratheus?" The lieutenant's voice only echoed back at her. She drew her sword and waited.

The bear finally emerged from the dark, shaking his head. "That wasn't the right tunnel. It should be this other one, but let me check it out first." He entered the second passageway the same way he did the first, marking the wall with his claws and sniffing the air. He was gone even longer this time but finally returned, nodding his head back to where he just came from. "This is it. I can smell vegetation from somewhere. It's faint, but I'm pretty sure I'm right."

"Pretty sure?" The lieutenant's eyebrows shot up.

"Yeah, pretty sure," Ratheus said.

"Okay then. That is good enough for me! Let's get going." She clapped a hand on his shoulder and they entered the tunnel.

Forty-five minutes later, they were once again able to recognize where they were on the map. "Told you," was all Ratheus had to say.

"Did I say I doubted you?"

Ratheus gave her a good-natured grin in answer.

"Okay. Maybe I worried a little, but I admit you were right." She smiled. "Having your nose along for the trip was definitely an asset and I'll never doubt you again!"

"Liar."

Finally, hours later, the lieutenant turned to Ratheus and pointed to the map. "If this is correct, the way out is up ahead!" she said. They rushed forward and entered a shallow cave that led to the outside. The entrance was covered with dead brush and vines and took a while to remove. Once the opening was free of detritus, they stepped out into the fresh air and tried to get their bearings.

"From the looks of it, dawn can't be too far off, so we need to get going!" Ratheus said. He put his nose in the air and sniffed the cool breeze in several directions while the lieutenant studied the stars. After one final sniff, Ratheus declared, "This way. Kerridin is this way."

"The Fates are with us," Kara said. "They gave us a clear night sky to navigate with."

"Who needs stars when you have a nose like mine?"

"It's not a contest, Ratheus. We can use both our strengths to get us there."

"You're right. It's not a contest, my friend, but if it was, I would win!" He snorted and laughed. "Before we leave, I think we should cover the entrance to the cave back up." The lieutenant nodded, and they dragged all the tree limbs, bushes, and leaves they had removed earlier and concealed the mouth of the cavern. When they were done, they were sure that no one passing by here could see the entrance.

Ratheus cocked his head at the lieutenant. "We spent longer than we thought we would in the tunnels and won't get there until tomorrow afternoon, and that's at the earliest by my calculations. How fast can you run? Do you think you can keep up with me, or do I need to carry you?"

She nodded westward and put her hands on her hips. "I'll have you know I outran everyone in my class at the academy and I *always* left them in the dust. Don't worry. I'll keep up. I may even beat you there, old bear," she said.

"Good elf!" he said. "We're off, then."

Pic and Samésh didn't have to travel as far as the others to reach their destination through the tunnels. Before them stood an enormous set of double doors, made of heavy oak, decorated with filigree gold, and Elven steel. Each door had a large gold "Z" mounted on it, and the entire area was in pristine and polished condition. Two brass lanterns hung on either side of the doors and as soon as they got near, the lanterns lit up. A chain hung on the wall to the left. Pic noticed another tunnel entrance to the right of the one they'd just come from and could smell a faint whiff of salt air wafting out of its entrance.

Samésh reached up and pulled the chain. "Ratheus told me that the proprietors of Zingett's have always used this secret entrance for deliveries of their finest, and most expensive collectibles from our port at the bottom of the mountain. The rest, of course, are delivered to the store at street level in crates. Ratheus said no one but he, and the proprietors of Zingett's, knew about this so we'll to have to give Rajari our word that we won't tell anyone, as well."

"Of course," Pic nodded. She loved going to Zingett's. It was a wonderful store full of exotic treasures, but Rajari always made her nervous because he was one of the grouchiest elves she'd ever met. Even though he had a reputation for being generous with local charities and good at his trade, he was crotchety nonetheless, never once cracking a smile when she'd been in his store. She didn't relish the idea of dealing with him now.

"Do you think he'll be willing to help, Samésh?"

"Rajari? Of course. He is fiercely loyal to the king, and he's a decent and kind elf."

"Are we talking about the same Rajari? He always seems so—" Pic scrunched up her face.

"Grumpy? Out of sorts?" Samésh smiled. "Sure, he can be a little prickly, but he's actually shy and just more comfortable on his own. Ever since his wife died soon after they were married, his store became his whole life. Except for a select few friends, like me, he stays to himself."

"You talk like you know him well."

"I do. Of course—" he said, reaching up and pulling down on the chain again. "I didn't know about this entrance down here. He did keep that from me, but this is a family-kept secret so I am perfectly fine with that. But, otherwise, we've known each other for centuries and he—he introduced me to Justa." He cleared his throat and wiped his eyes. "Believe me, Rajari will be more than ready to help. He's always been loyal to the crown and it is going to break his heart when I tell him what's happened. We will need the weapons in his basement. It's his private collection, some of which occasionally makes it into his shop, but he will be more than ready to use them to help out."

Rajari sure is taking his time to answer the door, Pic thought.

"Pic, are you and Princess Elswyth ready to show others some basic sword techniques? There will be many that want to do their part."

The very thought chilled Pic. "Yes, but Elly will be a far better instructor than me. I can teach them a few of the basics and they'll at least be able to defend home and family—hopefully." Pic looked into his eyes. "Samésh, I'm so sorry about Justa. I know she would be proud of you right now." He avoided her gaze. As a healer, she could feel his pain more deeply than someone else could, and her heart hurt for him.

Then they heard Rajari's high-pitched voice as he yelled from behind the door. "By the Fates! Quit ringing that blasted bell. I'm coming! This had better be important, whoever you are! Do you even know what time it is?"

SIXTY-THREE

Elswyth stared out into the moonlit sky, wishing she could will the map back into her hand, but it was gone. She closed her eyes and tried to slow her racing pulse. *"Okay. Don't panic. I can do this. We didn't make that many turns on the way here. Right? I can find my way back to the tunnel hub!"* After securing the door, she turned, gripped the hilt of her sword, and looked back the down corridor from where they had come. *Well, here goes nothing!*

She walked back through the tunnels, side-stepping an occasional rat or two, tried to retrace her steps and remember landmarks. *"Was that pile of debris there before? Did we turn here or did we use that other passage? I don't remember seeing this many missing tiles on the walls. Oh, just perfect—that door is new!"* She stopped and spun around. *"Fates save me. I'm lost!"* Standing tall, she gathered her resolve. *"Well, I can't stay here and mope. I just need to make a decision and commit to it."* She had to make a choice, and any direction was better than yielding to fear, because doing that meant she would give up on justice for her grandfather. It meant giving up on ever seeing everyone she cared about. Giving up on seeing Agnes again.

It only got worse the further she walked. *When did the tile on the walls change color? They were white before and now they're light blue. When did the ground start going uphill?* By now, Pic and Samésh would be back from

Zingett's with as many weapons as they could carry to the tunnels, so they must already be bringing the halflings to safety. She hoped they'd started without her because, unless the Fates gave her a miracle, she wouldn't make it back to them in time—if at all.

Eventually, Elswyth wondered if she was walking in circles, but couldn't be sure. She turned around to look at where she'd come from and fought the sense of panic fighting its way to the surface in her mind. Should she go back? One direction seemed as good as the other, so she continued moving forward and up, her steps echoing against the walls. There appeared to be more rats here, but instead of being alarmed, she welcomed their company. At least their presence made her feel less alone in the darkness. To combat her rising sense of panic, she replayed the many times over the years that Agnes told her she'd be okay, that she had all she needed inside her. *"I hope you're right, Agnes!"*

Then she heard it, off in the distance, but unmistakable. Loud voices. Laughter. Music. Somewhere there was a party going on! That meant she might be close to safety. At least she hoped so. Elswyth stood still, closed her eyes, and listened. The sounds bounced off the walls, making it hard to discern where they were coming from. *This way,* she thought and moved farther up the tunnel. She stopped at a passageway whose door had long ago rotted off its hinges and a rat scurried past her into the dark entry. *The sounds are coming from somewhere down there;* she thought. Taking quick but cautious steps, Elswyth made her way toward the noises, which grew louder the further she walked into the passageway.

The black-tiled walls in the new tunnel sucked up any light she made with her Majik, making it difficult to see well, but at least she knew she was still headed in the right direction. Or was she? Not only could she sense Dark Majik the closer she got but, could now hear some of what was being said, and it wasn't good. Whoever those elves were sounded intoxicated and were toasting their king—*King Terrick*! Over the drunken singing and shouting, she heard crashing, wood splitting, and glass breaking, so she made sure her shields were extra strong.

Elswyth stepped around a sharp bend and entered a narrow room. Along one wall there was a row of eight tall mahogany panels, and between each of those, set into the wood, were ornate floor-to-ceiling silver grates. The wall looked somehow familiar and the light coming through from the other side was bright, with shadows from the party moving back and forth in a frenzy. She moved up to a grate, peered through it to the room on the other side, and her heart stopped. No wonder the grated panels looked familiar. The other side of the wall was the throne room—or what was left of it. Terrick's drunken soldiers were destroying it, piece by piece. Between their raucous voices, the music, and the destruction they were committing, the sound was deafening.

She saw what was left of her grandmother's royal seat in hundreds of pieces on the floor, the velvet that had covered the cushions, torn and slashed. She watched as a slobbering; inebriated elf laughed with ugly glee while he continued to cut at the wreckage of her throne with his sword. He picked up a small piece of the splintered ornate wood trim and held it over his head as he sauntered through the mess. "Look at me! I'm the queen! Bow down to me, you worthless imps!" He laughed, obviously thinking himself clever. Elswyth committed his face to memory.

Her grandfather's throne was not in the room. Of course, with all the smashed furniture, torn draperies, and broken glass and wood, it may have already been reduced to trash. Long tables sat up against one wall for food and drink, but much of that was on the floor, stomped on or thrown across the room.

Not that anyone was paying them much attention, but the royal band was playing in a far corner. Her heart broke for them. The cheerful tunes they played were in stark contrast to their fearful expressions and tear-streaked faces. Her resolve to avenge her family, avenge Glenorim, reignited as she watched the debacle in front of her.

After careful examination of the wood panels, she found no latches or handles that allowed her access to the throne room from her side. This was going to require some thought, but she didn't intend to give up. It seemed far better to hide somewhere in the castle than to continue wandering the tunnels. She sat down in a dark corner to watch the scene play out and waited for them to either end the party and leave, or drop from drunken exhaustion.

So, how to get in? She could use a focused stream of Majik on the grate the same way she did against the iron bars in the storeroom. The metal was heavy enough, though, that it would sap her energy too fast, and she'd then need time to recover, time she didn't think she had. Cutting through the wood wall with her sword seemed like the better choice, but there was no obvious place to cut a hole.

While she sat in thought, two rats waddled in, close to the far end of the room, and stuck their noses through the grate, no doubt hoping for some of the discarded food to find its way to them. The royal family rarely served food in the throne room and, when they did, never this much! Even so, no one would have ever thought to throw it on the floor, as the soldiers were doing now. The rats must have thought the party was a gift from the Fates and wanted desperately to get at it. Three more rats joined the two, and they were so determined to get to their own feast that they began chewing on a corner of a wood panel. It didn't take long before their sharp teeth and combined efforts were successful and they all squeezed through their hole, one at a time. Several more showed up, chewed the hole even larger, and more of them slipped through.

Elswyth smiled. *Thanks very much, little friends. Your hard work is going to help me at least get a start.* She sat back, watched the debacle on the other side of the wall, and waited.

Sixty-Four

The party finally cleared and the only living things in the throne room were the rats feasting on the food strewn all over the stone tiles. After waiting to be sure no one returned to the room, she got up to inspect the wall. Thanks to her rodent friends, they'd continued to work on the hole in the paneling, making it larger. She pulled on a few pieces of the wood and much of it came off with a tug. When she'd removed as much as she could, she used her sword to cut more away. Even though no one was around, she was careful to make as little noise as possible, and worked slower than she would have liked. Finally, she had a hole just big enough to crawl through, and, after getting out, she pulled a large chest in front of the opening to hide it.

Looking out through the broken panes in the row of tall stained-glass windows across the room, dawn's light was just beginning to break, turning the sky outside a pinkish-gray. She'd been in the tunnels all night! Hopefully, Pic and Samésh had rescued as many halflings as they could.

The castle would come to life soon, so she needed to hurry. She stepped up to a broken mirror, glamoured herself as a blonde, and added some freckles, as well. With her sword drawn, she made her way through the trash and debris to the main doors, then peeked out into the dark main hallway. The only elves in sight were two soldiers at either end of the corridor. One sat on the floor up against the wall—no, not sitting—passed out, most likely from too much nectar at the party. The other soldier, elbows on the sill, was staring out a window at the other end of the corridor. *Two of Terrick's finest are hard at work, I see!*

Choosing the elf that was awake, she tiptoed up the hall until she was within reach of him with her sword. Her eyes narrowed and her fists clenched as she recognized him as the one that had mocked the queen last night. Stale nectar and perspiration emanated from him like a thick, invisible murk. She lifted her sword an inch at a time until it was level with her shoulder. *"Good morning!"* she thought to him. Startled from his reverie, he turned just in time to see her before she swung and hit his forehead with the broad side of her blade. He dropped to the floor, unconscious. *"Sorry,"* she thought to him. *"Actually, not really! I hope you like my dress because you're going to be wearing it!"* The soldier at the other end of the hall was still out cold.

As quickly as she could, she dragged the elf back into the throne room, traded her dress for his uniform, then used fabric scraps from the ground to tie and gag him. As a last-minute thought, she rubbed some of the food from the floor into the bindings on his hands. Deciding what to do next took no time at all. *"I think you might like the tunnels, soldier."* Sweating with the effort, she pulled him through the hole in the wall and down through the tunnels just far enough so she could find her way back out. *"Wow. You should think about losing some weight! Oh, and hey, by the time the rats chew your bindings off, I'll be long gone!"* She brushed the sweat off her brow and went back out to the throne room, once again hiding the opening in the wall with the chest.

Before she left the room, she sent a thank you to the rats.

Trying to appear as soldierly as possible, she strode down the halls, nodding a *good morning* to elves as they passed her. She needed to make it to Madam Teshka's apartment without incident. Not far now. Just around the corner—

"Soldier! Halt"

Elswyth stopped and turned around. Her heart leapt to her throat as she recognized the sergeant who was looking for her at It's A Date Cafe—the one who took Sweets and Dilly away. *Oh please, no! Dear Fates, protect me,* she prayed. She bolstered her shields and smiled. *"Yes, Sergeant? Can—can I help you?"*

He eyed her for a moment before speaking. "Were you at the party last night? I don't remember seeing you there."

"Um—yes, Sergeant. I came a little late is all. It was quite the party, wasn't it?"

"Huh. I'm sure I don't remember you. It was mandatory attendance for all elves in my platoon, you know." He squinted at her and crossed his arms.

"Honest. I was there. By the time I arrived, though, well, things were already long under way. Maybe you missed me in the crowd? There were a lot of us there. And, hey, that roast pig was pretty good, wasn't it? The band was okay, but it was hard to hear it over all our celebrating." She hoped she sounded convincing. Never mind butterflies. Her stomach felt like she had a herd of rabbits jumping around inside.

The sergeant rubbed his chin, still looked unsure but tilted his head to the side, "Well, I guess I do kinda remember you? Yeah, that pig was pretty good eating. Wasn't it?" Then, as if he just recalled something important, he turned to walk down the hall and said over his shoulder, "Remember, you need to report to the city square at 1100 sharp. We are going to be rounding up the halflings at 1400. Got that?"

"Yes, sergeant. I'll be there. 1100 sharp!" She waited until he rounded the corner before taking in a deep breath and leaned against the wall to steady herself. *I can do this. One foot in front of the other. Madam Teshka is just down the hall.* She almost ran the rest of the way there.

Before she had even reached up to knock, Madam Teshka opened her door, looked both ways in the empty hall and pulled Elswyth inside with a warm hug. "My dear! I am so relieved to see you!" She held Elswyth at arms-length and nodded. "Ah! I venture to say you've been through quite a lot lately. You've also been quite resourceful and brave, I see!"

This was one of those times Elswyth was grateful her teacher could read her mind, because the thought of having to recount the last two days felt overwhelming. Madam Teshka steered her to a comfy chair and lit the fireplace. "I'll get us some tea, my dear, then we can talk. It looks like the two of us are going to have quite a bit to do."

Elswyth had to admit, it felt good to do something as normal as having tea with a friend, but the pleasantries were going to be short-lived. They needed to discuss plans. *"Part of Samésh's plan was for you and I team up."* Elswyth hesitated and wrung her hands. *"Madam Teshka, it will be dangerous and I—"*

"Oh, hush, my dear," her teacher said, waving her slender hand in the air. "Remember, I'm quite capable of handling myself, and then some, so please, none of that. I believe between the two of us, we can put a very large kink in Terrick's plans." She turned to walk to the kitchen and Elswyth watched her leave, still believing Madam Teshka didn't walk—she floated on air. "And I think I have an excellent idea how to proceed!" she called from the next room.

Elswyth sunk back into the chair, relaxing for the first time in days.

It was already half-past one. The roundup would begin within thirty minutes. Elswyth and Madam Teshka stood just inside her apartment, each holding baskets full of small cakes. "Please hand me my bag, my dear, and we'll be on our way."

Elswyth picked it up from the floor, expecting it to weight at least as much as a baby dragon, but it felt as if nothing was inside. *"Um, I think you may have forgotten something. Your purse feels empty,"* she said.

Madam Teshka smiled. "Trust me. It's quite full. As a matter of fact, I should clean it out one day soon. I haven't done so in decades and I just keep adding to it." She slipped the handles onto her right arm. "Try not to look so nervous, dear. Except for the few guards in the dungeon and tower, most of Terrick's soldiers are going to be busy gathering the halflings in the city. We'll be all right as long as we work quickly. I've put quite a bit of my best sleeping powders in the cakes. You'll just need to give one to the guard and convince him you want to thank him for capturing the prince and doing his patriotic duty. Then wait for him to nod off. It should only take a bite or two, and then you can grab his keys. I will get to her Majesty and we'll all meet in the throne room. I know it's risky to go back into the tunnels without maps, but I think it's better than staying in the castle. Besides, I may have a way to find our way through those tunnels."

"Yes, ma'am. As soon as the guard is asleep, I'll look for Father and Caden first and then Sweets and Dilly," Elswyth said.

Her teacher shook her head. "For now, it's best to just look for your father and Caden and spend as little time as possible in the dungeons. Our combined armies will be here soon, and we can rescue everyone else then. Promise me you will just release your father and Caden!"

Knowing it would be useless to lie to someone who could read your mind, Elswyth agreed, and they went their separate ways down the hall.

SIXTY-FIVE

Her "borrowed" uniform enabled her to hide in plain sight, so no one paid any attention to her as she passed through the many corridors to her destination. When she got to the entrance leading to the dungeons, she took a breath, placed her hand on the latch and pulled, willing her nerves to settle. Once inside, she walked down a long hall to a desk where an older soldier sat behind stacks of parchments, ledgers, and a box of Majik-stealing shackles. He eyed her with suspicion while she made her way to his station. "What's your business here, soldier?" he said, when she finally stood before him.

Elswyth held up the basket so he could see its contents. *"I—er—am delivering some cakes to the elf guarding Prince Dayel."*

The soldier's eyes narrowed, and he sucked in on his teeth with a loud TSK. "Prince? He lost the right to that title when he took part in the king's death!" he said and leaned forward in his chair.

Elswyth gulped, then recovered and tapped her forehead. "You're right. How stupid of me. It's just all been so—you know."

"Yeah. I get it. Sorry I jumped at you, elfling. You're right. It's all been pretty crazy the last few days." He sat back in his chair and pointed down the hall on the right. "Go down that corridor to the end and you'll find the guard. Oh,

306

and hey, you couldn't spare one of those cakes, could you? They look mighty tasty."

This worked out well! She didn't even have to cajole him. "*Of course! Here you go. I was just going to offer you one. By the way, thanks very much for your help!*" She gave him her sweetest smile, handed him a cake from the top of the basket and then tried to not run as she made her way down the hallway. *Sweet dreams. And thanks for making our escape a little easier,* she thought.

Either the corridor was truly that long, or it just felt like it as she made her way to where her father's and Caden's guard stood between two cells at the far end of the hallway. The soldier watched her every step as she approached, so she tried to smile and act as nonchalant as possible. When she got closer to him, she held up her basket to entice him with the contents. "*Hello! I've brought some cakes for you. Made them myself and I always make too much, so I figured why not give some to the hardworking patriots down here?*"

He continued to stand at attention as he looked her up and down. "Why aren't you in the city with the other soldiers? They should be about ready to round up halflings and they'll need every elf on hand." His hand moved to the hilt of his sword.

Think! Think of something! Oh Pic, I could use your imagination right now. Elswyth's thoughts raced, then she spit out the first words that came to her mind. "*Well, hey. It's not that I didn't want to be there! I had planned to be part of the fun, but my sergeant didn't think I was ready. Said I'm too green. I mean, come on. So, what if I just signed up to serve two days ago? It's not fair!*"

Her eyes caught movement in the cell on the right, and she saw her father looking out from between the bars. He smiled in recognition of their shared energy, but she could also feel his worry for her. He nodded to the adjacent cell where Caden was, but she didn't dare look over there yet. "*So—is that the king's brother?*" She pointed to her father's cell.

The guard relaxed his shoulders, but didn't take his hand from his sword. "Yes, it is. The other one is his regent. Vipers, the both of them! Can't wait until we capture his halfling daughter."

307

"Yeah. Me, too. Maybe I'll be lucky and catch her myself then I can prove to my sergeant I am ready to be a full-on soldier."

The guard gave her a condescending grin. "Yeah, sure. Sure, you will. Look, I've got to resume my post here."

"Oh, sorry! Of course. I'll let you get back to your job," she said, stepping back. *"Oops. I almost forgot why I came here! The cakes. Want one? They're freshly made. I have chocolate or vanilla, so which do you want?"* She held the basket up for him again.

His hand moved from his sword as he looked into the hamper. "Uh, I can't decide. I like both." He looked past her to the door as if to see if anyone else was watching. "Can I have one of each?" he asked, his voice low. He still maintained his straight stance.

"Of course. I won't tell anyone. It would be an honor for me if you tried them both and I'd love to know which one you prefer."

He grinned from ear to ear, reached in and grabbed his two pieces of cake. The chocolate one disappeared in two big bites and his eyes rose to the ceiling in bliss. "Wow! That is the best cake I've ever—" He was flat on the floor, snoring softly, before he could finish his sentence, the piece of vanilla cake still clutched in his hand.

"Well then. I guess that is a yes vote for chocolate! You can save that other piece for later." The keys to the cells were attached to his belt, and Elswyth grabbed them.

Her father eyes lit up from behind the bars. "Elly! I'm glad to see you, but you shouldn't have come down here. It's too dangerous," he said while she fumbled with the keys. Finally, she got the right one in his lock and opened the door. The high-pitched squeal of the metal hinges echoed painfully off the walls and they all froze, waiting to see if the noise had alerted anyone. After a few heartbeats, Dayel stepped out into the corridor, his Majik flooding back into him. Elswyth hugged him tight, and then he took the keys and opened Caden's cell. "And, nice disguise, by the way. Where did you get a uniform, Elly?" Dayel said, pride showing on his face.

"It's a long story, and I'll tell you all about it later." Turning to Caden, she gave him a hug, too. *"Hi Caden. Pic is going to be so relieved to see you! Okay, now we need to make it to the throne room. Madam Teshka is going to meet us there with grandmother."*

"We'll follow your lead," Caden said.

Her father and Caden glamoured their faces, but they realized their clothing could still give them away, especially Dayel's. It looked a little too royal. *"I have an idea,"* Elswyth said. Within fifteen minutes, both Dayel, and Caden had their own uniforms, courtesy of the cell guard and the soldier at the desk. They stowed them both, snoring away, locked in the cells, the keys hanging just out of their reach on the stone wall.

"Don't worry. According to Madam Teshka, they'll be asleep for hours!" Elswyth said.

The three of them walked out of the dungeon entrance as if they were the soldiers they appeared to be.

SIXTY-SIX

Since most of Terrick's army was out gathering halflings, Elswyth, Dayel, and Caden made it to the throne room without incident and locked the doors behind them. Although the rats had eaten most of it, they were still feasting on what was left of the food lying on the floor. *"Hello again, my little friends,"* Elswyth said. She glanced at her father, and her heart ached when she saw the pain and disappointment on his face as he looked around the once beautiful room. They had little time to mourn the damage, though, and needed to get to the tunnels.

"Elly! Oh, thank the Fates you all made it!" the queen said through the grate. She and Madam Teshka were already behind the wall waiting for them. "Hurry! We need to get into the tunnels before anyone comes back. Some soldiers were in here before you arrived talking about bringing servants in to clean up." Elswyth ran over and pulled the chest away from the hole, stepped aside, and waved her father and Caden in.

Caden stepped up to the opening. "Your Highness, you and your father are more important and need to go first." Elswyth started to object, but he shook his head. "After you," he reiterated. "And quickly, please!"

Elswyth looked at her father, but he shrugged his shoulders. "I never argue with Caden. Let's go." He said and urged her forward. It was getting too crowded behind the wall, so Madam Teshka and the queen moved into the tunnel. Before her father could get into the opening, though, the handles on the doors to the throne room wiggled. Someone was trying to get in!

Whoever it was, called through the door. "Is anyone in there? Hello? Hey! Unlock this now!" They paused, but only for a moment. "I can hear you moving around!" The handles on the door jiggled again, but then they shook the door so hard, the frame vibrated with their efforts.

"Sorry, Your Highness," Caden said as he shoved his prince's backside into the hole. Dayel fell forward on the floor next to Elswyth and turned around, reaching out for Caden.

Someone was now trying to break the door down. They were out of time!

"Go! Get everyone away!" Caden said and pushed the chest in front of the hole in the wall as the door burst open. A soldier stomped in, brandishing her sword. Several servants holding mops and buckets stood wide-eyed behind her. Caden plopped down onto the chest, doing his best to act clumsy and hungover. "Ho there! Ow!" he said, holding his head. "You're making so much noise! My head feels like a wyvern chewed it up and spit it out. Woo! What a night!"

The soldier screwed up her face in disgust. "You should have been at roll call this morning! What are you doing in here?" she said and lowered her weapon.

"I know. Sorry. It was just such a crazy party that I guess I overdid the nectar last night. I passed out under the table and just now woke up. Please don't tell my sergeant!"

Annoyed and harried, she sheathed her weapon and crossed her arms. "Fine. You're the least of my worries today so I won't say anything—this time. Just pull yourself together, soldier, and get wherever it is you're supposed to be!"

"I will! Thank you!" Caden rose, pushing the chest even closer to the wall with his leg.

"Now, soldier! There is a lot going on and we need everyone at their posts!"

"Yes. Of course. On my way now." Then he sent thoughts to Dayel and Elswyth. *"May the Fates protect and guide you. Give Pic a hug from me and tell her we will see each other soon."*

Caden stepped in front of the soldier, groaned, and held his head as if he were in terrible pain. He then clamped his hand over his mouth, bugged his eyes, and choked, sending the elf stumbling backwards out of Caden's way. "Hey! Don't you dare get sick on me! If you can't handle your nectar, maybe you shouldn't be drinking it! Go on. Get out of here!" Then she turned her attention to the servants and barked last-minute instructions. "And you lot, quit gawking and clean this mess up!"

Before Caden left the room, he turned his head just enough to see the grate and winked. Elswyth and Dayel watched him go before they joined her grandmother and Madam Teshka in the tunnel.

Elswyth leaned against the wall outside the dark entrance to the throne room tunnel, relieved they'd made it out in time, but it broke her heart that they had to leave Caden behind. She dreaded telling Pic. Now they needed to somehow find the hub with the others. Elswyth, her father, and grandmother released their glamours and returned to their natural appearances.

Her father tried to comfort her in a hushed tone. "He'll be okay, Elly. Caden is resourceful and one of the most intelligent elves I know. We'll see him again." Elswyth could only give him a wan smile in reply.

The queen said, "We need to get moving. No telling when they may discover that hole in the wall and we should be as far from here as we can."

"I need to check on something first," Elswyth said. They followed her as she doubled back down the tunnel to see about the soldier she'd left tied up earlier. He was gone, and a lone rat sat chewing on the remnant of his bindings, its right ear torn at the edge. *"Well, he either went back out through the throne room or is lost in the tunnels."*

Araleia shook her head. "If he went back out through the throne room, he would have alerted someone and it would be crawling with soldiers by now. I think we can assume he's lost," she said.

"Agreed," her father said, nodding. "We'd best be on the lookout for him, though. He's going to have an axe to grind for the headache you gave him, Elly." He grinned and patted her shoulder proudly. "Madam Teshka, Elly said you might have a way to navigate the tunnels?"

Instead of answering, Madam Teshka stooped, picked up the rat and whispered something in its ear. It wriggled its nose at her and squeaked, and she nodded back as if responding to it. Elswyth thought her teacher could no longer surprise her, but once again, she was proven wrong because, obviously, this ancient elf and the rat were speaking with one another.

With their discussion finished, Madam Teshka cradled the rat in her arms and addressed their small group. "Apparently, the soldier went ahead, and did not return to the throne room. Our friend here thinks he took one of the tunnels to the left, well before the one that led back to where we were. But we should keep an eye out for him because your father is correct. He's sure to have quite the headache at the moment and not happy at all." She bent her head again to talk with her small friend. "Ah. Thank you, little one." She turned her attention back to their group and pointed ahead. "Our guide says we should go back up this way." Everyone stared at her and the rat, and she shrugged her shoulders. "Caden's wife was one of my students. I helped her with her gift of talking to animals," she explained, as if it was common knowledge. "Let's be on our way."

She floated past them and forward into the tunnels.

SIXTY-SEVEN

The rat and Madam Teshka chatted with each other (Elswyth positive the two were even trading jokes) as everyone made their way along the tunnels. They'd been walking so long through twists and turns in the many passageways the rat directed them to go that Elswyth wondered if they were, in fact, lost. Then their furry little guide let out a loud squeak and pointed its nose down a short tunnel on the right, where they saw a simple, rough-hewed wooden door set into the wall at the end.

"She says we are at a hidden entrance to one of the castle kitchens," Madam Teshka announced. "Our friend here also says there will be those inside who can help us."

"Um, Thanks Mr. Rat but I was wondering—and no offense, but—" Elswyth said.

"It's Ms. Rat, my dear," her teacher corrected.

"Sorry! Ms. Rat. Again, I mean no offense but—"

Madam Teshka translated a series of squeaks and chirps from Ms. Rat. "She thinks she knows what you're about to say and would like you to know that her friends and family have an agreement with the head cook. The kitchen staff puts food outside that door for them, and the rats, in exchange, leave the kitchen alone. It's an arrangement that has worked for over one hundred years."

"I see! Well, then. Thank you for getting us this far. Do you know how we can get to the hub?"

The rat offered a few more chirps, then Madam Teshka set her down with care and thanked her as she waddled away down the tunnel. "She offered her regrets but said this is as far as she can get us. At least for now we can rest and get some food and water to take with us to share with the others in the hub when we find it." Without waiting for them, she entered the tunnel, and they all followed her to the door at the end. She opened the door just wide enough to see into the room beyond and turned back around with a bright smile. "Isn't this grand! Come along everyone!"

Elswyth heard a familiar squeal as Madam Teshka went through the door before her. "Madam Teshka! Oh, my gosh!" Pic cried. When Elswyth stepped in, Pic exploded with delight. "Elly! We were so worried!" she cried and ran into her arms. Elswyth looked around the large rectangular table in the center of the room, and couldn't believe her eyes. Samésh, Sweets, Dilly, and the head cook were all sitting together, each with a steaming bowl of mutton stew in front of them, their mouths hanging open in surprise. When the queen and prince entered, they all stood up and bowed.

Elswyth turned and saw that, from the kitchen, the door to the tunnel was a false wall in the back of a broom closet. No one would ever know there was a secret exit hidden in there.

The queen went straight to Samésh and embraced him. "Oh, Samésh," she said. "I heard about everything that's happened and of all you've been doing. Thank you. I, and the whole of Glenorim, thank you! Garreth would be so very proud of you." Samésh closed his eyes as he rested in the arms of his queen, the emotion from so much sadness and heartbreak written on his face.

Elswyth was ecstatic to see all the familiar faces. *"Pic! Oh Pic, it is so good to see you! Did you and Samésh get the halflings to safety? Is everyone okay? Sweets! Dilly! I thought you were arrested. How are you here?"* Elswyth asked.

Pic answered with her usual fast-paced delivery. "Oh, Your Majesty! And Your Highness! We are so happy you're here!" She turned back to Elswyth. "The halflings? Yes, we did rescue quite a few. Some refused to come with us because they didn't believe Terrick would send soldiers after them, so we had to leave them behind. There were also some elves that wanted to come with us once we told them what had happened. They want to help, Elly." She waved her hand toward Samésh and continued, "Samésh wants me to teach some basic sword techniques to those that want to learn, just in case. I'm not excited about that but I will do what's needed. You'll be better at that than me, for sure, so I can't wait for your help! We got a lot of swords from Zingett's, and you know what? Rajari is not that so bad once you get to know him!"

Pic managed a full breath, but just as Elswyth was going to say something, she continued. "We used the maps to tell us how to get here to the servant's dining room and Cook is more than willing to share the larder with us, which is great because we've got a bunch of mouths to feed down there! Did Cis get away? We haven't heard from Ratheus and Kara, but I bet they're okay. Sweets and Dilly were assigned to the kitchens, since they can cook, otherwise, they'd be in the dungeon! Imagine my shock when I found them here! Oh, my gosh, I'm just so happy to see you." She started to tear up.

"Pic," Elswyth said, *"Slow down! We're all okay and glad you're here, too. And now we can get back to the hub."*

Pic held her at arm's length, when she finally noticed what Elswyth and the prince were wearing. "Um, why are you two wearing uniforms?"

"I'll tell you all about it, but first I need to let you know—"

Pic looked past Elswyth to the doorway, eyebrows raised. "My dad? Where is my dad?"

Elswyth took a deep breath. *"About your dad, Pic. He didn't make it into the tunnel when we escaped. "* It hurt to see her dear friend's expression fall.

The queen stepped up to Pic and put her hand on her shoulder. "Pic, you know your father. He is tough and intelligent and we'll see him again. I promise. Perhaps we can get Ruby to look for him. She can get him here to the servant's kitchen and then he can get to the hub." Dayel nodded in agreement.

Pic sniffled, still crestfallen. "S—sure. That's a great idea. I'll see him again," she said, not sounding entirely convinced.

Dilly came around the table and hugged her. "*Pic, you will. Of course, you will see him again!*"

Sweets spoke up from her seat, playing her usual Mom's-in-charge role. "Let's get you all fed before any of the soldiers come into the kitchens. We think the rounding up should be close to done and there will be a lot of hungry soldiers around here soon! We should be on our way well before they get here."

"*We? Are you coming to the hub, too?*" Elswyth asked.

"Yes, of course! Dilly and I can help bring supplies. We'll come back here later and no one will be the wiser."

The head cook walked to the stove and ladled stew into bowls. "Your Majesty, Your Highnesses, I regret I only have this humble stew to offer you for dinner!" she said.

Araleia sat down at the table. "If that amazing aroma from the pot is any indication, I am sure it will be a stew of the highest caliber. Thank you for sharing your food with us!"

When the cook gave Dayel his bowl, he scooped up a spoonful, ate it, and closed his eyes with delight. "Mother! I think we need to have this on our menus in the future! It is exceptional!"

The compliment made the cook blush from her neck up to the tips of her ears as she curtsied. "I am honored, Your Highness!"

Samésh cleared his throat. "Begging everyone's pardon. I don't want to rush you all, but I agree with Sweets and think we need to go soon. There is no telling when the soldiers will be back."

"Right you are, Samésh!" Madam Teshka agreed.

Cook took that as her cue and began grabbing breads and cheeses that they could take back to the hub. "I'm sure you've got some hungry mouths to feed down there so I'll gather all I can for you. Unlike the main kitchen larders, no one really checks our inventory and won't know what's missing. I might have some nectar in the pantry, too! If I kept it in the main kitchen storage, well, some of those soldiers would help themselves without permission and it would disappear quickly."

"Thank you! I'm sure everyone down there will appreciate whatever you can spare," Elswyth said. She pushed her chair back and got up. *"I'm finished anyway, so if you want some help, just show me what you want me to do."* While the rest of the group finished their meal, Elswyth helped to wrap loaves of bread and put them into bags. By the time she and the cook had packed multiple sacks, everyone had returned their empty bowls to the sink and headed for the broom closet door.

Samésh took his map from his vest pocket and went through with a sack in hand. The queen, Pic, Sweets, and Dilly each carried a full sack and followed close behind. Prince Dayel grabbed another two sacks, opened the door, and motioned for Elswyth to follow as he stood at the threshold. The cook put a finger up. "Oh! I also have some sweets I forgot to pack for you! It will only take a moment." She rushed to the pantry again.

"That sounds wonderful, and thank you!" the prince said.

"I'll help her and be right there, Father."

"Okay, Elly. We'll wait for you in the tunnel." Dayel smiled, and the door clicked shut.

"Princess, would you hold the sack while I fill it?"

Cook placed cakes and cookies inside the bag while Elswyth held it open and when it was almost full to overflowing, Elswyth tied a string around the top, then looked up at the cook. *"Thanks so much for these! The treats are going to be much appreciated and—"* She froze.

The cook's face had gone ghostly white, staring at something behind Elswyth's shoulder. Hand on her sword, Elswyth slowly turned around and saw a group of twelve soldiers standing just inside the entry to the kitchen.

Neither she nor the cook had heard them come in. *How could I have let my guard down?*

Instead of the traditional purple and gold uniform, they now wore red tunics with a black dragon eating its tail emblazoned on the chest. The soldier in front of the group put his hands on his hips and sneered at her. She realized, with a sick feeling in her stomach, she'd never returned to her glamoured look so they would know who they were looking at—Princess Elswyth.

And the lead soldier was recognizable to her, because he had a nasty black and blue lump on the side of his head.

"What do you know?" he said with apparent glee. "We thought we would sneak in here for some of the nectar we were told you have hidden, Cook. It seems we found something much more valuable." The soldiers moved so fast that Elswyth didn't even see them coming. Before either she or the cook could recover from their shock, soldiers had put shackles on them both.

They were powerless.

Sixty-Eight

E lswyth wasn't sure how long she'd been in the dungeon. Hours? An entire night? Without windows in the bleak stone walls, there was no way to measure the passage of time. She was thirsty, but the only water available was in a bucket on the other side of the dank room, and it looked anything but fresh. A second bucket was her only source of a toilet.

She sat on her wooden cot, staring at the barred wall of her cell. Her lack of Majik energy was almost painful and, more important, terrifying. No one could find you if they couldn't sense your Majik. You were invisible. She worried for the cook and prayed Terrick hadn't hurt her—or worse. Almost certain Cook wouldn't divulge anything about the secret tunnel door in the servants' kitchen, Elswyth felt at least a little relief. But, then again, she understood Terrick's cruelty knew no bounds. What if they'd been able to make the poor elf talk? She put her hands in her face. *How could I have been so careless? I should have been more aware of my surroundings. I learned that in my sword classes! And I should have stayed glamoured!* She was angry with herself. She was afraid, not just for herself, but for others she cared about.

Then she sensed it. Even without her Majik, she felt it to the core of her being. Terrick's dark energy. He stepped into view outside her cell.

"Look who we have here!" Terrick said, purring with delight, his fingers tented in front of his chest.

Elswyth sat up straight and looked at him with all the defiance she could muster. *"What do you want with me?"*

"Not afraid of me? Hm. Perhaps you should rethink that," he said. He threw her a frigid smile that matched his cold black eyes, then paced in front of the bars twice, appearing thoughtful, and rubbing his chin. "It seems I underestimated you, halfling. You've been very—resourceful! I have to admit it. I'm impressed. That is, as much as one could be about your kind."

Without her Majik, Elswyth wasn't able to see the black tendrils swirling around him, but she knew they were there. How she wished for her Majik back because, at least when she could *see* evil, she knew that meant she also had the power to protect herself. Protect others. Now she felt defenseless and vulnerable the way her mother made her feel when she was a child. She shivered. *"What do you want?"*

"What do I want? Oh, nothing much," he said, waving his hand in the air and grinning. "I simply want you, mother, and my brother here in the dungeon. Then I want you to admit publicly that you killed my dearly beloved father, the King. My brother and mother will admit they had a part in it, and then, you and my brother will be executed. Mother will spend her life in the tower while I rule the kingdom." His smile grew wider. "Your admissions will seal my rule as legitimate."

It sounded like he hadn't found her father and grandmother, at least not yet, and that gave her hope. Elswyth laughed and threw her shoulders back. *"And why would we do that? None of us are responsible for the king's death! You killed my grandfather. You're a murderer!"*

A small gasp escaped his lips, and he stepped back from the bars. "How did you know that? Who—" he quickly collected himself, his face hard and angry. "You will tell me where they are, halfling brat, or else. Where are my brother and mother?"

In answer, Elswyth leaned forward and glared at him.

Then he grinned and stepped close to the bars again. Almost imperceptibly at first, she felt the snake-like reach of his tendrils slithering into her
head—into her mind. *"No! I won't let you in!"* As a child, she'd learned to
mask her fear of her mother's cruelty and hid behind mental walls. She could
do that with Terrick. Elswyth met his steel gaze with her own and willed
herself to focus on the image of the rank bucket of water in her cell. He would
not have access to her mind! He would not see her fear!

Rusty bucket! Bugs floating water! Broken handle! Brown water! She focused on the images, the mental battle difficult, as if her entire mind and body
were on fire. Sweat trickled down her back, but still she resisted.

He raised his eyebrows and his grin spread. "Ah! Once again, you impress
me. Even without your Majik you have unseen strength. So, you want to
make this hard, do you? Very well. I have time and it will be more fun for
me." He looked down and casually examined his nails. "We'll see how you
feel tomorrow. Or—perhaps it will be the next day? You will weaken. They
always do." He turned to walk away.

The release of his energy was an instant relief, and she slumped back down
on the cot. *"Wait! What about Cook? Is she—?"*

"Oh, you don't have to worry about her anymore. She didn't fare as well as
you just did. She was no fun at all. I'll just say her loyalty cost her."

Elswyth clenched her fists. She would not give him the satisfaction of
seeing her tears, so she held them in. *"You are vile!"*

"Yes, I am, aren't I?" he said and left.

SIXTY-NINE

Elswyth had been in the dungeon for three days. Or was it four, maybe five—or more? She didn't know how long she'd been in that horrible place. Her cell was so squalid and dank she felt like the very air she breathed delivered sticky dampness and filth to her lungs. She either slept or lay on her cot, hungry and thirsty all the time.

Meals came with no set schedule and she was sure the guards did that on purpose to keep her from being able to mark the time. It didn't matter. The food was inedible anyway, so she didn't look forward to it when they brought it to her. She could sometimes hear guards talking farther down the corridor, but they were well out of sight. Except for Terrick's visits, the delivery of meals, and a few rats she'd befriended, she saw no one. Time crawled by at a cruel pace.

Terrick had returned several times and with each visit, he tried to invade her mind, searching for the answers he wanted, but she divulged nothing about the tunnels—about where her family and friends were. She could tell he was losing patience with her ability to block him, but despite that, she refused to give up and resisted his intrusions. The weaker she became, though, the harder it got to push back and the last time he walked away, she heard him instruct the guard to not bring her any food that night. She'd worried how long she could hold out.

At some point, Elswyth noticed one of the rats that wandered into her cell had a small tear in its right ear. It sat on the floor in front of her cot, looked up, and cocked its head at her. *"Hello,"* she said, praying it understood her. *"Are you the one that helped us find the servant's kitchen? If you are, could you get word to my father and grandmother? I'm sure they know by now I've been arrested. Just the same, if you could let them know where I am so they can find me? I'd be really grateful."* Certain the rat nodded a *yes*, she reached out to it and it squeaked and jumped up next to her. *"Sorry! I wish I understood what you're saying, little friend. Animal-speak is Madam Teshka's talent, not mine. But I do appreciate the company."*

Frustrated she couldn't find a way to communicate with her small guest; she sighed and laid down on the lumpy cot. The rat watched Elswyth for a moment and then snuggled up next to her. It chirped once, put its head down, curled up into a tight ball, and closed its eyes. Elswyth's lids lowered, and she fell fast asleep, grateful for the company of a new friend, even if it was someone so small.

Wake and sleep. Other than eating an occasional putrid meal and drinking fetid water, that was all she did. Elswyth felt her body and mind growing weaker. She woke up with Ms. Rat curled up against her shoulder, its little nose, and ears wiggling in slumber. *I hope you're dreaming of a more pleasant place than this one, Ms. Rat!* There were muffled voices coming from the corridor, but, as usual, they were too far away to make out what anyone was saying. Maybe there was a change of guard going on? She reached over to pet the rat's fur. It woke up, then squeaked as it sniffed the air and jumped to its haunches, alert.

What is it, little one? Elswyth sat up, taking it slow, and turned her face toward the barred wall of her cell. Just the act of sitting up made the room spin. *What is that aroma? It smells so good, and somehow familiar. Maybe it's another of Terrick's cruel taunts?* she thought through an ever-growing mental fog.

"*Can you hallucinate smells, little one? If I didn't know better, that smells like Agnes's venison stew! But that can't be.*" She choked on a sob and the tears she'd been holding back fell down her face. She missed Agnes. So much. She wanted Cis and Willow Grove. Her beautiful, safe Willow Grove. She also missed her grandmother and father. And how wonderful would it be to hear her grandfather's laugh again? And Pic. She missed her funny, kind, and often silly, Pic. She missed them all. *Terrick has won,* she thought, her spirit feeling the surrender. She laid back down and stared through the bars of her cell, while Ms. Rat squeaked again and curled up next to her. Elswyth squeezed her eyes tight, hoping that doing so would somehow block out the aroma filled with wonderful memories, because it hurt far too much to feel them right now.

She felt Ms. Rat freeze next to her on the mattress and Elswyth stilled on the cot. W*as that the sound of wings? Yes!* For a brief moment, she imagined it could be Cicero, but whatever bird belonged to those wings was far bigger than her Cis. Then Ms. Rat started squeaking again, but this time she sounded frantic, and Elswyth felt the little body shiver against her own. She opened her eyes and looked down at her small friend. The poor thing was terrified, hiding her face in Elswyth's shoulder, and when she looked out through the bars of the cell, she understood why.

An enormous white owl sat on the floor in the corridor and, as far as poor Ms. Rat was concerned, that was her mortal enemy. No wonder she was terrified. But the owl wasn't looking at her friend. It looked straight at Elswyth and it held a willow twig in its beak. *A willow twig?* She knew she was feeling woozy from lack of food, but—"*Is this a hallucination? If it is, then Ms. Rat sees it, too. What is happening?*" Elswyth shook her head to clear it, which only made her more dizzy.

She pushed herself up to a sitting position against the rock wall, scooped Ms. Rat to her chest, and glared at the owl. *"Go away. I will not let you make a meal of my friend!"*

In response, the owl fluffed his feathers and spoke up, his voice deep and proper. "I dare say, Your Highness. I had no intention of doing that." His enormous eyes blinked, and then his head swiveled back towards the far end of the corridor. "Over here! She's in this cell! I think you should hurry," he called out to someone.

Elswyth could hear footsteps running towards her cell. *Is this it? Is this my end?* She tried to be brave and stand up, but didn't have the energy. Instead, she sat up taller against the rock wall, ready to face whatever was coming.

The footsteps slowed and then—she heard the voice she was sure she'd never hear again. "My girl! Oh, my girl!" Agnes said, smiling broadly through her tears. She grabbed onto the bars and called out, "Here, Pic! She's in here. Quickly! Bring the keys!"

SEVENTY

I f this was some kind of dream or trick of Terrick's, Elswyth decided
she would enjoy it, anyway. She sat staring bleary-eyed at the visions
of Agnes and Pic as they entered her cell and stumbled against each other
at the threshold. It felt important to warn the apparitions. *"Careful.
You will lose your Majik once you step in here!"* Then she watched, mes-
merized, as they rallied and stepped closer to her. The smile on Agnes's
apparition made the dream blissful.

"Hi Elly!" Pic said, gently. "I can't believe we found you!"

Elswyth smiled at Pic's image. The hallucination then got even more
beautiful when Madam Teshka appeared in the corridor and stood next
to the owl. Elswyth blinked her eyes a few times. *Breathe,* she said to
herself. *It's okay. Just enjoy the dream!* But then, the dream dissipated
when she felt the same familiar, gentle embrace that had banished her
many nightmares over the years. The same one that had encouraged her
through bouts of crippling self-doubt and fear, that embrace that made
everything right. No, it wasn't a dream or a hallucination. Agnes—it was
Agnes! Elswyth squeezed her eyes shut and frantically hugged her back,
terrified of letting go.

Elswyth pulled back to sign to Agnes. *"How? When? Oh, Fates bless me! I've missed you so much!"* She couldn't control the sobs now racking her weakened body.

Just as she'd done when Elswyth was a child waking up from a nightmare, Agnes brushed back the sweaty strands of hair from her forehead. "I'm really here, my girl!" She pointed to the owl. "Tallon told me everything that's happened and I came right away. I needed some help since I'm not as young as I used to be," she said and winked. "The elves along the mountain path had to carry me most times, but they were very kind and they got me here quickly. I wasn't about to leave you to fight without me. Shush, now. I'm here."

Madam Teshka spoke from the hall. "My dear. We must be on our way. I've brought a strong healing potion for you and it will help you recover quickly, but we must move along! First things first. Come out of the cell so you can reclaim your Majik."

Agnes and Pic helped Elswyth to stand, and they all made their way to the doorway. *"Agnes, I—I smelled your stew. Was that real?"* she signed.

"Yes, it was real. It was a special batch I made for the guard down the hall," she said. They stepped out of the cell into the corridor and their Majiks rushed back into their bodies, but Elswyth was still felt weak from the lack of sustenance.

Pic rambled with happiness. "Elly, I am so, so glad we found you! You've been missing for two weeks! There is so much to tell you. Ruby found Dad not too long after you disappeared, so he is safe with us in the hub. Cis brought our army back and the Belnoir and Kerridin armies are here, too! Oh, and you should have seen how we handled the guard here. It was amazing! Agnes brought a powder that she mixed into the stew and then we fed it to the guard. Once he took a bite, he was more than happy to help us then and he actually *gave* us the keys. After that, Madam Teshka offered him a cake. He ate it and then, POW, he was on the ground in seconds. It was genius! We're all going to trade recipes later—"

Madam Teshka touched Pic's arm gently. "I understand you're excited, my dear, but I think we can discuss all that later. Don't you?"

"Sorry, of course!" she said, beaming.

Elswyth chuckled at Pic. She thought she'd never hear her friend; her adopted sister, ramble on again.

Madam Teshka pulled out a silver bottle and a glass from her ever-present large purse. "This should do the trick! Make sure you drink the whole cup, my dear! Once we get back to the hub, we will fill you up with some proper food." She removed the stopper and poured a generous amount of a thick green liquid into the cup. Elswyth had to hold her nose against the odor, but she drank it in just a few gulps and it instantly restored her much of her strength, mentally and physically. It may not have tasted or smelled good, but whatever it was, she felt grateful to feel more herself again. After Madam Teshka returned the bottle and cup to her purse, she reached back into her bag and pulled out Elswyth's sword!

"You found it? Thank you! I thought once they took it from me, I'd never see it again." Elswyth said, reaching for her weapon.

Her governess smiled. "That ridiculous guard actually tried selling it to us! Apparently, they stored it in a cabinet here in the dungeon, and he thought he was going to make some easy money. He would have been in a lot of trouble for doing that, I'm sure. Hm. Now that I think about it," she said, tapping her cheek, "I do believe he'll be in trouble for much more than a missing sword once they find out you escaped under his watch."

Ms. Rat interrupted with a squeak from where she sat on the cot and Elswyth looked at Madam Teshka for a translation.

"She says she's happy we found you. She is going to go back to her family now, but is sure you will see her again, if that is agreeable with you."

"Thank you, friend. And, of course, I hope to see you again. Any time you want to visit, my door will be open to you."

The rat nodded, jumped down from the cot, and scurried into its hole in the rock wall.

The hub had become the new war room. Now fully recovered, thanks to Madam Teshka, Elswyth stood at the enormous round table with her grandmother and father to her left and Agnes on her right. Cicero stood in front of her on the table. Samésh, Ratheus, Pic, Caden, Madam Teshka, and Lieutenant Kara had all taken their places at the table as well. Tallon sat perched on a tall log Ratheus and the lieutenant brought in for him. Also joining them were the leaders of the Glenorim troops, King Merrat of Belnoir, and Prince Tashir of Kerridin. The crowded room was charged with nervous energy while everyone talked amongst themselves, waiting for the meeting to begin.

Their three armies waited in the mountain passes and tunnels for the order to advance. Everything and everyone was in place to take back Glenorim and dethrone Terrick. It wasn't going to be easy—or bloodless—but they were ready.

The queen raised her hand, and the room quieted with an expectant hush. "I first need to say that Glenorim owes its deepest gratitude to those of you from Belnoir and Kerridin. We are honored that you've chosen to fight by our side," she began, bowing her head to them. "And, to my fellow Glenorim citizens, this is obviously a very dark time in our history. We have not only lost a great king," she paused, her head held high. "but our own son has betrayed us—betrayed our kingdom. I know there will be those of us with friends and family who've chosen to be on the wrong side of history. Many of them have discovered their mistake and may be ready to fight with us once we enter the castle and the city. There are others who refuse to take off their blinders. It pains me to my core to say that we'll be fighting against them. But, if we are to succeed, fight, we must."

Elswyth looked up at her grandmother, her queen, with respect and awe. Even now, with a grief still so fresh, her grandmother was the essence of power, strength, and poise. She was proud to be her granddaughter.

"Are there any questions before we give the order to attack?"

Prince Tashir cleared his throat, and Elswyth turned her attention to him. As young as he seemed, he exuded a strength and bearing she found intriguing. His dark Kerridin skin looked like burnt bronze in the light of the lanterns and she thought it beautiful. Tashir cleared his throat again, seemingly reluctant to ask his question. "I would like to know, Your Majesty—it hasn't been discussed yet, but do you want us to take the prince alive?"

You could hear a beetle breathe in the silence that followed his question. The queen hesitated and then answered, her voice strong and full. "Let it be understood by everyone here that the answer to that is no. That being said, I don't think he will have any intention of being taken alive, anyway. Are there any other questions?" The room was, once again, quiet. "Very well, then. It appears that we are ready. If you aren't directly involved in combat, stay safe as you perform your duties," she said, looking at Agnes, Pic, and Madam Teshka. To everyone else, "Per our plans, you may now give your troops the order to advance to their positions and attack—and may the Fates grant us all victory over darkness."

Agnes gave Elswyth's hand a squeeze and petted Cicero on his head. She then followed Pic and Madam Teshka out the door. Everyone else filed through the various doorways leading out of the hub. When the last of them were gone, Cicero hopped up on Elswyth's arm, and she and her father turned to leave as well.

"Just a moment," her grandmother said. She hugged them each close and stepped back, pride showing through her smile. "Be safe, my darlings. I love you and will see you when this is over. That includes you, too, Sir Cicero," she said, a hitch in her voice.

Earlier, she had been her queen. But at this moment, she was her grandmother, and Elswyth's heart swelled with pride and hope.

Even so, fear lurked in the shadows.

SEVENTY-ONE

Terrick sat back in his deep leather chair, glaring at the roaring flames in the fireplace. The room was sweltering, but he still pulled his collar closer to his neck and shivered. He swirled the nectar in his glass and grimaced, working to keep his fury at bay. It wasn't the cold he was angry about, though. *So, what if things haven't quite gone as I planned for the past two weeks? At least I've got the halfling, and it's just a matter of time until I find mother and Dayel. Surely, they won't leave her to perish in her cell and will come for her—if she doesn't die first, that is.* He growled and shook his head.

He slammed a fist down on the arm of the chair, spilling his drink on his clothes. "Damn the Fates! That brat has more determination than I'd bargained for. How has she lasted two weeks? More importantly, how did she know it was me that killed father? What Majik is that?" He wouldn't admit it out loud, but the thought of her being so powerful made him fear her like he'd feared no one else before.

Terrick rose from his chair, wiped at the nectar on his jacket, and stepped up to the mirror. He tried to calm himself as he stared at his reflection and noticed a definite change in his features. Were they sharper? His eyes looked somehow darker. The ever-present black tendrils swirled snakelike around him, but he ignored them. *Still handsome,* he thought as he turned left to

332

right, enjoying his image. Then his mind snapped back to his dilemma. "I just need to adjust the plan, that's all. Not to worry. I'll announce her execution in the morning and that should force them out of hiding. Yes! I should have thought of that before."

Someone knocked at the door, and he groaned in irritation. "I left orders not to be disturbed so this had better be important!" he yelled.

A young, trembling, bug-eyed soldier entered wearing a new red and black uniform that hung baggy on his slender frame, his voice a mere squeak as he tried to talk. "Your—Your Majesty." He said as he bowed. "I—um. There's a problem with—I regret to inform you that—uh,"

"Spit it out, you babbling imp! What is it?"

"It's the halfling, Your Majesty. She—escaped." The elf stood rooted to the ground, his trembling even more pronounced and his hair plastered to his head with sweat.

Terrick glared at the soldier in disbelief while the flames in the fireplace lept up and curled over the lintel, spewing smoke and embers into the room. "Say. That. Again?" Terrick said, going rigid and tall. He closed his eyes, the tenuous struggle for self-control slipping through his grasp.

"She—escaped early this morning, Your Majesty. I'm not sure exactly when it happened. I wasn't there and was just ordered to report it to you." The elf looked at Terrick, tears now rolling down his cheeks. There was a reason the others sent this poor, hapless elf in. No one wanted to be the bearer of bad news to Terrick. No one.

Terrick's guttural rants and screams rumbled throughout the halls outside his study. While everyone else ran in the opposite direction, someone hid in the shadows outside Terrick's door, waiting for his rage to die down.

"I am really glad you're okay," Cicero said, as he hopped alongside Elswyth up the spiral stairs leading to the forgotten gallery hall. "I was so worried when I got back and found out you'd been arrested."

"Let's agree never to be separated again, Cis. I was worried about you the whole time you were gone. But, hey! You're a hero now. How about that?" She shined her light over him, smiled and glanced back at Pic and Samésh, coming up the steps close behind. Following them, a platoon of a hundred solemn-faced soldiers trailed down into the dark spiral to the bottom of the passage, their lights flickering as they marched. All of them were counting on her leadership as part of the royal family.

Elswyth couldn't read Samésh's expression. She wished she had words that could somehow help him, but he would only discuss strategy or plans, and otherwise stayed silent behind his shields since the night they found him in the hub. She had expected him to accompany the queen and her group, but he came with her contingent instead. He'd lost so much and her heart ached for him.

Pic, she knew, was prepared to fight, but her primary job would be to aid the wounded. Agnes had insisted on doing the same alongside Madam Teshka with another platoon. Sweets and Dilly had gathered volunteers in the tunnels to wait near the entrance to the servant's kitchen. Although they too were armed, Sweets thought they should be ready to set up the main dining halls as temporary infirmaries, where wounded could be cared for. Many others volunteered to do what they could alongside the armies. For the hundredth time that day, Elswyth offered up prayers for all of them. *"Are you doing okay, Pic?"* she thought back behind her.

"Yeah. I'm as ready as I'll ever be," Pic said, and pulled her cloak back to reveal her sword. "I've filled every pocket of my cape, too, so I'll be ready to help anyone who's injured. Agnes also helped me gather what I needed. She had some brilliant advice and tips and stuff and—" Pic rattled on.

Elswyth smiled. It didn't matter whether Pic was happy, sad, nervous or scared. Talking always helped her relax and ground herself so, she let her friend chatter on. In reality, it helped her to focus, too. She glanced at Samésh again, who seemed to listen to Pic with a faint smile on this face.

Cicero interrupted. "Elly! Please keep your light up and your eyes forward! I don't think my heart could take another almost-disaster on these steps!"

"Don't worry. I don't want that either!" She trained her light up the stairway and Elswyth's thoughts turned inward as she calculated the progress everyone should make through the tunnels. The timing was critical. Before she was rescued, Ratheus, Lieutenant Kara, and Samésh spent several days making copies of the maps needed for the different routes. Each group had their assigned path, and based on how long their treks were, they would all be attacking very close to the same time. The three armies would cover both the city and the castle. At least, that was the plan, and it wouldn't be long now.

"I am not ashamed to say I'm afraid, Cis," she thought just to him. *"Determined, but also scared. I'm glad we're together right now."*

In answer, Cicero flew up to her shoulder and nuzzled her cheek. They climbed the rest of the way in silence.

SEVENTY-TWO

Elswyth put her hand on the lever that would open the door to the old gallery hall. *"It feels like it was just yesterday when we got in trouble for sneaking in here."*

Pic sighed and shook her head. "It also feels like a hundred years ago. So much has changed since then."

Cicero turned to her. "Pic, it's going to be all right and you need to believe that. We're all scared, but we will not let Terrick win. Okay?"

Pic straightened up and nodded. "You're right Cis. That is—I meant to say—*Sir* Cicero!"

Elswyth sent Cicero some love and then turned towards everyone behind her in the tunnel. With a jolt, she realized they were all looking up, waiting for her, as their princess, to say something that would inspire courage and strength before they went into battle. She took a deep breath and channeled the three women she admired most: Agnes, Madam Teshka, and, especially at that moment, her grandmother—her queen.

She remembered Araleia's word in the hub and began. *"We will advance shortly and I know you may very well find yourselves at a heartbreaking cross-roads. The enemy you encounter tonight could be someone you know. A friend. A family member. But remember who they have become. Some of you here have lost loved ones to Terrick and his followers. Others have been brutalized or tortured."* Many of the soldiers nodded, their faces pained. *"You didn't choose this path for his them. They did. Whether because of willful ignorance or greed, they turned their back on Glenorim and everyone—everything—they know. So tonight, you are being asked to stand up for your kingdom. For your loved ones. If the enemy resists you, they will have two options: to surrender—or not."* She could see grim determination on their faces. *"I wish, with all my heart, that we weren't faced with this reality, but we are."*

She tried not to show the nerves fighting to get the better of her. *"Now I am going to point out the obvious and get rid of the drunken dragon in the room. I didn't grow up here. I know that. But I've come to love this kingdom and everything about it. My place is with you all and I want you to know I pledge to fight alongside you. I will fight for everyone in Glenorim. For the Queen and my father."* She paused. *"And for King Garreth."*

The battalion commander placed his fist on his chest and bowed his head to her in respect. "Your Highness, my elves and I will proudly follow you into battle in defense of Glenorim." Then, almost as one, every soldier behind him put their fists to their chests and bowed as well.

Their act of respect filled her more than she could have imagined and she returned the bow. She then turned, pulled the lever down part way and peeked out the door. Seeing the way clear, she pulled the lever down all the way, put her hand up, and waved for everyone to follow her.

The commander insisted on staying at Elswyth's side, and for that, she was grateful. As confident as she was in the intense training she'd received, it couldn't compare with his many years of experience. Besides, his gift of superior hearing was an asset tonight. He had the unique ability to hear the smallest of sounds miles away, much less around a castle corner. Samésh positioned himself close behind Elswyth, and walking behind him, Pic carried Cicero on her shoulder. The soldiers moved single file behind them as everyone hugged the walls of the darkened corridors, careful to make no sound, every sword drawn and at the ready.

The commander's hand shot up and he stood still, eyes closed, listening to something ahead. The line stopped, and they all held their breath.

"Commander?" Elswyth thought to him.

"I hear soldiers—and they aren't ours," he said, his voice low.

She heard nothing yet, but trusted his skill. *"What's going on?"* Elswyth asked, as she opened her Majik wider to see what she could sense. Then she found it. Darkness! It lay somewhere ahead of them!

"What I can tell you is that they are all on alert. Terrick knows we're coming, and it sounds like they are being given orders to report to the ballroom now." He looked at Elswyth. "We've lost the element of surprise and we have very little time."

"But how could Terrick know?"

"Sadly, Your Highness, someone told him and there is no way to let the other units know."

"What do you suggest we do, Commander?"

"The only thing we can do. We move forward—and now, Your Highness. We can't wait for everyone to arrive at their assigned rendezvous. If we advance quickly, we could at least stop some of them or, at the very least, delay them from deploying, keep them from fanning out. That would give our side more of a chance. We need to keep them contained as much as possible. The other groups will arrive soon so we won't be on our own for long, but until they get there, well, I won't lie to you, this is going to be dire."

Elswyth nodded, and the commander informed everyone behind them about what was happening. Then, when he finished, every soldier raised their sword in solidarity. Still moving as quietly as possible, their shields high to avoid detection, they ran through the halls as one.

Who would dare to betray them to Terrick? Elswyth wondered, heartsick at the thought.

SEVENTY-THREE

Terrick sat on his throne and watched as several hundred of his soldiers poured into the enormous ballroom. At least two hundred more stood outside on the grand terrace, many still putting on their battle gear or attaching swords to their baldrics. Still others stretched and yawned, rubbing sleep from their eyes. "This is my army? What a ridiculous mess they are," Terrick muttered, his voice dripping with venom. Earlier, he'd felt confident in the army he had amassed, but as he watched them file in, he grew more and more irritated. He stood up from his throne and paced the dais. "Are you all imbeciles? You should have been in here faster and ready to deploy! This is an important night." Terrick's voice echoed against the walls and chilled every ear it reached inside and outside the ballroom. They all turned as one and stared up at him.

A few soldiers in front of the room noticed a quivering halfling, blond hair hanging in his eyes and secured in shackles, being brought to the stage. An elf left him kneeling near the throne and soon soldiers began to murmur and point at the poor creature. Terrick grinned, turned, and gestured to his prisoner. The murmuring in the crowd stopped, and they all waited for their king to speak.

"I see you've noticed our guest? As it so happens, we owe our little blond friend here a debt of gratitude since he is the reason you will have an advantage over our enemy tonight. I believe his name is Arthid, halfling traitor to his own kind, but yet, an asset to us. He's been in hiding with the enemy in the tunnels, that is until he came to my study earlier tonight." He turned back to Arthid and gave him an exaggerated bow with an evil grin to match. "We thank you for your sacrifice, halfling." Then he motioned to a soldier nearest to him. "Take him to the dungeons and put him in one of the old cisterns. We won't need him any longer."

Arthid's tear-streaked face went ashen as he shoved the bangs from his forehead with shackled hands. The whites of his eyes shone as he pleaded with Terrick. "What? But, Your Majesty. I—I've been loyal to you all this time! Whatever you've asked, I've done! I ran errands for you. I tricked elves and halflings into the dungeons. You said I'd be rich and comfortable— that I could have a place in your court. And—and I brought you the information about the attack! Doesn't that count for something?"

Terrick crossed his arms and tilted his head to the side, smiling at Arthid. "A place in my court? Did you really think I would allow a *dirty halfling* a place in my court, much less in my kingdom? And, no. The treachery you committed against your own kind really doesn't count for anything. You're a halfling. Your usefulness is done."

"NO, TERRICK. YOU'RE THE ONE THAT'S FINISHED. BY THE AUTHORITY OF HER MAJESTY QUEEN ARALEIA, I ORDER YOU TO SURRENDER OR SUFFER THE CONSEQUENCES!" The Glenorim commander's order reverberated off the walls from the back of the room.

Terrick whipped around to see the commander, Elswyth, Pic, Samésh, and the loyalist soldiers pouring in from the entrance to the ballroom.

Elswyth looked up at Terrick and sneered. He stood gawking at them from the dais, his shock obvious. She watched Terrick's face turn deep crimson with rage as his tendrils whipped through the air and spittle spewed from his mouth. He pointed at them and shouted to his army. "WHAT ARE YOU WAITING FOR? ATTACK YOU IDIOTS! LEAVE NO ONE ALIVE, BUT BRING THE HALFLING TO ME!"

Bloody chaos erupted.

Brutal Majik energy cracked and flashed through the air, releasing the heavy, sharp odor of ozone. Shards of glass fell down from the chandeliers as energy crashed into them from below. Soldiers on both sides brandished swords, making cruel and mortal contact. Fists flew and hands grappled with their enemies. Angry roars and anguished cries became one painful cacophony that ricocheted off the high ceilings. Elswyth wondered at the scent growing stronger in the room. Then she recognized it. It was the metallic tang of blood. Like the horrible pandemonium around her, it was everywhere.

Elswyth fought her way through the enemy around her as her training took over, muscle memory doing the work. *Parry! Thrust! Attack!* She felt searing, painful energy shoot down her arm every time she met sword against sword. For now, she was holding her own. She caught sight of Pic as she ran through the melee trying to help their wounded while defending herself. Cicero flew above her, darting and pecking at those trying to get at Pic as she ministered to elves in need.

With horror, Elswyth looked around at her compatriots and saw some were already mortally wounded. There sheer number of Terrick's soldiers were too many for them to hold out much longer and more of his elves were rushing in by the minute. *"Please, dear Fates. Please get our reinforcements here soon!"* she prayed.

Then she knew what she had to do. Find Terrick. If they could get to him and capture—or kill him—then his army would fall. She looked at the blur of lunging, fighting figures around her for her commander. He was only yards away, but embroiled in a bitter battle against two enemy soldiers. A few loyalist elves fought nearby, but they too were in a battle for their lives, so she was going to have to do this alone. It may be reckless and stupid but, they were desperate. She pushed harder through the crowd of combatants, slashing and moving with more purpose than she'd ever felt in her life.

By the time Elswyth made her way onto the dais, Terrick was gone. Then she saw Samésh near the throne, his sword raised over the head of the shackled traitor who was curled up in a ball on the floor. Elswyth ran to him and laid a hand on his arm. *"Samésh?"* Even though the halfling on the floor was a turncoat and deserved punishment, she knew Samésh was not a killer. At least not this way. The prisoner was chained and defenseless. *"Samésh. We will arrest him and he will pay for his treachery."* But Samésh didn't move. As if he hadn't heard Elswyth, he glared down at the halfling, his sword still raised over his head.

Samésh's voice quavered as he shouted down at the object of his anger. "Did you even check on her, Arthid? Did you know she was already dead? That they'd taken her body? How many more did you betray? How many?"

"Who? Who are you talking about?" the halfling wailed. "I don't know who you're talking about! Please don't kill me!" He was now openly weeping, his cries blending in with the tumult in the room. He looked at Elswyth, pleading. "Stop him! Please!"

"My wife! My Justa! I paid you to get me into her cell that night, but she was already gone! You could have at least told me. Instead, you took my money and left me to find that she was—dead!" His voice was getting higher and louder. Elswyth now understood who this was. The sword in Samésh's hands shook as he raised it higher above his head. She knew he was moments away from bringing it down on the halfling.

The traitor screamed. "I swear! I didn't know! She was just one of many and I never went back into the cells. Terrick just paid me to trick elves and halflings into being arrested. I never actually put them into the cells. Please! I was just doing my job."

"One of many?" Samésh's face grew purple with rage. "Justa was more than *one of many*! She was my wife! She'd done nothing wrong!" His sword shook even more now, his eyes wide with fury.

Elswyth touched his shoulder. *"Samésh, you want justice and so do I. We all do. But, don't do this. Take him to the dungeons so he can be tried for his crimes. There are many that will need to see justice done here. The Belnoir army is surely down there by now, releasing prisoners and on their way up. Put this traitor in a cell. We'll make him pay for Justa and for all the others."* He didn't lower his weapon. *"Samésh?"* She gently pulled his arm down, and he let her. He looked at her now, his face full of sorrow and pain. *"I promise. He will pay, Samésh."*

His shoulders fell, but his jaw remained set. "I will do as you ask, Your Highness. But I'll do it only because I know he will receive judgement for all he's done. For all the others, but especially for Justa." He turned to his prisoner. "Get up. I'm going to put you where you will never see the light of day again." He pulled the sniveling halfling up and ushered him behind the throne to the doors that would lead Samésh and his prisoner to the dungeons.

Once Samésh had made it out of the ballroom, she peeked out from behind the throne and looked for Terrick in the tangle of fighting. Not seeing him among the mob, she opened her Majik to scan for his dark energy.

"Found you!" Across the roiling tangle of clashing swords and soldiers, she saw him through the doors to the terrace. He was out there standing atop a stone pedestal, his arms spread out wide like some kind of spectral conductor, looking right at her—and smiling.

SEVENTY-FOUR

Elswyth fought her way through to the terrace, stepping over the wounded and dodging grappling hands as she moved forward. Terrick's elves did their best to fight her—to stop her—so they could deliver her to their king. Her Majik was stronger than they'd expected, though, and her skill with her sword not only matched theirs, but bettered it. No doubt Terrick had told them she was nothing but a weak halfling and they had must have believed him, to their shock and detriment. Their surprise at her skill only gave her more courage, and she continued to fight, leaving many of them injured, unable to continue the battle.

Finally, out on the terrace, she could hear the same sounds of battle echoing from the city below, the night sky alight with the thunder and explosion of deadly Majiks. That meant the Belnoirian army must have made it up from the tunnels and were defending the city! The rest of the Glenorim soldiers and the Kerridin army would be up here soon, but would it be soon enough? Their own soldiers were losing ground, but as long as she could get to Terrick, they could win.

"I'm coming for you, Terrick. Your reign will be the shortest in history!" she thought to him. Then she felt his darkness attempting to enter her mind.

"Go ahead, halfling. Try to come at me. I welcome it!" His laughter rang out above the din. Still, she moved towards his dark energy. She bolstered her shields more and pushed forward, darting behind fighting soldiers, tables, and chairs. Anything to keep out of Terrick's view and get closer to him.

A black and red uniformed soldier stepped in front of Elswyth, and she raised her sword. He quickly put his hand up and motioned for her to follow him. *"This way, Your Highness! Please! I can get you closer!"* he sent her the thought. She felt his Majik reaching out to her, and it felt safe.

"Who are you—"

"Your Highness, my name is Banor, and I was forced to enter the prince's service," he thought quickly to her as they ran in between ongoing skirmishes. Elswyth noticed the elf did not address Terrick as king. *"He had my family in the dungeon and threatened to kill them if I didn't join up. There are others like me. He thought he could control our minds, but we've resisted, hoping for help to come. And you have!"* An injured Glenorim soldier fell directly in their path, grasping a grievous wound in his arm. Out of nowhere, Pic rushed to his side, pulling aside her cloak for medicinal aid while Cicero darted at those trying to attack her and keep her from ministering to the wounded.

Elswyth felt a tug on her arm. *"Hurry, Your Highness. This way!"* Still feeling the red and black soldier's Majik to be safe, Elswyth left Pic to tend to the wounded and followed him as he led her behind some columns on the terrace. There was a group of eleven more elves, also in Terrick's uniforms. She stopped short, but before she even had a chance to read their Majiks, they bowed to her. "Your Highness!" they said in unison.

Banor now spoke aloud for the group. "We saw you trying to make your way to Terrick and assumed you were planning to attack him. We thought we could act as a shield for you so that you could get closer to him. You'd just need to stay low in the center of our group so no one sees you, then we will fight by your side."

Elswyth took a deep breath and smiled at them, grateful for their courage. *"Let's do it!"* she said.

Banor took the lead as the soldiers surrounded Elswyth and she huddled down low in the center of the group. They pushed out as one towards where Terrick was standing on the pedestal. It looked like it would work until they had gone about twenty feet. Then Terrick invaded her mind again.

"Ah, my little halfling. You think I can't sense you hiding there? You're making this too easy for me! Watch me take care of this!" She stood up tall and saw Terrick, less than a hundred feet away now, raise his arms in the air. The inky black tendrils snaked out over the terrace and entwined themselves around his nearby soldiers. One by one, those who weren't already fighting turned towards Elswyth and her group. *"You see, they are so easy to manipulate! I offer them strength, power, or wealth, and they're mine to control. If those incentives don't work, fear is also a handy tool. The rest is easy,"* he said to her, laughing. Then he spoke out loud over the noise and raised his arms wide. "KILL THE TRAITORS AND BRING HER TO ME!"

"Protect Her Highness at all costs!" Banor called out as they formed a tighter circle around her, blades facing out. The first of Terrick's soldiers had reached them when a roar rang out over the noise from the ballroom. Everyone inside and out turned to see the rest of the Glenorim army, led by her father and Caden, and the Kerridin army, led by the prince, as they flooded into the ballroom. Elswyth's heart surged with relief even as the battle intensified. Through all of that, she could feel her father's Majik reaching out to her, telling her he was coming to help her.

A blast of rage-filled, dark energy shot out from Terrick, shaking the ground and the castle walls. The glass in all the ballroom doors shattered over enemy and patriot alike, and soldiers on both sides stumbled to the ground from the shock wave. "NO!" he screamed. "This is MY kingdom and you will not take it from me!" He looked down at Elswyth, his face twisted into a livid, evil mask. "Bring her to me! NOW!" The nearby soldiers doubled their efforts and began slashing at her guards. Their numbers were far greater than her twelve soldiers, though, and the enemy soon had her by the arms. She could feel her father's anxious energy fighting through a wall of red and black uniforms to get to her.

Then it happened. Everything in her changed. All the things she'd always believed she had no power to fight—lost their hold on her. The anger. The helplessness. The fear. The insecurities. Agnes taught her she could overcome it all—but she hadn't believed her—until this moment. Until right now. She finally understood she did have the power. Her Majik began building in her heart center, a deep, power-filled, pulsing energy. She looked at the guards holding her on either side and grinned. *"I would let go now!"* she thought to them.

They laughed, and one of them jeered at her. "Oh really! And you're going to make us?"

Elswyth shrugged. *"Have it your way."* White hot energy shot from her heart out to her arms, knocking the two guards on their backs yards away from her, their hair crispy and smoking. The fighting in the immediate area ceased as everyone, enemy and patriot alike, stared at her. Instead of the drain she expected to feel, Elswyth felt a refilling of power in her chest. She stretched out her arms, stood tall, and walked closer to where Terrick was. She enjoyed his momentary look of surprise. And something else. She sensed—fear. Terrick was afraid of her!

Pic ran up beside Elswyth, eyes wide. "Elly, be careful! You're going to drain all your energy!"

Cicero landed on her shoulder, staying close to the side of her head. "Elly?"

"I'm fine, you two. Never better!" She turned her head to them with a smile to reassure them.

Terrick laughed. "So, the halfling has honed her abilities, I see," he said, no longer looking stunned.

"Yes, SHE has! And your days of greed and cruelty are done," Elswyth said, and continued to walk towards him.

"That's close enough!" Terrick raised his arm, and she felt his dark Majik build. A tremendous blast of black-tinged energy shot from his hand and she ducked just in time. She turned to look back at the hole Terrick had made in the castle wall and saw through the crumbling, burning opening to the ballroom.

Turing back to him, she grinned. *"Is that all you have to throw at me?"*

"Elly, do you really want to tease the dragon like that?" Cicero asked nervously.

"Don't worry, Cis. I know what I'm doing." At least she hoped she did.

Terrick roared, and the ground shook. Elswyth could sense his Majik becoming erratic and unfettered, his frustration, anger, and fear causing him to abandon all self-control. He raised his arm again and sent a volley of blasts at her, his face wild with fury. Each time, she deflected his attacks with her own Majik, but soon felt the inevitable draining of her energy. She stumbled backwards and Pic ran to help her as Cicero flew up to peck at a nearby soldier, who tried to pull Elswyth from Pic.

Terrick raised his eyebrows and his face split in half with a wide grin. "Feeling a little weak, halfling? You still think you will hold out against me?" She was still trying to regain her stance when Terrick raised his arm and sent a crackling stream at her.

"ELLY, WATCH OUT!" Cicero cried and flew up to block the deadly shot. Elswyth watched in horror as he plummeted to the ground, unmoving, his chest bloody.

"Cicero! Oh Cis. NO!" Blinded by tears, Elswyth felt the connection to his energy ripped from her heart center.

Pic ran to Cicero and knelt over him. With gentle care, she picked him up and felt for a pulse.

"Pic?" Elswyth couldn't move. Cicero was so—still. And there was so much blood.

Pic looked up at Elswyth, tears pouring down her face, and she shook her head no.

Anger and grief roiled up inside Elswyth. For herself. For Cicero. For everyone she cared about. She looked up at Terrick, at his horrid, smug face, and felt the red, furious energy building in her chest. The composure and confidence she felt earlier were gone and replaced by searing anger. A need for revenge. But her shields were failing, along with her energy. She was now vulnerable to him, body—and mind.

Terrick raised his eyebrows and spoke into her mind. "Ah! Now I can see who you are. Who you were. I can see it all! Thank you!"

Elswyth felt the tentacles as they bored deep into her hidden memories. The pain almost sent her to her knees, but she squeezed her eyes shut and fought back. She stood her ground and resisted his reach as best as she could. From somewhere close by, she heard her father calling her name above the roar of the battle and Pic crying out to her. But above it all, she could hear Terrick's laughter. Finally, she pushed him out and opened her eyes.

Her heart stopped as she saw, standing in Terrick's place on the pedestal—her mother! "Can't ya do nothin' right, brat?" she yelled at Elswyth. "Ya ain't natural, I tell ya! I wish I never birthed ya! Evil is what you are! Worthless!" Terrick's laughter mixed with her mother's as Elswyth stared, transfixed. The vision swam in front of her eyes.

Elswyth's pulse raced, and nausea threatened to overtake her. She fought against the desperate need to fall to the ground and curl up in the once-familiar protective ball. That panic from long ago threatened to pull her down, but then she saw her father running up to her. She saw Pic holding her dear, lifeless Cis! Her life flashed inside her head and she saw the image of Agnes in Willow Grove. Her dear, sweet Agnes, who taught her to be strong, and that she was not the victim anymore. Then more faces lit up her mind. Her grandmother, grandfather, and Madam Teshka.

She looked up at the visage of her mother and understood it wasn't real and couldn't hurt her. It was Terrick trying to control her, and she refused to give him the satisfaction. Pulling from a place deep inside, she found the strength to stand tall, gritted her teeth against the pain of his brutal reach and then, from her heart center, she felt power coming out of her mouth. GET! OUT! OF! MY! HEAD! The words boomed across the terrace and into the ballroom.

The battle froze as everyone turned and stared at Elswyth. She had spoken—out loud! *Was that my voice?* she thought, as shocked as everyone else. *How can that be?* She looked around and realized everyone was looking at her, enemy and loyalist alike.

The image of her mother morphed back into Terrick; disbelief plastered across his face. And then—fear. No, he wasn't just afraid of her! He was terrified.

"I've had all I can stand of you, halfling. It ends here!" he said. He reached towards her, trying to gain access to her mind again while building energy to fire at her. At the same moment, she found the strength for one last try, and raised her hand to him. Before his Majik could get far from his hand, her blast hit it and blew his energy back at him with a thunderous BOOM. An enormous ball of black flame and smoke erupted on the pedestal, sending everyone to their knees. When the flames and smoke finally cleared, only ash and rubble remained where Terrick had stood; the pedestal obliterated.

Terrick was gone. He'd been destroyed!

Elswyth knees buckled just as her father reached her. He carefully helped her to the ground as she looked over at Pic and reached for Cicero. *"Father! It's Cis! He's—"*

"Yes, Elly. I know. I'm so sorry!" he said, cradling her in his arms, his face lined with sorrow.

The last thing she remembered was Pic weeping and placing Cicero's body within the folds of her cloak.

SEVENTY-FIVE

*W**here am I?* Elswyth wondered, her head foggy. She opened her eyes against searing white sunlight and squeezed them shut. It took her a moment, but she tried again, and her eyes finally adjusted to the brightness. *I'm—I'm in my room! How did I get here?* She looked down and saw she was covered with the quilt Agnes had made for her, and she clutched it in her hands. Her body felt weak and sore, but her throat hurt worst of all. Reaching for her neck, she discovered a warm, soft cloth filled with fragrant herbs wrapped around it. Then she turned her head to the side and her heart leapt to see Agnes asleep in a chair pulled close to her bed. Elswyth reached out and rested her hand on Agnes's shoulder.

"My girl!" Agnes cried and jumped up, which sent the chair crashing to the floor. "Oh, bless me! My girl's all right!" She smothered Elswyth in a tight hug, and they both wept. "You've been out for two days and I've been so worried! We all have been!"

Her father and grandmother rushed into the room. "Agnes? What happened? Is everything okay?" Araleia asked, panicked. They saw the chair on the floor and then Elswyth and Agnes. "Elly? Oh, Elly! Thank the Fates!" More tears and hugs mixed with laughter while Dayel brought in more chairs.

Her father's face was drawn and his voice sounded strained. "Elly, we are so glad you're awake. We haven't left your side since we brought you up here. How are you feeling?"

Elswyth touched her throat and winced. *"I feel kind of weak and my throat really hurts, but, otherwise, I think I'm in one piece"* she signed for Agnes's sake as she sent her thoughts out. *"Why does my throat hurt so much?"*

Her father moved to sit next to her on the bed. "You don't remember? Elly, you *spoke*! Or, more accurately, you *shouted* with a voice everyone could hear," her father said. "Actually, everyone felt it, too!" Agnes and her grandmother nodded in agreement.

That can't be. Can it? I spoke out loud? Elswyth thought back to the battle, and the memories poured into her mind. Rushing into the ballroom, the fighting, Terrick. Then her eyes flew wide open and her lip quivered. *"Where is Pic and—"* she signed. Tears started falling as she remembered what happened to Cicero.

"Somebody looking for us?" Pic said, walking in with Caden. Elswyth noticed her friend's white hair now had a very noticeable black streak down the right side. And she was holding something in a small blanket. "I was coming to check on you again. But I couldn't leave my other patient alone, so I brought him with me." Pic uncovered the coverlet and there, in her arms, sat Cicero.

"Cis!" Elswyth reached out for him.

"Elly! Oh wow, am I glad to see you awake!" Cicero sounded hoarse and tired.

Pic handed him over to Elswyth. "Careful. He's still healing, but he'll be okay," she said.

Elswyth took him in her arms and brought him up to her chest. He rested his head in the crook of her neck and they stayed that way for several minutes, everyone looking on with smiles. When Cicero pulled back, Elswyth noticed he had a patch of white feathers on his chest. She remembered that was where the wound was. She looked at Pic for answers. *"I thought Cis was—"* She couldn't even say the word.

Pic fiddled with a button on her blouse for a moment. She didn't look at Elswyth at first, but then turned to her and explained. "Yes, Elly. Cis was—he did die when Terrick's Majik hit him. I know we're supposed to obey the second tenet, but I just had to try." She looked at Cicero, who tilted his head towards her. "I used my healing gifts to bring him back. It was really difficult, but it was soon enough after his injury that I could. Anyway, Madam Teshka said that's why I have this streak in my hair. It is a reminder, a marker, from the Fates of breaking that tenet."

"Did I hear my name?" Madam Teshka said, as she floated into the room. "Hello, my dear. I'm so pleased to see you awake and recovering," she said, her smile broad and warm. Elswyth noticed her teacher's sparkling silver eyes were also a little misty. "And Pic, my dear, what else did I say about all that?"

Pic got up, hugged her teacher, and stood next to her. "That even though it's a reminder to never break that tenet again, it is also a reminder that I did it out of love. Cicero's mark will be a reminder that it was love that saved him. I had to try for you and him, Elly. Well, for me, too."

Madam Teshka broke in. "Elswyth, Pic made a sacrifice for Cicero, that she's not telling you about. Breaking the second tenet takes years from the life of the healer who broke it and depletes a measure of their Majik." She hugged Pic again. "But I will say I have been interceding on your behalf and the Fates are not cold to your reasons, Pic. You have many, many years ahead of you. After all, it's imperative I have my new apprentice by my side for as long as I can have her. We need more teachers in the kingdom, and who better than you? You would continue your calling as a healer, but learn to teach others as well. That is, of course, if you are interested?" She tilted her head at Pic.

"What? Really? Oh, yes! I don't know what to say! This is going to be fabulous. Thank you! I can't wait to get started and—"

"All right, my dear." Madam Teshka laughed and placed her hand on Pic's arm. "First lesson will be for you to learn to calm yourself and contain the chatter."

"Yes, Ma'am."

Elswyth didn't think Pic's grin could get any bigger, and it made her happy. Then she put her hand back to her throat. *"What about what happened to me? Does this mean I now have a voice?"*

Madam Teshka spread her hands wide. "That will be entirely up to you, my dear. Of course, it will take some very hard work and practice on your part. After all, you've never spoken aloud before. You will need the appropriate medicines to help you with the transition, but I believe my apprentice is more than qualified to assist you with that." She gestured at Pic, who nodded with enthusiasm.

Cicero asked, "If Elly learns to speak out loud, will we still be able to talk just between ourselves?" He snuggled closer to her.

"Absolutely, my dear, absolutely. Nothing will change with that."

Elswyth felt Cicero relax into her arms and she gave him a light squeeze; mindful he was still healing. She looked around the room at everyone gathered around her bed, grateful to the Fates for all of them. They were her family. They were her strength.

Pic ordered Elswyth to rest in bed for several more days to give her body, and her Majik, a chance to completely recover, which Elswyth agreed to since she was still feeling weak from the battle. Cicero had to abide by the same orders, but insisted on staying with Elswyth for his confinement, which Pic, of course, agreed to. Each day, Cicero acted as a voice coach, making Elswyth stop and go back to thought-speak if he thought she was overdoing it.

Once she was up to it, Elswyth's grandmother and father brought her through the castle to tour all the reconstruction being done. It pained her to see the destruction Terrick and his army had caused, but it was just as encouraging to see elves and halflings as they worked together to bring things back to life. The royal gardens had been hit especially hard, the trees charred or slashed, and plots trampled or torn up, but Samésh took it upon himself to supervise its restoration and Elswyth sensed it helped him feel connected to Justa.

The city below was undergoing its own rebirth. Everyone worked together to rebuild their beloved streets, buildings, homes, and parks. Neighbor helped neighbor by sharing resources, food, and labor. Sweets and Dilly worked with other food vendors to make sure they kept everyone fed until they could get back on their feet. The royal family even came down multiple times, ready to work and helped with everything from cooking to digging to hammering nails.

The recovery effort was a kingdom-wide effort that brought everyone together.

But they had help from the outside, too. The Belnoir king sent elves to assist with all the work, and Prince Tashir even brought a contingent of workers with him. However, Pic had mentioned to Elswyth, with an impish smile, that the handsome, bronzed-skinned prince seemed to spend most of his time helping with whatever project Elswyth worked on.

Ratheus was happiest in Prince Dayel's study, reviewing the old maps of the tunnels and overseeing the research of which ones were still viable, which were repairable, and which should be permanently closed. Much of the tunnel system needed remapping, a huge undertaking that would take time, but he loved the work.

As for Terrick's army, those that had willingly followed him were sentenced to live out their days on Kyper, the island prison off the coast of Glenorim. Elswyth went to see them being loaded on the ships in the harbor at the bottom of the mountain hoping to witness remorse or sadness over what they'd done, but shocked to see just the opposite. As they boarded the ships, they sang the praises of Terrick, not seeming to care about the pain and harm they'd caused. For those that were forced into service, Madam Teshka made it her mission to help them return to their lives. It took a while for many of them to recover from that trauma.

SEVENTY-SIX

"Are you really going to go back to Willow Grove, Elly?" Pic asked while they strolled through the gardens. In the months that followed the battle, the kingdom had slowly returned to its former glory. The gardens were responding to the love and care of the cultivators, and it made Elswyth happy to see it. "And what about your royal Majik? I thought it was so strong that Markan would know you're in Carthia right away? How are you going to handle that?"

"I'm not leaving right away, but yes, I do plan to go back at some point. When they're ready to return, I want to help Agnes and Tallon bring Majik back to humans." Speaking aloud was still a strange sensation for Elswyth, but as her throat healed more each day, she could use her new voice for longer periods of time. "I know it's dangerous because of King Markan, but people need to reclaim their Majik, and I want to be a part of making that happen. And, who knows, maybe with my father's help, we can join our kingdoms again someday. Besides, Madam Teshka thinks that since I'm half human, she might come up with a way to shield my Majik there. She and Agnes said they'll test that out before I ever go back."

"One step at a time, Elly," Cicero said as he hopped along with them. "Let's continue to enjoy the peace first! Besides, here in Glenorim, I'm a knight!

When we go back to Willow Grove, I'll just be good 'ol Cicero again," he said teasing. Elswyth suspected he was only half joking.

"You'll always be our knight in shining black feathers, Cis," Pic said, laughing.

They walked up to a gated garden plot full of beautiful purple roses, and their delicate scent wafted up to greet them. Elswyth admired the gold plaque that hung on the entry that read *Justa's Garden,* and not too far from the entrance, they saw Samésh on his hands and knees, weeding. He looked up and waved, a bright smile on his face.

"We brought you some lunch, Samésh," Cicero said.

Pic handed him the basket she brought, and he brushed off his hands, accepted the hamper, and peeked inside. "Thank you very much! Pic, it looks like you've outdone yourself, as usual. I can't wait to eat this. " He set it down and squinted up at her in the sunshine. "But first, there is someone here that has been waiting to meet you."

Elswyth smiled. She and Cicero knew what was coming. Madam Teshka and Agnes told them this morning and had sworn them to secrecy. Elswyth was sure that Cicero would have exploded with excitement before they ever got here, but to his credit, he never let the secret slip. Samésh was in on it, too, and was playing his part well.

"Really?" Pic asked. "Who would that be?" She glanced around the garden, curious.

"That would be me," said a small voice. A red squirrel with tall, tufted ears stepped out from between the roses and sat on its haunches. "Hi Pic! My name is Miki. I'm your complement."

THE END

EPILOGUE

For all the twenty-four years of his life, Lord Callan only knew his Uncle Markan—King Markan of Carthia, to everyone else—as a drunk and an addict, disheveled and inebriated whenever he held court. That paled, however, to his insatiable greed and cruelty, and Callan held only contempt for the man who raised him. So, that day at court began like any other in the throne room.

A line of petitioners, both poor and not-so-poor, stood waiting their turns, hapless subjects who hoped for a ruling in their favor or a compassionate act of clemency. Things rarely went their way and Callan hated he was required to attend court as a witness. He had learned years before that it did no good to intervene on any supplicant's behalf. On the contrary, it often resulted in making things worse for them, so he kept his peace.

After taking a few gulps from his flagon, the king let out a loud belch as a guard brought a middle-aged woman in shackles closer to the dais. She held her head high and stared straight ahead, her jaw set, not looking at the king until he spoke to her.

"Do you know what you are being charged with, woman?" Markan asked.

She stiffened, her nostrils flared, and she replied with a sharp edge to her voice. "You accuse me of not being a healer, Your Majesty, but I have always done my very best for those in my care. I've helped many of the people in our village over the years. Many. That is, until you took me from my home and brought me here."

"If you are so—gifted—then why is it," the king said and took another gulp of his drink, "that you could not make *me* well? I still feel weak and sick. I say that makes you a sham and only pretending to be what you say you are." The tension in the room rose, some holding their breath, others shaking their heads with furrowed brows. Everyone knew what happened when the king was unhappy with yet another healer.

The woman raised her head higher, her voice loud and clear. "I have done my best for you, Your Majesty. But it is you who chooses to keep yourself in darkness and ill health! There is no one who can help you until you change your ways. I say again, I have done my best and will go to the Fates proud of my efforts to ease the suffering of others!" Several people gasped at her defiant response.

As much as Callen admired the woman's strength and fire, he knew what was coming. No doubt she did, too. King Markan's bloodshot eyes narrowed to slits as he stared down at her for several long breaths.

"Go to your Fates, then," he said. He pointed to her guard. "Hang her."

The woman pushed her shoulders back and sneered at him even through her tears. Callen felt sick at heart as he watched her being led away. How he hated his uncle.

The next person to be led up wore a shabby black cloak, their face hidden in the shadow of its hood. Bent over and limping, it took a while for them to make their way closer to the dais where the king sat. Something about the figure made Callen deeply uneasy, and he moved backwards a few steps until his back met the wall behind him.

"Speak up! State your reason for coming before me!" Markan said. Callan could tell his uncle was growing tired and his patience wearing thin.

The figure bowed, but did not remove his hood. "I am a healer, Your Majesty. I can do what no other healer has done for you before." He then stood silent, waiting. Callan thought the raspy voice sounded male and wondered who was under that hood.

The king took another swig and eyed the figure. "You know what has happened to healers who have failed me and yet you come willingly to offer your services? Are you so certain of yourself, or simply a fool?" Markan let out a loud snort.

"I can prove my worth to you, Your Majesty," the man said and pulled the front of his cloak aside. The guard next to him grabbed the healer's arm, and the figure stilled. "I have no weapons; I'm only reaching for a sample of my medicine. Please allow me show it to you."

The king nodded to the guard. "All right, but move slowly. My guard will run you through if you try anything. Pull out your medicine and let me see it," the kind said, intrigued. The hooded man brought out a silver bottle with a crystal stopper and held it up. Callan noticed the man's hands were arthritic and covered with scars. The healer held the bottle higher. "A drop of this in your drink will restore your well-being almost instantly. You would need to take it only once a day. Would you like to try it? I promise it will not disappoint."

"Do you take me for a fool? It's probably poison!"

"Your majesty, may I suggest you give it to someone here as a test, then? You will see I am not lying," the healer said, his hoarse voice oddly reassuring.

Markan looked around the room, choosing a victim. "Bring that guard a flagon of mead!" he said, pointing to the soldier next to the healer. The guard's eyes widened and his brows knit together. "Put some of your potion in his drink and I will see how it goes."

The healer poured only a drop into the cup and waited for the guard to lift it to his lips. The soldier took a deep breath, then sipped a little of the liquid. He lowered the cup.

"You must drink the whole thing," the healer said, nodding his hooded head. The king gestured for the guard to finish, so the soldier sighed, closed his eyes, and drained the cup. Everyone in the room held a collective breath and watched to see what would happen next. The soldier stood stark still, clutching the empty cup, surely thinking he was about to die.

Then, "Your Majesty! I feel good. Better than good!" the guard said, smiling from ear to ear. "This is a wonderful elixir!"

Markan's eyes lit up, and he pointed to the bottle. "I will try your medicine! Give me a dose, and if it works for me, you will have the position of Court Healer and all the honors that go with the title!" He gave his cup to his servant and let the stranger add a drop to his drink.

Callan still felt uneasy and considered warning his uncle from doing something he may regret. But, then again, why bother? Not only would Markan not listen to him, but Callen truly didn't care what happened to the man, family or not. Besides, he was the only one in line for the throne. So, there was that.

Markan swallowed every drop in the flagon and waited only a few moments before his skin took on a fresher, more healthy tone. His eyes became bright and clear and he sat up straight in his seat. Callan stared in awe. He'd never known his uncle to look, or sound, so full of health and vigor.

Markan leaned forward on his throne. "What is this Majik? I have not felt this alive in—actually, I cannot remember when I felt this good! You are a miracle worker, healer! The position is yours if you want it. What is your name?"

With stiff and deliberate movements, the figure reached up and pushed the hood back from his head. No one in the room was ready for the person who stood before them. Even the king let out a small gasp. The man in the cape looked as though he had survived a horrendous fire. Black scars covered his entire face and bald scalp; his ears reduced to maimed holes on either side of his head.

But the healer's eyes! Those eyes glittered with darkness as they peered up at the king. Callan shivered and felt as if he'd been plunged into ice. *That is evil standing before us,* he thought, pressing into the wall even more.

"I am called Terrick, Your Majesty. And I humbly accept your offer," the healer answered, as a grin split across his face.

LITTLE PICS CANDY RECIPE

Little Pics Candy (Dilly's Birthday Gift To Pic - Chapter 47)

Ingredients

8 dates (pits removed), finely chopped (Tip: cut each date in half length-wise and then chop the slices)

1 cup finely chopped pecans

¾ cup dried cranberries

1 cup toasted unsweetened flaked coconut

12 ounces (1 Bag) of white chocolate chips

Coarse sea salt

You will need

2.5-quart microwave-safe bowl for melting and mixing chocolate

Spatulas for stirring melting chocolate

2-quart bowl for mixing chopped ingredients

Knife and cutting board

Measuring cups

Large cookie sheet covered in foil or parchment paper

Two teaspoons or a teaspoon-size cookie scoop (it will be much easier with the scoop!)

Optional: 1 inch candy cups (I highly recommend those made by Celebrate It Baking Cups sold at Michael's craft store. The paper is thicker than some other brands and holds up well.)

Directions

*Chop and prepare ingredients one through four (dates through coconut) and mix thoroughly in the 2-quart bowl. Set aside.

Melt chocolate on the stove in a double boiler or in a microwave in the 2.5-quart bowl. (Microwave method: Heat at half power for twenty seconds at a time. Stir with a spatula after each heating and keep going until chocolate is melted and creamy.)

Pour prepared mix into the chocolate and stir to distribute ingredients evenly.

Working quickly, use one full teaspoon at a time to scoop up the white chocolate mix and a second teaspoon to scrape it off the spoon (or use the cookie scooper) into a candy cup or just drop onto parchment paper. While the candy is still warm and soft, sprinkle sea salt over them. Let cool. It will harden into perfect Little Pics.

Makes 25 to 30 candies

*For the mix, you want a little less the same volume as the melted white chocolate. I sometimes have a bit of the mix left over and just save it. You can also use it in your oatmeal.

ACKNOWLEDGEMENTS

Before I acknowledge anyone else, I want to first thank my wonderful husband, Lar, who is always supportive of my creative efforts, whatever they may be. From encouragement, to helpful critique, to sharing household chores, to even the occasional dad joke to cheer me up, I know I can count on him being there for me. I love you for all you do, Lar!

To our daughter Heidi, thank you for believing in me more than I did myself while I wrote Elswyth's story. You are such a bright star and an amazing woman. I love you tons!

Thank you to our daughter Caitlin for telling me she was proud of me and knew I could do this. I love you and am beyond proud of you, too!

This book may not have happened without the two very special women in our three-person writers' group, Tiffani Hockett, and Jenn Krajack. Thank you, ladies, from the bottom of my heart. Every two weeks, since the spring of 2024, we've met and shared stories, ideas, encouragement, and milestones. You are both amazing writers and have inspired me since day one! And Tiffani, both Jenn and I are so grateful to you for opening your home and providing such a perfect place for us to meet. You are the best!

Of course, I need to thank author Teresa Widdowson for sharing her stories, encouragement, and helpful critiques of Elswyth and friends. You are a gem, Teresa! (P.S. dear reader, if you've never read one of Teresa's books, do yourself a favor and look her up. You won't be sorry!)

To my beta readers, Heidi Strock, Rhonda Dicksion, and Pat Pierce. Thank you so much for reading Eslwyth and Cicero's story before the final polishing. Your input and encouragement meant the world to me.

Finally, a huge thanks to the Watermark Book Company in Anacortes, Washington for creating the Watermark Writing Company, which is a super special organization that inspires, teaches, and helps writers to find their voice. Our community is brighter because of Watermark!

ABOUT THE AUTHOR

Jan Fagan is an author, artist, illustrator, and dreamer of fantastical worlds who enjoys giving life to the many characters that crowd her creative mind.

A lover of all things fantasy, she relishes stories that highlight the power of strong role models and unlikely heroes. She writes and creates her art in her home studio next to the Puget Sound in the Pacific Northwest and lives with her husband, their English Shepherd, and a cat that may possibly possess magical abilities.

To contact Jan via email, go to jafaganauthor@gmail.com

Instagram: www.instagram.com/artworkbyjanfagan